DAWN OF ASH

THE IMDALIND SERIES, BOOK SEVEN

REBECCA ETHINGTON

IMDALIND PRESS

Copyediting by C&D Editing
Production Management by Market Street Books

ISBN (e-book) 978-0-9964632-3-2
ISBN (print) 978-1-949725-05-6
Printed in USA
This Edition, February 2016

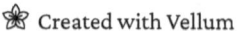 Created with Vellum

CONTENTS

To Duck

Who showed me sunshine,
Who reminded me how to laugh.

THE COMPLETE IMDALIND SERIES

BOOK ONE: *Kiss of Fire*
BOOK TWO: *Eyes of Ember*
BOOK THREE: *Scorched Treachery*
BOOK FOUR: *Soul of Flame*
BOOK FIVE: *Burnt Devotion*
BOOK SIX: *Brand of Betrayal*
BOOK SEVEN: *Dawn of Ash*
BOOK EIGHT: *Crown of Cinders*
BOOK NINE: *Spark of Vengeance*
BOOK TEN: *Flare of Villainy*

CHAPTER I

ILYAN

"Ilyan! Watch out!" Risha's shout cut through the roar of the violent explosions that shattered the building to my left; bricks and dirt flying over us. The ancient structure answered her scream with a groan of warning.

"Move!" I yelled, swiping my hand to the side and throwing both Risha and two of the other Skříteks who had come along on this mission out of the way of the collapsing brick and stone. The entire side of the building was crumbling down on top of us.

Pater and Mara flew into the air before landing in a heap on the opposite side of the alley, beside Risha who was already pulling herself to her feet. Risha and the boys had gone one way, and Edmund's men had gone the other, all of the bodies scattering as I sent another explosion into the next wave of both Trpaslíks, Edmund's Chosen, and now Vilý who had been led there by the noise.

I could have been more careful with the explosion, but with so many of Edmund's diseased beasts heading our way I had a few other things on my mind. Like the fact that there was no way we could fight them off with just the four of us.

The more noise, the more Vilỳ.

We were already outnumbered and hundreds more would come.

All of this for a bit of food.

I refused to lose any more of my people, from starvation or otherwise.

Edmund's men streamed through the alleys, magic streaming from me and Risha as we took them down in blasts of red and white. The power from the two attackers faded away as their destruction turned them into nothing more than shadows.

The two had barely fallen before a blast erupted behind me in a spark of grey, the air buzzing with the magic that was heading right toward me. I leapt to the side, narrowly avoiding the attack that smacked into the same building.

Brick poured over us like hail, mixing with burning sparks of magic and singeing my clothes and hair. The building wheezed as it tipped over, the sound of collapse ricocheting with the loud Trpaslíks' laughter.

With one sure movement, I grabbed my would-be assassin by the throat and slammed him into one of the other buildings that lined the alley. My jaw was a hard line of anger as I stared him down, my hand clenched around the soft flesh of his neck, pressing, restricting. My lips twitched into a smile as his turned blue, the pulse of his heart beating against my palm in time with the staggered explosions that surrounded us.

"How did you get in?" I demanded, letting my magic warm through him in warning. He only stared at me, his eyes bulging red and wild as I held him in place. "How did you get past the barrier? Tell me, and all this ends."

He gasped for breath, but not in an attempt to answer, his lips were already curling into a smile as he jutted his chin out. The threat was obvious, even if the fear in his eyes didn't make it believable.

A streak of red light erupted above my head, and I turned, keeping the Trpaslík debilitated under my palm. Edmund's men were nothing if not ballsy. You would have to be with as bad of aim as they had.

A cavalcade of my father's bastards was emerging between the destroyed buildings, magic flaring, eyes murderous as they cut off our easiest route for escape.

Wonderful.

The skies were already black with Vilý, and the brick from the collapsing building that had effectively trapped us in.

We needed to get out of here, but this dead end was making it difficult with the alleys and streets that were feeding into it like some sort of river basin. How was I to know they had built a new high rise last year? This street had always gone straight through.

Screaming in frustration, I sent an attack into yet another of the Trpaslík attackers with my free hand, the other still holding the little man, his smile fading as one of his comrades collapsed to the ground lifelessly.

"I don't like killing innocents," I growled as I turned back to my captive. "Tell me where Edmund is, and I will protect you."

The man's smug smile twitched and my chest tensed in fervent possibility, perhaps this one would tell me. Perhaps this one would crack.

Then I could reach my father and end everything.

He opened his mouth just as an explosion erupted at

our feet, rubble flying through the air and knocking him from my grip. So much for answers.

"I obey only my master. He has saved me, he has taught me what it is to be truly strong." His voice echoed from where he stood behind me, the sound loud and disjointed. "You are not my master. We will defeat you. We will defeat all!"

The man proclaimed his last words as I turned through the dust filled air, shooting my magic into him, ending his life with one flash of power against his heart. Quick and painless.

It was the humane way. They weren't all Trpaslíks, after all. Many of them were Chosen—it wasn't their fault.

Stepping over the body, I rushed back into the battle, killing man after man as my fury grew into a dangerous rage. Controlling my temper had never been my strong suit. Normally, Joclyn's magic would fill me, the silver glint in her eyes warning me when I was getting too out of control. But she was asleep. Something that didn't happen too often anymore, even with her Drak blood.

With an explosion of sound and an eruption of power, a single stream of red light exploded from my hand, flying right into one of the many abandoned vehicles that was left rotting in the dark, forgotten city. The broken thing erupted into the air and jammed itself in the narrow opening of an alley to our left, blocking the way for thirty or so men behind it.

It wouldn't hold them long.

"Risha," I yelled as I raced toward her, heart pounding as I evaded another attack, sending one right back toward the source without looking, the hollow thunk that followed promising me it had hit its mark.

"Help! Ilyan!" Pater's voice ripped through me as the

black cloud descended, the hissing creatures surrounding him.

My hands sliced through the dusty air, sending another beam of light from my palm. The first wave of Vilỳs turning to ash and smoke as the earth reclaimed them.

Damn. We were done for if we didn't get out of here.

"Risha!" I rushed to her side. The tall Skřítek woman didn't so much as look away from the fight.

Determination bled from her eyes as attack after attack ripped from her and she protected the Chosen who sat huddled behind her. One, a young woman who had insisted on coming with us, sat crying as she bled profusely from a large gash in her chest. The elderly man she was leaned up against was already gone judging by the glossy look in his eyes.

"Focus your magic on the skin to stop the bleeding," I yelled at the panicked female as another explosion sent my vehicular blockade into us. Hand extended, I caught it moments before it landed on top of us and with a burst of light I sent it to the left, right into two of Edmund's men, pinning them between brick and twisted metal.

"I'm never leaving the cathedral again," Risha growled from somewhere behind me as yet another blast of magic streaked through the air, my magic alerting me to the danger late enough that the bright red blade cut through my hair, long lengths of gold falling to the ground.

For a moment, my heart stopped, scared the délka vedení královsk had been severed, but the long length of ribbon was still wrapped around my wrist, kept safe in the only way I knew how in these situations.

"You said that last week, Risha," I reminded her as I destroyed another man, and sent him crumpling to the ground.

"This time, I mean it."

Another Trpaslík crumpled, my magic scurrying in a mad attempt to keep us ahead of the fray, only to freeze as the entirety of the narrow street lit up in a bright yellow blaze. The air caught fire as the brilliant glow reflected over every lifeless body, illuminating every smear of blood, revealing the destruction that Prague had become.

The ribbons of light made the dilapidated city all the more frightening, it also preceded an attack that would easily kill us all.

"Stupid untrained bastards," I grumbled as the light began to fade, waves of iron following behind and wrapping around me and everyone else, seeping into bones and muscles and freezing me in place.

This attack was not one I would ever use. Uncontrollable, powerful, and downright idiotic.

Shouting in pain and exertion, my magic pushed away from me, glittering trails of crimson streaking through the air and breaking through the attack to wrap around my men. Holding my magic as though it was a rope, I tugged the bands back, pulling at the powerful magic that had soaked the alley and releasing them from the deathly bind moments before the attack unveiled its final blow.

My chest ached as I gasped, falling to the ground only seconds before Edmund's men's attack sliced through the alley and Edmund's deformed army fell dying, their own foolish assault taking both Trpaslíks and Vilỳ lives in a slow painful end.

I wasn't going to rejoice yet. I was going to get us out of here.

"What in the world are they doing playing with the reverse flame?" Risha was snarling, slowly pulling the others to their feet. We clearly had the same idea.

The light would bring more Vilỳs to us, and with no quick escape route, our only chance was to soar up as Vilỳs were coming down. A fun game for myself, perhaps not for the others.

"Risha, I need you to take them up. Fly to the 'Young Prince', keep your head down, and move on to the 'Old Man'. Use the river as a guide to mask the magic. Meet me on the 'High Point'. Patar and Mara will go with you, cover you for anyone that follows. They are coming." I didn't need to say anything more. Risha and the two Skřiteks nodded, understanding the instructions and the code that we had set months before.

Ropes of green shot from her fingers, each line of magic attaching to the Skřiteks and Chosen who had survived this battle.

The poor, undertrained Chosen screamed in fear as her magic moved into them, connecting them to her in a tether they could not break. Risha's grating yell followed her into the air, her powerful magic swirling in a flood of wind as it swept her and her charges up like a rocket, our broken armies the tails of her kite.

The sound of wings were returning, the pounding of feet growing as the next wave of attackers came closer.

I stood still as Edmund's men broke into the dead end of the alley and faced me; the lone man who stood amidst destruction and death, long hair swaying in the breeze Risha left behind.

They froze, anger dripping from them. It snarled in their lips, and tensed in their shoulders. But the fear, the fear was clear in their eyes.

I would be scared of me too.

I needed to give Risha enough time to get ahead, but without anyone to protect I could at least have some fun.

My magic unfurled into the monsters that surrounded me in a wall of electric flame. The swirling magic of the attack felled man, woman, and winged beasts.

It was beautiful in its own way, until out of nowhere a familiar scream broke through the death, broke through the light, broke through the battle I was trapped in.

Joclyn.

Her screams hit me like a wall of stone, even though she lay miles from me, trapped in one of the many nightmares her sight had plagued her with for the past few months.

Her scream ripped through me as I continued to fight, my chest constricting painfully as her pain mixed with my magic in a deadly concoction that felled one after another, many of fading into nothing.

Teeth clenched, chest heaving, I fought through them. Fought my way back to her.

"Joclyn!" I yelled aloud, confusing the next line of Edmund's men that were flowing through the streets, flooding the quickly shrinking alley.

So much for games. I had more important things.

With one spark of my magic, I snapped the broken foundation of the building that was threatening to collapse, sending it to the ground.

Right on top of me.

Joclyn's magic erupted through me, the power joining with mine in a shield so strong that I stood underneath it, watching the tons of ancient architecture crumbling around me. Dust and stone settled over me in the remains of something that had once been beautiful as I stood in an upturned fish bowl.

My heart rate increased as Joclyn's did, images of her sight flashing in my mind, showing me a battle eerily similar to the one I had just ended.

"Wake up, Můj kamarád." My plea echoed through the shield as I surveyed the damage, making one last sweep for anyone that might have survived before breaking through the shield and taking off into the sky, dust falling away like snow.

"Wake up!" My worry was as palpable as the blood of her sight that flowed through my mind, mixing with the red tinted night that I soared through. I twisted around buildings and death filled air before landing on the rooftop of the 'high point', the tall lookout building that I had told Risha to meet me at. My tension was still taut with the possibility that she and the others might not have made it.

The battle was far below now. It was only the faint red of the world, only the hot breeze that moved through my hair as I stood looking over the city.

'Wake up, mi lasko!' I tried again, this time sending the call right into her mind, grateful when her heart rate slowed, the heavy influx of her magic regulating.

"Mi lasko?" I breathed. "Are you all right?"

'Ilyan.'

My heart relaxed with the word, my soul calmed. I stood over this unrecognizable city, watching as buildings fell, and Edmund's men destroyed and tortured us all under the cage that my father had built. I hated what it had become, but it was still home.

She made it that way.

CHAPTER 2
JOCLYN

Distorted sobs bounced off the cool grey stone in a sound so mangled that I wasn't sure if the crier was laughing or crying.

Especially here in this cave, with the smell of blood in the air.

Laughing-slash-crying in a blood soaked cave never led to anything good. I needed to get there and save them, or stop them, or pull myself out of this nightmare. I didn't care which came first.

Peering through the black and blue striation of light, I tried to find the source, but the deep blue of the moon cast confusing shadows over the rocks of the cave. For all I knew everything could be a person, a monster.

Rock walls shook as the deranged sob mutated into a scream that rattled against light and stone and brought everything crumbling down. Dust fell like snow, covering me, smothering me, surrounding me until it was all I could see; the vision shifting, buzzing in my ears like television static that pulled me out of the nightmare.

Or sight, because this clearly wasn't your everyday 'go

to school with no pants on' drama dream. With my track record I should have seen that coming.

Static flickered through the dust as the deep red glow of my sight took hold and everything became the same derelict, red-tinged streets of Prague.

A crash of an attack resounded over the tall buildings, the sound pulling me forward, guiding me through a tight alley and right into a fray of death and magic, Ilyan and Risha right in the middle.

Magic exploded everywhere, colors and blood and screams all blending together as Ilyan and Risha spun against them all, sending bricks and even cars flying through the air.

Ilyan spun as a bright yellow light filled the space and then everything came to a halt, magic and stone freezing in air, sparks of magic sticking against bodies and brick as silence drenched the battle.

I was stuck, watching as an attack sped through the air, right toward Ilyan.

"No!" I yelled, sure my magic was sparking, sure I could get the magic to move away.

Then, with a pop, the battle sped forward, everything moving in double speed as a tall, muscular figure walked through the battle toward me, their body shrouded in a dark cape, their face lowered and hidden in shadow. No one else seemed to notice they were there.

Not again. Not freaking again.

I was so over this nonsense.

Sound drained from the world, leaving only the thunder of my heart to pound in my ears as the figure took one step after another. Closer. Closer. I swear I could smell death on him. Death that spread as they lifted old gnarled hands and slowly pulled down the hood, revealing not the man I expected, but Wyn with a wide, nefarious smile. The look was so similar to Edmund's that before I knew it, I was screaming.

Wyn stared at me, the smile spreading to reveal blood-stained teeth behind thin lips. The smile grew as the magic changed to fire, as everything behind her began to burn and scream as though she had opened up the gates of hell.

I was pretty sure I ripped my throat open with how much I was screaming in my attempt to get away from the image of my best friend in demon form.

Nothing worked. I was stuck, watching her turn and leave everything to burn behind her. Cobbles boiled, bodies turned to char, and I was left behind in the sound of my scream. I was left with Ilyan who bled as he looked into the nothing before him; who lay with Thom who stayed lifeless against the red-tinged asphalt. They were there with my mother, Ryland, Talon, Risha. They were all there, their blood seeping into the leather of the worn shoes Ilyan had made me so long ago.

My scream froze in my chest as the bodies faded, shifting to rock and darkness as the sight became the cave that had haunted me for months. Dark and damp, with the deep crimson blood that flowed over the jagged rocks like a river. Ilyan's body spread-eagle over those same rocks, the river pouring from him, his eyes vacant, mouth agape.

My scream had been bad enough, but now it was replaced by Edmund's laugh, trapping me, pulling me deeper into the sight...

"Wake up!"

With a jolt, I sat straight up in bed, my eyes wild as the sight vanished into a wobbly bedroom, my chest heaving as I caught my breath.

'*Mi lasko?*' He was as panicked as I was.

'Are you all right?' he asked from the rooftop deep inside Prague. The old, battered building was his favorite for a lookout.

"Ilyan," I spoke aloud between heaving gasps, my eyes flashing to his side of the bed, despite knowing he was miles away.

Didn't stop me from wishing he was. He would surely be holding and singing to me if he was.

'Always,' he whispered in response to my thoughts, his magic moving into me in a thick wave. *'I will wrap my arms around you the moment I see you.'*

I could practically feel his arms around me now while his hushed voice drifted into my mind in the melody that was embedded into my soul.

Even though the nightmare had left and I wasn't quite as freaked out, I still wrapped myself up in the song, and fell back onto the bed to curl up in my blanket, warm and safe.

For now. The first light of day was filtering through our tiny, blown glass window, making the ancient iron light fixture and plaster cracks in the walls and ceiling that much more prominent. Beautiful. But there would always be that underlying panic, and a bit of anxiety that I had grown used to. War would do that to you.

"They are getting worse," I whispered more to myself than to him.

'I know. Who was in the cloak this time?'

I tensed at his question, knowing it was coming, and turned over in the bed, pulling his pillow into me like a teddy bear, silently thanking the stars it still smelled like him.

It wouldn't have taken much for me to drift back to sleep.

'Wyn.' Wyn hadn't been featured as the freak in the hood for a while, especially with that look.

Death, seduction, and doom.

I may have been wrapped in a warm blanket but I still shivered.

I was sure I was seeing what was to come, some hints as to how to get out of Edmund's zit. How to defeat him. But *someone* didn't quite agree with me.

'Are we calling him someone now?'

Fine. Sain.

'It's either that or 'the jerk who wouldn't shut up about how I was breaking all the sights and destroying his future.'

'That's a mouth-full Joclyn.' Even Ilyan was chuckling now. And for good reason, the name fit him. We knew he was doing something to my sights, we just couldn't figure out what. Months of training with Dramin and I didn't feel any closer to figuring it out, either.

'Did it look like Wyn?' Ilyan asked, getting us back on track.

I cringed. I really didn't want to pull up the recall and see that again. Unfortunately, I wasn't about to forget. The look in her eyes, the way she smiled, it was too close to Ryland, or the Ryland Cail had created anyway.

"Not really."

I could practically hear the gears turning in his head. I could even imagine him dragging his hand through his hair as he always did.

'You know me too well.'

I smiled in spite of myself. He was right; I did. But that was how it was supposed to be, after all. When you love someone.

Cue the cheesy romance music.

'We could ask Sain ...'

And... end cheesy romantic music.

I was certain I heard a record scratch as my gushy soundtrack came to an abrupt end.

'*Unless you are saying we can ask Sain for a recipe for baba ghanoush I would suggest you don't finish that sentence.*'

Thank goodness Ilyan laughed, I don't think either of us wanted to ask Sain about my sight-dreams and see his smug little face, with that smug little voice telling me the same thing I had heard whispered around the cathedral for the past few months.

That my sights were broken and I couldn't control my magic.

Sain better hope I didn't run into him any time soon.

I rolled off the bed with the full intention to get ready and join Ilyan on his rooftop, only to be met by a million aches and pains and a frustrated growl to go along with it.

I sounded like an angry bear. Ilyan's dislike of mornings was rubbing off on me. I felt like I had been tossed around in a cement mixer for the last twelve days.

"How long was I asleep?" *Please let it be more than two days. Please let it be more than two days.*

'*Enough, mi lasko.*' He was sidestepping, and part of me didn't care. I had already pulled the pitiful 'thirty-six hours' answer out of his head.

That wasn't nearly enough time.

I had been awake two weeks, and from what Dramin had told me in our semi-secret 'how to be a Drak' lessons, I would need four days to get my body back into shape. It took time to heal broken bones and bruises from days of battles and raids, after all. Those four days were very much needed.

And thirty-six hours was just a bit short.

Draks hardly slept as it was, and I *really* didn't sleep

thanks to the sights that love to wake me up and keep me from sleeping. Oh well, thirty-six hours was better than nothing.

"Maybe next time, then," I muttered as I made my way to our battered dresser, dull aches and throbs rippling over my body.

'You can sleep now,' Ilyan whispered, despite knowing the answer to that. *'You aren't due to run a raid for the next few days.'*

He had a point. Running through the city, facing waves of Edmund's men was definitely not what I needed right now.

I did know what I needed, however.

"I want to see you." It was only half a lie. My heart was already beating faster, a tense knot of eager anticipation forming in my belly at the plan that was bubbling in my mind.

'I want to see you, too.' His voice was deep and throaty as it came back to me in heavily accented English.

Hot darn. That voice. I needed that voice. Everywhere. I needed his hands everywhere, too. A plan was growing more detailed in my mind, and I was starting to blush and heat and giggle like a freaking love sick girl.

The sound was far too loud and embarrassing for my own good.

'Hmmm. Sounds like you want to see me more than a little bit.'

"It's mostly those arms I want to see," I teased, moving over to an old, antique mirror and the odd, fuzzy object that Ilyan was still trying to convince me was a brush.

Great, my cheeks were flushed, my eyes were sparkling, and I was sure my smile was tickling my earlobes. I knew full well he was looking at me through my eyes. I tried to wipe the smile off my face, but it was no good.

'Oh, is that all?' Ilyan's voice filled my mind as I pulled the long, black tangles of my hair into a messy bun, wrapping the délka vedení královsk around the ponytail holder a few times before letting it trail down to the floor.

My hair was a mess no matter what I tried to do with it, but I really didn't care. I was sure Ilyan would remedy the situation the moment he saw me.

'I will, but you better hurry. This rooftop is awfully lonely.'

'Is it now?'

He didn't answer, but he didn't need to. I could hear it in his voice, feel the longing in his heart. It set me on fire, a heavy wave of desire running through me.

Dagnabit! What was I waiting for?

Getting a moment alone with him was impossible most of the time, I wasn't going to miss this. Ilyan would win over sleep every time.

'It could be more than a moment, but you need to get here.'

Still smiling, I tore from the room, sipping from a mug of freshly pulled Black Water.

"Mmmmm," I sighed as the heat from the deep magic moved through me, soothing away the last of the aches and pains. Everything felt light for a moment, and for one second I was worried another sight would come, but it was only me and the slap of my shoes against the old, marble hallways.

'Sometimes, I wonder about you and that stuff.'

"It's my food, Ilyan. I mean, you like to eat food." I laughed, taking another long sip before refilling the mug. *'I'm always willing to share, you know.'*

This time he laughed, the deep, rippling sound shivering through me enjoyably before his voice went silent, his magic withdrawing as Risha arrived on the rooftop with several others. His focus changed as a million images flashed to mind mixing with what I had seen in my mind and rebuilding their most recent 'raid'. Or rather, an attempt at one.

I knew as well as anyone, that if you stepped one foot outside the cathedral you were going to be attacked. The attacks had gotten worse over the last few weeks, and we had lost more than a few Chosen. I knew Ilyan could handle himself, but I really needed to see it for myself to know he was okay.

I should have never let Ilyan put the block on the shield around our compound. I could have already Stuttered to him, but no...

'Mi lasko, we are all fine. Jsi moje láska, můj život, já budu s vámi brzy.'

"You are my love, my life, I will be with you soon." I quickly translated back to him. I just wished his promise could make all the fear go away.

All the sweet nothings and romantic interludes were gone.

'Did everyone make it through alive?' he asked as his focus shifted to his second-in-command. 'We need to get them back before another wave comes. Go by way of the large department store to the old warehouse near the wall and back.'

The quick Czech was like bees in my ears, so I tuned them out, looking out the high windows that lined the hallway as I rushed to him. Our private interlude may have been cancelled, but my destination hadn't changed.

Maybe I would add a side destination. I had time.

Taking another drink, I turned into a different hallway, and to the large oak doors that were set with metal hinges and grating. The ominous portal made the tiny hall look like the entrance to a dungeon. If I didn't know better I would say that was where I was, and I was sure certain people within this hall would agree with me.

And by certain people, I meant Wyn.

Of course, she might not feel that way if I could get her to leave the room more than twice a week.

The door creaked with a harassed sigh as I opened it to a near abyss. Dust motes danced through the ribbon of light that trailed behind me; the cluttered, derelict room seemed alive for a moment. Well, until the door closed and the depressing space sucked everything away.

I didn't know how she spent so much time in there. I was here every week to see my brother, but Wyn was in there more and more lately.

The longer Thom was unconscious, the more she was there.

Dramin lay, feigning sleep, on the other side of the room. His small twin bed was pushed into the corner, surrounded by bookcases that were covered with dusty, leather-bound books. Large earthen mugs of Black Water were tucked between them like a child who was trying to hide candy bars. It looked like his room at the Abbey had, much as I imagined his little alcove in the cave had. Full of food for mind and body, all of it intermingled in an ordered mess.

Dramin was like a mad scientist. A mad scientist who wasn't doing a very good job of pretending to sleep given that he gave me a wink before he rolled over to give us privacy. Not that you could get any in a room the size of a closet.

I would feel bad, but he wasn't who I had come in there for anyway.

It was for Wyn.

She lay over the foot of Thom's bed, her arms wrapped around him as though she was afraid he would slip away if she didn't hold on.

Part of me hoped that one of these times I would come to check on her and I would walk in and find them sitting and laughing as I was sure they had done so many centuries before.

There was sure to be quite a few bad jokes flying around.

The chances of that happening, however, were becoming less and less every day.

Boils covered all of his arms and part of his chest now. His body sunk together, collapsing in on itself as though he had been deflated. It was all part of the Přetížení dávka—the magical overdose. And, according to Ilyan, it was something with no known cause or cure.

Which of course meant that I had tried more than once. I had healed Wyn. I had healed Dramin. But with Thom, everything I had tried had bounced around inside of him like a ping-pong ball.

Not even my magic reacted to tell me what to do. It was as stumped as I was. Which made me even more pissed.

So he laid still, the same dreads, the same smug smile plastered to his face as though he had told one of his little jokes and closed his eyes to enjoy it. You would think everything was fine, except his side of the room looked nothing like him. Dramin's was a glimpse into the soul of the ancient man. Thom's was littered with a wild assortment of flora and fauna, poultices, and salves that sent a violent aroma into the air. Even a few battered mortal pill bottles lay among them all, a saline bag someone had tried to figure out how to use thrown into the corner. It was a hospital room of the worst sort, one formed in desperation and panic.

Anything to keep him alive.

I pulled the door shut behind me with a loud click. Wyn jerked away from Thom, her magic flaring in the air, ready for attack. Not that she looked ready for it; the rough blankets had left heavy lines against one side of her face, and her hair was plastered into some kind of a half Mohawk.

"Talon," she mumbled, calling out in longing as her wide eyes searched the dark, swallowing the world until they adjusted from sleep and saw me standing there in the darkness, staring at her, smiling.

"That good, huh?" she said with a laugh, her hands automatically moving to flatten whatever mêlée had occurred on her head.

"I wouldn't bother." I chuckled, still trying to keep my voice low. "I think you are fighting a losing battle."

"You are probably right. I would have to sleep in a real bed every once in a while for it to do what I wanted, anyway." She said the words, but she didn't stop trying to flatten her hair.

"You could keep it going and get yourself some matching dreads." I smiled at her as I took a few quick steps over to the still feigning Dramin, putting my half-full mug on his nightstand.

A little gift for my intrusion.

"Don't think that the thought hasn't crossed my mind." She twisted her hair around her finger, mindlessly staring at the tangled strands with a look of mild disgust. "I don't think I'd look good with dreads."

"Sure, but you can give it a shot. Who knows, you might fall in love with it."

I tried to smile, as did she, but neither stuck.

REBECCA ETHINGTON

I extended my hand to her in comfort. After all, I didn't think any words would help. They hadn't for the past few months, and they wouldn't now.

Sometimes words couldn't heal the way you thought they would. Sometimes they made you bleed more.

"When was the last time you left him?"

Her shoulders stiffened at the question, her hand tightening around the sheets as pain and irritation moved through her in waves.

"Left the room, Wyn. When was the last time you left the room?" I quickly clarified, even though it didn't seem to help. The reaction was the same.

"I took a team to the yellow sector last night. We thought we saw a light …" Her voice was stiff, dangerous, and I cringed against it. "I need to leave again in a few hours."

"Another raid?" I would like to say that it wouldn't happen given the fight that Ilyan had survived, but I knew better.

"Grocery run," she said, her focus still on Thom. "We need more apples, and beans, and anything else I can find in a can. I hope we don't lose anyone this time."

I nodded numbly as I tried to think of anything to say besides *how are you?* If I was tired of that question, I knew she would be, too.

"I have to go meet up with Ilyan, but do you want to spar later?" I knew I would end up with a broken bone with the way she was brooding, but if I could avoid it and not bring too many onlookers to the cathedral, I would call it a win.

"I'd like that." She looked back to Thom as she answered, her mind already leaving the conversation.

Part of me didn't want to leave her alone, but I had no

choice. I had to walk away from the darkness and back into the hallway. I had to walk away from her, from Thom, and in some strange way, from the hope that Edmund would stop hurting those I loved.

It was a dumb hope, really. No matter how much I tried to push the images of everyone dead in the street, of Ilyan bleeding in the cave, back into the black pit of my mind …

Edmund would still come.

It was why I kept sparring with Wyn. She was a warm up act.

CHAPTER 3

JOCLYN

The hallway was far too bright and active for this early in the morning. Every turn closer to Ilyan, the more people emerged. Staring at me, bowing, mumbling, and even tripping over their own two feet as they stared.

No matter what Ilyan had said, I still wasn't used to it.

If anything, it was worse than before because those mumbles and head bows were now accompanied by wide eyes, hushed whispers, and sideways glances. All that nonsense belonged in the hallways of a Junior High School, not the corridors of a massive church complex in the middle of a war.

Grow up people.

Says the youngest Queen ever.

Yep. I was still not used to it.

I quick-stepped into a longer, and much busier, hallway and instantly froze as the sound of thunder and drums resounded through the sky and ripped into the old building. Stone walls shook and groaned, lead windows rattled, and the ceilings released a cough of dust that fell over everyone like confetti.

My heart clenched as the recall from this morning's sight burst right to the forefront, my eyes dipping to black for a moment before I was able to push it away. But not fast enough, a few people to the left of me had already started to whisper, staring, one even pointing.

Wonder what lie about me Sain had told them this week...

'How many?' I shook my grumps away as I asked Ilyan, sure he had a better vantage point of what was causing the explosions from the roof he was perched on.

I couldn't see much from where I stood along the line of windows with everyone else, all eyes turned to the sky and the black specks that were circling around Edmund's zit.

More than a dozen planes circled around us, bombs falling from their bellies like insects. Months ago, after their attempted first bombing, there had been nothing for weeks. Then about a month ago they had started up again, every day.

Another bomb smashed against the barrier, shaking the ground beneath us and sending the building that Ilyan was standing on rocking dangerously to the left. I clung to the windowsill, sure I was going to fall over with Ilyan even though both he and the building were more than a mile away. Another blast, another shake and I pushed my magic through Ilyan, into the stone and foundation below him, searching for cracks or breaks or anything else that would spell trouble. We really didn't need another one of our tall, lookout buildings to come down, the 'Young Prince' was already unstable after the bombings of last week.

'They are coming from the west.' Ilyan tensed, my magic snapping back into my heart as he took off into the sky, soaring toward another of the high buildings. *'Looks like there are about twenty bombers today.'*

Twenty. That was almost double from yesterday. They must be getting desperate... or scared.

Silly, really. The mortals were scared of the cage Edmund had made, but we were the ones trapped inside of it. And we were terrified of what would happen if they brought it down.

Of what they would let out.

I'm sure they thought they had some idea what was inside, but even their imaginations couldn't predict the horrors they would be unleashing. Powerful dark magic and thousands of poisoned Vilẏs.

Their tiny, mutated faces were probably trained to the sky as ours were, waiting, hoping, and praying the barrier would break so they could feast on the new batch of victims on the other side.

The barrier was a ticking time bomb, one the mortals were trying to detonate.

Everything shook with the next round of explosions, the sound of thunder rumbling with a high groan that made it sound like we were trapped in a bass drum.

That one was big. Maybe too big.

'It looked like a nuke, but it can't be...' Ilyan provided, and my heart sunk. 'It didn't work.'

They had never used one of those before, I hadn't assumed they ever would. It didn't matter. Man's most powerful weapon of destruction was no match for Edmund and his freaking zit. The bombs held little more destructive power than a child banging pots together.

Guess I was going to have to up my game to pop that thing. I had gotten close twice before now, so it was possible.

In the meantime, the mortals could keep playing their war games.

One after another they came, lines of little black planes dropping bombs against the barrier and erupting into spirals of color that blossomed over the surface like oil on water.

Purple, blue, gold. A mesmerizing rainbow of movement. It was beautiful, or it would be if it wasn't for the massive destructive power behind it.

The colors blossomed like flowers, my head spinning as dust continued to fall over my head.

Specks tickled against my neck, they fell over my nose and kissed my eyelashes. I barely cared. I wasn't even seeing the colorful dance anymore.

All I could feel was the comfortable weight of my magic, the warmth as it pulsed through me spark.

Like lightning trapped inside.

'Do you feel that?' Lightning sparked as another bomb dropped and the world went red and yellow and wobbly.

'Feel what?' Ilyan was so focused on the planes, on the bombs that they were dropping on us, that he hadn't even noticed.

Before I had a chance to explain, the second bomb hit and the ripples of color spread. The red of the zit fell away as the dome vanished. Popped like a soap bubble.

Blue sky spread like a blanket, the chill of a winter we weren't experiencing rushing on the back of a wind we hadn't felt in months. Birds sang and I saw a cloud for the first time in years. Okay, not years, but it sure felt like it.

They had done it!

I had no idea how, but they had done it. I would rejoice, but I knew what happened next and I was already drifting into full panic.

'Done what?'

He was as scared as I was, but I didn't know why he

wasn't moving. We had talked about this before. If they were successful, we needed to act. We needed to lock as many of the rats in as we could. We needed to get to Edmund.

'Come on Ilyan! We have to move!'

Hordes of black wings were already taking off from the ground, millions of the screaming things rushing out of their cage and ready to attack, ready to create a new army.

'Not gonna let that happen! Come on, Ilyan.' "We have to move!" I yelled that last part aloud, pushing off from the windowsill as I pulled one of the Chosen after me. I was ready to lead this army, kill Edmund, and end all of this.

Ilyan didn't seem quite as keen as I did. In fact, none of them did. They were all staring at me with wide eyes, side glances, and those dratted murmurs that had followed me around most of my life, and gotten so much worse after the fountain.

Whatever. I would defeat Edmund and that would shut them right up.

'Joclyn?'

The roar of the planes grew as the large, black birds came closer, their bellies bare and open. The zit was gone and they were ready to drop more bombs, to stop whatever they had unveiled. Only this time, it would hit us. This time, it would destroy us all.

"We have to move! Guys, come on, before they attack." I was trying to use some kind of a Queen voice, but it didn't work. The entire hall was still looking at me like I had lost it.

'Ilyan,' I gasped, as I tried to push a few more Chosen and a Skřítek towards the door. It did about as much good as pushing a boulder through a river. *'They did it. You need to get back ...'*

'What are you—'

"It's time!" I yelled over him, still not mastering the Queenly command. I was begging now. Awesome. "They've done it. We need to move!"

'Joclyn! What?' Ilyan's confusion was mounting, but I couldn't think through my own worry, through the Vilÿs screams that were ringing through the open window.

And still, not one of my supposed subjects moved. We weren't that ill prepared, were we? We had trained for this. They had all trained for this.

"The barrier is down. We need to move."

I tried to pull power into my voice, but all of my confidence ebbed away as everyone gaped at me with downcast eyes, whispering to each other as they looked at me in fear and pity.

Okay, that look I hadn't seen before. What the heck?

'Mi Lasko...'

"What are you waiting for?" I had run out of steam, my hands were spread out in front of me in a plea. Fear and confusion grew as they looked at each other, and then at me.

"Perhaps we are waiting for the barrier to break."

That voice. That slow, snide, and overly calm voice. It was poison against my soul and brought on an incessant need for punching. My lip twitched, the false calm that always followed him around pulling my agitation and panic back up to full throttle.

Freaking hell.

Sain.

'The barrier isn't down is it?' My heart sunk to my toes as I glanced back out the window, to the blue sky and clouds and the flying Vilÿ. It all looked real. It sounded real.

'No, it is not.'

Sain stepped through the crowd, everyone parting to welcome him like he was some holy man. He certainly looked the part. He had ditched the tweed suit for a long Drak robe he had pulled from who-knows-where; mix that with his unkempt hair and scruffy beard and he certainly looked the part. People swarmed around him, hovering, smiling. All while taking a step away from me.

'Ano,' Ilyan swore. 'Don't rise. I'm coming.'

Don't rise? Who did he think he was talking to?

'I know exactly who I am talking to, my love. Don't rise.'

Okay he was probably right, just looking at my father was making my blood boil.

Sain looked at me with concern and fear that I believed about as much as I believed Ilyan was hiding wings in his spine before whispering something to the girl next to him. Her eyes popped before he took a step forward, worry deepening in his face even if it didn't hit his eyes.

"What did you do? The barrier is down!" I snapped at him. Having to deal with him never did anything good for my temper.

'Don't rise.'

"Child," Sain cooed. We had moved into the condescending tone quicker than usual this time. "Daughter, my child, can't you see ...? The barrier ..." He gestured toward the window, his eyes sad.

Right as he said it the screams of the Vilÿs stopped, the sky rippled with red, and the sounds of the planes faded to a resonating rumble of television static. The grinding, electrical noise that had taken over my sights, invading my reality.

I didn't need to look out the window he was gesturing to. I already knew what I would see.

'Joclyn, just breathe. Just get away from him.'

I should have just raced to Ilyan as we had planned, to forget all of this, but I couldn't. Not with the way my anger pulsed, not with the way my muscles seized. Not with the way he was looking at me.

"What did you do, Sain?" I growled, the anger in my voice causing several around me to flinch.

"What do you mean?" His feigned innocence ground against me. "I didn't—"

"I know you did something!" I may have been a little ragey, but it was like this every freaking time. I couldn't let him get away with this again.

'Don't rise.'

I had gotten one step in before a strong arm wrapped around my stomach, pulling me into a hard chest that I knew all too well. Those rugby muscles had come in handy over the past few months, and now they were holding me back with all the strength of a hippo on a rampage.

Him, not me. I doubt I could hippo anything.

"Let me go, Ry," I growled as I fought against his hold.

"Not going to happen, Jos." His grip may be tight, but even I could tell by the tension in his voice that he was having a hard time keeping a good hold on me. "You're making a fool of yourself, *Your Highness*."

Two words and the reality of what I had been about to do, of what I had done, came crashing down on me. Fear and pity. It was what I had seen in their faces before and it was echoing back at me as they all looked from Ryland, to Sain, to me. But mostly at me, the queen who had, for all they knew, hallucinated the fall of the barrier then turned and attacked her father.

Great.

I stopped pushing against the wall that Ryland had captured me in.

He didn't let go, and I didn't blame him. I still felt dangerous.

"What did you do?" I asked my father again, trying to stay calm even though rage was grinding through me.

Sain looked at me, his eyes pushed open, his mouth agape as he shook his head, looking to those around him in loss and confusion. "I didn't do anything, darling."

Darling? That was a new game to his repertoire.

It boiled my blood.

"Are you okay?" Sain seemed genuinely concerned. I wasn't going to feed into that. "What can I do?"

'You can face him, my love. Be who you are. Handle him like the queen you are.'

"You can tell me what you did." Keeping my voice calm and diplomatic was the equivalent of pulling teeth right then. I wasn't sure it worked. "With the sights. First the Vilỳs, that attack last month, a hundred other little things, and now this. What did you do?"

I was getting angry again, and Ryland sensed it, his arm tightening in warning.

"I did nothing. The sight was broken with the choices you made, dear child. It is one of the Zlomený now. I have explained this all before." And there it was, the same excuse he had used for months. "Perhaps, if you cannot control your power, you are not fit to be a Drak."

This was clearly not going to be a badass queen day.

Lightning shot threateningly from my fingers as Ryland pulled me away again. Everyone else took a step back, several ready to turn and run.

Okay, so maybe I was still a bad-ass queen. I just didn't want to bow down to His Royal Highness: The First of the Drak right now.

"The power is too much for you," he continued,

standing as though nothing had happened. "I am worried about the risk you are putting us all in."

"I am not—"

"Even your behavior is not fit for what you are. I stand by what I said before: 'You are going to kill us all'."

"Sain!" I yelled, but he said nothing more before turning and walking away. More than half of the people in the hallway followed him like sheep. The other half lagged behind for barely a moment before they, too, turned away.

Great.

I tried one last time to escape Ryland's hold, but he held on, his hands clasped one over the other like he was going to wrestle me to the floor, something I was sure he had very seriously considered.

"What was all that about?" he asked, as the last of the Chosen turned the corner.

"What was *what* about?"

"Oh, I dunno ... you screaming that the barrier was down and then trying to attack your father—"

"I've decided I'm calling him 'the jerk who wouldn't shut up about how I was breaking all the sights and destroying his future' now."

"Not funny Jos," he sighed, rolling his eyes in exaggerated frustration. "Be serious."

"I am being serious. I saw the barrier come down Ry. I saw it so clearly I thought it was real, and I know he has something to do with it."

Ryland gave me the same look that he always did when I brought this up. We stood on opposite sides of team Sain.

"How can he have?"

"I saw it, Ry."

"I'm not saying you didn't." Ryland dragged his hand

through his curls, his blue eyes growing dark as they darted down the hallway Sain had vanished down and back to me.

"It's just ..."

"What?"

"Is what Sain is saying true? About your magic? About you?"

I blinked, my jaw clenching. I hadn't expected that.

"I know he's your friend, but I wouldn't believe all the garbage Sain spews," I said, taking a step in full expectation of continuing down the hallway as though nothing had happened.

"But he's your father."

"I've told you not to call him that, Ry. You of all people should know how I feel about him." A small bubble of hurt was forming in the pit of my stomach as I turned back to Ryland. His eyes had an odd mix of hard and sad. "You had a crappy father, too."

"Sain is my friend. He has his own demons. If he is doing something I can promise you—"

"Ryland!" Ryland's rebuttal was interrupted by an overexcited voice, the sound of steps loud as we were bombarded by Ryland's protégé and full-time shadow. The kid was nearly a teenager now, and so lanky it was hard to find clothes that fit him. He didn't care, though, the smile that spread over his face squished the kiss on his cheek together until it looked like a burn.

He was as energized as he always was. That was, until he caught sight of me and his smile faded to something akin to horror, his youthful eyes wide, lanky limbs freezing in place. Then everything about him was more irritating than endearing.

Gossip travels way too fast when you are trapped in an apocalypse.

Thanks, *Dad*.

"Hello, Jaromir," I hoped the calm greeting would take the edge off, but he took a step back, his eyes widening more, if that was possible.

Jaromir stared between Ryland and me like a confused child trying to gauge which parent to side with. In the end he chose to stay still, attempting to communicate nonverbally with Ry.

"I don't care what good he's done. You know me better than anyone. Why would you believe him, when this is how people treat me now," I gestured to Jaromir. "I would pick who your friends are more carefully, Ry."

"Interesting advice coming from you."

My focus snapped to him, my eyes hard as he met me with a smile, the grin tentative as he pulled his hand through his hair.

"I'm sorry?"

"I mean... You're my friend, Jos," he said with a sigh, his eyes looking to the chain that still hung around my neck before turning back to the barrier that had caused all the problems in the first place. "I still choose you to be. I don't think you are a bad choice."

I stared at him, my tongue tied in a large knot, shock pressing against my chest in an oddly comforting weight.

'*Joclyn,*' Ilyan pressed into my mind, his worry over what had happened paramount. Either that or he wanted to get me away from his brother. '*I want you here.*'

"Right," I finally said, knowing it was a lame retort. "I would still be careful."

"Okay, Jos." He smiled in that goofy way he always did. "I'll talk to Sain. We'll figure this out."

"Okay." I wasn't sure I believed him, but I smiled anyway and ran past him and Jaromir, keeping my head high and focus away from everyone. One step into the courtyard and people were already staring.

Ryland's quick Czech followed behind me as he and Jaromir talked about lesson plans and sparring. I walked faster, pretending I still didn't understand the Czech, though I did. It took me three months, but I had mastered it. I could officially ask for more than the bathroom and not tell people they looked like dumplings. Although I would gladly choose to speak nothing except English any time I could.

'Joclyn?' Ilyan was desperate now. I felt bad he was trapped there, unable to leave the rooftop while all of this was going on. *'Are you okay?'*

'Did you see?' I asked, already knowing the answer.

'Yes. All of it.' His tone said it all. *'I want you to come right to me.'*

'You don't have to ask twice.' I was fully aware he had already asked at least five times.

Everyone was already watching me, so I had no qualm with taking off on a full sprint through the courtyard. Heads turned with every step, and the murmurs followed behind me, picking at the back of my head like lice.

It took way too long to recognize the heat, the spin, and the magical weight of my sight. Now, in the court-yard was not the best time for this, especially with what had happened with Sain's challenge of a few months before.

But I couldn't stop it. My emotions were drained and my magic might as well have been a tsunami. I barely made it to one of the tiny alcoves when the whole world spun head-over-heels and my vision shifted, my magic coming to life.

"Crap," I hissed, grabbing the wall right before I fell into it and my magic pulled me into a sight, and the world around me sunk to black.

The derelict streets of Prague drifted through the red, the streets I had run through so many times I had lost count coming into focus.

I already knew what was going to happen. I knew what was coming.

The cloaked man.

The figure ran from street to street as I tried to follow, waiting for him to turn and remove the hood as he always did. This time, he kept running.

Over one more turn, one more flash of the tail of his cloak.

I turned with him, following him. Ready to see who it was this time. My money was on Ryland, it always tended to be the last person I had talked to.

In place of the same scene I usually faced, there was a lone man, someone I recognized all too well.

Edmund.

My heart accelerated to a vibrating pace, my entire body tensing in fear. I couldn't move, even if I had legs to do so. I was a floating ball of magic, staring at him as he stood in the middle of the street, Ovailia beside him. Sain was huddled off to the side like a wounded kitten, a small child I had never seen before standing before him, staring down at Sain like she was scared of him.

Red and black skittered over my vision before the street came back into view, my heart plummeting at the way the child fidgeted, the way she tried to move away. Something holding her in place, something keeping her there. She twitched and tried to run, but she could only stare at me crying with a sound I had heard before.

A sound I had heard minutes before.

The closer the sight took me, the more in focus the little girl became. She was no older than five, a long, tattered nightgown hung over her emaciated frame, dirty brown hair hung past her waist. Blood dripped from her fingers in a slow rhythm that fell into pools of scarlet that covered her feet, sprinkled over her bare calves like a Jackson Pollock painting.

The red of the blood splattered down the front of her nightgown, seeping from the ragged gash in her throat, her eyes crying tears of the same color.

"Auntie," she whispered, and I recoiled, the alarm in my sight increasing. "You've got to stop him. He has it. He's going to hurt her."

I wanted to scream at the sound of her voice, at the way she looked at me, but the sound never came.

The sight melted away in an ember burn, leaving me standing in the alcove, the low chatter of Ryland and his protégé still echoing toward me.

I was frozen, trying to process what had happened, what I had seen. It had changed again, but this time, it hadn't changed in the normal way. It wasn't just a different face behind the hood.

It was a different street. A different day. It was an actual sight.

It was like the first time Dramin had pulled me into sight. It felt real.

'Ilyan,' I called to him, needing his connection. Judging by the way his heart beat thundered inside of me, he had already seen. He already knew. 'Did you see?'

'Come here, now.' He hadn't needed to say it.

I was already running.

CHAPTER 4
JOCLYN

I moved at a dead run, my ribbon pulling against my sloppy bun as it trailed behind me in a bright line of color. People flashed by me, turning their heads to stare with a combination of horror and fear.

They would have to sort through their emotional constipation and prejudices on their own. I had bigger things on my mind, like that dark, blood covered street.

Throwing up a shield, I ran past the thin, white line that covered the cobbles and plunged through the barrier Ilyan and I had surrounded the cathedral complex with. The thing was like a suction cup powered by a vacuum.

Air pressed against me like a lead weight, making it hard to breathe, hard to think, but I didn't stop. I kept moving, propelling my feet through the pea soup tunnel and out into the open where I prepared to breathe and continue my chase.

That first gulp was always the worst.

I don't think it was possible to ever get used to sucking in the aroma of rotting corpses and forgotten life and not feel like you had been transported to hell.

Inside of the complex, there were still shadows of the war we were stuck in, streaks of blood no one could remove, broken windows and shutters still waiting for repair. But it was clean, it was safe. Outside of the barrier, however, underneath the bright red glow of Edmund's dome, you couldn't ignore that we were still trapped in the city that he had designed to be a death sentence.

Out here, silence poured over the streets making every creak of an abandoned building and chitter of the Vilý a siren to danger. Fresh streaks of blood splashed over the carcasses of the ancient city; burned out cars sat rotting, belongings scattered over bloodstained streets from when people had attempted to escape. Out here, it was an active war.

A tight knot formed in my gut as I turned back to the cathedral that was as dead and forgotten as the rest of this place. All signs of life were wiped out by the shield, the cathedral and courtyard as broken down as the one I now stood in. Exactly how it would look to Edmund's men.

I leapt into the air, my wind and magic catching me, propelling me toward the heavy pull of Ilyan's magic.

'Be safe,' he whispered, his magic filling me as he tracked my movements, as he traveled alongside me.

My magic carried me up toward the rooftops, the broken shingles and collapsing spaces stretching before me like a deranged, rotting garden.

Speeding up, I kicked off the corner of an old wrought iron balcony, the ancient structure shaking underneath the pressure. I had already moved away from it when the sound of metal against stone ricocheted through the crippling silence. The balcony crumbled to the ground, landing against a street cart, the old food vendor's stand collapsing under the pressure.

Grinding, heaving, explosive sounds boomed through the dilapidated city, growing louder as bricks and wood continued to collapse.

Darn it all. I had kicked against the balcony a thousand times before... which was probably why it collapsed. And of course it had to do it with the loudest racket possible, guiding everyone and their dog right to me. Double darn.

'What was that?'

If he had heard it, then so had any other living thing within a twenty-mile perimeter.

Great.

'I'm fine. Just making everything twice as hard as it needs to be.'

'You seem to have a knack for that,' he chuckled, even though it was laced with panic. *'Just get here.'*

Black clouds of Vilÿs were already zooming through the streets below me, heading right to the crumbled remains of seventeenth century architecture.

For the time being, it had pulled their focus. Too bad Vilÿs could track magic like nobody's business. It was why I was so good at it. Why all the Chosen were. They bit us and infected us with magic, and that little bit was what had decided to stick.

Minutes.

I had minutes.

I pushed my flight, soaring faster, right into the warmth that was Ilyan's magic. The tall building he stood on peaked out from behind the ruins of the city. I was almost there, not that it mattered, I could already hear them snarling behind me. I could feel each speck of their power as they streamed behind, determined to destroy me.

I should have burned the trail.

'They are coming.' I pushed myself faster, knowing it

wouldn't do much. I had tried to outrun them before and failed.

'*So am I.*' A small, black shape appeared between the buildings as Ilyan sped toward me, hair and délka vedení královsk swirling around him like he was a falling star.

Maybe he was, with the magic that was already blazing from his fingers. Powerful. Beautiful.

His heart pounded along with mine, every muscle tight as he soared closer, his bright blue eyes searching for me.

'*Can you see me?*' I asked. I could see through his shield, but Ilyan couldn't see through mine. That was one ability Ilyan didn't have.

'*No,*' he responded, '*I can feel you.*'

As he was about to collide with me his arms opened, wrapping around me in an iron cage of comfort and security. I had barely felt him against me before he changed direction, his magic carrying us high into the air, above the buildings, above the Vilỳs who continued forward blindly, for the moment anyway.

"Ilyan," I whispered into the hollow of his neck, the momentary calm shattered as the creatures stopped, their bodies jittering around in a manic need to find the trail again.

"My love," he growled in deep Czech, the sound lighting me on fire.

I gave him a smile he couldn't see before I shifted my weight, ready to take off after the Vilỳs and set them ablaze. Ilyan held me tighter.

"Wait."

"But..." I hissed, cut off when he smiled back at me. Or smiled at what he thought was me. He was more grinning at my nose, but whatever.

"Wait," he repeated with a grin as we hovered high in

the blanketed sky, the planes from this morning still patrolling the perimeter in a slow circle like vultures waiting for flesh to rot.

Ilyan's arms were a sweet pressure against my spine as his lips pressed against the crown of my head, a calm wave washing through me.

'*How can you be so calm when...*' The thought was cut short when he laughed, a building several blocks away from where the Vilỳs had congregated collapsed.

The sound was louder than the small balcony mishap, as loud as the bombs as it called the Vilỳs to it, all thoughts of us forgotten.

"What did you do?" I asked as I turned, my shield dropping.

His hand left my back to gently push the wild strands of my hair out of my face, a mischievous smile spreading at the question, his magic gently setting us down on the roof of one of the many buildings of the city. The two, long, golden ribbons of our royalty tangled around each other, clinging together as if they belonged that way.

"Don't worry; it's not the first building I've torn down today." His voice was gruff even as his eyes danced.

"What?"

"It was coming down, anyway," he clarified, as if that made it all better. "Are you okay?"

He took my hand, the burn on his skin pressing against mine. I would happily drown in the warmth of him, the heat spreading as he moved closer, his arm snaking around my wrist and pulling me against him and making the rest of the world fall away.

"Ilyan," I whispered, the tension of the last few minutes melting into nothing.

"Můj kamarád." His voice was rough and deep, his arms

pressing me into him, stomach against hips and shoulder against chest.

I fit against him as he looked down at me with a blazing light in his eyes that ignited something explosive. Tiny pinpricks of light burst to life around us like fireflies. The colorful specks danced as the strength of our connection energized them.

I would never get tired of this light show. I would never get tired of him.

Which was probably why I was having trouble focusing on anything other than kissing him right then.

"Ilyan." His name was a groan, a plea for further contact I knew he couldn't ignore.

He wanted it, too.

His lip twitched in response, the soft, wet, kissable smile mercilessly too close to mine, his breath hot against the tender skin of my lips.

Oh goodness, when did everything get so hot?

His eyes flashed before he pressed his lips against mine, before his magic swelled and the lights became a freaking half-time firework show.

We were clearly not good at hiding. So much for being responsible rulers.

'Ilyan.' I tried to get his attention, tried to pull away, but the effort was half-hearted, just as the silent plea inside his mind was.

His lips trailed over my jaw, down my neck as he traced a line down my spine, down, down until he gripped my hips, pulling me into him roughly. I moaned.

"Miss me?" he whispered as those kisses trailed back up my neck and to the tender skin below my ear. "Yes."

Another moan. He chuckled, the sound only driving me more mad.

"You know I want to continue..." his voice was raspy as he nibbled at my earlobe and my knees almost went out from underneath me. Thankfully he hitched my thigh over his hip, holding me up. "But we have something--"

"You are not going to make me watch bloody children over kissing you, are you?" I interrupted him, grinning as I pulled back.

I could already see his answer in his eyes. More later. When hot water and squishy mattresses could be involved.

He was right, of course, picking rubble out of your butt-crack was never fun.

'I agree with that.' His smile faded into a low frown as he looked at me, his hand soft as the tips of his fingers traced over my face. "Show me again what you saw."

Exhaling heavily, I placed his hand against my mark, gasping as the strength of his magic ripped through me, my knees shaking. My recall flared inside of me like a flame. The same scene played before our eyes: the cloaked figure running, my vision flowing around a corner to face Edmund and the child. The girl had barely started to turn when Ilyan's hand pulled away from me, the recall severing along with the connection.

"I thought so..." he stuttered, his thoughts moving so fast I couldn't pick up on any of them. "But that shouldn't be possible."

He staggered away, his magic leaving as the skin contact did. His eyes were darker than I had seen them.

I had thought the sight of the girl was frightening, but somehow, Ilyan's reaction to her was even more so.

"Ilyan?"

"Have you seen her before?"

I flinched at the fear in his voice, at the wide eyed stare he was giving me.

"No." I regretted asking what came next. "Do you know her?"

"It's Rosaline."

Wyn's daughter.

No, Wyn and Thom's daughter.

"What? Isn't she ... dead?" I couldn't compute it. It didn't fit. Nothing about it fit. It wasn't past, not with the city the way it was. And Rosaline was already gone, so it couldn't be now, and it couldn't be future.

I looked up to Ilyan, the alarm in his eyes making it clear he was following my train of thought perfectly.

"Is she alive?" I asked, Sain's claims of my broken sight pounding on the back of my skull.

"No. There is no way she can be, but something is going on," Ilyan answered, his steps wide as he gathered my hands in his. "Did the sight feel like the others? Did it feel real?"

"Yes," I whispered against him. "It had that pull ... like it's trying to tell me something. And there was none of that static ..."

Ilyan stiffened, a violent pull of warning and magic moving through both of us from somewhere on the other side of the city. It was magic we had only set up days before in an attempt to more easily track the movements of Edmund's men.

"The proximity alarm?" I asked, turning toward the magic and narrowing my eyes, as if I would be able to see on my own from this far away.

It was just a red tinted destruction zone.

"How did the alarm miss it?" Ilyan asked, following my lead to the edge of the roof. "They are set up to track armies entering from the barrier..."

"Not the middle of the city," I finished for him.

I dropped to my knees, magic scanning the red-tinted rooftops and the shadowed labyrinth of streets for whoever triggered the alarm. It was gone before my magic could get there, only to be replaced by an identical alarm, many more miles away and to the left.

"What in the world..." My heart dropped as I turned, eyes narrowing as my magic soared away, only to jump again a mile in the opposite direction.

"You are feeling this too, right? I mean, I'm not losing it?"

"No," Ilyan responded, crouching beside me and peering into the city, albeit in a completely different location.

The same magic was shifting around the city as if it was playing a game of hopscotch.

No, as if it was Stuttering.

Stuttering. Seamless movement from one place to another.

Only Ilyan and I could Stutter inside the dome. But besides us, there was only one other person we knew of who could move so swiftly.

Edmund.

"It can't be..." Fear gripped me, it pulled through my muscles as I froze, crouched against the ancient rooftop. "Edmund."

A hot wind wound around us, ribbons tangling as we both stood, feeling the magic pulse again, feeling it move and shift.

"Is it the same?" Ilyan whispered, his voice rumbling inside my head. "The magic, is it the same as his?"

I knew Edmund's magic as well as Ilyan did. I had been trapped with it. I had been tortured by it.

And I knew that the magic below us wasn't the same. It

felt different. The power was different. The malice and rot within it was different. If only judging by that, it wasn't Edmund. It couldn't be.

And yet ...

"No one else can Stutter."

Ilyan's muscles tightened, his thoughts going into a speed so fast I couldn't help flinching at the onslaught. "But it's not him."

"I don't recognize this magic, Ilyan. It's someone new."

New, and yet somehow familiar.

The anger, the poison of its emotional depth, it was the same as the Vilỳs', the same as what I had removed from each Chosen who we brought into the cathedral. The same as what I had felt from Edmund's men before they attacked us.

It might not be him, but it was one of his, which meant one thing ...

Someone in Edmund's new army could stutter. Some newly awakened magic was strong enough to do one of the most difficult magical skills.

I looked to Ilyan, the look on his face making clear he had heard my thoughts.

I wrapped my hand around his, letting his magic fill me as he pulled me into a Stutter, pulled me into the dark void between worlds as we chased the magic.

CHAPTER 5
SAIN

Everything was going perfectly.

Joclyn's madness was becoming more active, and thanks to this morning's little 'episode', more public.

It was a spur of the moment decision to feed her that vision, but it paid off, working its way in nicely with the rumors I had been spreading since the fountain.

I couldn't stop the smile.

First, she couldn't call her magic at the fountain.

Now, she can't tell sight from reality.

Perfect. Perfect.

One step closer...

"Sir! Excuse me, Sain! Sir!" A voice erupted from behind me, concerned, deep, feminine.

I tensed before I turned, unsurprised to see the pretty Skřítek I had whispered to in the hall a few minutes before rushing toward me.

'Look at her eyes,' I had whispered, the low voice agitating poor Joclyn more. *'That's how you know her magic is destroying her. You can see the madness there.'*

Seeing the woman now, it was clear she believed me. I

knew she had already spread those few simple words around.

Little seeds of doubt, planted everywhere, ready to grow.

"Yes?" I asked, the sound of her approach echoing in the mostly empty courtyard. Normally, it was full around that time. I supposed everyone had left to see what the commotion was about.

Forget growing, this was going to spread like a weed.

"I'm sorry, sir," she mumbled as she reached me, eyes falling to her toes in respect.

It had taken far too long to get these Chosen to treat me the way I should, finally it was starting to take hold.

"I ... I need to know. Is what you said before true? About the queen's magic destroying her mind?"

"I want to say that it isn't," I sighed dramatically, placing my hand on her elbow in what I hoped was a fatherly way. "But I have seen this before. It is a common ailment of my kind. When the mind cannot handle the power of sight, it begins to destroy itself—"

She gasped, the horror on her face evident. "Our poor queen."

I bristled, anger and agitation running through my spine. She may have bowed, but she had not learned. She should not be showing worry or sympathy for one so pathetic and volatile. Disgust, anger, fear—those should be lining her face, the reality of the weakness of her queen filling her.

Instead, she was worried.

Unrelenting anger moved through me, numbing my better logic as I pulled my hand away, grateful not to have to touch her anymore. My anger kept growing, but I tried to make the emotion in my face mirror what she was obviously feeling.

Sadness. Devastation. The emotions were there, even if I didn't feel them. She melted into putty in my hands.

"Will she be all right? You are the first of the Drak; your magic is pure. Surely you can see what is coming for her."

This time, I couldn't disguise the smile. I didn't even try. This was the response I wanted—this dedication, this awe. To me, not to the ones who had stolen my throne.

"I see nothing. When one of the Drak compromises our magic, all sight is broken." Well, when one of my kind didn't let me control what they saw, anyway, but I wasn't going to get into that with this woman. "The sight will not become clear again until after the magic has left her."

'We need you.'

I visibly jumped as Ovailia's voice filled my mind, my heart rate accelerating as I cut off the story. Ignoring Ovailia would not end well.

The woman looked at me, alarmed by my sudden reaction. I could tell by the look in her eyes that she expected my eyes to fade to black, and me to give sight right before her. The eagerness, the awe, it was all there, as it should be.

She would have to drown in her disappointment.

"I'm sorry, but one of the Chosen is in need of my help," I gasped, forcing as much emotion in my voice as possible. "If you'll excuse me."

I didn't wait for her response, I immediately turned and left. I had learned hundreds of years before not to keep Edmund and Ovailia waiting. While I had given them my fair share of defiance before, now was not the time to risk what I was building there. I needed them as much as they needed me, not that they knew any of that. They still assumed that I was the one being manipulated.

Shield up, I darted through the people in the courtyard and made a beeline for the tiny passage hidden behind the main barracks. Heart pounding, I moved into the shadowed, overgrown narrow that war had rendered forgotten. It was like walking into a jungle. It was the perfect place to escape, to store a certain piece of incriminating black fabric.

Grabbing the latter, I took a few more steps before opening the old, wooden door that had served as a servants entrance, and then as an escape during the coup in the twelfth century. Ironic that I was using it for much the same purpose now.

The doorway glimmered with a faint sheen of white, Ilyan's barrier. Most people avoided it like the plague. Most people would get a shock if they even got close without permission.

Not me.

There was one design flaw that the foolish man had overlooked. One little loophole that suited me perfectly.

The shield was made to keep all of Ilyan's people inside, to keep them safe. However, to keep Edmund and his men from finding us, all of those who served the tyrant would see nothing of our camp if they were to cross the invisible line. They would only see the destruction of the city.

Ilyan, in all of his naïveté, never assumed someone could be inside the barrier and see the world as it was yet pass through without his blessing into the destruction of Prague.

He had never assumed someone could serve two masters or, in my case, none at all.

Grinning, I plunged into the torture chamber, air sucked from my chest as heat and pressure assaulted me from all sides.

Like a struggling infant, I fell through to the other side,

collapsing to the ground as my hands spread on the cold, bloodstained road. The shadowed darkness swallowed me as I coughed in an attempt to catch my breath.

'Begin at the third mark.' Her voice was a growl as she gave me the instruction for the starting place. Obviously, she wasn't looking forward to seeing me.

The feeling was mutual.

Coughing, I lifted my head toward the alley and a dozen pairs of hungry yellow eyes that peered at me, teeth glinting through the dark. The tiny, infected creatures took off into the air, making a beeline for me.

"Zdechnout." One word and the tiny things froze in mid-flight, their bodies falling to the ground with a dull thud. Blood seeped out of the tangles of flesh and bone, staining everything around them with shimmering pools.

The heavy material rippled like thunder through the silence as I unwound the fabric, throwing a heavy cloak over my shoulders. The hood lay low over my head as I shrouded myself in the dark.

'You have ten minutes. Get to the third.' Her voice dug into me. I didn't like being ordered around, not with what the divine magic of the earth had created me for.

Soon, even she would bow to me.

Silently, I ran over the streets of the deep red city, the sound of the cloak echoing over abandoned buildings and forgotten streets. The fabric was heavy, perfect for the prickly harshness of cold that was familiar for Prague this time of year. Once I was outside the barrier, it would be needed, now, it was nothing more than a hindrance.

'To Kozi, near the river,' she snapped right as I turned the corner, the street lamp that marked 'the third' just ahead. Kozi, however, was on the other side of the city. Same as always.

53

I uncaged my magic from where I always kept it hidden, letting the full strength of it erupt as I Stuttered across the city, right to where Ovailia had commanded. The Kozi: the long, historic street that extended straight from the Vltava River. The banks had overflowed weeks ago, leaving bright red water lapping against the historic buildings, eroding the cobbles and thousands of years of history.

One place to another, without the faintest bit of effort.

A perfect Stutter, as they were meant to be.

Ilyan could perform a Stutter because of the magic of his father. The weak strain of Drak magic the Chosen possessed gave him access to the ability. It was why Edmund could Stutter so flawlessly, and Ilyan was able to because the whispers of the same power ran through his own veins, the tiny magic amplified by the magnitude of his power. It was only the Drak who could truly Stutter, who could truly manipulate time and space.

Drak power Edmund had stolen, that Ilyan had befouled.

For centuries, I had let them believe it had something to do with the amount of power a body held.

It was an easy lie to let grow, as with all the others.

Like the 'sight' that had led Edmund to order the murder of all those bastard Chosen. They were like his siblings, but one word to him about their danger and he had killed them all.

I needed them gone, and Edmund had given that to me.

It was needed seeing as I couldn't control the Drak power within the Chosen as I had in my progeny, as I still struggled to do in Joclyn.

Letting that much power roam free would risk the future I had planned. The magic was too powerful for them, anyway. They did not deserve it. No one, not even my precious Dramin, deserved it.

At least I could control him.

So they had to go.

Joclyn would go, too. I had already groomed Edmund for that task centuries before. They saw her as nothing more than a threat, not what she really was. Edmund would destroy her, and thanks to sight, I already knew how Ilyan's life would end.

They were the only two who could stop me, and they were half-dead already.

Everything was coming together.

I sped through the alley, moving dangerously close to the high wall of the dead end, as her voice came again. The false sugar she was so good at coating it with grew deeper. *'Near the wall, on Na Ostrohu.'*

The blood-splattered stone wall was inches from me before my magic surged, pulling me from one side of the city to another. This time, it was to a large street nestled beside the wall, the red-tinged light so deep you could barely see through it.

I should have enjoyed the imagery of a beautiful scarlet world, but something was wrong. Something felt different. Something was here.

I froze in place, the constant movement Edmund believed was required in order to move me through his cage breaking with a snap.

'Why did you stop? You are running out of time.' The rare panic in Ovailia's voice surprised me, but I didn't let it show. I looked toward the rooftop, toward the building where a faint popping noise of another Stutter had resonated from.

Ilyan.

And I was sure, knowing him, Joclyn would be with him.

I had never been able to track her magic.

It was too pure, too close to my own. Besides, she was learning to master it faster than I could figure out how to block her, even though she had no idea what was happening. To her, everything was broken, not that everything was starting to work properly.

"Hello, daughter," I whispered, a grin spreading over my face. It was only a matter of time before they would see the cloaked figure from her nightmares in person. I had flitted in and out of supply runs for months, ever since that run in with Ryland had almost revealed me. But now, she was here.

It was the perfect opportunity to play with her already fragile mind.

'You need to keep moving. Get to Nový židovský hřbitov.' The old Jewish cemetery. Perfect.

They would follow me there, but I knew the place well enough that he would never catch me. See me, yes, but not reach me. Besides, what was more haunting than an apparition amongst tombstones?

Moving through the Stutter, I kept my eyes wide, ready to begin running the second I reappeared in the old graveyard. The lines of past and present that existed inside of a Stutter moved through the darkness, the colors bright against my vision before they left me staring at the red world again.

Darting through the old, broken tombstones, my heart thundered as I waited for the faint pop of magic to signal the chase had begun. I ducked behind a large mausoleum when I heard it, the sound followed by a low grunt of pressure as someone fell to the ground.

Wonderful.

Now I needed them to see me, to see the cloak, to have Joclyn feel my magic. With my magic fully charged and broadcasting, she would never know it was me. She had never felt the full magic of the Drak before.

No one had. I was the only one who possessed it, after all.

But soon, everyone would feel it. Everyone would know what Draks were fully capable of.

Darting from behind the large cement building, I ran between two smaller tombstones, attempting to give them the best possible view while trying not to laugh as her gasp of fear and surprise hit my ears. Moving faster, I darted behind the large headstone directly in front of me, the massive thing perfect to dodge the single stream of stunning magic they fired my way.

The top half of the stone was blown away, rocks and dust showering over everything as the scream of thousands of awakened Vilỳ's echoed through the graveyard. Swearing under my breath, I plastered myself to the back of the pillar, gasping for air as my heart raced. I hadn't counted on that.

So much for stunning. The bastards were prepared to kill.

The soft crunch of dying grass bounced off the forest of headstones, their steps slow as they approached me. The heavy pulse of my heart was comical against their slow stalking pace.

'Last one.'

Perfect. The last jumping point was always the same. It had to be in order to intersect with the underground pool of magic that gave me enough power to pull through the barrier.

Sucking in a breath, I steeled myself against what was

coming, knowing I didn't have much choice. I couldn't throw up a shield if I wanted to make it through the barrier. I had one shot, so I had better make it good.

Running out from behind the old headstone, I darted between a garden of ancient statues as stream after stream of their magic was sent my way. Disappearing with a snap, the Stutter pulled me into the long, endless street of old town, the high buildings surrounding me on all sides.

I had run down this street a million times before, run to the same intersection, burst through the barrier unscathed. For the first time, however, I was excited. This was a challenge!

They had already shown they weren't afraid to kill me. Here, there was no cover, no alley, nothing more than a straight runway until my next Stutter when I would exit the tepid confines of the dome.

I ran, everything tense and fearful as Ilyan landed right before me, his long hair twisting over his face ominously. It was all I could do not to attack.

Anger and hatred gleamed in his eyes, his hands fanned open as they sparked ominously. He looked right at me, but I knew he couldn't see me, not with the hood shadowing my face, not with the darkness and shadow that surrounded us. The glow of power sped from his hand in a brilliant purple flame that would incapacitate me if it had time to make contact.

My magic flashed and the faint pop of the Stutter surrounded me, sending me out of the city and into a field just on the other side of the wall. Here, in the dead of winter, it was little more than endless rows of withered corn stalks. The cape was a necessity, now.

The other side of the barrier.

"Hello, Sain." Her voice was distorted silk, the sound of

seduction, pleasure, and gain clear. So fake, so forced. I had heard her true nature, and I would always prefer it to this. She seemed to think whatever she was putting into this façade was an asset, however. She was all acid and vice, everything about her coated with so much malice that any lust she tried to conjure was cracked.

It still affected me the same way, though, perhaps because she had been my mate. Perhaps because we were both hiding something that no one else understood.

A perfect match, which made the fact that my magic was trying to pull into hers more irritating.

She moved toward me slowly, her gaze never leaving mine as her ridiculous heels crunched into the dead undergrowth. Her eyes were dark orbs of plum blue as she leaned closer, running her finger over my lips, my heart tensing in confusion and irritation at the gentle touch.

"I was beginning to think you weren't going to show up." Her finger didn't leave my face, her magic continuing to wind around me like some poisonous snake that I could tell neither wanted me, nor wanted to let me go.

"Hello, Ovi." I kept my voice low and fearful, back to the cowering role she knew. Easy enough to accomplish with the bitter cold.

I inhaled, savoring the pain of the icy air as the wind moved over my skin, tugging at the cloak, at my hair, and taking any hope of warmth away from me.

"Why did you stop?" she snarled, the calm of my greeting unheard as she moved even closer, her hand wrapping around my neck in a violent warning.

"It wasn't my fault," I cowered, letting my voice warble as I fought against the strong waves of pride that rippled through me at her accusation.

She turned away at my denial, her hair swinging over

the pristine white of her fur coat like a flurry of snow. White against silver. It was beautiful.

I would give her that; her beauty was still hard to resist.

Something foreign swirled through me as I stood, lost in thought. Two of her guards appeared from the air around us, flanking me so close that, for a moment, I was truly afraid they were going to take me to Edmund. I didn't need that. Not yet.

I still needed Ryland's blade. I still needed Thom.

"You stopped moving. You almost severed the magic—"

"I was being followed."

Her eyes narrowed for the briefest of moments before they widened in understanding.

"Ilyan." It wasn't a question, though it probably should have been. He wasn't the only one who could Stutter anymore, but she didn't seem to care, even though I knew that she too possessed the ability. "And the girl?"

I nodded, Ovailia's shock leaching back into disgust as a loud hiss slipped past her lips. She turned away from me in anger, her hair fanning around her like a blizzard.

"How did they find you? You told us that your sight is clean."

"You know how he found me. That girl can track magic better than most Vilÿs," I snapped, regretting the outburst the moment Ovailia turned back to me, her eyes dark in warning.

The guards increased their holds at her look, hands digging into my arms as they held me in place. I grimaced at the pain, at the pressure.

None of them cared.

"Did he see you?"

"Not that I could tell." I nodded, shivering in the bitter

wind, letting the weak movement move through me like a wave.

Ovailia studied me for a moment, obviously skeptical, before she narrowed her eyes. Her hand drifted to the side as she dismissed the guards, the burly Trpaslíks fading back into nothing as they pulled their shields around them.

"So you are still good for something."

Before I could get a chance to answer, the look changed, her eyes drifting in and out of focus until they were a million miles away, the anger falling from her face as though it had been melted.

I knew that look. I knew that movement. It had happened to me enough over my life and even more in the last few days. She had received her instructions from Edmund.

I couldn't help the odd mix of eagerness and fear that took over my body. The idea of playing the game was hauntingly desirable.

"What does he want of me?"

Ovailia smiled, her hand lifting as she brushed the back of it against the bare skin of my jawbone, her fingers running through my beard in a touch so soft I couldn't stop the shiver.

Our magic connected, the skin contact giving the power free range to move between us; something that, by the look in her eyes, she enjoyed.

"What do *you* want of me, Ovailia?" I couldn't help the question. I couldn't help the low grumble of my voice, the twisting of my stomach making a powerful play.

She smiled more, her eyes dancing as her magic continued to penetrate, and the chill of the wintry breeze became a distant memory as the warmth of her hand heated my insides like a hot water bottle.

"I want the same thing my father wants." The honey of her voice melted into me, despite knowing what was coming. "Information."

My magic attempted to curl back into me in disappointment, but I kept it there, inside of her, a strong force as magic and souls danced in a tango that could never be completed.

"Haven't I given you enough?"

"There is always more."

This time, it was my turn to smile.

She was right. There *was* always more.

She leaned into me, her breath hot on my lips as her blue eyes attempted to swallow me whole.

"Give me more." Her request was a whisper, a flutter of heat over my lips, a twist of pleasure against my heart. I was sure anyone else would have caved.

I wasn't as weak willed as she assumed me to be. She didn't know me well enough to know the difference.

She knew what I let her see, and what I let her see now was the reaction she had expected of the person she thought she knew: the buckling, the giving in, the whimpering plaything she could mold.

"Anything." The word was more a moan than an agreement.

"We need to know more of Joclyn's magic, specifically her sight: how it works, how it connects to Ilyan, or even if it does. We want to know how we can use it to end them. If they are so connected then surely we can end them together." The honey slipped from her voice as Edmund's instructions rattled through the air.

The warmth that had settled in my stomach disappeared into vapor as the air became lead.

I had known from the beginning that Edmund would

want Joclyn's power for himself. I had hoped that he would see more use for her dead, as I had intended. But that was obviously not the case.

He had inadvertently stumbled into the plan I had cultivated so carefully.

That information was mine.

My lips pressed into a tight line as I hastily attempted to find the smallest bit of information I could give him. I had to give them something. I had to figure out what I could sacrifice that didn't give them too much of an upper hand in this delicate game.

"Do we have a problem?" Ovailia asked, the graceful dance of her hair in the wind the only movement amongst the frozen and dead world.

"No."

"Sain." My magic reacted to the sound of my name on her lips, to the touch of her fingers against my cheek as she brought me back under her spell. "Please don't forget. I hold the cards. I always have. I can control your magic."

No, you can't.

"I can control your sight." *But you can't see what I do.*

"I hold the key to Thom's life in my hands."

Thom.

The word, the reality that was clenched behind it, was a knife twisting into my spine, the bones creaking as I straightened to my full height. The fearful, broken man I always played was gone for a moment.

"Yes, I thought as much," she soothed, her smile spreading.

Whether it had been done on purpose or not, Ovailia had played her cards right with that one. She needed a way to control me, and thus, she chose the person everyone perceived as my best friend. I guessed, in a way, it was true; except, I didn't believe in friends.

I believed in using the right people in the right way, and she had taken out one of my most valuable assets right when I needed him the most.

I had told Wyn I had made a mistake moments after it had happened. Only, she had no idea how truly damaging that mistake had been.

I had let the man I had been grooming for centuries to play as bait be incapacitated beyond all hope. All my work with Rosaline was rendered useless in that one moment.

I had needed him. I still did. I hadn't found a suitable replacement yet.

I had tried to use Ryland, but while he still remained loyal to me, he had risen above his father's control before I had expected him to. That raw power and anger he'd had before was gone. Now, he saw me as someone to help.

Me! Need help!

Ryland was useless.

Wyn was too headstrong, and no one else was emotionally broken enough for me to manipulate in time. So, I had to keep playing into Ovailia in the hopes she would give Thom back to me, awaken the dead so he in turn could kill her.

I ground my teeth together at her threat, my heart racing angrily in a display of emotion she did not miss.

"Strange you care more for the life of one whose blood is as distant from yours as can be, while you would willingly feed your own progeny to the wolves."

"She was not bred for life. She is nothing more than a pawn." The words came without thinking, my head spinning with power, with the deep Drak magic and imagery of that first sight. The truth I had concealed flashed before my eyes in a recall so powerful that, for a fleeting moment, I wasn't certain if I was the one who had summoned it.

When Ilyan had come to me that day, all those centuries before, he had been a weak boy searching for a mate. I had looked into the water to see what he sought. While I had seen his future with this powerful urchin with unrestrained magic I instantly recognized as Drak, it was not the future I had shown him.

I had shown him joy. I had shown him light. I had shown him possibility.

But I had also shown him death that had not existed.

I had turned the precious girl who was meant to be the liberator of our people into a martyr.

I had seen her sent from the mud to restart the realm of magic, with Ilyan by her side.

I could not let such power be free in the world. I couldn't. So I changed it.

I changed it and created a war that would end in her death. I set brother against brother and father against son. I took the image I had seen of Joclyn beside the well, of her magic restarting all of the power. I took the battle that ended in hope. I took it all away and showed him death and destruction, instead. I showed him her dead body as he held her, as he screamed. I took his future away.

I took any possibility Joclyn had to use the Drak magic that she was not worthy of holding. I took it all away and gave them something different... because I could.

After all, they had taken my future away. Before the false words had even left the mouths of the Draks who had surrounded me, it was done, and it would be that way because I had 'seen' it.

Oh, how suggestible everyone was.

I could say I 'saw' a three-legged medusa come forth

from the mud, and they would all sit around and wait for it to happen.

Fools.

"She is disposable." I finished the thought with a snap, Ovailia's eyes widened as her shock wound through her, the look gone before I had even fully registered it.

"To more than us, it would seem," she whispered.

I smiled, and so did she.

For the first time, I had let her see a sliver of who I really was, and although the glimpse into my reality didn't scare her, it was definitely a surprise to see it so well received. To see that, even through everything she had seen of me and all the falsehoods, she liked it. She liked me.

And, in that moment, I liked her.

For the first time in my life, I actually wanted to kiss her.

What an odd feeling.

CHAPTER 6
OVAILIA

S creams carried through the frigid air as I made a beeline toward my father.

Building an army of Chosen strong enough to defeat Ilyan took work. We had to beat the weakness out of them and turn them into something we could use.

The agonizing bellows increased as the large field of burlap tents drifted into view, the beige forest wavering in the cold like a mirage. Broken and stained canvas rose from the ground, surrounded by a sea of brown and red snow that was nestled between the wall and the forest.

The forgotten farmland was the perfect hiding place. A hidden army, shielded from the mortals who flew overhead, from Ilyan who couldn't see beyond the barrier.

Snow crunched under foot, my guards dropping their shields as we approached the first tent, a large, broken mess of fabric housing the weakest of the filth the Vilÿs had infected. If they survived the first few weeks in that endless graveyard, then they would be moved to another tent, one with marginally better conditions. First, they had to get through week one on their own. Sympathy was not a treasured trait, no one was going to tuck them into bed and tell them it was going to be alright. If they couldn't make it, we didn't want them, and having the tent on the outskirts made for easier clean up in those cases.

"Someone needs to take a hose to that," I growled as we passed, the smell of blood and human excrement overwhelming as the tent walls rippled in the violent wind.

"Gladly." One of the guards laughed from behind me, the sound deep and callous. Last week they had done just that, by the sound in his laugh it had been a source of much-needed entertainment.

The vile smell grew deeper into the camp, but this time, it did not come from the tents. It came from the people who had begun to flow out of them. Their dirty faces eager as they sped through the broken city toward me, their eyes bright and desperate.

"My lady," a ragged woman mumbled as she bowed beside me, the tattered sheets she used as a coat slipping off her bare and bloodied shoulders.

I looked away in disgust, fully aware they were coming faster now, drawn to me like a moth to a flame. Mumbled greetings, pleas, and tears of desperation repeated as the guards closed ranks around me. Their massive, burly figures a protective barrier as they kicked and shoved the slowly intruding garbage back.

"Please, my lady. I have fought twice. Food... It's all I ask." One voice raised above the rest as a muscular man attempted to break through the guards, only to be shoved into an already collapsing tent, the burlap folding around him like paper.

It was always the same: food, safety, loyalty. All those things must be earned, and they knew it. It was why they bowed, why they cowered. It was why they threw tattered coats down for me to walk on, muttering long forgotten Czech prayers.

"My lady," a blonde girl mumbled as she pressed against a guard, her hand stretched toward me in frantic need to touch me, worship me.

Lips snarling in disgust, I pressed one finger against her palm before she backed away, tears streaming down her face in a revered look. It was beautiful, the fear of what I could easily do to them.

Voices begged in one final plea as I reached the tent my father would be holed up in. The massive structure loomed over us, screams emanating from somewhere inside so loud I could barely hear the pleas of the refuse I was surrounded by.

"My lady," my guards echoed in unison as they flanked the doors, lifting the tent flaps and allowing me to duck into the open warmth of the reception room, the wails of the masses muted by the heavy canvas that fell closed behind me.

"Ovailia," a short, darkly colored man greeted me the moment the flaps had closed, his voice a hollow reverberation as he moved toward me.

He was obviously happy to see me, and judging by his body language, he expected some sort of embrace or handshake. He really was a fool if he thought he had a chance at that.

"Damek," I practically growled, opting to check my designer heels for any unwanted filth instead of looking at him.

Damek was a Trpaslík older than myself, his face battle worn and scarred, some of which I was sure he had given himself with the reputation he had earned. He had served on my father's forward guard for centuries, and I had never really cared for him, something that had increased since he had taken over Cail's role after his death.

He seemed to think such a simple advancement awarded him the same stature as my father and me. It was something I was getting very tired of reminding him otherwise.

"We did not expect you back so soon," he tittered, his authoritative voice far too happy.

"We?"

"Edmund and I."

Good to know he was speaking for both of them now.

"I didn't know you were expecting me. Was there something you needed, some information vital to our cause that you require, Damek?" I straightened as I looked at him, eyes full of warning as the tiniest of smiles played around the corner of my lips.

"Well ... I ... that is to say ..."

My smile lengthened, the power in his spine tightening as a flare of my magic wrapped around him. Judging by the way he shivered, I was sure he could feel it, even if he didn't know what it was.

"I suppose my father sent you to wait for me, to escort me if there was any problem?" I was snide, bored even, my irritation toward him bared.

Silence.

"Good. Well, seeing as there wasn't any problem, you can be on your way." I smiled as his pride bristled. As he ground his heels into the loose dirt beneath him.

"I can't do that Ovailia, your father..."

"I'm sorry. Are you speaking to me?" I snapped, and he took one quick step back.

I stood still, our two solitary bodies comical in the massive space that had been used as Edmund's ornate reception hall, back before this war had even begun. All the gold inlaid furniture had been swapped for barrels of bright purple fire. All of the tapestries had been removed except one, a massive piece that was hung over the main entrance. The ancient thing was now only echoes of the vibrant colors it had possessed centuries ago, the scene a depiction of the ritual I was sure my Father was surveying.

The tradition he had demanded this damn arena be built for in the first place.

Removing my coat with a grin, I handed it to the awakened filth who stood cowering in the corner, waiting for my instruction.

The Chosen who had cowered before me outside the tent had bowed before me for a reason. And that was it. They wanted a place. They wanted to serve. This girl was one of the lucky few who had braved the pits, who had won, and who had received the right to live.

"My lady." Her words were barely above a mumble, something I would normally punish her for. I had punished her for it in the past. She obviously remembered the large gash I had left in her flesh with the way her shoulders tightened, the way her back curled.

Good.

She was learning.

"Try again," I soothed, careful to keep my voice soft, kind, while also making it very clear she was moments away from the same beating.

She heard the warning.

Her back curled farther as she took a step closer, her filthy hands wrapping around the pure white of the fur. I couldn't help cringing.

"My lady." Her voice shook, but it was louder, calmer. Her place known.

I made sure Damek was watching, watching the way she served me, the same way I was going to have him do. My eyes burned into him and the woman bowed before scuttling away, broken and controlled.

"Anything else Damek?"

"No." He swallowed, backing away a step.

"Good."

I said nothing more, merely stepped toward the now broken man, not willing to let him think he could be anything other than a servant.

"You can finish your task now," I soothed, my voice calm, sweet even, the acid behind it seeping through in warning.

Damek bowed his head and turned from me, opening the next flap and holding it open to the large, open underbelly of the stadium.

A thick layer of magic and heavy canvas had dulled the sounds of the pits, but now that I was on this side, crippling roars of excitement and catcalls assaulted me as hundreds of Trpaslíks screamed in joy and frustration.

It was an exhilarating sound, those of death always were.

"How many have fought today?" I asked as Damek caught up with me, the clack of his shoes echoing over the underside of the risers that stretched above us like an ancient wood and steel bridge.

I was glad I had chosen to leave my fur. It was warmer in there, the heat mixing with the smell of blood that reminded me of what I had been raised in, what my father had taught me to love.

What I had learned to love.

"There have been over twenty, Ovailia ..." he began, and I stopped, fixing him with a hard look that, considering the way his shoulders pulled into his chin, hit him hard in the gut. "*My lady*, he is in his usual box."

A cheer boomed down to us from the stadium, the loud and riotous scream of the winners mixed with the moans of defeat of the losers.

"I hope the take was good."

I didn't even have to ask if my father had won or if he had bet. He always did, and he was always right. For the centuries that the Trpaslíks had been fighting in the pits, he had been right. It was how he had kept his guard so well trained. He only picked the winners.

If I remembered correctly, even Cail had killed ten men without the use of Edmund's Štít in the pits.

Everyone had to prove themselves. The more you proved yourself, the higher you were in the ranks of the Trpaslíks' magic.

"Earlier, he won over twenty thousand Euros," Damek answered, his voice eager again.

"Perfect." At least he would be in a good mood. I was about to make it an even better one.

Heels clacking as my pace picked up, I raced toward one of my father's other guards. The handsome man stood outside of one of the many entrances, his body shrouded in a heavy, black cloak.

I had taken advantage of those handsome features before, perhaps I would again.

"Ovailia," he greeted as we approached, his voice heavy against the shouts of betting, taunts, and hollers that were thundering from the arena beyond him.

Another match must be starting.

"Sir," I greeted him, knowing I should have corrected him yet choosing to leave the overly familiar greeting hanging. The single word bristled poor Damek's insecurities further. "Is he expecting me?"

The man nodded with a smile, moving to the side to let me through before moving back, blocking Damek from entrance.

"His majesty does not grant you further entry," the younger man growled.

Oh, this just became even more wondrous.

"How unfortunate." I gave him a pout and pushed past the canvas, leaving him slack jawed behind me.

Thankfully, I wasn't the only one who was getting fed up with the boundaries Damek had been pushing. After hundreds of years of service, he should have known better. No matter. From what Sain had just let slip, he would be gone in a matter of days, anyway.

The bones of the stand fell away as I walked past a second set of guards, revealing rows and rows of metal bleachers that rose both above and below me, the towering stands threatening to swallow me like the ocean of people they were. The icy sky peeked out from behind a partial canvas roof, wind sneaking in through the opening. But it wasn't enough to wipe away the smell of sweat and blood that mixed with the joy and exuberance of the crowd.

The sound of raucous bidding was deafening as I made my way up to the large glistening box in the middle of the stadium. Rows stretched down to a large, open pit where mud that was more blood than dirt lined the floor.

"Ovailia!" my father bellowed the moment I entered his box, another guard snapping the door shut behind me. Edmund smiled with a dangerous grin that pulled a shiver of warning through my spine. Anyone else might have turned and run, but the eagerness of danger, of reward, pulled me forward.

He was surrounded by pillows and platters of food, his guards flanking him in such a wide berth that he was an island amongst the shiny, silver bleachers. An island that was draped in an ornate cloak I hadn't seen since before we had been banished from Imdalind the first time.

I recognized the fur-trimmed relic as what he used to wear to council when I was a child. It had been given to him by some king when he had saved their country, or so the history books said. In reality, it was him taking over, a coup he would run from behind the scenes.

Another kingdom we had claimed for our own.

Like this one.

"Father," I began, his eyes lighting up at the greeting, "you seem quite comfortable."

His nefarious smile grew, hand waving to the bare bleacher beside him in an invitation to sit. Without missing a beat, one of the Chosen who served him rushed forward to place another pillow there, his head bowed low, his hands and arms covered with bruises. At least it wasn't dirt, or I wouldn't have taken a step closer. He shook as he moved, as if every step was a trial, the shake in his back growing the closer he moved to my father.

"Was your task completed?".

"Yes."

I expected him to reply, to demand more information, but instead, he drank, smiled, the maniacal greed in his eyes matching my own.

"He gave you something."

"He did not mean to." My lips twitched into the smile my father always brought on, my own eagerness to tell him mounting.

"Was it the location of Ilyan's camp?"

"No. You know as well as I do he cannot give that. Not that we would use it, anyway. We need those brats alive."

He looked at me with a scowl, his displeasure obvious, but I just leaned in, smiling.

"I saw the sight." That pulled his attention.

"The sight?"

"Yes, the one he's been hiding from us, the one concerning Joclyn." I leaned closer, screams and catcalls erupting around us with the start of the next battle, but neither of us turned. "When I was standing in the field, the water inside of me pulled me into it—his recall."

The stadium was a wall of sound, my own heart adding to that, but all I heard was silence, all I saw was the look of stunned shock on my father's face.

His eyes darkened to a color I hadn't seen before, the depth of them almost black, the bottom of an endless pool of death. A lustful look of longing took over his face, fear spreading into me in an electric spark that straightened my spine.

"What did you see?"

"I saw you standing with Joclyn as companions at the banks of the deep wells of Imdalind. I saw Ilyan's death. I saw the Vilÿs, untarnished, sweeping through the city in joyous revelry. I saw you and me and Ilyan sitting with Joclyn in the four-headed throne, the one that was destroyed in the seventeenth century."

"But that is not what he has told us. Are you sure that's what you saw?" His words were slow, calculated, the pits and all the bloodshed not so much as pulling his attention anymore.

"What I saw, what the poison within me showed me, was nothing like what I had seen before. Yet, from what he was speaking of, from what the magic told me, it's true. I don't know how, but do you think he could have changed it before he gave the sight to Ilyan, before he showed it to me?"

I could barely get the words out as the fear knotted through my shoulders with each shade my father's eyes darkened.

"What are you saying?"

He already knew the answer. He needed me to say it.

He needed me to unleash the anger.

A cheer broke through the crowd that surrounded us, the sound deafening as it filled the canvas tent we sat in. I didn't know if someone had won, if someone had died. I didn't bother to look. I didn't dare break away from my father and the eagerness in his eyes.

"If what I saw just now was the true sight, then Sain has been playing us all, all along. But now I have seen what's coming. We have the upper hand."

The eagerness in his eyes faded to anger, the emotion tensing his shoulders as he turned back to the arena and the two small figures who battled in the pits below.

Children. They couldn't have been older than twelve. These fights were always the most entertaining.

"You saw the sight. Did you also see enough to know what he is planning?" I barely heard his grumble above the roar of the crowd, the sound almost incessant now. Something must have happened; I could smell the blood in the air.

I knew the tone in his voice well enough not to turn away.

"No. I saw enough to know what the real outcome is … or, rather, what it was supposed to be."

"Supposed to be?" He jerked toward me, his eyes questioning. "Do you not think that it will?"

Utter disbelief ran through me, shock at the unexpected question. He had never asked for my opinion.

"Sain prides himself on his infallibility. He has always been vocal about that. But even he cannot believe in his own ability if he is giving false sights to those who seek his counsel."

A small, feminine scream rang out from the pits, the boisterous yell of the crowds drowning us as my father turned to me, a grimace spreading over his face.

"Unless he believes that, by feeding us the information he chooses and preaching of its truthfulness, it thereby will become." Edmund had put the outcome together before I could, his words poignant as he turned back to the pits, watching the two children—a boy and a girl—as they clawed and battered each other in an attempt to draw more blood.

"Ovailia."

A pleasurable ripple moved up my spine at the sound of my name on his lips. I sat up a little straighter, letting my hair fall down my back as I scooted closer to him, eager to hear what he had to say, eager to be what he needed me to be.

"I need you to arrange another meeting with him. If what I have done to you has allowed you to see this sight, then you can see more. Use it. If Sain won't give us the information, then maybe you can get it for us."

"He has lied to you, Father; do you think showing him mercy is wise?"

"Normally, no. But he has already shown he does not fear us, so we need to give him a reason to love us, a reason to work alongside us."

"But, Father—"

"*Then* we will crush him," he interrupted, a smile

stretching so that the white of his teeth bled through. "He is still a valuable pawn to us, just as we are to him. It all depends on how we make our moves, who gets the king first, so to speak. I will use him to the very fullest until the moment he becomes disposable."

"But how do—"

"Look to the pits, Ovailia," he interrupted again, his tone, while kind, warning me of the storm beneath the surface.

My muscles tightened as I turned toward the children. They circled, lunged, bled, and screamed as they battled for a place in Edmund's army. For their life.

"Take these children," he began with a small gesture of his hand. "Young, innocent, they don't want to hurt each other. They don't want to kill. But they want to impress me, and they will do anything to gain that honor ..."

His grin stretched as he stood, the bright red cloak unfurling beneath him, revealing him as the royal monarch he was. Heads turned toward him, the stadium quieted, even the children who fought below us slowed to a stop, their eyes turned toward their king in expectation, their backs bent in reverence.

"This fight is a good one, so let's up the ante, shall we!" His voice rumbled as the crowd went wild, and the tiny frames of the children shook in anticipation. "The victor of this fight will move beyond Imdalind and gain the right to be trained as my new, personal bodyguard."

Gasps, awe, cheers, they filled me as they did the crowd around us, a pride and exhilaration flowing freely at what was about to occur.

"There is only one exception. The fight, is now, to the death."

More screams, more cheers. The children looked at each

other in horror. They knew this was a greater prize than what they had originally been told. As much as it scared them, they had begun to fight with more fervor and desperation before Edmund had taken his seat on the billowy nest.

"Will you look at that?" Edmund chuckled darkly as the children attacked each other, jumping and clawing and tearing and biting. "They were doing as they were told before, but now ... with a promise of victory, a promise of a better goal, they truly fight. Their hearts are in it now."

"And what can we possibly give him?" I scoffed. Short of giving him Joclyn's head on a pike I wasn't sure what he could possibly be after. And I wasn't about to suggest that to my father. He already had plans of his own.

"Tell me, Ovailia, is his magic still reacting to yours? Did it try to connect again?"

"It did." I was hesitant, that connection had been cultivated for other reasons.

"So his desire for you is strengthening?"

"Yes, Father, as you asked me to do."

"Wonderful," he cooed, his focus finally pulling back to the pits where a lone child stood over a lifeless shape, tiny fists smashing into bloodied flesh again and again. "Use him. Even go as far as completing the bond if you must. Anything to access his sight, to get the information we need."

"Complete the bond?" An odd mixture of desire and disgust rumbled through me, the twisted emotions making me feel vile.

"He has secrets we need, Ovailia, and with the magic I have embedded in you, once a bond is complete, you will have full access to whatever I wish. You need to give him a greater reward. Give him a reason to fight to the death, and you have always been his reason. You need to show him you still are."

He looked away from me as the girl was pulled off the heap of the body she had destroyed, her eyes wild and manic. She knew she had won. She knew she had gotten what she wanted. And all because my father had given her the opportunity.

"Give him a reason to do anything I say," I whispered more to myself than to my father, but he heard, anyway.

His face broke out into a smile, the same mania darting to me as the pit master brought the child to him. "Give him a reason to fight for it."

He was right, and what was more, I knew I could. Sain had shown me something in himself I had never seen before. His eyes had become something different, someone I had never seen, a magic I had never felt. Even when we were bonded, I had always felt that something was missing from the man, something he kept so deeply hidden I had even convinced myself it wasn't there.

But today ... Today, I had seen it.

Today, I had wanted it.

I wanted to exploit it—exploit him.

"Our King, our lord," one of my father's many servants announced loudly from beside us, his voice carrying over the now silent stadium as he presented the child to her new master.

She was filthy, every article of clothing stained, every bit of flesh smeared with rot and blood. Her blonde hair was barely visible from underneath the mud that coated it. She did not cower. She did not even try to hide. She stood still and tall as she met my father head-on, her focus solely on him.

It was as he had said. She knew what she had done; he needed to give her a reason to do it.

"What is your name, child?" Edmund asked, his voice calm, obviously taken aback by the loyalty the child was already displaying.

"Míra," she said, her voice strong as the gaze she had fixed him with.

Edmund said nothing as he walked toward her, placing his hands on her bare arms to look at her.

Her steady gaze wavered as his magic filled her, as a new Štít was placed against her heart, taking away any chance of a life that the girl had held before.

Turning the child into something more.

As my father had me.

As I would Sain.

It was as my father had said: it was all in how you played the game.

And I was going to play.

CHAPTER 7
RYLAND

"**G**ood job, Jaromir! You are going to be a pro at this in no time!" my voice boomed through the red-lit courtyard, the deep sound echoing off the cobbles and broken stone work in a weird ricochet.

Everything was different close to Ilyan and Joclyn's barrier. The small patio was bathed in a golden light that filtered over the already painted world. The light made everything look real, closer to how things were on the outside. It wasn't perfect, but close enough that for brief moments I could believe that everything was normal.

'You will never get outside.'

That was probably why I preferred to do my work out here, even though Ilyan asked that all magical training take place within the cathedral so as to keep the signs of our presence as shrouded as possible. I understood the reasoning, but the ancient space was too dark for me. I always felt trapped. Here, I could pretend it was nothing but a never-ending sunset and not trapped in my father's death bubble.

'Don't worry; I'll keep reminding you.'

Even if it wasn't for the restrictive prison we were

trapped in, there would still be that. That incessant voice in my head.

I was reminded of it every day as I trained Jaromir, as I trained all of the other newly awakened Chosen, preparing them for what no amount of fantasy could conceal.

At first, I had rebelled against the job, before I realized I was one of the few people here who knew what my father was capable of, who knew what they were up against. And someone needed to prepare them for the war that was ahead.

'My war. The war you are going to help me win.'

No.

'We shall see.'

That training was as good a daily reminder as any.

"I didn't quite get the flick like you taught me, though, sir," Jaromir spoke in quick Czech as he approached me, shaggy hair bouncing as his voice rattled on with all the eagerness and excitement he'd possessed since the first day I had started training him.

"What flick?"

"You know, how you move your wrist to the side ..." He smiled with a crooked grin, before stepping away and pushing his hands before him.

I could see the gears in his mind twist and turn as he thought about what he was about to do, as he twisted the magic to perform whatever wrist flick he was talking about.

With a bang like a gun, the magic erupted from his palms in sparks of colors that went wide, much wider than it had the time before, thanks to the odd jerking motion he was trying to accomplish.

Even with the large spray, the magic was still accomplished perfectly.

While all the other Chosen had fought against their

new abilities and life, mourning what Edmund had taken from them, Jaromir took to it like a duck to water. He mastered complex tasks easily and quickly, surpassing all the others who had awoken around the same time.

'You should use him. Use him to help us win this. To defeat Ilyan. To kill Joclyn.'

Of course, his acceleration was partly to do with how far he had pushed himself. He refused to move on to another task until he had perfected it, and he would get quite upset with himself if things weren't honed in record time. It was a lot for a boy of twelve to take on.

That insatiable quest for perfection, while valiant, was sometimes fruitless, which was what he was stuck in now —a search for perfection that was focused on a wrist flick not required for the task I had set him.

I recognized what he was trying to do. That particular movement was one I had done since I was ten when my father had broken my wrist in a fight and demanded I heal it, breaking it repeatedly, until I mastered healing every break, every mutilation of the bone he could think of.

'And you whined like a baby the whole time. I should have broken both your wrists to teach you a lesson. How I could have been stuck with such a—'

I cut the voices out with a cringe, something that wasn't easy to do considering the strength of the memory. It was hard to forget the full year of constant bone breakage and pain he had inflicted on me. I guessed it was a good way to teach a task if you were a sadistic monster, which my father was.

'You are more like me than you think.'

In the end, I did master healing. I was also left with a few ticks within my magic, something that was bound to happen when you perform magic with nothing more than splinters of bone and tendons instead of a working hand.

'You could always break his wrist. Then he would be able to master it.'

"That movement isn't required, Jaromir."

"What do you mean it isn't required?" the boy asked, the greasy mop of dirty brown hair quivering as he shook his head. "That's how *you* do it."

"Yes." I tried to keep the frustration out of my voice, but it leaked out, anyway. Jaromir wrinkled his bulbous nose in response. "But that's because it's how I was trained."

Jaromir narrowed his eyes at me. I wasn't going to tell him what my father was capable of, not yet. Right now, magic was still new and amazing to him, and I didn't want to be the one to destroy that.

It was like Santa Claus—no one wanted to be the one to ruin the secret.

'Then let me.'

"So train me that way."

"Not going to happen, kid."

'You can't stop it, son. You know it is the best way.'

"What do you mean 'it's not going to happen'? It's how you were trained, and I want to be trained like you. I want to be as good as you."

'Even he knows what you are capable of, what you were made for. He sees it, and he wants it for himself.'

No.

"You *will* be as good as me," I said with a laugh, the forced sound resounding back to me with the same awkward ripple the barrier always gave. "But that doesn't mean you have to do everything exactly like me."

'Why not, Ryland?'

"But I want to," he said, half-shocked, half annoyed, his eyes squinting together as he wrinkled his nose.

I once again found myself fighting the need to smile, to laugh.

It was an odd feeling to be looked at by someone that way, like I was Santa Claus instead of the magic.

An unfamiliar knot formed in my gut with the realization I could be that to someone. With scars all over my body and a brain that was addled and frightening, that they could look at me and still want to be like me.

Jaromir still looked at me like that: eager, waiting, his eyes full of so much life it was infectious.

I really didn't want to deflate that magic from him. And yet, hadn't it already been?

He was still young, yes, but he had also been pulled away from his dead mother's arms. He had watched his family being destroyed by mysterious, winged bats, only to be cursed with immense pain. He was a child who had chosen to survive, to live, even through all that pain.

He had something to fight for, too.

Like I did.

Like we all did.

Maybe, I thought with a cringe, *it is a bad thing I am trying to sugarcoat it the way I am.*

'Yes. Be more like your father, Ryland.'

I couldn't keep the disgusting truth of what was coming from him forever. Besides, I didn't have to tell him all of it right now.

"I twist my wrist that way because of how my father trained me," I said with a sigh, keeping Jaromir's focus on me, no matter how much I wanted to look away. "He broke my wrist every day to teach me how to heal while still teaching me other abilities, so things like the wrist flick are because I couldn't move my body the right way and had to make do."

'That's a good boy, Ryland.'

Jaromir's smile faded little by little with each word I spoke. This tiny, little fact about my father and what he was capable of seeped into him and replaced his awe with worry.

"Your father broke your wrist?!"

"My father is not a very nice man, Jaromir."

'He doesn't seem to think so. Look at him, Ryland.'

"Every day for a year?" He continued speaking as though I hadn't said anything, like he hadn't heard the little asterisk mark that I was attaching to that or, worse, like he didn't care.

"That is not a good thing, kid," I reiterated as I turned back to him, my heart dropping to see the awe seeping back into Jaromir's eyes. *Please don't let it be for what I think it is.*

'It is Ryland. It is exactly what you think it is.'

"My father is ... well... He's not very nice."

"I know that."

I froze.

"How do you know?" We had been very careful to shield him from knowing my connection with Edmund, something that had been nearly impossible, all things considered. "You don't know my father."

Jaromir smiled, his lips spreading to reveal rows of perfectly straight and white teeth. "Yes I do," he said through the grin. "It's Edmund."

I felt like I had been punched in the gut. My mouth opened automatically, my brain struggling to catch up, to find something to tell him, some way to respond.

"I figured it out," he laughed, the smug look growing as he rubbed his fingers over the mark on his cheek, as though if he pressed hard enough he could make it disappear. "It wasn't that hard. I knew Ilyan was his son, and you and Ilyan are brothers, what with your weird eyes and the crazy things you both do and everything ..." He smiled broadly at that, his hand dragging over his hair before he pinched the bridge of his nose, his smile increasing in mockery.

He laughed.

"Were you *trying* to keep it from me?"

"Well ... yeah ..." I dragged my hand through my hair in embarrassed frustration again before stopping halfway through and dropping it to my side. *Of all the things to give us away ...*

Jaromir's smile stretched to inordinate proportions.

"There are some things you probably shouldn't know yet," I finished in a desperate hope he would let it drop.

I was a fool to think there was even a chance at that.

"That's bull," he spat, the quick change in demeanor taking me by surprise.

The awe had gone; the pity had gone. He was just a lanky boy who stood before me in angry defiance.

I didn't miss those mood swings.

'You were always more powerful with them, like he is.'

Whoever said only girls got those during puberty had never tried to control the magical rage of a boy trying to figure himself out.

"How so?" I was careful to keep the hesitancy out of my voice.

"You're training everyone for war, right?" He already knew the answer to this, but I nodded my head in agreement, anyway. "Which means you are training me for war, too, so why hide things? Why lie and say things are different than they are?"

'So that it's easier for me to defeat you.'

"So we can protect you."

"Also, stupid," he said, a smug, little smile springing over his face, his nose turning up at me as if he smelled something disgusting. "If you are training me to fight, to protect myself, then why keep stuff like that from me? I can't protect myself if you aren't going to tell me everything. Saying it's for protection when I can't protect myself without it ... It doesn't make any sense."

He had spoken in circles the way he always did when he was agitated, the way I used to when I was his age. Despite the circles, however, I knew he had a point, one I was foolish for having missed.

I stared at him, the obviously blank look on my face causing him to smile even more.

'I know how to wipe that grin off his face.'

He was smug. He had won. I didn't know why, but that made me uncomfortable—being upped by a kid.

Risha and I had gotten in far too many conversations about what to tell him when he had figured it out all on his own, understanding the ins and outs of it enough to make what I thought had been sound, simple logic; seem fickle.

I turned away, my hand moving toward my curls, ready to drag its way through. I pulled it away quickly, not really wanting to be compared to Ilyan by a twelve-year-old again.

'It's pathetic that you have picked up so much from your brother. You were supposed to destroy him.'

No.

'Kill him, Ryland.'

"Don't worry; you don't have to say it. My dad didn't like it much when I was right, either." The words came out so easily, the certainty of truth behind them, spoken with a grin and a flip of his hand.

Like it was nothing.

Yet, I felt responsible. Felt so... parental?

My stomach flipped.

Is that what this was? This weird feeling of uncomfortable failure and of failed responsibility? I had never really had a parental figure to know. In fact, the closest I'd ever known to a *dad* was Sain, and I was currently plotting to kill my biological father with him.

I was way too young to be dealing with this stuff.

It was too late now.

"You're right." Those two words were so much harder to say than I would have thought.

Who would have guessed that accepting defeat to a kid would be so hard?

"Whoa," Jaromir gasped, his eyes popping exponentially. "My dad never did that."

"Did what?"

"Admitted it."

'It's because you are weak.'

I narrowed my eyes at him. It seemed like the logical thing to do. If you made a mistake, you owned up to it. Then you made it better. Wasn't that how this stuff went? I could already tell this was going to be a lot harder than I had thought.

Thank goodness I wasn't his real father.

"Well, I made a mistake, didn't I?" My voice was much harder than I wanted it to be. It was more with frustration from trying to figure this out than from anger.

"I guess."

This whole thing was getting complicated.

"Well then, I'm sorry for it." While I paused awkwardly, he gaped at me uncomfortably, and I did the only thing I could think of. "Now try it again."

"Try what again?"

"The inverted flame."

"But I thought—"

"You already seem to know more than your fair share, I promise no more secrets. And anything else you want to know, we will talk about it later. I promise." And preferably not when I was still trying to figure out what in the world had happened and what role I had taken on.

Besides, I knew he had been dying to talk about what he had seen with Joclyn all afternoon. It was not something I wished to discuss quite yet. I still needed to talk to Sain and figure out what in the world he had been thinking.

What he was doing.

I supposed it was a good thing we had already scheduled dinner tonight, even though we had planned on card games and trying to figure out where the rest of the Soul's Blade was. I would have to add a Q&A to the schedule.

Jaromir caught my meaning quickly and grinned before running back to the center of the courtyard, leaving me trying to catch my breath while the space filled with streams of smoke and fireless flame.

"Why do I feel like I have run a marathon?" I asked the question to the empty courtyard, jumping when someone responded.

"I didn't think we had the space to run a marathon."

I spun toward the voice, toward Risha who was walking through the dim red light toward me, her arms filled with what looked like sandwiches and water.

I simultaneously smiled and cringed, something she did not miss.

"Everything okay, Ryland?" Her voice was sweet, and the disgust that had filled me at seeing the food left quickly. "Is it okay that I am here?"

"More than okay."

"Good," she said with one of her grins that twisted through my stomach, "because, with the look you were giving me, I was sure I had grown a lizard head out of my shoulders."

She laughed at that, but I gawked at her, trying to get my mind to pick up the pace and form coherent sentences.

"No!" That was too loud. "It's just that you smell ... I mean the food smells ... I mean the food ..." I let whatever mumbo jumbo I had been trying to say fade away as she laughed, her green eyes sparkling as the bell-like chime of her amusement made my stomach flip around a few more times. All thought was slowly draining from my mind like goo.

There was something about her—about Risha—that had been troubling me. Risha brought out a whole new, awkward side of me I hadn't even known existed, one that stammered and blushed for dumb reasons and somehow forgot to be suave. It was something no guy should ever be, especially over a girl. It drove me crazy, though she found it adorable.

Considering the way she always appeared with food when I was training Jaromir, despite having all of the responsibilities to tend to as Ilyan's second, I would venture a guess that I wasn't the only one fighting off an overly strong attachment.

"What is it, Ryland? Don't you like food?" She could barely get the words out with how much she was laughing. Her eyes danced as the loose curls of her strawberry hair swayed over her back.

"Something like that." I tried my hand at subtlety again, this time keeping my voice low, something that was made easier by the deep Czech we spoke.

My stomach flipped as her cheeks tinged with red, her eyes piercing mine as she took a step closer, her head held high as she offered one of the sandwiches to me.

"Or was it this supposed marathon you were running?"

My mind went blank. "What marathon?"

"When I came in ... You were talking about a marathon." She smiled, pushing a lock of hair behind her ear as she looked at me.

"Oh." It took me a full minute to catch on. "It wasn't a real marathon."

"I didn't think so." Her eyes glittered even more, staring at me with some message I couldn't quite decipher before she looked away, toward Jaromir who was still shooting smoke away from himself, still trying to accomplish that darned wrist flick.

I pinched the bridge of my nose, fully aware it was also something I had picked up from Ilyan yet not really caring at the moment.

"Jaromir is the marathon, I take it?" She took another step toward me, her sudden change in proximity making it very hard to concentrate.

Come on, Ryland, what's wrong with you?

"I think I realized how much more he sees me as a father figure and less like a ..." I struggled to find a word.

I could feel the heat of her skin radiate against me, making it very hard to focus.

"Friend," she supplied.

Close enough.

I nodded.

"Well, to be fair, Ry, I don't think he's supposed to be your friend or you his."

I turned toward her quickly, my eyes narrowing in question, but all she did was smile and move to sit on the old, bloodstained cobbles, her hand waving beside her in welcome.

I sat beside her without question, my heart continuing to hammer uncomfortably in my chest.

"You can't really be his friend and teach him everything he needs to know—to fight, to win ... You have to train him, not play with him."

She was saying things I already knew, things I should have been more careful about from the beginning. However, it was so much more complex than that, and I felt more than a little awkward admitting it to her.

I exhaled heavily and turned back to Jaromir, a small smile sneaking out at the boy. The streams of smoke were gone, replaced by tiny, little rings he had somehow figured out how to conjure all on his own.

"He figured out my relationship to Edmund and what we are really training him for." My voice was dead.

I heard her exhale beside me, her own frustrations rattling through the red-tinged air.

"I guess that would be a marathon. What did you end up telling him?"

"The truth."

"The truth?" She was frustrated, and I didn't blame her.

My focus snapped to her at the panic in her voice, not surprised to see the aggravation that normally came before some kind of reprimand. Even if we were crushing on each other, she couldn't let that side of her go all the way. I didn't blame her.

"Calm down, Risha." I was careful to keep the irritation out of my voice, but she fumed more. "I didn't tell him anything. He had already figured it all out himself. I'm sure all the other Chosen know. We were silly to think they wouldn't talk."

"So much for shielding him."

"That's the thing, though," I sighed, scooting a tiny bit closer to her as I lowered my voice, careful to keep him from overhearing.

She leaned forward, and my brain tried to melt out of my ears again.

Keep it together, Ry, I ordered. It was becoming my mantra around her.

"He doesn't want to be shielded, Risha. He wants to be prepared."

She was obviously expecting something else. Her eyes widened with a little headshake, and then she pulled away from me in shock. I scooted away, desperate to get some fresh air instead of inhaling that deep perfume she always wore.

"So he wants to know?"

"Every word."

"Do you think he's ready?" she asked me curiously, her eyes filled with the same sparkle I had seen on the very first day.

"Why are you asking me?"

"Well, it's like before ... You aren't his friend. You can't be. But you are something, a guardian, maybe. Something like that. It seems like a decision such as that would be up to you. I mean, he can't have a government raising him."

"Don't you think I'm a little young for that?" My voice was shaking violently, but I didn't even try to conceal it. I wasn't too happy with the sudden turn this conversation had taken.

"I think you are as old or young as you want to be, but sometimes, when hard things happen, we have to grow up a little bit, whether we want to or not." She stared at me intently, my heart racing even faster at the look in her eyes, at the little dimple that played around the corner of her lips. "Besides, I think *he* is older than we give him credit for."

"Risha!" Jaromir's shout rippled through the courtyard as the boy intersected with Risha, tackling the beautiful woman out of sight, leaving me staring blankly into the courtyard as Jaromir began regaling her with everything that had happened over the past few hours.

I barely saw.

I barely heard.

I sat beside them, one word echoing through my head.

Guardian.

Minutes before, I had realized I felt like a parent to this boy. I had felt responsible. And now, with that one word, everything from before kind of fit into place.

Risha was right.

More than responsibility, more than some twisted parental relationship, sometimes you had to grow up and do what was needed of you.

"Some marathon, huh?" Risha said as I looked up to where Jaromir was still occupying her, some weird pink smoke seeping from the palm of his hand.

I stared at them, her eyes sparkling as my stomach flipped again, the pungent smell of Jaromir's magic filling my mind. It may have been the fumes of the smoke, but I was fairly certain that being around Risha had turned Edmund's voice off in my head.

Some marathon, indeed.

CHAPTER 8

JOCLYN

The cloaked figure was right before me.

Except, this time, it was not a sight. It was reality.

We had been close in the graveyard, and now he was right in front of us. Running down an empty street, the heavy fabric rippled behind him as he ran. Ilyan was only feet from them, magic soaring.

Then, with a faint pop, they were gone. Disappeared into thin air.

"No!" I screamed as they vanished, my hand millimeters from pulling the cloak from their head, Ilyan inches from tackling them, the violet stream of his attack still moving uselessly into the darkness and toward me.

Ilyan and I shouted in unison. I sidestepped as he pushed a wave of counter magic after his attack, the black smoke swallowing it whole. I knew it was pointless, magical attacks didn't work against mated pairs, but even though it wouldn't hamper me, it would still hurt. I wasn't in the mood for crippling pain right then. We still had a chance to find them.

We needed to catch up before it was too late, before we lost them.

I closed my eyes, magic stretching away from me and spreading through the city as I desperately searched for any trace of the magic I had been tracking, eager to catch them. We were so close. I couldn't let them get away.

I tried to control my breathing as the deep vein of the earth's magic filled me, the force of it so much stronger than I had ever felt. My body swayed abruptly as my power reacted to it in a frightening wave of power.

"Can you feel them, mi lasko?" Ilyan whispered from beside me, his hand winding around my waist as he leaned against me, his chest pressing into my back, his magic filling me.

Closing my eyes, I let our magic move through the city, through streets I had never seen, through houses that lay in ruins, searching for any trace of the cloaked man, of where he had gone.

Every other time he had Stuttered, it was a quick search, but this time he was gone.

"Nothing," I said, my eyes snapping open to the street before us. "There is nothing left."

Edmund could somehow track that magic past the blackness of a Stutter, that ability obviously did not lie with me.

"Nothing?" he asked, his voice shaking in my ear before he moved away from me, his hand still resting on my hip.

"No, I can't follow the Stutter," I said slowly, glaring at the looming red wall of the dome at the end of the street. "It's like they ... left."

"Through the barrier," Ilyan said slowly, his mind following right along with mine. "Whoever it was can Stutter through the barrier."

"One of Edmund's men." My teeth ground together. "The shield must work just like ours. Keeping us in, while they can move between."

We had always had a hunch about that, but now we knew it.

"Still, the strength of the magic required. I've never felt magic like that before, Ilyan."

Ilyan turned away, the muscles in his shoulders tensing as his temper pulsed through me. His thoughts moved so fast I couldn't hope to keep up with them.

"He's done something to them. Whatever he did to those Vilÿs, he's mutated their magic, strengthened it. Strengthened them." He turned back to me, the quick movement making me jump.

"Do you think it was one of his Chosen?"

"It could be, or it could be someone who is working for him." Ilyan's thoughts stabilized as he spoke, images flooding into me as his mind moved someplace we had visited many times before.

"And us?" I asked, knowing where he was going.

We had questioned Sain's motives enough. It would make sense. But besides him being a disagreeable, old man, we couldn't do anything without proof.

"We need to get back," he announced, his voice heavy with the same authoritative tone I had gotten used to when he went into war mode. "We need to do a count, find out if someone's missing."

"You mean we need to check to see if Sain is there." My voice was hard, the anger that always erupted at his name taking over.

"Yes," he agreed, his bright blue eyes meeting mine with a whip of energy. "It might be what we need."

My heart pulsed heavily, my hands in tight fists around

the soft fabric of my jeans. After months of waiting, of having our hands tied behind our backs, we might have something. If that was Sain, then Sain wouldn't be at the cathedral telling everyone I was an undead, bleeding puss nugget.

He wouldn't be able to control my sights.

Or whatever he was doing.

Ilyan's lips twitched at that, his hand moving quickly as he took a step toward me and wrapped his arm around my waist, pulling me into him.

'You're not an undead, bleeding puss nugget.'

'And you're not the king of France.'

"Well, not now. Many years ago, however …" he said with a smile, the emotion fading quickly into a pained grimace as the deep stress of what we were really facing plowed into us.

I cringed against it, leaning against him.

"We need to go," I gasped, not only because of the urgency of the task before us, but because of the painful wave of magic that had moved through me. The heavy heat that spelled danger.

With one quick sweep I felt them, twenty of Edmund's men were one street over, looking for us.

I was sure it was no coincidence they had chosen this exact spot at this exact time to attempt to stage an ambush.

With a gentle kiss against the skin of my forehead, my magic reached to meet his. The colored specks of light flickered in the darkness just as the army of Trpaslíks rounding the corner. Ilyan smiled at them as his magic pulled us into the void, away from the striking ribbons of colorful magic that would have brought our death.

Well, would have if Edmund's men could aim.

Everything tightened as we were pulled into the suction

cup of the Stutter, my heart tensing in preparation from the pain, for the black.

Except this time everything was different.

The pressure was gone, my body calm in a space that felt more open, more alive. More than that, it didn't end. A stutter that usually took seconds stretched on, my anxiety and confusion growing as I tried to understand what was happening.

Forcing my eyes open, I expected the black of nothing. Expected to be trapped and alone.

But I wasn't alone, and I wasn't in the dark.

Ilyan held me against him, his hair flowing around him, eyes closed, face at peace. He was beautiful, frozen as he was in the space between time.

I could have gazed at him until we returned to Prague, let him be my anchor to the disorientation that was still plaguing me. But, something else pulled my attention and slammed into my chest like a ton of bricks.

It was my magic.

It was ribbons of smoke and color that stretched away from me like cloth and air. It felt the same as every time I used my sight.

But this time, I could see it.

Ribbons of sight swirled around us, playing the past and future like a movie reel.

I watched it twist around us, a heavy weight taking over my body as my head spun. The ribbons of sight shifted, their movements speeding up into a blur that I couldn't focus through. Heart pounding, I clung to Ilyan, gasping for breath as the reels of sight moved so quickly I wasn't sure which way was up or down or what was happening... until it stopped, leaving Ilyan and I hovering amid the sight of our first meeting. Of him, watching me in my high school classroom. They twisted again, speeding up to the same image I had seen before of all of us standing on a mountainside, facing the wall as I brought it down.

A sight.

A sight inside of a Stutter? The thought was as ridiculous and far-fetched as a bad sci-fi movie, but I couldn't shake it.

Before I could look further, the colors faded to nothing, spiraling into the ebony abyss as the pressure of the Stutter slammed against me in disorienting dizziness as we were pulled out of the void and back into reality.

Everything was spinning so fast I could barely make out the church, or the great archway to the left. I was certain there were people in front of me, but even that was indistinguishable behind the ember burn now blocking my vision, the red and black of my sight growing darker.

The cobbles against my knees were the first things I felt as I collapsed to the ground, Ilyan's hand a hard pressure against my back as he tried to support me, his magic attempting to connect with mine. I felt the power, felt the heat of it only to be met with a wall of sight so powerful I screamed as the world within my sight did, as everything turned to red and fire and death.

The red city swam below me, my vision drifting lazily from above the rooftops as though I was attached to the belly of an airplane. Watching with thundering anticipation, I waited for the bomb to fall, waited for the city to burn.

Instead of what I had always seen, however, I continued, flying right through the barrier, into a world that was shrouded with a deep blue sky and covered with a blanket of white snow.

My sight had never taken me beyond Edmund's barricade before. Even when I had tried, I had never been able to penetrate its surface, my magic had been as trapped as we were.

Now, as I flew through the bitter wind, snowflakes falling over me in wet, little specks that shook through my spine, I could see. What was more, I could *feel*. I could feel the cold, feel the wet. I knew they were not there, because I could still feel the hard, cobbled courtyard against my knees, hear the voices of whoever was at the church, mumbling over us like a garbled song.

Everything was real.

The sight was *real*.

Shivering from the snow, I soared over the barren wasteland as I searched for whatever I was meant to see. There was nothing other than snow, until the beautiful, untouched drifts of snow were trampled with mud, the flattened earth speckled with tents I had seen scarcely a few months before outside of Rioseco when Ilyan and I had gone to destroy one of Edmund's many camps.

My sight soared through the tents, the howling of the icy wind broken up by voices, one deep and guttural, another high and whiney, both mixed with the mumbling groans of fear and trepidation.

I trembled at the emotion behind the sounds, something in my heart tugging at a familiarity I couldn't place with the heavy Czech they were using.

The heavy, Slavic accents drifted up from a small group of people directly below me. The man in the cloak stood in the middle of them, and directly before him stood Ovailia.

Everything in me tightened, my throat frantic for a scream. The creature who had been in so many of my sights was right below me. Not in the streets of Prague as he usually was, not inside the barrier as he had been moments before. But right below me, with Ovailia.

Ovailia looked at him with a smile that spread over her face in reprehensible greed. The smile was so opposite from her usual sneer that it made me jerk, my shoulders folding up to my ears as I fought the distress that smile gave me.

I waited, eager to hear, to find out who Ovailia faced. But before I could see, the whole vision changed, the clear sight broken up by familiar static.

The electronic noise buzzed in my ears, screamed through my head as the sight became distorted, broken images that ripped through me the same as they had for the past months.

Blood on rocks as it seeped into an already red river.

A cluster of people standing in the snow, a woman screaming over their silently moving mouths.

Wyn, just as I had seen her this morning, sleeping beside Thom. When she raised her head to me, however, it was her daughter, instead.

Children crying in corners, a little, blonde girl laughing as she tortured them. The cloaked figure removing the heavy hood to reveal Dramin's pained face. Edmund standing beside me, laughing joyously as we looked into an unfamiliar, underground pond.

One after another, they came, spinning through me uncomfortably until I felt like I was trapped among them, my body fighting them, my mind breaking down inside of them.

New sights mixed with old, the old sights changing enough I wasn't even quite sure what I was looking at.

What was true.

What was false.

What was when.

I watched the new pieces mix with the old, my magic screaming at me to pay attention, screaming it was real and not the same as the distorted sights.

"Here is where it starts again." The unfamiliar voice was clear in my head, ringing clearly as the sight flashed back to the pair in the snow. Ovailia walked away from the man, a smile spreading over her face.

"Don't fail me," Ovailia said as another flash of blood, of red, filled my vision, Edmund's laugh echoing inside my head before the sight was gone, leaving me staring at the red-tinted world of reality.

Gasping, head swimming, I tried to let the real world come into focus as I stared at what I was sure was regurgitated Black Water seeping through the valleys of the cobbles I kneeled on.

"What's wrong?"

"What's going on?"

Voices ricocheted around in my head like they were coming from a tin can, the hollow sounds of what I believed were Ryland and Risha sounding far too loud and far too foreign against the confusion I was still trying to recover from.

"Zůstávat," Ilyan growled in warning as he pulled me closer to him, the contact welcoming, even if it made it harder to breathe.

My body ached as I gasped, my throat burning with a distinct taste of blood, my fingertips raw from clawing the ground.

"I saw him ... the man ... cloak ... with Ovailia," I gasped as I looked up at Ilyan. "They are working for Edmund. You have to find him, Ilyan."

"What's going on?" Ryland erupted, obviously scared.

He wasn't the only one.

'I know you are worried about me, but you have to go. You have to find Sain.' I pushed the words into his mind as I collapsed back to the ground, everything spinning, everything aching.

Ilyan's thoughts froze with conflict, worry, and fear, his hand clenching against my back, his hesitancy clear.

"Go." I could barely get the word out. "I'll be fine."

"We need to find Sain," Ilyan announced as he stood. "Ryland, go check the far courtyard and the catacombs. I'll hit the dorms and then the tombs. Risha, I need you to take Joclyn to Dramin and then do a perimeter sweep. We will meet at my tomb." He spoke very quickly in Czech, and I was having a hard time keeping up, especially with the way my head was still spinning.

"Is she okay?" Ryland asked, his worried query catching me off guard.

"She will be fine," Ilyan answered in English, his fingers pressing against my back comfortingly. I focused on the contact, letting it strengthen me, letting it fill me. "We need to get moving."

Ilyan knelt beside me and I turned to face him. His piercing, blue eyes full of so much love and concern that, for a moment, I forgot how to breathe. The intensity of his look swallowed me before he lowered his lips to mine.

I kissed him deeply, my hand reaching around to grab his neck, the soft, golden ribbon he had woven through his long braid falling between my fingers.

'Stay with me,' he insisted as he pulled away, looking at me passionately, his meaning clear. *'I may need your help.'*

'I know.'

He was gone before I had even finished the thought, with a grunt I sat back, jaw tight as I pulled myself to stand.

"Can I help you?" I had, however, forgotten Ilyan had asked Risha to stay behind and help.

"I'm actually okay," I said stubbornly, legs shaking as I tried to push myself up, eyes focusing on the long, golden ribbon that fell down the side of my neck, circling elegantly through the stones below me. "It sucks to say I'm used to this. But I'm used to this..."

My legs continued their violent shaking as I forced myself to stand. Part of me was secretly grateful when she caught me, her hand strong around my bicep. I hadn't even realized I had been falling.

"Okay, I guess I do need some help," I admitted quietly, grateful when she chuckled, the sound musical rather than condescending.

Taking her arm without question, I leaned against her as she led me toward Dramin and Thom's room, my mind running over everything that had happened.

I hadn't been around Risha outside of our weekly meetings, and had avoided her most other times thanks to her unsuccessfully hidden crush on Ryland. The whole ex-girlfriend vibe was a little too high school given our current situation, but I couldn't shake it. Besides, it was more than that. I really didn't know much about her besides the whole Ryland thing. That and the fact she liked to eat meat.

Both of those were public knowledge, no matter how hard the two of them tried to hide it. Not about the meat, but about the crush. I was fairly certain everyone knew. After all, Ryland had never been very good at hiding those types of things. I should know.

Contrary to public, or Wyn, knowledge, I was happy for him.

Wyn had even taken a betting pool at one point to see how long they would last or how I would act when I found out. Everyone was kind of waiting to find out the results of it at this point.

"That's okay," her voice was soft. "Everyone needs help from time to time."

"Some more than others." It was said in mostly a growl. Considering everything I had been through over the past year, it fit.

Sometimes, like right then, I was ashamed of the fact that I still needed help.

I had grown so much. I had done so much. I had defeated so much.

I was supposed to be the "most powerful."

I was ready for all of this growing and trials and learning stuff to be over, but I wasn't naïve enough to think it ever would be.

All this junk was just life.

Even when I hit a thousand, I was sure I would still be learning new things and conquering new trials, and I would probably be messing them up from time to time, too. If anything, I was getting better at handling it, and I was going to wear that like a badge of honor.

After everything I had faced, after everything I had done, the badge had been well deserved. And to be able to look at myself and see how much stronger I really was... I didn't even think my own mother would recognize the 'me' I had become.

"But needing help, that's okay, too," I whispered, knowing it was more to myself than it was to her.

She smiled, anyway.

CHAPTER 9
SAIN

"Zdechnout."

Tiny teeth gnashed inches from my face, the creature falling to the ground in a lifeless heap at the sound of the word, a thud of flesh and stone ringing throughout the cramped alleyway.

It wasn't often that one of those things would slip back through the barrier with me, and I wasn't sure how it happened when it took so much effort for me to move through the space on my own. Yet, it did.

Luckily, I could kill them easily enough.

Stripping off the heavy cloak, I dropped it in the same weeds I always kept it in, grateful to be rid of it now that the winter chill was trapped on the other side of the barrier.

I didn't even check to make sure it was hidden, I was in too much of a hurry.

Joclyn was a smart girl—sometimes too much so—and thanks to her personal vendetta against me, I was sure they had moved past the first stages of assuming they were being double-crossed by whoever was under that cape, and moved to solid assumptions of me being the culprit behind the cape.

Now I had to find them before it was too late, discredit the brat even more.

"Pošetilý Ilyan," the words were a grumble as I walked away from the door, and into the large church complex of his people.

The brainwashed herd wandered around as if the world on the other side of the barrier wasn't trying to kill them, as if they had forgotten why the light was red and the air was hot. There was more laughter than training, more joy than fear. It was a stark contrast to what little I had seen of Edmund's camp.

It was kind of exciting to see how ill prepared they were, how secure they were in the delusions I had been force-feeding them for so long.

The attack won't come until spring.

The barrier will fall months before the danger finds us.

The lies made me smile, my grin catching the eye of a few members of the tittering horde who were wandering through the courtyard.

"Sain," a Skřítek I had met several hundred years before called to me from across the large, stone square. He was one who had always stood and fought by Ilyan's side. If I remembered correctly, his mate had perished in one of the many battles Ilyan had led them into. Now his eyes were dark with questions and doubt.

Several others perked up at the boom in his voice, their own questions buzzing through their heads as they, too, made their way over, and I waited for them. Part of me knew I needed to get to the bathroom in order to check that I held no incriminating evidence on my body of where I had been, while another part was grateful I had been stopped—

at least they could provide some sort of an alibi if Ilyan found me before I found Joclyn.

"Yes?" I questioned as they grew closer, the soothing nature of my voice completely contradictory to the thunder of anxiety that had taken over my insides. The tall man's eyes darted toward a few of the people who surrounded him in waning confidence.

"We are sorry to bother you ..." he began before stalling out.

"It's no bother," I assured him, stretching my hand out to rest on his shoulder, noticing a small patch of dirt near my thumb. "I was seeing to some of the children in the ward." The group was awed by the lie, their worry softening as the doubt began to fade. "What can I help you with?"

"We were wondering if you could tell us what happened to the Queen this morning ... if she had a sight, if we are safe here."

Of course they weren't safe here.

Wiping my hand off on the leg of my faded dress pants, I turned my face down into a frown. "She did see into the future, but there is no way to know if that sight is true."

"What do you mean?" the man asked, his face opening in horror. "I thought the sight of a Drak is infallible."

I sighed heavily, the exaggerated sound seeping from me as I ran my hand over my forehead. "It is when the magic is pure. Hers is not pure. It is uncontrollable at the moment. Her sights are dwelling in the depth of the Zlomený."

They began whispering, the word known to a few of them, even if they didn't understand its true meaning, they still understood the impact. Even the ones who didn't understand could grasp the fear around them, their eyes wide as they looked to their peers for answers.

"So everything she sees—"

"Broken? Yes," I clarified. The looks of shock and fear deepened with each lie I spoon-fed them.

"But yours ...?"

"I am of the first, and I can fight the Zlomený better than any of my kind, but it is still hard. Because of her foolish choices, everything is muddled." I wasn't even going to give the older man a chance to say anything more. I didn't want anything other than what I gave them in their heads. "I hold the Drak magic deep within me, I will do everything in my power to restore true sight. To stop Joclyn from this tirade and save us all."

Calm, relief, and awe washed over all of them. The fear slowly dissipated at the knowledge, their own minds putting the pieces together that I wanted them to. After all, who would want someone with a broken sight leading them when pure magic stood right there?

"So we are safe?" a young Chosen asked, the look on her face making it clear she didn't fully understand what was happening.

"For the time being," I answered, my hand heavy as I placed it on her arm. "Do not worry; I am watching."

I smiled, waving away any further questions as I walked from my captive audience, my eyes scanning the courtyard for my daughter, despite knowing she wouldn't be here. Hopefully, I still had time to find her.

In a few steps, I moved into the vast marble and stone hallway that led toward the catacombs, leaving the still tittering crowd behind me. Centuries ago, this space had held long kitchens with ovens similar to those at Rioseco. However, sometime in the early twentieth century bathrooms had been added with running water, flushing toilets, and all. Thankfully, the ceramic palace was as empty as the hall outside, the room already filled with the echoes of the ambient noises my very presence was causing.

Locking the door with a snap, I ran past the basin sinks to the mirrors, the glass old and rusted out near the corners. Some were harder to see through than others, but it didn't matter.

I didn't need to see much other than if there was more than the dirt I had already found.

Blood, snow, grime.

Signs that I had been on the outside.

"What did I bring back with me this time?" I queried, peering through the specks of red and brown that littered the mirrored surface.

Luckily, thanks to the heated air, the snow had long since melted from my hair and all that remained was a soggy hem around my dark, frayed pants.

With one small spark of perfectly placed magic, the damp cloth dried with a small tuft of smoke, the smell of singed cotton mixing with the smell of borax soap in an oddly enjoyable bouquet.

"Beautiful," I sighed, my eyes closing against the lingering scent of death. Unfortunately, the smell would give me away too quickly.

"Joclyn, foolish girl, where are you?" I growled at the thought, my heart tensing in impatience. I needed to move.

I had seen a few people gathered before the cathedral when I was on the other side of the barrier, preparing to return. I thought I had a good idea who they were, but even if I was wrong, it was a good place to start.

With one last check in the mirror, I tore from the bathroom, pushing my magic into my heart as I moved. Teeth clenched and heart pounding, I fought the need to yell as the familiar pain ripped through me like someone was trying to tear me in two. I growled, anxious for the agony to end yet also needing to restrain the power, to hide it away where Joclyn couldn't sense it, couldn't sense me.

Finally breathing normally, I peeked in doorways and hallways as I raced through the complex at a sprint, growing more and more eager to find her with each slap of my shoes against stone, like the ticking of a clock.

My anxiety had grown into a panic, when I turned the final corner to find Joclyn and Risha huddled together on the other side of the long corridor. Joclyn was leaning against Risha heavily, her body sagging so deeply I was sure she couldn't walk very well on her own. My heart rate sped up at seeing her so impaired, but not for the fear or anxiety I had felt up to this point.

Yes, she was my daughter, and deep down, I wanted to say part of me really, truly cared for her in that way, cared for her as I cared for Dramin. As a father should. But, I didn't.

She was nothing more than a liability to me, a liability I needed to keep under control. I had to keep *her* under control until Edmund disposed of her. She stubbornly thought her magic was *telling* her to break rules the Draks were raised to obey, every rule the Skříteks and Trpaslíks were taught to fear.

I was sure her magic *was* actually telling her all those things because what she was saying was actually true, which was why the need to control her was so necessary. Discredit the queen and my step to the throne was that much closer.

"Joclyn!" I yelled from the end of the hall, my voice terrified, even though the beat of my heart said otherwise.

Risha looked up as I yelled, relief washing over her as she held Joclyn close to her. "Oh, Sain, thank all."

"What happened?" I yelled as I continued to move closer. "Joclyn? Are you okay?"

Joclyn looked up, but where Risha's expression was one of relief, Joclyn's was one of anger and frustration. Her silver eyes flashed, her jaw tightening as she bit the inside of her mouth, something I was sure Ilyan found endearing. To me, however, the lack of self-restraint and poorly handled mortal outbursts angered me more. She was a Drak, and she needed to act like one.

"Joclyn?" I asked, trying to conceal the loathing that looking at her gave me. "Are you okay?"

"Where were you?" Her response was a snap as it rebounded across the stone to me.

I knew what she was referring to and doing my best to make it seem as if I was as clueless as she was to the world.

"Where was I? I was with the children... What are you...?" I reached my hand out to her, desperate for the skin contact I needed in order to check her magic, to regain control of her sight and know what she had seen.

She flinched away from me, and my stomach wound together.

I had obviously misread exactly how weak she was, exactly how much sight she had regained. I couldn't be sure without touching her, but if I had to guess, considering the look on her face, the thin layer of sweat rolling down her pale skin, I would say she had seen something.

Something more than I had been force-feeding her.

Something real.

"You look terrible, Jos. Did you see something?" I swallowed, trying to stifle the panic that rose up in my stomach as I reached toward her again, anxious for contact.

"Where were you?" she snapped again, the pale red of her anger coloring the ash white of her face.

I fought the smile that little detail gave me. She was getting angry, and I knew as well as anyone how volatile her emotions were. Combine that with the instability of her sight, and it would take very little to plunge her back into another vision. It was something that, given her power, would be dangerous, but not now, not with me here. It might be what I needed in order to gain skin contact and regain control of her.

"Where was I when?" I looked to Risha in question, pushing as much innocence into my voice as I could, knowing it would aggravate Joclyn more.

"Before," Joclyn growled.

"Risha, what is she talking about?" I asked, but Risha looked as confused as I did, her bottle green eyes darting between Joclyn and me so quickly they looked like a blur.

"An hour ago, a few minutes ago." Joclyn stopped for breath. "All of this morning? Where. Were. You?"

"I was here ..." I spoke slowly, condescendingly, hoping to increase her anger, knowing I was close. I could already feel the strong light-headedness that usually preceded a sight. The heavy power of her Drak magic was trying to join with my own. "I was helping some of the new Chosen children understand what the future held for them."

She knew I was lying. Risha probably did, too, but Risha was more concerned with what was happening to Joclyn at that moment.

So was I; except, my concern and help came in a different packaging.

Joclyn exhaled in a low, painful moan, her eyes snapping shut in an excruciating grimace, to open again with the bright ember glow of sight, her eyes dark and deep, the contrast stunning against the blank canvas of her face as she saw into past and future simultaneously. It was beautiful to watch her magic work the way it was intended. Still, it was a beauty I would not allow.

Especially not with her.

I didn't even care if Risha noticed the smile spreading over my lips. I let the grin grow at the glow in her eyes, the anger in my gut howling in success as I reached my hand forward and wrapped it around her wrist. My magic plunged into her as my sight connected with hers, as my magic connected with her soul.

It was easy to do as long as I was connected to her. She was my child, after all.

The snow-filled world outside the wall blossomed in recall. The dead corn fields, the barren trees, they all stretched before me as the bitter wind tugged at the two figures huddled in the middle of the wasteland, a small army of guards surrounding them.

I recognized the moment. Ovailia standing before me, my tall frame shrouded in the black cloak I had been haunting Joclyn with.

This was more than a sight, more than recognition; it was remembering.

I had stood before Ovailia hours before and felt the power of prescience, but not as though I was one who saw, rather in the way sight was being taken from me. And now I understood why.

It had been.

Joclyn's sight had taken her right to us.

Joclyn had pulled true sight from me.

She had tapped into a sight I had so carefully concealed I was sure no one would ever find it.

Yet, she had.

I watched the perfect recall of those moments play again: Edmund and Joclyn beside the wells of Imdalind,

Joclyn fighting, the blood, the screaming. I watched in horror before I acted, letting my magic take control and infect the sight, to change it, as I had so many times before.

The image of her and Edmund standing beside Imdalind was now Edmund drowning her inside the muddy waters. The boy fighting was now the boy dying. Some little girl I did not recognize running to Joclyn in help was now the child running to her with a knife.

One after another, I changed them, intertwining them with the image of Ovailia standing in the snow, her caped companion changing from one person after another—from Wyn to Ryland to Risha to Ilyan.

A sight that was so perfectly clear before was now nothing more than the maze she had learned to fear.

I could already feel her alarm as the sight crippled her, the image becoming more twisted as her magic tried to rebel against the changes, rebel against the ironclad lock I was placing on it.

"Here is where it starts again."

I twitched, jumping away from her as though I had been burned.

I had heard that voice before, when I had pulled Dramin from the mud, when the sight had crippled us both, and he had started crying for the first time.

'You have done the wrong.' The same words echoed again as Joclyn collapsed in an unconscious dead weight right into Risha. The woman held onto Joclyn's tiny frame for dear life.

"What is it?" she exclaimed, obviously concerned. "What happened?"

It took me a moment to realize the question was directed at me and not Joclyn.

"She had a sight," I said, fear still running through me.

"What was it?" Risha asked, the panic in her voice shaking through the air. Interesting, I might be able to get more information out of Risha with Joclyn out of commission.

"Is she okay?" Risha asked when I didn't answer, her hands pressing against her skin in an obvious desire to heal her.

"Yes, she's going to be fine," I lied, knowing my plans would deter that. "Sometimes, this happens after an especially intense sight."

"She's been having them an awfully lot lately—"

"I know." *I have been helping that along.* "They seem to be doing her some damage."

"Why don't you pass out after your sights?" She looked away from Joclyn, her terror easing as she looked at me in wonder.

"Because I know how to control my magic. Drak magic can be powerful, and if you are not strong enough, it can destroy you."

"Is that what's happening?" Risha asked, concerned. "Her magic is destroying her?"

"I believe so. Normally, I can help my people, help them restrain their magic, but she won't let me. She knows what the vision about the end says, and she's trying to change it. It makes all her sights unreliable when she goes against one like that, when she doesn't listen to her magic. It destroys her ability." Yet another little lie, yet another worried glance.

My lips shuddered, though I tried to stop the grin.

"Did she have a sight before?" I asked as innocently as I could, my head spinning slightly at the prod of a sight I would never let come.

"Yeah"—she was hesitant—"right when she and Ilyan came back ... She couldn't really stand—"

"It was the same sight," my voice growled as I looked at her, the hatred for her coming back even in her partially unconscious state. "I saw it as she did."

"Did you see it then?" Her eyes narrowed at me, a question behind the words I didn't quite understand.

I didn't know what I had said wrong, but my guard went up, my eyes narrowing as I tried to decipher where this was going.

"See what?" Better to feign my innocence again.

"The sight ... Did you see it when you were with the kids?"

I was sure Risha had no idea why Joclyn had been so concerned with my whereabouts; I could see that much on her face. But she was still going to take every chance she could to find out the information Joclyn could not.

"My sight is not hindered by her inability. I can control what sights come to me, and I was with the children. It was not the right time to see."

Risha glowered at me, eyes hard, all thoughts of the injured girl she held gone.

I had never liked Risha before. She had acted more like a spoiled brat than the powerful Skřítek she was. Right then, though, I was sure Ilyan had chosen wisely for his second.

She hadn't missed anything.

"I don't know what either of you are getting at, but I was helping the Chosen with their futures. I was here. I don't have anywhere else to go. I don't have anywhere else I *can* go." I had tightened my jaw as I looked at her, waiting for her to say something, when a sudden pulse of powerful magic alerted me to the arrival of someone I really didn't want to see. Luckily, I had already stepped into an easy escape.

"Now, if you will excuse me," I growled like a lion, stepping around Risha and my invalid daughter, determined to put as much space between me and them before Ilyan's arrival. "You should see that she makes it to someone who can help her."

It was harsh, but right then, I didn't care.

I needed those seeds to grow, and I would do anything to make sure it happened.

CHAPTER 10

DRAMIN

I sat against the headboard of my bed, stagnant air pressing against my skin as the dim, red light faded to a deep black as the sun set.

Everyone stood around the tiny room Thom and I shared, refusing to make eye contact. Each of us were lost in the new development Ilyan had thrown at us. Not that it should be surprising; it was one more thing to add to the list of many.

One more thing I couldn't help with.

I couldn't see where we were headed, I couldn't warn them. I couldn't say anything.

"So, when you say this ... *person* ... Stuttered ..." Ryland began from where he leaned against the wall, the muscles in his arms tensing as he folded them over his chest.

"There one second, gone the next," Joclyn said from where she sat at the foot of my bed. "I couldn't find his magic after that, so either he moved through the wall, or he found some secret world within a Stutter that neither Ilyan nor I know about."

"Can we say this mysterious, cloaked person got caught

in some other dimension?" Wyn mused acidly before Ryland had a chance to retort, leaning her head against Thom's headboard with a thud. "If only to get Ryland to stop asking the same thing again and again?"

"I'm not asking the same question again and again," Ryland snapped, his voice hard as his focus jolted to Wyn, who raised her eyebrows in some kind of challenge I didn't understand.

"He's asking questions as a good leader should," Risha interrupted the fueled staredown that the two were having. Children.

"As we all should." Ilyan's loud, commanding voice took over the conversation with a snap, causing Ryland to collapse back against the wall.

It had only been a few hours since Risha had brought her here, half unconscious and weak as she fumed about 'stupid sights' and 'stupid fathers'. She had been 'attacked by a sight.' according to Risha. But I had known better. I hadn't seen Tatínek all day.

I needed to tell her, but Risha had refused to leave her side, and with the amount of questions she asked about our father it did not seem like the smartest company to be having such a conversation.

I would have been more concerned for Joclyn's well-being if she hadn't been fuming about 'stupid sights' and 'stupid fathers'. Even though she had been weak, she had recovered quickly enough. That was probably more thanks to her stubborn temper than actual well-being.

Then again, without that stubborn temper, I wouldn't be alive. It was something I was still torn over. After all, we had seen my death in the very first sight she received, and yet, here I sat. She had listened to her magic and saved me.

And nothing exploded.

"Here," Joclyn whispered, my old metal bed frame creaking as she handed me the mug we had been sharing. I quickly finished what was left of the contents.

"So this man," I began, my hands wrapping tightly around the old, earthen mug, "you are sure he works for your father?"

"I don't see any other reason for someone to attack us. Besides, even the possibility that he moved through the barrier cements it," Ilyan answered in Czech, his voice growing deeper as he began to pace through the tiny room. "I don't see how they could know *how* to move through the barrier unless they were."

I nodded, knowing he was right. Wyn asked some questions about motive, but I stared into the dry and cracked bottom of the mug, silently wishing I had the ability to fill it myself, that the next question would never come.

"—and he's one of us," Wyn finished her thought, her voice drifting away as she avoided the obvious.

Too bad I wouldn't.

"You believe this cloaked man to be Sain." I spoke into the mug, my voice echoing. It wasn't even really a question.

I didn't often get nervous, or I hadn't for all my life until a few months ago. Right then, as I sat with a dozen eyes on me, the only sound in the room was that of Wyn's heavy breathing and Ryland uncomfortably shifting his weight, I was sure that I felt it.

"You know where I stand," Joclyn spoke only to me, her hand extended to cover the mug as she refilled it. Her eyes were bright as she stared at me. Yes, I knew where she stood, and I was fairly sure she knew where I stood too. Or where I would.

We weren't alone. Wyn was clearly in agreement, meanwhile Ryland looked as torn as I did.

"In some ways, having our culprit be Sain would be the lesser of two evils," Ilyan's voice cut through the silence, but I sat, staring at the swirling black water in my mug. At the image that was just on the surface. Me, sitting in that alley. Sain, right behind.

It was the closest to sight I had gotten since I had been pulled from near death, but I quickly drank from the mug, not wanting to see more.

Not wanting anyone to see.

The liquid burned as it went down, something that had gotten worse over the last few days. I kept my face impassive as I drank, silently praying that no one would notice.

"Being double-crossed by your own man is the lesser of two evils?" Wyn asked, the smug smile the same as I had always known from her. I couldn't help the shiver that ran up my spine. "If that's the case, then I think I want a do-over. Let someone else take the fall for my 'lesser'."

"I hate that I am going to say this, but being double-crossed by a condescending, old man would be much better than having Edmund's entire army knowing how to move through the barrier." Joclyn was snarling again, the bed jostling as she slammed her back against the footboard.

"As if they don't attack us enough on our normal raids. We lost three people this morning," Wyn conceded from where she sat, squished against Thom's endlessly sleeping frame.

"I can't believe he would do that," Ryland muttered from where he leaned against the wall. "He has the same goals as we do; why would he work for someone he wants to kill as badly as the rest of us?"

"But do you know that he does, Ryland?" Ilyan asked as he stepped toward his brother. "I know what you two have been through. I know you have become very close to him.

Regardless, we have to keep every possibility open, and his behavior with Joclyn as of late, with our queen, has been highly inexcusable."

Ryland cringed as Ilyan spoke, his bulldog stance sagging as the strength of Ilyan's words sunk in.

"No, I will give you that," Ryland sighed, running his hand through his hair. "I just find it hard to believe he would be working with Edmund after everything he put him through."

Risha was nodding, even Wyn sat back looking guilty. But I was frozen, guilt raging through my system. But for a different reason.

Grumbles and groans and whispered agreements moved through the small group as instances and possibilities and facts about Sain were thrown around. Everyone trying to find their own answer.

I sat back, only to face Joclyn who was staring right at me, the question she had asked a dozen times staring right at me. I clamped my tongue between my teeth and pretended to drink as I gave her a little shake of my head.

Sain couldn't do that... I didn't want to believe he could do that... And yet...

I turned to Thom, my mind filled with that moment in the street where everything had gone so fast, time sped up. I had been bitten, so my memory was addled by pain, but I could have sworn I saw Sain talking to someone, someone who had poisoned Thom.

"What makes you think it is Sain?" Ryland asked, pushing himself off the wall as he too began to pace.

"Joclyn saw him within a sight in the cloak, running through the city. She's seen the same figure a few times. After what we saw this morning—"

"She saw him in sight? Or she saw him in real life?"

Risha interrupted, her voice quivering as she glanced to where Joclyn sat. I could feel my sister bristle from here.

"What are you asking?" Joclyn snapped, her face draining of color.

I straightened, a tense knot forming in my spine as I looked between the two women, obviously missing something.

"Well, after this morning, I feel it's necessary to look at other possibilities."

Joclyn cringed, her shoulders pulling into her neck, her face wrinkling in the way it always did before she erupted at our father. Except, this time it wasn't father; it was Risha.

"Joclyn?" I whispered as I leaned toward her, the mug all but forgotten. "Are you okay, my dear?" Placing my hand on her knee as I always did, I pulled her attention away from the beautiful Skřítek who looked like she had walked into a men's locker room.

Joclyn looked at me, her eyes pained. The wrinkles in her brow intensified as her eyes shined with tears. That was new.

"Wait. What happened this morning? Lightning bolts erupt out of her head or something?" Wyn asked, putting voice to the question that, thanks to Joclyn's heartbroken expression, had been about to leave my lips.

"She had a sight," Ryland provided, moving away from the wall, his hand running through his shaggy hair again. "She couldn't tell the sight from reality."

I froze; everyone did. Everyone but Ilyan, who moved back to Joclyn's side. His arm draped over her shoulders, his chest expanding as he stood beside her, strong and defiant while she sat beside him, her eyes narrowed, brow hard, willing to do the same for him.

"She couldn't tell ...?" Wyn began, her eyes drifting in

obvious worry to her best friend. Joclyn said nothing, and Wyn didn't pry, even though I could tell she wanted to.

"And that makes her untrustworthy?" Ilyan asked of Risha, the power in his voice pressing against her as she cowered in respect.

"Not to me, My Lord," she clarified, her shoulders heaving as she stepped back toward Ilyan, her jaw clenched tightly. "But to others ... There are things that have been said. That I have heard."

"You mean the rumors?" Wyn asked, her fingers gripping the edge of the bed as she sat up a little straighter. "Everyone's heard them; that doesn't mean they are true. For all we know, it's some jealous Chosen who is mad they can't 'see' like Jos can."

It was the reasoning we had always used. What was said, what was being spread around, was so vague there wasn't any basis to think there was any concern, any basis in fact. Joclyn caught my eye again. We knew the truth.

"I think I may know for certain where they are coming from." Risha looked right at Ilyan, her eyes narrowing in an anger that was not meant for him. I guess we all knew. "When Sain stopped me and Joclyn in the hall, when Joclyn had that other sight, he said some things."

"What *things*?" Ilyan's voice had grown even harder, and this time, I saw Risha's confidence dip.

"That, as she won't listen to her magic, the Drak in her is dying."

The room went quiet. Wyn sat still with a clenched jaw. Ryland was caught between looking at Risha and Joclyn in some kind of shock. Ilyan stared at Joclyn with such severity it was clear they were deep in silent conversation.

"I don't believe him, Your Highness, but it was too close to what we have been hearing, to the rumors that have been going around since you first—" Risha stopped halfway through, her own confidence failing from what she had been about to say. "But he's your father; he wouldn't say such things ..."

"But he's been saying them since the beginning," Joclyn snarled, she and Ilyan exchanging a sharp look. "That's why I've broken things. That I'm broken. Ranting about the Zlomený. This is nothing new."

"The Zlomený," I whispered, pulling Joclyn and Ilyan's focus right to me.

"Yes, we know, broken sight." She rolled her eyes at me, and I knew why. That was all she knew. That was all she was allowed to know. I looked between them, my chest aching as the path before me became clear.

I knew what I had seen: that little boy in the alley.

I knew what I needed to do.

"I think it is time to tell you the truth, dear sister. I must tell you of the Zlomený. Of what Sain did..." Everyone froze at my words, all of them leaning in. My heart rattled in my chest, screaming at me to stop, but my father's bind was weak.

I knew this was right. I couldn't let this knowledge die with me.

"What did he—" Joclyn began, only to have her eyes gloss over, her mouth dropping open in fear. "Sain is coming."

As though someone had shot a bolt of electricity into them, everyone moved. Wyn jumped up, obviously ready to pin the old man to the ground if she had to, Ryland and Risha shifted around to face the wall, although they were both still clearly torn on what to do.

I sat still as I watched them, Ilyan clinging to Joclyn as my own anxiety rose to inhuman levels. His bind... it was stronger than I thought. How much had he heard. How much did he know?

"Umlčet!" Ilyan commanded, his voice a loud boom as his magic washed over everyone in the room, pressing into them and taking control. As one, everyone turned to him, their bodies unable to disobey the control he had taken. "Ryland, Risha, I need you all to watch. Watch the movements of everyone around you. Not just Sain, *everyone*. We cannot act until we know beyond doubt who is beyond this. We need to find this person before anything happens. No one else can know of your task. Wyn, you are the guard for the night. I had to tear down the Little Prince, so you will need to use the Old Man."

The three nodded before they left, leaving the room in a flood. Joclyn didn't move from her perch, Ilyan beside her, his fingers twisting through the tail of her braid as he leaned down to kiss her. The four of us in the same places we were every time he found us.

It was a weird feeling to be a thousand years old and still sneaking around your father as though the worst thing you have ever done is hidden some wine coolers under your bed.

Ilyan pulled away from Joclyn with a grin, the gaze they held between them was long, deep, and loving, their arms wrapping around each other, absorbing each other, as if they couldn't get enough, as if they were scared to let go. It had been so long since I had seen love that deep. In fact, I didn't know if I ever had.

It was beautiful, and yet...

"It's times like this I wish Thom was awake. I could sure do with one of his snide comments about propriety right now."

Joclyn laughed, the sound deep and free, a welcome

sound after the tension that had invaded my room for the last few minutes. "Are we bothering you, Uncle?"

"Well, you are my sister ..." I smiled, lifting my mug toward her in a twisted toast that I wasn't sure she saw as wrapped up in Ilyan as she was.

Her lips met his as lights flashed, popping around us all in a beautiful array that was almost comforting. I lay back as I watched them, content to observe the dancing sparkle of the earth's magic, sad when they left as Joclyn breathlessly pushed Ilyan away.

The normally stoic man laughed, stealing another kiss.

"Seriously, will you *get a room*?" I groaned, "or at least break it up before Tatínek storms in here."

"Oh," Jos blushed, leaning against my bed frame again. "He's not coming. We just didn't want to share information."

The two laughed before Ilyan swept out of the room, leaving Joclyn and I alone, staring at each other.

"The Zlomený," she whispered, twisting the long, golden ribbon through her fingers. "What are they really?"

I paused. If the bind hadn't called him to us, then we should be good. Still, I hesitated, the desire in her eyes swallowing me whole. The silver had gone from their depths, replaced by a color so dark it was almost black. I expected the ember glow, expected the sight, but she sat still, staring at me as if she could see into me, as if she really was.

Draks had been taught to use our magic for a slow recall in order to peer into someone, to understand who they really are. I had seen the deep looks, the knowing glances, many times before. I had performed them many times before. With Joclyn, however, it was different. It was as though she was peering into the deep hidden caves of your soul and connecting with them, understanding them, rather than exposing them and poking around.

"Are you sure you want to know?" We were both aware I was hesitating, and she grinned.

"Well, I am your younger and much wiser sister." She said it with a laugh, her eyes sparkling.

"Siblings is a very loose word for what we really are, dear Joclyn."

"Drak, then?"

"I'm not sure that fits, either," I said with a growl, trying to ignore the deep longing that flamed through my soul.

"Why not? If you haven't been able to see, and my sights are broken," she growled back, one look pulling her right back to the battle in Rioseco where our father had claimed their bonding had broken everything.

"Your sights are not broken." I grabbed her hand, my knotted fingers curling around her as I pulled her focus. "I have told you this before."

"How do you know? Tell me. Because, I know you know, Dramin."

I swallowed, not liking the massive pit that had grown in the middle of my chest in the last few seconds. I couldn't back down now. She needed to know. She had waited long enough.

"What Sain told Risha, the rumors that have been spread, they are things the Drak are told never to repeat: about the Zlomený, about the weakness of a Draks' power. We tell everyone they are the sights that are broken by the acts of others, by the mortals. But that is not true."

She stared at me, obviously waiting for more, but I couldn't seem to find the right words. Everything was trapped behind a mental block, something keeping me from telling her the truth.

"So what he is saying is true?" The anger behind her voice was heavy, but still I smiled. Sometimes, I thought Father was right—that she did need better control over her emotions. "That by creating a Zlomený my magic is dying. It's killing me."

"That's just what we are told." I repeated the words the same way I had for years, but this time, they pressed against me, igniting something deep inside. I was going to have to be careful. "We say that Zlomený are sights that are broken because the Drak magic is too powerful for those who hold it. They can't control it, so the magic devours them. But that..." my throat felt as though it was going to close up. "But that is not the truth, the term Zlomený does not refer to the sights, but rather to the people who have them... the people who... control."

That same barrier I had felt before became a well, whatever block my father had put on my slamming into place. Joclyn's hands wrapped around mine as she watched the block slide into place, her jaw dropping into a wide 'o'.

"A block?" She asked, her jaw tight as she leaned forward, as if she could pick the answer out of my mind. Maybe she could.

"The Zlomený is not a sight." I spoke slowly, trying to get the words across, finding a way around the block before it snapped into place again. "It is a Drak with magic too strong..." It faded out again, but this time it was enough. I could have sung to the mud as I watched her frustration shift to fury.

"The people he cannot control," she said, my heart light as I nodded furiously. "The sights he cannot control."

"So, I'm too powerful..."

"The Silný." I whispered pulling her into me, staring at

those dark eyes as they widened, her breathing going shallow as the full meaning, the true meaning, hit her.

"Most powerful. Not because I am the strongest..."

"But more powerful than him," I finished for her as she leaned back against the footboard, her hand sliding from my grasp as the bed shook.

"Do your sights still change?"

"Obviously, I'm a Zlomený, remember." I couldn't tell if she was trying to be funny, or still stunned from the weight I had dropped in her lap.

"I'm quite serious, Joclyn." I hissed as that memory of the alley came back again, the sound of my father's shoes. Of his belt as he whipped me... "Do your sights still change?"

She nodded, "Some of my sights have been changing. It depends on if I am near him."

"Have been?" I asked, even more confused now. "You mean they have been changing after you have already had them? Showing you something different?"

Again, a nod before she said, "I know they are the same; I can feel it. It's like the sight before you woke up. I saw it. I saw the roofs. I saw the Vilý. But when it came again, when I pulled it through the recall it was different. It's the same roof, but it's like the picture was taken with a wider lens. It's the same attack, but it shows it from a different angle. People are in different places. Some are missing. Different things are shown. So I know it's the same ... but not."

She leaned in again, wrapping her hands around mine as I felt her magic flare and another shield snap around us.

"Like I said, it depends on if he is there."

I nodded, we had talked about this before. I just did not know it had grown this bad.

That he was working so hard to regain control. I should

have guessed, he didn't seem as angry as he had only weeks ago. Last week he had brought me a cupcake, something I should have known had not come from in here, no matter how many times he told me otherwise.

"How often ...?" I could barely get the question out, my mouth was dry.

"That's all there is now. I don't know what to follow anymore. I don't know what's right. Everything contradicts each other, and it all looks different. More than the clear and static images, it's all distorted, like a television with bad reception."

"So he hasn't gained full control," I hissed to myself. "When I was a child, fresh from the mud, my Drak abilities had come on strong, much as yours did after I gave you the water. They were as strong as our father's when he had first awakened, or so he had told me." I stopped then, my focus pulling from the intently listening child before me to the mug in my hands.

"I don't remember much of those days," I admitted. "But I do remember one. One day, I was probably nearing one hundred at the time, I saw a girl, a Trpaslík. She was tall and fair, so different from the rest of her kind. At first, I had confused her for a Skřítek, but then the sight came ..."

Joclyn leaned forward as if she would be able to tap into a recall. Except, there was none, not anymore. Only a memory of the girl remained, only the painful bite of the sight that never was. I had written them all in my journals, every sight that had snaked through. But those were gone now.

At the time, the sight had come on as strong as they had been in the beginning. I had felt my father tense beside me as I saw the girl on the street; except, in the sight, she was older, her hair long, her face lined. She stood beside a man, and in her arms was a baby boy. I had seen the boy grow before my eyes. A strapping Trpaslík, he was strong, and you could easily tell he was one of their leaders. I had watched as he found a mate of his own. Her appearance was so sweet and stunning it was burned into my memory.

My father had gasped as he tapped into the sight, as he saw what I had. His anger was so quick that, before the sight had even finished, he had dragged me into an alley, the shadows of the city buildings hanging over us like cobwebs, drowning us in darkness.

His voice had been a hiss of anger I had never heard before as he pressed me into the wall, jeering in my ear to forget what I had seen..

I am the first of the Drak, and it is my responsibility to make sure all of the Draks below me see what I approve and do what is allowed. That starts with you, Dramin. Never question me, son. Don't be a Zlomený. Those will be killed.

He had been so kind before that moment, so loving. He had given me life and raised me, everything he had said was true, so I agreed.

I had wanted to.

And I had never questioned him again.

Not until this moment, not until Joclyn looked at me and told me her sights were changing. Told me of the television fuzz that two thousand years ago would have made no sense, but now I understood, because I had seen it.

"I saw the girl's son find a mate, a beautiful Skřítek. The boy was a Trpaslík, and I saw their magic join as one."

Joclyn's eyes widened at the admission. Even she knew the story about how our father was the first to mate with someone outside of his magic.

And here I was, telling her otherwise.

No, here I was, telling her why.

"Before Ovailia?"

I hesitated as I recalled the boy's chosen mate and her face that, at the time, was like any other. Just another woman. Just another man.

I had seen the Skřítek standing with the Trpaslík she was meant to be bonded to. I had seen it clearly, and yet barely minutes later, with my father hissing in my ear, the sight changed. The static Joclyn had described took over as the sight of the woman changed. Her face shifting to one of hundreds of other women.

"I saw it, but then it changed, exactly as you said."

"So, he is changing them." It was a statement filled with the downtrodden weight of one trapped in a painful reality. "Now, I need to prove it."

"And that, child, may be your hardest task to date."

Her nose pinched as though she smelled something bad, though her eyes were dancing.

"Of all the tasks I have faced, Dramin, I think this is far from the hardest." She smiled, and I couldn't help smiling with her, regardless of something inside me that was screaming, something that was nagging at me.

It wasn't as simple as proving Sain was debilitating her sights; it was finding the reason why. Why he was so scared of her sights, and why he was so scared of a child who was stronger than him.

I was sure I already knew the answer.

"Joclyn," I sighed, the tension of fear spreading through my back. "I'm sure I don't need to warn you of this, but just in case: Don't underestimate him."

"I never have."

CHAPTER II
WYN

G litter and light bounced off the cathedral's barrier, showering me in the residue of an attack that had barely missed its mark. Blossoms of magic spread over the surface as I looked at my best friend, unsurprised to see her standing on the far side of the cathedral now, the same smug smile on her face.

Of course she was smug.

I had barely deflected that attack, and judging by the color and movement of the remaining magic, it would have knocked me out for a few minutes if it had made contact.

Leave it to Jos. When I said, 'Don't hold back, but don't kill me, either,' she had taken me at face value.

Good. I was up for the challenge, and it was better than sparring with Ilyan. I liked breaking rules, and he liked being boring.

Now, if I could stop worrying about Thom and whether he was still breathing or not or if that new boil that had appeared on his neck this morning had grown ...

Ugh.

I needed to focus.

Besides, we both needed the escape, and this was better than the mass murder I had resorted to after Rosaline's death.

I needed an escape from Thom; Jos, an escape from... Well, everything: her little breakdown from a few days ago and the rumors that had multiplied since then.

It was upsetting.

Whatever Sain was doing was really starting to piss me off. It was a good thing I hadn't run into him. Even though I knew Ilyan had already ripped into him, there was nothing stopping me from doing the same.

Or torturing him ... That would probably be a good release, too.

After all, thanks to Sain, everyone acted like Joclyn was broken. Everyone treated her like she was somehow too weak to do anything. That wasn't the case, however. Not really. At least, not the way I saw it.

She was actually *too* powerful. Her magic had grown too much, she was having a hard time controlling it.

It was something I knew all too well. Mostly because I had experienced it.

In the beginning, controlling the fire magic was scary. I would blow things up. Heck, I had even blown myself up a few times. It was undoubtedly why Ilyan was so insistent that I glue myself to her, maybe help her try to figure out what the heck was going on.

Despite her crazy-powerful magic, controlling it *was* possible. It would take time to figure out her own set of rules to make it work.

It was like 90s grunge—you had to find a way to make the loud, confusing mess work for you.

"If you keep messing up like that, I *will* get you," Jos said, a massive smile plastered across her face.

"If you keep taunting me, you *will* pay." My smile was as big as hers, but not for the reason she thought. I spoke calmly, plainly, distracting her from the fact that a powerful attack was already heading toward her, slithering under the old stonework of the cathedral floor.

I smiled wider as I fought the need to laugh, especially when her eyes narrowed in sudden realization.

She noticed too late, however, the magic shot into her before she could act, leaving her screeching in pain, jumping around like her shoes were on fire.

"No fair!" she yelled as she pranced, her retaliation attack coming seconds later.

The attack, while powerful, was so poorly planned all I had to do was sidestep, my laugh echoing against the old, stone walls.

"Nice try."

The bright yellow streak burst into a firework of green and gold, glitter splattering against the barrier with a crash, leaving both of us staring at it in disbelief—me, laughing maniacally; her, on the border between humor and frustration.

"Stop doing that! Let me get you!" Joclyn screeched with a stomp of her foot, her movements making it clear she was already lining up her next attack.

"Ha!" I laughed loudly, purposefully pushing her buttons. "You would have to play a lot harder than that for a flimsy attack to work, Jos. I am a master assassin, after all."

"Oh! Is that what you are calling yourself?" she prodded, her face twisting into a half smile. Her steps were slow and calculated as I matched her step for step. "I thought more like, 'poor, little, cursed child' was a better fit. I mean ... Your attacks are a little weak!"

With one step, her magic exploded toward me in a wall of purple flames, dancing with the black of death I recognized all too well.

Jumping into the air, I countered, my own magic spreading over her wall with a crash that beat against my ears painfully.

Her wall exploded into wisps of smoke, long tendrils of green and grey drifting toward the ceiling as what she had hoped would end me faded into oblivion, leaving me staring at a slack-jawed mongrel again.

"Come on, Jos," I teased. "I've watched enough TV to know better. You can't play the old 'talk and distract' thing on me. This isn't a Saturday morning cartoon."

"It was worth a shot, Wyn," she admitted, laughing knowingly before she shot up into the air like a bullet. Her wind pulled her up like a carnival ride, the brilliant gold ribbon of her crown trailing behind her.

I followed, wind moving around me before I soared over the smooth, marbled floor. Where Joclyn had chosen to jump, to rocket through the buttresses and stained glass windows of the magnificent cathedral, I went low. My body a straight arrow as I sped inches above the ancient floor, focus scanning through the red-tinted light for the shadow of that bird I was going to ground.

"Kill the Wendy-Bird!" I screamed as she came into view, rolling onto my back and sending a string of flames from my hands before she could even notice it. She didn't even have a chance to dodge.

One line of fire. One flying best friend.

Or so I expected.

Except, the attack exploded against the barrier instead of her. Light and sparks fell like a million shooting stars, the same as hers had done. It should have been beautiful. I knew better.

My heart thundered painfully in my chest, everything tensing in expectation as I waited for the attack, certain this time I wouldn't be able to escape.

"No fair!" I growled into the space, certain she had shielded herself. "A shield *and* a Stutter. Don't you think that's a bit much?"

No answer.

My chest tightened in agitated fear as the minutes ticked by. I looked around me, spinning on the spot as I tried to feel her magic, but nothing was there.

She wasn't there.

"Nice try, Wyn."

I moved the second I heard her, but I wasn't fast enough. An attack slammed into my gut, heat and force moving through me as I soared through the air like a puppet, arms and legs flailing in my frenzied attempt to gain control of them before the floor found me. It was no use. With a dull thud and a loud scream I collided with the hard floor.

"Is that the best you can do?" I grunted, body aching as I tried to push myself up. At this point, the lone weapon I had was snark. I had better use it considering I could hardly see straight.

I attempted to find my feet, Chuck Taylors squeaking loudly against the marble floor. I hadn't even stood before sparks of colors and sharp, conjured knives fanned toward me with a bang like a cannon.

Falling back to the ground, I held my arms up in a shield, magic spreading from my skin in a bubble that wrapped around me in a sheath of grey.

Tiny pokes of the knives strained against the shield

before falling to the floor with a clang. I waited for her attacks to stop before the shield gave out, but instead the attacks increased, explosions and knives and who knew what else coming at me.

I was vulnerable, crouched down like this with the shield up, and she knew it. Forget that silly rock and its dumb hard place. There was nothing worse than a weak shield and a powerful best friend with no shame.

I was doomed.

"Give up yet?" she shouted in a lull of attacks, her exaggerated villain laugh pulling at me in all the wrong ways. "Or are you still pretending to be a master assassin?"

"Ha! I'll never surrender!"

Darn me and my stubbornness. I could kill myself for getting into this position, and if this had been a real fight, it would have killed me. Of course, if this had been a real fight, I would have killed her by now.

Either way, it was a stupid move, like eating cheese out of a can.

"Come out, come out, wherever you are ..." she taunted, the laugh poorly concealed in her voice. "Come and face your reward, Wynifred!"

I guessed I deserved the full name. I had started all of this in any case. I would have to be grateful she didn't know my middle name.

"You can't call this ..."

Mommy?

Crap.

My spine straightened, magic sparking dangerously as her voice hit me.

"Rosaline." It was a whisper, but I regretted saying it instantly. It was as though the shard of blade in my pocket could hear me. No, as if *she* could hear me.

Mommy! I'm here!

I had heard her multiple times. I had reacted to her, but this was the first time I could have sworn she was responding to me. Just hearing her talk to me snapped something inside, some primal rage I hadn't felt in centuries... since that day...

"What did you say? Did you say you give up?" Jos asked playfully, her voice a million miles away.

Everything was warm, too warm. Heat was radiating from the tiny shard in my pocket as it had the last few times I had heard her. This time, however, it felt as if it was going to brand me.

Mommy? Where are you?

"Wyn?" Joclyn's voice came simultaneously with Rosy's.

"I'm here, baby," I whispered foolishly, all that ache and heat growing worse.

Mommy?

My hands ground against the floor as my magic boiled, ready to explode out of me. To save her. I needed to save her.

No, I needed to get out of there before I did something stupid. I was starting to feel uncontrollable.

"Are you okay, Wyn?" The humor was gone from Joclyn's voice.

I flinched, a fear I couldn't quite place taking over.

"Are you crying?"

Was I crying? I couldn't focus on anything beyond her voice, beyond the memories.

Mommy! Save me!

"No!" I snapped, uncertain if it was to Rosy or to Jos.

"You better not be messin' with me ... I'm not going to fall for it, Wyn." Jos was worried; I could tell. But I couldn't look up at her, I couldn't reassure her. It was taking everything in me to keep my magic calm. Why was it reacting like this?

"Wyn?"

Mommy? She was crying, too. *Please.*

I needed to go. I didn't care how; I needed to go.

Fingers digging into the stone, my back arched as my breathing turned ragged. My magic grew, the heat of it, the desperation taking over. A small voice in the back of my head screamed at me that the magic was too strong. If only it was louder ... if only I cared...

In a burst of fire, my magic spread over the floor so fast I wasn't sure Joclyn could avoid it even if she was paying close attention. The raw power of the fire magic moved into stone, the floor shifted underneath her and sent her tumbling to the ground.

Rosaline screamed in my head, Joclyn yelled in panic, but I couldn't think.

Suddenly, it was another job.

It was another body to claim.

Another beating heart to deliver to my master.

Heart thundering in eagerness, I burst from the shield that had become a prison, my hand raised in preparation for attack, turning to face Joclyn who was inches from me, face hard, hair whipping around her as she hovered there.

"Wyn! Stop this!"

No!

This wasn't just a job. It was a game.

"No!" I yelled as the voice left, the frightening reality implanting itself within me. "No," I said again, my magic withdrawing back into me in one swift pull.

The stones of the floor solidified themselves, Rosy's screams fading as Joclyn gripped my forearms, her magic flooding me. My fire magic flooded to the spot, pressing against hers in an angry shock that zinged its way right into her. She grit her teeth, hissing in pain, but she did not pull away.

The same thing had happened in Rioseco when her magic mixed with mine. Before, we had laughed it off, saying our magic must be enemies or something. That was getting harder and harder to believe. I knew there was something else there, as she did.

Staring at her, her hands holding me in place, I saw what I had missed before. It wasn't just shock. It hadn't just been my magic reacting to hers.

She had seen something.

I opened my mouth to ask, but she cut me off.

"Wyn?" Her voice was the roar of a Queen, the power behind it matching what was inside of me. "Are you okay?"

I glared at her, my jaw locked as the battle continued inside of me. I had attacked her, and she was asking me if I was okay.

"What do you mean?" I was defensive, too defensive.

"Correct me if I'm wrong," she began, her voice shaking, "but I am sure you were trying to kill me for a second ... and you were crying."

To anyone else, the combination might be seen as normal. In a way, it was for me—well, the killing people part. Strangely, the crying was more out of the ordinary. It was an odd reality when she was more alarmed by that than the 'almost murder' I had 'almost committed'.

"I'm fine." My voice was a growl, and she rolled her eyes recognizing the stubborn assassin instantly.

"Wyn," she prompted, "you can tell me."

I froze, mouth open as I almost revealed everything. Could I? Could I tell her about the blade and Thom and how scared I was to lose him, about Talon and how he still came into my dreams every night, about Rosaline's voice echoing in my head. No, I couldn't. Not if I was going to free my daughter. I doubt they would look kindly on me having a sliver of a soul's blade. They were dangerous... because of stuff exactly like what had just happened.

There were stories of them driving people mad, of the souls inside taking control of those who held them. It was probably why Edmund had his wrapped in a heavy cloth and not in his pocket.

It was a risk I would have to take. I needed it to release Rosaline's soul, to release Cail's. Besides, it wasn't my daughter beside me, not really. It was her memory. I could handle it.

I had handled it this long.

"I'm fine, Jos. Please." I tried to remove her hands from my arms. She just held on tighter. "I think I got nervous, what with the impending war and everything."

I added a shrug and a smile and she finally let go, her silver eyes studying me far too closely.

"You're not the only one," she groaned.

My shoulders loosened, though the knot in my stomach stayed firmly in place.

"I think I'll take fake wars to actual ones any day," I tried again, I really wished I had something better to say than 'I'm sorry I almost killed you'.

"Then again, we may be looking at a war once Ilyan sees what we did to the floor." I sighed as I moved to stand beside her, my shoulders dropping dejectedly as I caught sight of the pile of rubble she was trapped in, the beautiful floor smashed to bits.

I was so dead.

"I'm not accepting responsibility for this," Jos moaned from beside me.

"That's fair," I said dejectedly. It was. I couldn't wait for Ilyan to unveil that little temper tantrum unless ... "Maybe we can blame it on Edmund. Then Ilyan could be so mad at him he would just explode."

Seemed legit.

She looked at me out of the corner of her eye, before she laughed at me. Yeah I knew it was ridiculous.

"Well, I can hope," I said with a shrug, falling to my knees to begin digging her out of the pit I had trapped her in. "I will hope that Edmund will take the strength of his son's wrath from me and that I will survive this unfortunate incident."

"Oh, boy."

"It is the only chance we have to save us all." Laying the melodrama on thick, I swept my hand over my shoulder from where I knelt below her, letting a bit of an American accent shine through the dull shadow of my Czech one.

I expected her to chuckle, but she sighed, with a sound that was more like a groan. Just like that, the playfulness in my voice evaporated.

"Oh, bother." Her eye roll was obvious. "I guess we should have left it to you all along."

"What, you don't like being the breaker of all sight?"

Her lip twitched, "Don't even get me started."

"I wasn't planning on it. I'm just hoping one day the future will open up to you and show you everything. But mostly how to heal Thom." Or maybe free Rosaline. But I wasn't going to share that.

"I'm trying." She was dejected, and I didn't blame her. Sometimes, Joclyn's sights had a habit of putting a damper on any situation. All she saw was what was coming; she forgot to look at where she was.

"It's okay not to see everything," I whispered as I continued to pull rock away from her partial tomb, her legs shifting around as she tried to free herself.

"I've seen too much, Wyn. I know you can't see everything. No one can, not even a Drak. But you can see too much. Sometimes, I think I have."

With a snap, I looked up to her, a warning of temper rumbling through me as agitation twisted through my spine.

"So have I, Jos. We've all seen too much." My voice was dead. It barely got above a whisper before it was swallowed by the vastness of the room. "It may not be the future, and it may not be what's coming, but I've still seen too much. I've seen years of Edmund killing and destroying and manipulating and …"

Mommy? Can you see me? Why didn't you come for me?

"I've seen my own daughter murdered before my eyes. I've seen the blood running over her cheeks as I screamed, fighting to get to her as she pleaded for Mommy to rescue her."

Joclyn was staring at me from where I still crouched below her, her eyes as wide as saucers while the truth of what I was saying hit her.

But I didn't see that.

I saw Rosaline: her eyes pleading, her cries soft and defeated as she was taken from me.

I pushed the memory away, looking away from the woman before me, from the concern in her eyes, and went back to removing the rocks with renewed vigor and freeing her in ten seconds flat.

"He deserves to pay for that, Wyn. I'm ready for all this

to be over. I'm just..." she hesitated, looking at the door before continuing. "I'm not really ready for everything that comes between now and the end."

"I know," I said as I stood, patting the dust from my jeans, even though it was a lost cause with how dirty everything was. "But you have to get through the bad in order to find the good."

"You sound like a mom." I stuck my tongue out at her.

"Okay then, full 'mom-wisdom' coming up." I cleared my throat dramatically and put my hand on her shoulder. Giving her the biggest mom look I could. "What did you do before there was magic? When it was just you and no magic and no sights and no Drak, when it was just us going off into the night to crash Ryland's graduation party?"

"We crashed Ryland's graduation party." She repeated my words back to me so sarcastically that, for a split second, she actually sounded like a teenager.

I tried to restrain the eye roll, but it came, anyway. In that way, we were a lot alike.

"Did we know if we were going to succeed?" I asked, plowing on in a desperate need to get to my point.

"No." She grinned, she was catching on, even if she didn't seem happy about it.

I plowed on before she had a chance to stop me. "Did we have a definitive outcome?"

"No ... But, Wyn, we ... We didn't succeed."

I turned to her with that same sly smile. She grumbled again.

"You're right. We didn't. We failed. But did the world end?"

She glared at me, the silver of her eyes so full of irritation I couldn't help laughing, something that pissed her off more.

"No." It was a growl more than a word. "You can lay-off the 'mom voice' now."

"Not going to happen." I laughed harder. "Did we keep trying?"

The lines in Joclyn's forehead increased with every word. She needed to stop that. We might be immortal, but that didn't protect against wrinkles. I mean, had she seen Dramin?

"Did we keep fighting?"

She knew the answer to all of these as well as I did—yes, yes, we did—but I could already tell she was firmly standing her ground, too stubborn to say it, too scared to admit what came after.

"But what if we fail this time, too?" Her voice was a whisper.

"Then we try again."

"But the sights—"

"And what if there were no sights, Jos?" I interrupted her steadily, not letting her disrupt my flow. "What if we had nothing to guide us and no guarantee of victory? We would still try. We did for centuries before you came along, and we will for centuries after if we need to. So what if you can see the future? If you've told me anything, it's that what you see isn't set in stone. Let Sain have his cult and Zlomený. You've changed it before, so let's change it again. Let's make it what we want. Stop trying to guess what's going to happen next and find out for certain. There is more to see in life than the future, Jos. Sometimes, we have to look to the past to see the whole story."

There it was—the answer that not only she needed, but I needed, as well. It scared the bejesus out of me that I could lose Thom the same way I had lost Talon, the same way I had lost Rosaline. In the end, even if I did lose them, I would do as I always had. I would keep moving. More than surviving, more than trying, I would find another way to succeed. To save Thom. To free Rosy.

Nothing else was more important.

"You're the queen, Jos. Ilyan chose you for a reason. The magic mud hole chose you for a reason. The Vilỳ that bit you chose you for a reason. Who cares what the reason was? Accept it, own it, and be it."

It was the pep talk of the century. At least, that was what I was going to label it as. And judging by the way Jos was staring at me—with the look of someone who had been slapped—I was going to have to count that as a win.

"Ilyan says you're right," she grinned, shoving my arm playfully.

"As he should. I'm the smartest one here." I grinned, chest out, sure he was still listening.

"He takes it back, and says he will never forgive you for the floor."

"Jeez, love you too Ilyan." I grinned at her, but this time she didn't grin back. Her jaw was set as she stared at me. Her breathing even.

"What? What is it?"

"Wyn?" Joclyn's voice was barely above a whisper, so soft I could barely hear her. "What did you take out of Ryland?"

CHAPTER 12
WYN

I froze, everything tightening as the alarms in my head went off.

"Take from Ryland? I don't know what you are talking about." I knew the shake in my voice was a dead giveaway, but I didn't care. Right then, it was all I could do to keep me from attacking, from running away.

So that was what she had seen when our magic had reacted.

"Wyn?" she asked again, and for the first time, I could tell how scared she was. "What did you do?"

I could scarcely look at her. All I could think was that she wanted to take away my daughter, that she wanted to hurt her, too.

I wouldn't let that happen.

Not this time.

"Wyn? What did you take?"

Mommy! Don't let her take me!

The heat of the blade singed into me, and all the rage and fury that I had shoved away before came racing back and I couldn't focus past the fury of the blade. I couldn't focus past the break in reality.

I could think of one thing.

I only knew to do one thing.

Attack.

"I took nothing. I have nothing!" Power surged through me, speeding right to my best friend as her hand wrapped around my wrist and our magic reacted the same as it had before. This time, however, because I had already been ready to fight, it exploded.

It exploded in a wave of blue ice and flame, the eruption like cannon fire as it threw us apart and sent rocks and rubble flying. The air exploded with sound as my magic hit against the barrier, the rattle echoing as the barrier split apart.

Spread out on the floor, I watched in horror as the barrier faded away and the attack slammed into the ancient stonework of the gothic chapel. Everything shook so violently that I expected the whole building to come down on top of us.

Instead, it was just the head of a statue, and half of the glass from a stained glass window. It wasn't much better.

"Oh, Ilyan is going to kill me." And I had thought a few loose tiles would be bad.

I was dead.

Disembowelment was in order.

It was the solitary fear I had until I looked down at Joclyn, to where she was spread out over the rubble a few feet from me, her eyes black as she convulsed violently.

"Joclyn!" I yelled, panic shooting me over the rubble strewn floor. "Joclyn?"

I had seen her have sights before. I had watched her slide off tables, writhing in agony and crying over what she had seen behind the black of her eyes. But this was different. This was wrong.

Hands fluttering around her, I tried to find a way to help, tried to find a way to get her to snap out of it, something. She was jerking around so much, so fast that I couldn't even get a good grip on her, and even when I did I was met with the sharp burn of her magic.

"Joclyn!" I yelled again, but she kept writhing.

Her black eyes stared toward the sky, her face haunted and broken as if she was looking into her very own death.

"Give me," she said, her voice the deep hollow that I had heard from Draks before. "Give it to me."

"No..."

The fear from before slammed into me, my worry for Joclyn evaporating in the boil of my blood.

I needed to run, fight... hide... something. I knew it was illogical, but I couldn't shake the feeling. I tried to fight it, after all, I couldn't leave Jos. She was my friend, and I knew what these sights did to her. I needed to help her.

"Wyn—" The word seeped out of her before she began to shake again, her joints twisting in ways that shouldn't have been possible. She looked broken.

"Wyn," she gasped as she sat up, looking at me with the same black eyes, her voice twisted between normal and the hollow Drak tones. "You need to give me the blade. You don't know what you've done."

"No!" I snapped as I stood, backing away.

Mommy! Save me!

"Wyn, please." Her voice was normal now, but her eyes had not changed. The same dark depths of nothing were staring at me as if they could see me, as if she was looking at my future, too.

Mommy!

I jumped at the terror in her voice, the tenor of it taking me right back to that day when Rosaline had lain on that table, Edmund hovering over her, Ovailia laughing in the background. And Sain ... Sain chained in the corner, his eyes as black as hers.

His eyes as black as hers.

Something in me flipped.

"Wyn," Joclyn gasped, her voice broken and scared, so much like everyone else when they had begged for life, when they had begged for their end to come.

And so would she.

"No! I have to save her!"

Mommy! Please! Stop! Rosy's voice shot through me as my magic did, the attack speeding through the air and right toward Joclyn to stop her, to end her.

Joclyn screamed as the light erupted, the blazing flash impacting against the stone as she dropped to the floor.

"Wyn! What are you doing?" She was screaming, begging, but I couldn't hear it anymore. I couldn't think past the sound of Rosy's voice, past her fear.

I needed to save her, and I wasn't going to let anyone stand in my way.

I would stop her first.

One attack after another shot toward Joclyn, but again, she shifted away right before the attack would have made contact.

"Wyn!" she screamed as she tried to back up over the stone, her black eyes looking into me, digging into me. "You must give it to me ... you can't—"

"No!" I didn't even let her finish; I attacked, expecting her movements.

This time, I hit her. This time, the magic hit against her leg, the denim jean burning away.

Closer.

I needed to get closer.

"You can't have it!" I screamed as I attacked again, volley after volley flying toward her as she tried to move away.

She wasn't fast enough. She never would be. I was more powerful than her. I had the fire magic, and now ... Now she was going to feel it.

"You can't have my daughter!"

Mommy? Save me!

One last powerful ribbon of fire and death streamed away from me and right into her, seeping into her gut, spreading through her, destroying her.

Mommy!

"You can't have her!" I spat, ready to attack again, ready to end her.

Mommy, Rosy pleaded, freezing me in place. *Mommy, don't hurt her.*

Shock filled me like warm water as I watched my friend writhe, watched my magic attempt to end her, watched her scream.

I knew I should do something. I knew I needed to. I had attacked her. I had hurt her.

I needed to get out of here. I needed to save my daughter. I needed to leave Ilyan in order to save her.

I turned, running away from Joclyn, away from whatever she had seen, away from what I had done like the coward I was deep down inside.

I ran because it was the only way to save her.

I needed to save my daughter, and I needed to keep moving toward that, no matter what I ended up running away from.

CHAPTER 13
WYN

Joclyn's screams echoed around the hall as I ran, stumbling over rubble and broken chunks of stone in my need to get out of there.

I needed to get away from her, away from where I would hurt her, away from where she could take everything from me.

Part of me—the sane, logical side that was never loud enough when I needed it—was screaming at me to run back, to help her, to give in and trust my friend.

But I couldn't, not with the way my daughter was screaming, her voice as loud as the terrified pleas ringing from behind me.

I raced down the stairs of the cathedral and across the small garden and turned another corner, picking up the pace as I tried to decide what to do, what course of action to take, when I ran right into Sain.

"Watch where you are going you bi--" He stumbled back as I did, his face full of rage. The hem of his weird suit-robe combo was wet, and in my panic I could have sworn that he had snow in his hair.

"Wynifred!"

My heart beat louder, the knot in my stomach tightening as I met his gaze. Seeing him there, in front of me, brought back the image I had seen moments before of him ... in that room. Watching my daughter die, as though it was nothing.

I swallowed, my brain already tallying him up as another casualty. Then my spine aligned as I rushed him, afraid someone would hear him. Someone would find me. I was sure Ilyan was already looking.

"Shhhhhhh!" I hissed, pushing the old man into the wall as my magic spread away from us, searching for any signs of magic, for anyone who might be looking for me.

Sain glared at me with a combination of fear and interest as I held my hand over his mouth.

I expected to calm down, being so close to him, we had been through enough after all. Instead, my panic increased, the reality of what I was feeling, or rather, what I wasn't feeling become alarmingly clear.

"I can't feel your magic."

"Is that what's got you so spooked?" Sain asked as he shoved my hand off his mouth. Part of me did not even care he was dodging. "You looked like you've seen a ghost."

Mommy, don't let them take me.

More like I heard one. Between Joclyn's pained pleas and Rosaline's cries, I was starting to think *I* was haunted.

"I'm fine," I lied, sucking in air through my teeth with a sharp snap that sounded more like a smack against skin.

"Fine compared to what? Compared to before in Imdalind? Choose light, Wyn, because murder doesn't really qualify—"

"What do I look like, Sain?" My voice hissed in clear warning as it had done for centuries.

He didn't miss it; he glowered at me from where I held him against the stone of the old hallway. His lips twitched in a way so unlike him I was momentarily worried it wasn't really him at all.

"It's about what's in your pocket, isn't it?" His voice was that deep, gravely wave of knowledge it always was, and where before, in the dungeon and in Spain when I would stop and listen, I reacted this time.

"What do you know about it?" I snapped, pressing him into the wall with a thud. The sound ricocheted around the enclosed space, a loud ripple that came right back even louder.

He cringed at the impact, his face cinching together painfully. "I know what Joclyn saw a moment ago. I know you are running from her."

"What did she see? What did *you* see?" My eyes narrowed as I held him against the wall, Joclyn's cries echoing around us while we glared at each other.

"Where did you get the blade?" He asked smoothly as I panicked, trying to convince myself not to attack him right then and there. It would be much easier to kill him, and I wouldn't mind killing this one.

Mommy!

I looked at him, my eyes narrowing dangerously. "Why should I tell you?"

"Because I know what's coming." He stared back with the same calm he always had, his face almost disinterested.

If it wasn't for the way he continually looked toward the window that opened to the courtyard, as if he was expecting someone to come bursting through the barrier at any time to attack us, I would say he was positively bored. He moved to look again before I grabbed his chin, forcing his head back to me, and his eyes widened in shock.

I was running out of patience and time.

"I got it from inside of Ryland," I was careful to keep my voice down, the words a low groan as they reverberated off the stone wall.

"Ryland?" he asked as if he hadn't heard, all signs of his previous boredom gone. "She saw what the blade is meant for. And she knows what you are planning. She wants to stop you."

So, she saw everything, then. Great.

"You are going to help me much sooner than I had planned, Wynifred. I believe I have finally found my replacement for Thom." His voice was dark, terrifying, and the murderer inside of me reacted accordingly: hackles up, warning lights blazing.

"What about Thom?" I slammed him into the wall again, placing the palm of my hand against his neck, letting the fire magic inside of me heat to a temperature that was more pain than warning, but he didn't even flinch. He looked at me with that same darkness as before.

"What are you talking about?" I growled, sending another warning flare of my magic. This time, he smiled.

"Don't worry... You'll like this." Sain soothed, his eyes fading to black as he shifted underneath me and his hand slammed into my stomach.

I gasped, curling against the impact as magic colder than I had ever felt flooded me. Ice ripped over my body, it tore at my muscles and pressed against bones. I had never felt magic like this. Never felt an attack like this.

Except it wasn't an attack. It was a flood. It was strings that wrapped around me, pulling all of that anger to the surface. There was so much. I was going to drown in it.

"You don't want to kill Joclyn," Sain said as if he was reading my mind, his voice distant as the cold liquid in my veins burned like fire. "You need to run as far as you can. Run to the edge of the barrier. Run to the river. He will find you. There, you can make him pay. You can make him burn. If you make it, if you run, then you can have it all. You will have your precious daughter back. You will succeed."

His hand pulled away, all of the icy burn moving to my head as his words repeated themselves.

Cemented themselves.

As they became everything.

Succeed. I could still save her.

The fire in my blood sparked abruptly as a new magic shot into where we were, close enough I could feel it. The power behind it was unmistakably Ilyan.

I was out of time.

"Run, Wyn!" His arms broke free of where I had held him down, his grip like a vice against my forearms as he pushed me away. "After centuries! Everything is starting! Run Wyn, you don't have much time!"

I ran, my feet fast as I continued in the direction I had been traveling, while Sain raced in the other direction, right to the place he had been glaring at, as if it had somehow offended him.

The sound of Joclyn's cries faded to nothing as the sound of my shoes grew in my ears. I knew someone would hear me, knew Ilyan would hear me. I knew he would find me.

And if he did, there was nothing I could do.

Joclyn, Sain—anyone else, for that matter—I was confident I could defeat. But Ilyan ...

I would lose every time. And if what Sain said was true, I had to stop them all.

My sole choice was to keep running, to escape this cathedral and get outside where Ilyan couldn't reach me.

Easy.

I had done it before. Anytime I needed an escape, anytime I couldn't look at Thom's slowly deteriorating face, I left. And considering the way Joclyn's cries had somehow disappeared, Ilyan was very much preoccupied.

I needed to get to the tear in Ilyan's barrier before anyone saw me.

So, I ran.

I darted through unsuspecting Skříteks, their faces horrified as they looked toward the cries, their focus on whatever might be going on over there. As I darted through them, the questions started flowing, the shouts of fear loud as they asked me for information, begged to know if we were under attack, what was going on. Drawing attention to me, to the person who should be running toward the Queen instead of away.

The more they yelled, the more they looked, the more I ran.

"Wyn!" I recognized that voice. Risha always sounded like an elementary school teacher.

I glanced back, my toe pressing against the hole in my shoe, against the bare ground and sending magic right to her.

I didn't even see her fall.

Sain had said not to let anyone stop me, and I wouldn't. Risha was the start of that.

I threw up a shield with a flash of magic, disappearing from view as a dozen or more attacks flew right towards me. The bangs and explosions of colliding magic ignited the courtyard in waves of color. I raced away from them, flying down a corridor as I climbed the stairs of the old bell tower, taking them two at a time in my desperation to escape those I was confident were following me.

Mommy! Don't let him hurt me! Daddy! No!

The top of the bell tower opened like a fan, the tightly wound staircase expanding into the small, cylindrical room that led to the red sky, to the small crease in Ilyan's barrier that would let me escape without his help.

A slight shimmer in the barrier hung right over my head, the glistening patch of white so faint I probably would have never seen it if I hadn't been hiding up here, staring blankly out into the city as often as I had. But I had seen it. And it hadn't taken me long to figure out what it was.

A tear. A way out. An escape route.

With one leap, I soared off the old bell tower and into the air, letting the wind catch me as my magic supported me, throwing me toward the shimmering line of color. I braced for the impact, for the way Ilyan's shield would grip against my body and try to trap me inside of it.

With one strong push, I shot through it, feeling the heat and weight crowd against me before it released me to the other side, my wind disappearing with the weight, sending me into a free fall. Hot air and an endless nothing soared past me as I tumbled to the ground below.

With a snap, my magic moved fast enough to stop me from hitting the hard ground on the other side—well, hitting it hard enough to do some damage. I still hit too hard, my knees slamming into stone, hands barely able to stop me from face planting into the loose gravel.

Heaving, I froze, staring at the old, filthy asphalt as I waited for some scream, for some shout, for some clue someone had seen me.

There was nothing except the scream of distant Vilỳs, the silent horror of the city.

I might have been safe from Ilyan, but I was far from safe.

Moving myself to standing, I pressed my hand against my jeans, making sure the hard ridge of the blade was still in place before I turned, staring at the place that had become both a prison and a sanctuary.

"What have I done?" The panic gripped me, the question screaming. I shouldn't have left. Ilyan should have been able to help me. He could... I took a step forward before ice twisted up my spine, Sain's promise burning in my ears. I took a step back. Sain had said this was the only way... the only way to succeed.

My heart ached as I backed away from the cathedral, away from Thom.

Somehow, I had been the one to leave this time.

But I wouldn't abandon him. I would come back.

After I found the rest of the knife. After I made Edmund pay.

"I will save our daughter, Thomas. I will free her. I will free us all."

CHAPTER 14
JOCLYN

"Wyn?" The single syllable sounded all distorted and wobbly as it reverberated around the cathedral, the fear in my voice causing it to tremble even more. "What did you take out of Ryland?"

She stiffened as I did, "I don't know what you are talking about."

"Wyn? What did you do?"

She still wouldn't look at me, her lies pulling at my sight, of that flash of her pulling something from Ryland. Something that was screaming. Something that was evil.

Except that feeling from the sight had shifted to her. Now she was the one who felt dangerous. I had never felt anything quite so out of control before: the strength of her power, the fury behind it. It scared me.

My magic buzzed to the tips of my fingers, as if it was going to explode out of me. As if it was going to attack. Stupid.

"Wyn?" I asked slowly, grabbing her wrist in a move I hoped would calm her. Instead, everything exploded.

A blast of flame shoved against my chest, pushing me back as everything went dark. I crumpled against the stone, the pain only a shadow as I gasped for air, fire erupting in the dark of my eyes. Sight blazed through my mind as screams echoed in my ears, a pillar of light breaking through the black as red flames engulfed the city, licking the red roofs and engulfing the decimated buildings.

I had seen this vision before. Except, this time was different. This time, Edmund's red barrier was gone, and the peaceful yellow sun hovered over the city as if it wasn't being eaten by ash and flame.

With a bang, the sight shifted to an army, thousands of men, women, and children marching into the streets of Prague as it burned. The sound of their march echoed through my sight, the heavy thuds of their advance divergent to the gentle snow that fell over where Ilyan and I stood on top of a snow covered hill, surrounded by a dozen tattered people.

We stood, watching the army, waiting for an attack we knew we could not win.

I had seen flashes of this before. But those times had been different, they had not included the mounds of dirt behind where we stood, the single red rose resting upon a fresh grave.

My heart pulsed in my chest, my back arching as the haunted echo of a scream grew louder. The sight shifted, this time to my brother, his lips blue as he lay in the snow. A handkerchief was placed over his face, bright red blood spreading over it. The delicate white flakes mutated to heavy wet drops of the deepest crimson as the sight zoomed out to us on the hill again. The color cascaded over us all, staining our faces, our skin, our clothes. They asphyxiated us in the smell of iron, each drop mirroring the stabbing pain that filled my chest.

No one moved, they just let it cover them until everything was red and white.

"Joclyn?" Wyn's voice broke through the sight with a jolt, her hand pulled against my arm, the hot air of the cathedral running over my skin, I could smell the familiar aroma of smoke from a magical explosion taking the place of the iron and blood.

I was aware.

I could feel it all.

Wyn's magic had burned through me, and the sight shifted back to that same image of her covered in blood as she knelt beside Ryland. This time, however, I saw what was lying in the pool of blood in her palm.

It looked like rock, the jagged fragment a little larger than the size of a thumb, the deep red color vibrant even against the sheen of Ryland's blood.

The whispers of my magic screamed in horror as I watched the heavy fluid drip over her fingertips; the deep Drak magic screamed inside me, the warning clear. I knew what this was.

The Soul's Blade.

The sight shifted with a snap, my chest tensing from the abruptness of it. Now there was an image of her with the blade, kneeling over a bloodied body, the jagged thing protruding from her hand. Another snap, another jolt and now she was in a foreign forest, hunting something I was certain was also hunting her.

Sight after sight came, raging through me as the warning flowed heavier.

"Give me," I gasped, unaware if the words had actually

broken through the sight and made it out of my throat. "Give it to me ..." I looked toward her, gasping from the pull of the magic, knowing she had the blade on her.

I had to change this.

My mouth opened in a wide, panicked scream as my sight shifted to the image of Wyn, standing in the middle of the cathedral, shrouded in the shadow. The image mixed with bright flashes of her with the blade, her fighting, and Edmund smothered the image of the real world as if the magic of the Drak was projecting itself over reality.

"Wyn. You need to give me the blade. You don't know what you've done." My voice was a hollow gasp as I watched a bridge crumble into a river, the image swirling through the air as she came into focus. She kneeled beside me, worry and horror staring back at me.

"Wyn, please."

She jerked as Ryland once had, before she had removed the blade from him. Before the power had infected her instead. The anger on her face mutated into the image of Ilyan's death as I was pulled back into sight, the same haunting vision that had been stalking me coming to full force.

Blood flowing over rocks, away from his lifeless hand, his eyes lost and forgotten. I stared at it, wishing I could look anywhere else, wishing I could see anything else.

"Wyn," I gasped, a heavy desperation leaking through me as the sight that was bleeding through reality shifted. The image of my best friend split in half, two different people kneeling before me—one who raised her hand toward me before the other one did.

I felt my magic flare in fear, my heart racing as I looked into the face of what Wyn used to be, who she was raised to be. For the first time I saw the eyes of a killer, and instantly knew what she was going to do.

What she wanted to do.

What the blade was telling her to do.

Ilyan! I screamed his name, as Wyn attacked, the image so distorted I couldn't tell if it was her who was attacking me, or just a shadowed remnant of sight. I rolled, the powerful blast hitting against the stone I had been sitting on moments before.

"Wyn!" I tried again. "You must give it to me … you can't—"

"No!" she screamed, another blast rumbling around me. This one was so close I could feel its heat against my leg, I could smell the singed jeans.

I could barely focus on what was going on in front of me. The overlay of sight became confusing as it altered even further, her motions moving forward and back in quick succession.

"You can't have it!" she yelled, another attack moving toward me.

My joints seized in agonizing strain as they tried to fight the weight that sight always gave me.

"You can't have my daughter!"

Joclyn!

My sight shifted yet again, pulling away the superimposed image of my friend and taking me right to where my mate was, his terrified face clear as he stood still in what looked to be an abandoned department store.

Ilyan! I called again as Wyn attacked again. There was no way I could move fast enough, no way I could have dodged.

Violent waves of heat ripped through me, the magic

ripping through my flesh as though I was being torn in two. Warm blood spread over my skin; I could smell it.

"Ilyan!"

Her running out of the cathedral was the last thing I saw before I collapsed to the ground. The sights took control with more force than I had ever felt. Sight after sight flashed before my eyes, accelerating until they were embedded in my soul, speaking to me, a part of me, as if they *were* me.

Ilyan, I gasped, screaming his name in my desperation to get his attention from where he and Risha were off surveying another part of the city.

Nothing came in return. Not even the whisper of his fear. I lay there, paralyzed by the agonizing pressure in my bones, by the weight of the visions.

Children laughing in a field, strips of a grey-green sky, Edmund laughing, Ovailia crying. Images I had seen before, all of them different. All of them real.

Sight faded to the cathedral, but not the cathedral I lay screaming in; instead, the chapel was still full of ancient pews filled with men and women cowering in fear of a god they didn't understand. They moved around me, apparitions of smoke and past, people of a time long forgotten, surrounding me as though they were real.

"Ilyan," I gasped aloud as I watched them, watched as time shifted.

The robed men were replaced with Victorian women in high lace collars and frilled dresses. A tall lady with her hair in curls walked past me, a white parasol flung over her shoulder. I looked from her to a child in knickers and a cap who ran away from a very haggard looking nun. A chill of ice rippled up my spine as he ran right through me, his body swirling into wisps of smoke at the collision.

"Ilyan!"

My arms gave way as I crumpled to the floor, my face compacting against the tile in a thwack. The pain of before increased, the strain so much now I could barely think through it.

"This is sight. This is real. This is pure," an unfamiliar woman said, the loud boom crashing through me as the sights did.

"Ilyan," I gasped, anxious to hear him now.

Joclyn! With a nauseous rumble his voice broke through the sight, broke through my mind in a rush of panic. I relaxed at the sound, at the flutters of his magic that I felt moving through me, only to have them vanish, the connection breaking up like a flickering light bulb.

Where ...? Are... Okay...

His question faded as the sight gained control, the magic coming on so fast I screamed with the force of it, the strength of the vision suffocating.

A man, Edmund maybe, holding a baby as he stood near an ocean. It was calm, relaxing, yet my body didn't feel the emotion. I didn't feel the cool air of the sea. I felt heat, felt the heavy thump of fear that moved through my chest. I couldn't ignore the fear that perhaps he was going to throw the wriggling infant into the ocean.

The vision faded back into the distorted haze of the cathedral, to the medieval workers who had built the magnificent building. Ilyan stood before me as he worked amongst them. His hair was the short cut I had seen before, his face spread with a wide smile as he lifted the massive stones.

Ilyan. I wasn't certain who I was calling to: the man before me or the man in reality. It didn't matter; neither answered.

"You must move." That voice came again, the foreign familiarity of it frightening.

I looked up, expecting to see the woman standing there, but it was nothing more than a few boys fighting with wooden swords, Ilyan and his fellow workers long since faded into history.

"You must move." The forceful voice echoed from behind me, and I turned. No one was there, nothing but a dense space of white, the oddly shifting mass calling me toward it.

My vision shifted to the cathedral of today, pieces of glass and stone falling from the ceiling like rain. The white shape still stood near the door, the shifting mass looking more human the longer I looked at it.

"Move."

I did, even while my joints were aching, even while every pull of my body over the stone cut into me, glass and rock and who knew what else falling down from the heavens. With each desperate pull of my arms, flashes of sight surrounded me: flickers of blood, sun-bathed beaches, children laughing, and dying and crying and bombs.

I dragged myself forward as I screamed to Ilyan over and over. He never responded, though I could feel his magic, feel his concern as snippets of what sounded like his voice broke through. A rumble shook the world, the floor shaking as I screamed, clinging to bits of broken stone as if it was going to collapse underneath me.

"Keep moving!"

Tears streamed down my face as I reached the doors to the massive hall, my hands sore, knees screaming in agony. I didn't want to move any farther. I wasn't confident I could.

Clawing at the old, wooden frame, I pulled myself up, my legs shaking as the world shifted. Turning, my heart plummeted as I faced the cathedral. The ancient architecture lay in piles of rubble and clouds of dust.

And there, in the center, was a spot of white, the brightness of it consuming me. Everything glowed with a white-hot heat before tongues of red and yellow began to burn everything.

Burning. The word stuck against my ribs as the light continued to move into me, my muscles constricting painfully at the realization of what I was surrounded by.

A bomb.

I was inside of an explosion.

I gawked at it, waiting for the sight to change, waiting for it to give some answer.

But it didn't. It didn't even so much as deviate.

It simply burned.

"You must move," the voice came again, so close I turned, expecting again to see the formless shape of white. Instead, I faced myself.

I stood in the white space, staring at the vision of myself. A crown of red blood dripped over her face from her hairline, her eyes a hollow black staring, yet unable to see.

I fought the need to scream at what I saw, at the blood, at the sight, at the death that echoed from her.

"Hurry, Joclyn," the other me spoke, the voice I had heard making sense.

My heart rate accelerated in agonizing fear before she disappeared into a speck of black against the brilliant white. Black so dark I was convinced it was devouring the light, sucking it into a vortex of nothing.

"Hurry," the other me said again.

Before I knew it, I was running toward it, running despite my aching joints, despite the hollow ache in my chest. The fear mounted at what had happened and what I would be facing.

There was only the sound of my frantic breathing, the black spec before me taking shape, molding itself into the bodies of two people.

I could see their outline, see the way they held each other, feel the way their power moved around them.

No, not around, not between. Away. Away from them.

I had been wrong before. They weren't consuming this power; they were creating it.

They were the bomb.

Continuing my run toward the pair, but no matter how much I ran toward the two figures, I wasn't getting any closer.

"Joclyn!"

The familiar scream pulled me out of the world I was trapped in, the two figures replaced by one I would recognize anywhere—the way he moved, the swing of his hair so familiar to me now.

"Ilyan!"

He ran toward me as I ran to him, my body stuck within the blinding sight, his running through it until I could see the wild worry lining his normally bright blue eyes.

I saw him, but I saw so much more.

I saw him from two hundred years ago, running like a shadow through the ancient halls, his face wide in terror as he raced away from something. The fear in him was more than I had ever seen before, the strength of it infecting me.

"Ilyan!" I sighed, collapsing in his arms as the frightened shadow of the ancient man continued to run past us, a scream breaking from the sight and ringing in my ears. "What's coming?"

I felt his strong arms, but all I could see now was the fear in his eyes, the scream on his lips. Before I knew it, the scream was coming from me, the same voice I had heard before yelling from somewhere around us.

"Run!"

CHAPTER 15
OVAILIA

"He's late." My father's voice was a growl from where he stood beside me.

"I'm aware," I growled right back, even though every part of me was on high alert.

Of course he was late. Sain was partially reliable at best, it would make sense he would pick today, when my father had chosen to meet with Sain inside the city, inside the dome, to push the limits of what was acceptable.

"I did not want to have to beat the information out of him, but if I am forced to stand in this alley much longer, I will."

I forced a breath through my nose and took a few steps away from him, the sound of my heels clicking loudly in the deathly silence of the decimated city. I chanced a quick glance away from the relative safety the alley gave us and into the red-bathed street, even though I didn't know if that was where he would emerge since we had no idea where Ilyan's camp was.

It was one of the many reasons I didn't like this plan.

We were too exposed, too vulnerable inside the city.

Even though my father didn't go anywhere without his guard, and the powerful men were already hidden by their magic as they surveyed the streets surrounding us, I didn't feel comfortable. Especially with how close Ilyan had come to capturing Sain the last time. For all I knew, my irritating brother had already gleaned information from the pathetic Drak and was standing on the rooftop right above us, watching.

Waiting.

It wouldn't have been the first time in the last century he had done something so brazen.

I wouldn't put it past him.

With a groan and a glare, I shifted my view, taking one quick glance at the roofline before looking back to where my father stood in the shadow of a dilapidated store overhang, the words *poslední z květů* barely discernible. If it wasn't for the rotted twigs and wilted roses, I wouldn't have even been able to tell what it was.

"Leave it, Míra," Father snapped, as though he was controlling a dog. I supposed, in a way, he was.

He had barely finished the warning before the fair-haired beauty he had made his forward guard snapped to attention, running to his side and looking very guilty for having picked up the remains of a red rose.

"Sorry, master," she grumbled, deep and fearful, obviously expecting a strike.

Smirking at her reaction, I took a step away, not really wanting to see what would come next. She was lucky my father was more concerned with Sain's absence than her foolishness, or a strike would probably be the least she would receive.

She stood beside him like a rail, her head just below his shoulder, her hair a long sheet down past her waist. If it wasn't for the dirty rags she was still forced to wear, I would say she looked like a life-sized porcelain doll, right down to her bottle green eyes. It would be a much nicer sight when she completed her training and was allowed to wear real clothes.

"Find him, Ovailia," Edmund growled, the depth of his voice pulling me away from the child and right to him. My scowl deepened at the intense look he was giving me.

"He's coming," I spat, feigned confidence spilling over my lips as I flattened them into a tight line.

The anger in his eyes intensified as he took a step closer to me, his fingers flexing by his side. "You would do well to make sure that is not a lie, Ovailia."

He stepped around me, my head held high as I waited for whatever was coming.

"Find him for me," Edmund hissed in my ear as he moved a step closer, a shiver moving down my spine at the icy chill of his hand moving over my neck as he swept my hair away from my face. His scowl deepened as I peered at him from out of the corner of my eye. "I want to know definitively."

You are trying my patience, I sent to Sain through the shard of blade that was embedded in his spine. The piece matched with the one my father had placed in me, as well as in Ryland. I wasn't even sure that Sain knew he had placed it there.

I turned toward my father with a flick of my hair, my eyes meeting his dead-on, and I smiled. "Do not worry, Father. He is coming. You will get what you need."

"Wonderful." His lips twitched into what I hoped was a smile before he moved away from me, back into the shadowed overhang of the flower shop.

The girl who had gone back to her inspection of the

dead and blood-soaked flowers snapped back into obedient attention.

"I would hate to discover this little game he is playing is tied to you, as well. We still need him, Ovailia. I would hate to make you prove your loyalty to me... again."

Ice trailed down my spine at the warning. The hatred in his words moving over my spine and I shivered, his smile expanding.

"That won't be necessary," I cooed, keeping my voice gentle as I tried to pull his focus from my fear. He simply smiled more. "I am yours, Father."

"Good, because he may be my key to procuring Wynifred as my mate." The greasy grin on his face spread wider. It was why he was here after all. It wasn't the first time he had tried this either, but I wasn't going to be the one to remind him of how that had ended. "Once that is done, we can attack Ilyan and his pathetic pack mules. Then we can end this."

My smile broadened with eager anticipation as he turned back toward the girl. The way he was looking at her and the way her eyes glossed over made it obvious he was taking control through the Štít he had placed in her heart.

"Why wait?" I asked, the enjoyment of the creature's fears igniting my desperate need to cause more pain.

"Soon, my precious girl." His voice was a smooth whisper as he moved toward me in three quick steps, his finger resting against the side of my face with a touch so gentle I forgot who he was. "Soon, the war will come, our thousands will crush Ilyan's handfuls of rejects, and then all of this will be ours again. The magic will be mine again, and no one will be able to stop me."

"No one deserves that more than you. You are my king."

"Good."

Looking away, I walked back toward the end of the alley, avoiding a puddle of what looked like fresh blood that had pooled in the middle of the cobbled street.

Everything here was too red, too wet, and too dirty. I wasn't about to touch anything; it was bad enough I had to smell it.

"Father ..." I began, stopping short at the crash that moved through the city.

A loud bang and a flash emanated from the old, broken cathedral that lay a few streets away, the already debilitated city shaking with groans and bangs as a mist of dust moved over us like a fog.

I raced back to my father, hands outstretched as if some unseen assailant was hurtling toward him. Míra was right by my side as my father's guard appeared before us, their bodies popping into existence as they surrounded the three of us in a wide human shield.

We stood still, waiting for the attack, but the alley was empty except for the dozens of Vilỳs that poked their heads out of their hiding places, too scared to come out all the way.

"You fools. It's not an attack. At least not on us," Edmund snapped as he pushed his way past our open arms, his stride wide as he gave his guard one look.

With shivering veils of magic they vanished back to their patrol, the single glance all they needed as far as instructions went.

Edmund sneered as he continued to walk away from us all, disappearing from view as he moved toward the middle of the street.

Remaining still, I followed the sound of his shoes. The soft sound all that was left to tell me where he was. I knew better than to follow him without request, Míra however followed blindly, hand on her chest as she tried to locate his magic, even though she could no longer see him.

The moment he reappeared, she rushed to his side, her feet moving like little patters of rain. Instead of moving into the protective stance she was being trained for, however, she moved behind him, her shoulders hunched as she cowered.

"You pathetic fool," he snapped, as she shrieked, hand over the Štít as he hurt her. "I am your king, your lord, and your master. You would not be alive if not for me, and you will do well to remember that. Do what you have been trained to do, or I will kill you. I always enjoy watching things bleed." He kicked her away from him as he finished.

The child whimpered as she fell into a pool of blood and excrement, her hair fanning around her.

"She will learn," I said as he laughed, his toe digging into her arm before he moved away, leaving her in a heap. "What did you see? What was that?"

"What do you think the chances are that Ilyan has all of his *army* holed up in the cathedral?"

I shook my head, "It was the first place we checked. We had all the churches checked shortly after the wall was placed..." I hesitated. I could already see the warning in his eyes. "There was nothing there."

"Nothing, as in it was empty? Or nothing, as in they were destroyed?" His smile continued to grow, the greasy mess twisting down my spine, and I shivered pleasantly.

"There was no one within them." My voice was barely above a whisper.

"So they were empty." His smile grew. "And yet, your brother loves churches."

"Which is why we checked them first."

He said nothing more before walking back to the middle

REBECCA ETHINGTON

of the street, this time without shielding himself. A tense knot rippled through me and I smiled, the long-ingrained fear of this man growing.

"Come, Ovailia."

Leaving the still sniveling girl in a heap of dried blood and what looked like fresh vomit, I joined my father where he stood in the middle of the road, facing the pillar of black smoke that spiraled from the cathedral.

The lazy circles of black and blue drifted through the air, even with the red tint of light, the smoke was an unnatural shade of blue, which could mean one thing.

"Magic."

"Yes," he hissed. "And if the smoke is magic ... Well, there is only one way it would be there, wouldn't it?"

"But we checked—"

"And your brother is one of the most powerful Skříteks, mated to a more powerful Drak. Imagine what together they could do with that power." He spoke with the same hunger I had heard before, the same eager desire he had whenever he spoke of Wyn's gifts, except this was more.

I cringed against it, already knowing what was coming.

"Imagine what *I* could do with that power. She is worth more to me alive than dead. I must have it."

The awe that had loosened the knot in my stomach tightened up my spine like a poorly made corset, twisting as the poison inside of me reacted to his words.

"Shall I bring you Joclyn's heart?"

"No." He stepped away from me, toward the smoke that was quickly dissipating, his eyes wide with greed.

"No?"

"This one I will get for myself. At the very end, when Ilyan is nearly dead, I will make his mate mine, and I will force him to watch. The same way I made you watch. The same way I made Wynifred." He turned toward me in one swift movement, the dark cloak of his shadow falling over me.

I watched him, watched his smile, watched his icy eyes flash as he took a step forward. The horror on his face brought back flashes of memories that ran from exhilarating to traumatizing. I flinched and his smile increased as he stepped right up to me, his hand twisting around my waist before pulling me closer to him.

"Would you like to see that?" he asked, his breath harsh against my face. "Would you like to see me break your brother? Finally break him as I did you? As I did Sain? As I did Wyn?"

"Yes," I hissed in eagerness as he smiled deeper and pulled me closer still.

"Would you like to see me hurt him as he did you for all those years?" His teeth lashed with a smile so deep I was positive he expected me to pull away, to turn into the same sniveling heap of a girl.

But I didn't.

I couldn't.

Not after what he had said. Not after the fire that had erupted inside of me.

Ilyan had hurt me.

Ilyan had lied to me.

Ilyan had controlled me.

As my father had asked of me when I returned to his service a year ago, 'Would I like to see him pay?' The answer was still the same.

"Please."

Edmund's grin spread as he released me from his grip, my heels clicking loudly against the road as I regained my balance.

"Good."

He left me standing in the street as he moved back to the girl who flinched and whimpered the closer he came.

"Get up," he demanded of her without so much as a hint of compassion.

"But it hurts." Her moans were barely audible over the sobs, over the way she clung to her own chest, clawing at it as though it was hurting her.

I was convinced it was.

"Get up," he insisted again, his voice harder this time.

"Hurts …" she moaned again, her body twisting more, as if the movement would help her escape it.

"It will hurt more unless you get up," he warned, a harshness in his voice as the child slowly moved to attention.

If there was one thing she knew, if there was one thing she would continue to learn, it was pain. Edmund delivered it better than any other.

Her body shook as she forced herself to stand, her eyes downcast as she refused to look at her master. Her hand still clutched against her heart, against the Štít.

"Good." The sneer in his voice had deepened. "Life is pain, little one. You either rise to the occasion, or you fall beneath it. Work hard and perhaps that pain will end, but until you can stand on your own two feet, get used to the agony." He leaned over to the child, hissing in her face as she recoiled, her shoulders digging into her ears.

"We need to get in there," Edmund announced eagerly as he turned toward me, the swaying child all but forgotten.

"Into the cathedral?" I clarified before continuing without waiting for a response. "But we've been in there—"

I stopped short at the look in his eye, the danger mixed

with frustration I understood all too well. I was obviously missing something.

"No, Ovailia. We need to get past his shield, past whatever he is using to block us from seeing what is really in there."

I narrowed my eyes in question. We had sent so many of our men into that space, looking for any sign of Ilyan, and they had all come back saying they had seen nothing. They had walked through the old basilica, through the monks' quarters. There was nothing there.

Such a thing could not be, yet I could tell with one look that it could.

That it was.

"M-Master?"

I turned at the voice, at the timid traitor who walked into the darkened alley, practically falling over his own feet at the sight of my father.

I would guess it was good I hadn't told Sain who would be meeting him, if only for this show alone.

Sain stood next to the still swaying child, his frame as broken and beaten as the girl's. They were a good pair—two beaten dogs, bred to do anything my father asked.

"Sain." Edmund turned to him, his voice a menacing growl. They both recoiled. "Glad you could join us. We've been waiting."

"If I had known ..." he began as he cowered away from Edmund's approach, trying to gain some sort of favor with the man who now towered over him. "I tried to ... I mean ... I was held up—"

"You were held up?" Edmund asked with a condescending lilt.

Sain practically collapsed to the ground in fear. I would guess I wasn't the only one who knew where this was going. No matter what act he had been playing, he could not escape this, and he knew it.

"Was it all the smoke? All that beautiful, blue smoke?"

"Yes," Sain whimpered as he folded into himself more, knowing what was coming.

"It makes me wonder, seeing as you chose this exact minute to show up. I'm convinced you could tell us ..." Edmund paused, the tension so tight it gripped against my abdomen, twisting around my spine and awakening the poison inside me even further, my magic reacting to Sain's close vicinity with a painful, caustic burn. It was all I could do not to call out.

"Yes, master?" Sain questioned obediently, his back bending even farther.

"What happened." It was not a question, not really, and even Sain knew he could not avoid it.

His whimpers turned into cries as he collapsed to the ground, shivering under the weight of his oppression, under the fear Edmund had ground into him with just a few words.

"Joclyn," he stammered, his cry matching that of the child who was now leaning against the wall, her eyes closed as if in prayer. "Something with Joclyn."

"What *with Joclyn*?" Edmund hissed at him, his hand jutting out to grab the old man by the hair, lifting him to eye-level. "Don't think for a second you can get away with that answer."

Sain cried out in pain, a hiss and a sob echoing around the old, stone alley. His eyes closed as Edmund moved toward him, his face so close that I was momentarily concerned he would bite him.

"Look at me," Edmund growled, his anger increasing by the second. "What did your bastard child do?"

Poor Joclyn, child of a weakling. If Sain was my father, I would do him in. Heavens, he was my mate, and I had handed him over to my father without question.

"I ... I don't know ... I didn't see—"

"You have sight, and you didn't see?"

"It's broken, she broke it..."

My heels tapped against the ground as I moved toward them, hair swinging down my back as I circled them. Father looked up at me, his smile matching mine for a moment before returning to his prey.

"Would you like me to check, Father?"

"Perhaps that is not a bad idea—"

"It was Wyn!" Sain stammered, his voice breaking as my magic attached to his. "Wyn has a piece of the blade. Joclyn saw it, and Wyn attacked her."

Edmund's eyes shot to mine and mine to his, his expression one of shock I had never seen in him before it faded to the familiar greed.

"She has a piece of the blade? Where did she get it?" Edmund asked eagerly, his desperation rattling the man he still held.

"From R-Ryland," Sain stammered before Edmund released him, sending him tumbling toward the ground.

Greed.

Even I felt it now.

"So that is why my connection to him has been severed."

After everything, Wynifred had made a misstep. She had done something even she should know better than to do. If she had a piece of the blade, father could control her, control the girl with the magic he prized.

With one last grin, he closed his eyes, his face serene as he did what came naturally to him, as he searched out the blade that held the souls of so many he had killed, their magic now inside of him, a direct line if you will.

"She's close ..." he whispered, stepping over the heaving, gasping man as he took my hand in his and pulled me back into the middle of the street. "It is not within her, so my control is limited, but not for long."

He gestured forward, eyes trained into the darkness. I looked between the street and my father in confusion before a small, black figure cut through the red tint of the world before us, stumbling, running, screaming. I knew who it was and that my father was in control of her.

Wynifred.

We had originally come so as to command Sain to bring Wyn to us. And yet, here she was. An assassin had walked into our control.

"Wonderful." I smiled, my eyes wide as she continued toward us. "What are you going to do with her?"

"I'm going to get you past Ilyan's wall." Edmund smiled "If she can get out, then she can get you in. Together, you will destroy his army before he has a chance to attack us. He will be crippled, and all because of Wyn."

"Brilliant."

"Make sure to come back with my new bride, Ovailia. I would hate for dear Wynifred to miss her bonding ceremony tonight."

"I thought you wished for Joclyn?"

He grinned, "I see no reason why I can't take the magic of both."

This time, I laughed, the sound loud as I danced before the woman who had been my archenemy for several centuries. I had been forced to pretend, to cower to her. Now I would return the favor.

She staggered towards us, her eyes wide as her body

propelled her forward without her permission. Her hand wrapped around a shard of red blade I recognized immediately, the panic clear on her face.

She could see us.

She knew what was happening, yet there was nothing she could do.

"Hello, darling," Edmund cooed, his voice the same he would use before he forced all of his wives into his bed. "I told you I would make you mine eventually."

Wynifred looked at him in terror as he grabbed her hand, her palm opening to reveal the jagged blade. She couldn't even move as he lifted the shard and plunged it through the center of her hand.

There was silence for the briefest of seconds, and then her mouth opened wide, a high-pitched scream seeping through the hot air around us as we laughed.

CHAPTER 16
DRAMIN

The mug was dry. It had been dry for the last few hours, but I held it, anyway—clung to it as I listened to the screams that had been resonating through the halls for the last few minutes. The pain and agony behind them increased with each wave.

I didn't need to be told whose they were.

Joclyn.

I could only hope the powerful Drak magic that even I couldn't help her understand wasn't taking control. That whatever it was that Sain had done to her, to her sights, wasn't ripping her apart.

I hoped she would be strong enough to control it, to defeat it.

To defeat him.

That it wouldn't devour her.

The scream came again, louder, the sound swallowing the footsteps that were racing toward me, opening the door with a bang so loud I was surprised Thom didn't jump.

"Wyn!" Ryland yelled angrily as he barged in, Jaromir

on his heels as he searched for the Trpaslík who normally occupied the space.

"Ryland?" I asked in a panic as his eyes swept over the room to meet mine. "What's going on?"

Ryland turned to me, his bulky frame even more powerful as he pulled to his full height. "Have you seen Wyn?"

"No."

"Damn it!" His voice was loud, louder than the fist that hit against the door frame, his powerful strength leaving a long crack in the old wood.

"Ryland!" I yelled his name with as much authority as I could. "What is going on?"

"Joclyn," he panted, the obvious answer frustrating me. "She was with Wyn. Ilyan thinks she attacked Jos."

My eyes widened in shock. I hadn't expected Wynifred to attack her best friend. Six hundred years ago, the thought would not have made me bat an eye. Now? That was not the girl I saw every day.

"Ryland?" I asked, pulling the blankets off my old, useless legs before I even got a response. "I need you to take me to her."

"But I—"

"You can find Wyn after. I need to be there with her now."

Ryland glanced down the long hall, looking toward wherever else he was supposed to look for Wyn, before glancing back to Joclyn's screams. "Fine. I've already looked everywhere. Come on, old man."

My emaciated body sagged awkwardly as he lifted me, holding me against him with a firm grip. I almost asked him to let me go, but then Joclyn screamed again, the sound worse than before, the pain and agony behind it cutting through us both simultaneously. He tensed as I did.

Without another word, he ran, carrying me as Jaromir followed us at a sprint. The flush on his face made it clear he had been running after Ryland since the screaming began.

Hallways streamed past me, clusters of people gathered in corners and against windows as they looked toward the screams, as they gossiped. My father's name traveled with us, the rumors that he had spread sprouting into a forest as we reached the people who gathered outside the King and Queen's chamber.

"Move!" Ryland growled, his patience gone as he burst through them.

The door swung open and shut behind us before any of the rubberneckers had a chance to see inside. It was disgusting how they tried.

"I brought Dramin," Ryland announced as he rushed into the tiny room, the sound of Joclyn's pain mutating into a deafening call now that we were within the heavy walls.

I had expected healers to be crammed into the tiny space. However, it was only Ilyan who sat on the bed, Joclyn wrapped in his arms as she screamed, as she cried, as she writhed. Ilyan held her and soothed her, as he had all those months ago when we had been trapped in the cave.

I watched in horror, trying to find some sign of physical injury as she turned toward me, her eyes encompassed in a thick black sheen, seeing and unseeing as they stared into me. Her sight had taken her, Wyn might have attacked her, but it was her sight that was destroying her.

"It's coming," she gasped before she whimpered again. "You must run."

"Good," Ilyan said, ignoring the words as if they were

meaningless. "There is a chair there. Did you find Wynifred?"

"No." Ryland's voice was hard as he sat me down, Jaromir tried to blend in with the doorframe as if he was unsure if he should be there. "I've looked everywhere."

"I had a feeling she would do this. With what I was able to see, and with her magic... She could be anywhere. She could be underground. Risha is still looking..." Ilyan's voice faded into an uncharacteristic weakness as he clung to Joclyn, her body writhing as her breathing picked up.

"Your další v příkazu will find her. She couldn't have gone far." Ryland was confident in Ilyan's alarm system. I hoped it wasn't in vain.

"Your feet are not fast enough," Joclyn moaned from Ilyan's embrace, her voice deep and hollow before it broke into the same scream that had been echoing around the halls.

"Has she said anything... helpful?" I asked hesitantly, my chest tight in fear of what could possibly be breaking through her.

"No. I can't make any sense of it," Ilyan sighed, his hand pressing against the mark on her neck, the same way he had done so many times before.

She gasped at the contact, her back arching abrasively, but her eyes stayed black, her face blank.

"It sounds like she is talking to someone, mostly things about running and traitors."

"And screaming," Ryland provided, his voice solemn as he moved to the foot of the bed. "Lots of screaming."

"And her sight?" I asked as Ilyan fixed me with an expression of such hopelessness that I temporarily found it hard to breathe.

"She was in sight when I found her," Ilyan answered,

his voice heavy, "running through the halls like she was trying to reach something. Her eyes were black. I'm not even certain if she could see me. It hasn't stopped since."

"Have you been able to see anything?"

"Flashes, but it's mostly white."

"I need her, or else it will not break," she moaned out, cutting him off. Ilyan pressed his forehead to hers, his lips mumbling a song I couldn't quite make out.

I watched them, the helpless feeling growing more painful in my chest. I fought the need to grip the chair, knowing by the way Ryland had begun to pace I wasn't the only one feeling agitated.

"I need to find Wyn," Ryland whispered from the foot of the bed, his hands clenching the bed rail so tightly his knuckles were turning white. "I need to find her."

"Wyn can't help." My voice was dead as I stared at Ilyan who was now rocking my sister, his face burrowing in her hair before it snapped up to me.

"No," Ilyan growled, his mind going right to where I expected it to, and judging by the intensity of his response, we shared the same opinion.

"He can't help, either."

Ilyan's eyes widened, Ryland looking between us as he picked up the pieces to what we were talking about.

"Sain?" he asked, but neither Ilyan nor I looked in his direction. "What do you mean Sain can't help? He's a Drak. Of course he can help."

"Think, Ryland. Do you really think he would?" Ilyan snapped, his focus shifting back to Joclyn who had finally calmed in his eyes.

"Joclyn is his daughter; they are of the same magic..." Even Ryland didn't seem convinced.

"Yes, but just because he can help us," I said, my voice

calm as I looked Ryland in the eye, "it doesn't mean he should. His help has done damage to this child. I will not let him do more."

"You sound like you know more about this than I do, Dramin." Ilyan asked, a terror I hadn't expected seeping into his voice. I thought Joclyn would have told him what we had discussed. Perhaps she hadn't found the proof she was so desperate for.

"He's also changing her sights," I sighed, my voice as heavy as the weight that was pressing against me.

"I know," Joclyn whispered, her voice soft as it seemingly answered my statement, her eyes black as she stared at something none of us could see. "I have seen it before."

"How can... but... what do you mean?" Ryland looked between Ilyan and I in a panic. But Ilyan just nodded in confirmation.

"It's happened to me before." I swallowed heavily, Ryland's eyes wide. "I was only a child ... long before you were born." I hesitated. I had only told Joclyn part of this before. "I saw Ovailia's true mate, and then I saw it change. No, Sain changed the sight."

"Ovailia's true mate?" Ilyan could barely get the words out.

"I saw Ovailia, saw the joy and happiness she was supposed to have ..." Then he had changed it, and it was devoid of all the joy I had seen that day. She always was sour and angry after that. Even on the day when she had bonded herself to Sain, the man she was not meant to marry.

And he knew it.

He knew it because he had seen that sight.

"He changed it," I whispered, my focus drifting to Joclyn. "He changed what I saw so he could have her.

Different angle, different point of view. The same sight, distorted enough I couldn't really tell what was going on."

"He's changing more," Joclyn gasped. The words were so perfect that again I was sure she could hear me. But she still lay there, eyes black as she looked into the void of sight, face blank as tears rolled down her cheeks.

"He couldn't have." Ryland's voice was dead, as though he himself was piecing it together yet refusing to accept it.

"He is," Ilyan began, his voice distorted through his clenched teeth, "I have seen it."

"He's spreading rumors about her while he controlled her enough to make all those rumors seem viable," Ryland's voice was dead as he put it all together, staring out the window at the now pitch black sky, his face as hard as Ilyan's. "Have you ever heard Sain talk about the theory of magic? About how it's all connected? About the waterfall?"

"You mean like the délka vedení královsk?" Ilyan asked, his anger evaporating.

"No," Ryland sighed, turning back to face us, guilt riddling his face as he dragged his hand through his curls. "It's something Sain told me about how magic is connected. He said he let Edmund *think* he controlled his sights when he was in prison. He told me magic is connected through the races, through the family ties, like a waterfall, or a ribbon. Magic is really carried by one person —the first person. The mud birthed your grandmother and your father and so they held the end of the ribbon of their magic, controlling it and all the magic of those below him. All the magic moved down through him. One after another, all tied to the first, to the top."

"Sain *told* you this?" I asked, barely able to get the words out as everything clicked together in my mind.

A ladder, a connection of magic, and a man who might or might not be controlling it all.

"He said all the Drak magic flows through him, that he controls it."

"Controls." I looked up to Ilyan whose anger was returning with a force I could feel consume the room.

"No," I announced, something clicking into place. "He's not. He *can't*. He's trying to, but he doesn't have full access to her magic. That's why she's reacting this way, why her sights are doing this to her. Someone is trying to control them, and her magic is fighting it. *She* is fighting it."

"What do you mean he doesn't have full control?" Ryland asked. I was actually surprised he hadn't put it together yet.

"It's not a ribbon. Not for her. I'm actually surprised Father doesn't see it," I mused. "Or maybe he does, but after so much time, he's too stubborn to believe otherwise."

They both looked at me, obviously not piecing it together yet.

"Joclyn is one of the Chosen with all of the different strains of magic flowing through her. All of these different abilities are tied to a dozen different people. For her, it's not a ribbon; it's not even a straight line. It's a spider web that is wound through everyone.

"Edmund is the first of the Chosen. Ilyan, the son of him, but also the eldest surviving descendant of Frain. Joclyn's magic is connected through Edmund because she is Chosen, but also through you, Ilyan; not in binding, but in carrier, as well. The first of the four over all of the Chosen. Silky strings tying everyone together."

"A web," Ilyan repeated, his face blank as he put it all together. "And Sain ..." He stopped short, the unspoken words clear.

It was one thing to realize how magic was connected and another to know what Sain was doing, to have Ryland confirm Sain had known it all along.

"What is he up to?"

I could only shake my head, all of us falling into silence. The hush was interrupted by a sob that ripped from the girl Ilyan held in his arms, her black eyes gazed into his as though she could see him. As though she *was* seeing him.

"Joclyn?" I asked aloud, unsurprised when she turned toward me.

She was here.

"Ilyan," I gasped, my body tipped toward her so far I was convinced I was going to fall. "I think she can hear you."

"What? How?"

I watched her, trying to find some clue that would tell me what to do. If I had my magic, I could connect with her sight, see what she saw and guide her through it like I had done when she had seen for the first time.

We just needed a Drak. Or someone close.

Simple.

So simple.

"Ilyan," I whispered the moment Joclyn had calmed, the last note of Ilyan's song fading into the nothing. "Do you remember when I told you about the water? About how the more you put into—"

"The more I come in contact with it, the more I have in my body? Yes. Are you suggesting Sain can somehow control me, too?"

"No, I was actually going to suggest the exact opposite. Because of the Drak magic your father holds, thanks to his kiss and the magic you hold in your body from the water that has touched your skin, *you* could control *her*."

"I don't want to control her."

"Perhaps control is the wrong word," I spoke in a rush, my hands twisting as I shifted in the rickety chair. "When we were in the cave, when Ryland had pulled her into Cail's mind you tried to connect with her magic to pull her back."

"Yes?"

"Do it again," I gasped out, the tension in my chest growling with anticipation. "But this time, connect with the Drak inside of you to see what she sees. Give her the Drak magic you possess in order to strengthen her, to help her find a way out of whatever my father has done to her."

"*My* Drak magic?" He was obviously skeptical.

"Yes, that magic that is tied to your father, your mate, and the Black Water that flows through you. Connecting to magic is how Draks share the sights. Perhaps it is what she needs—someone to share the sight with her, not control it. Someone to help her find the base of reality and take control of her ability. Break whatever bind Sain has placed over her. Set her magic free. Set *her* free."

He gawked at me. No one knew anything about Drak magic. Even I knew nothing about my own magic or even what it could do. I had no tools to give him beyond what I had already shared. Sain's rules had kept everyone pinioned under a control so deep they never saw the sun. Now I was breaking the rules. I was going to set them free.

"I have been fighting," Joclyn moaned, the broken speech drowned by the tension in the room. "I'm going to keep fighting."

"Sain is trying to restrain her for a reason," I went on as Ilyan broke his contact with me to look from Ryland to the girl in question. "What her magic is doing is more powerful than any Drak magic I have seen, any Drak magic I have been told exists. Perhaps her magic is what Drak magic truly is. Perhaps it is what Sain has kept hidden all along."

"If you don't try, Ilyan, I will," Ryland spoke up from the foot of the bed, his voice shaking a bit. I was confident he was fighting with whatever demon still dwelled inside of him. "She's my best friend, and our father's blood is in me, as well."

The two brothers looked at each other, locked in a gaze I was positive was not built in competition for the first time, but in understanding. In support.

"No, this is my place," Ilyan contested, his hands shaking as he pulled the burned one out from underneath Joclyn. "I will do anything to save her. I have already proven that time and time again, and this isn't so much saving her as unlocking her."

We all stared at Ilyan as he pressed his hand to the nape of her neck, the burn on his hand connecting again to the mark on her skin with a jolt that, considering the way he moved, was filled with enough electricity to charge a city street.

He gasped at the contact, hissed at the power, and his eyes flew to mine in request for guidance.

"Find the burn inside of you, Ilyan. Find the water. Follow it."

It was advice he would never want to hear. There was so much water in his body, burns and poison that had caused him agony for centuries, pain I knew he had fought against since the day the water first scarred his chest. And now I was telling him to follow it. Now I was telling him to feel it.

He didn't hesitate; he closed his eyes, gasping and hissing in agonizing pain as his body tensed, arms stiffening around Joclyn as the agony became worse.

My muscles were tight as I leaned forward, wishing there was a way I could be closer to them, connect with them, guide them through whatever was about to happen.

But I was left to watch as Ryland was. His hands were wrapped tightly around the old, iron footboard, leaning toward them with a look on his face that made it clear he had forgotten to breathe.

Ilyan closed his eyes as the pain became too much, a yell breaking from his chest in a growl filled with the same agony, the same feral sound ripping through the space. I cringed, scared of what was about to happen when Joclyn's voice joined his. The tone of her pain matched his in perfect harmony. It was a song of a scream that ripped through the hot air, ripped through my heart.

And then Ilyan opened his eyes, orbs as black as Joclyn's looking back at me. I saw them for one moment before a painful weight in my chest ran through me. An agonizing weight ripped around me like fire that absorbed me, fire that ruled me, fire that pulled me right into the same sight Joclyn had been trapped in, right into the same sight Ilyan now saw.

Right into the sight that had left me so long ago.

CHAPTER 17
DRAMIN

Flames ran over me, drowning me in sights that flashed with the speed of a strobe light: images of death, joy, war, and peace. There were moments from hundreds of years ago and images that had not come to fruition. I watched them all, my chest tightening with the realization of what I was looking at.

It was more than being in sight; it was seeing *all* sights. I was seeing everything that had ever been given by the mud. It was a recall of extraordinary proportions.

A calm took over as the visions shifted, not to all sight, but to my sight. Moments of my life. Every moment of my life flooded me; my wife on the night of our bonding, the births of our children. So many moments, some of them forgotten. I watched them, no doubt crying, about to burst with the strength of the emotion.

It was all gone in a flash of white as fire pulled me in. I was no longer sitting in a room with my sister and her mate, no longer broken and weak. I was there, among the nothing, the happiness of my sights still swirling through me.

"Hello." The feminine voice came out of nowhere, so familiar, but I could not place it. There was wisdom in it that did not seem to fit.

"Hello?" I asked, looking through the space in an attempt to find the owner, facing only the bright white of the world.

"Your sights are beautiful," she said, the voice seeming to come from inside of me.

"Are they?" My confusion was melding into something closer to panic.

"Yes."

"Who are you?" I asked, still looking through the nothing, still trying to place the voice, still trying not to lose my calm.

"You know me," she said, her voice indicating a smile. "Everything will be alright, Dramin."

"Will it?"

"Yes," she said with a sigh, the joy in her voice fading away. The single word echoed hauntingly off the nothingness surrounding me. "It will hurt, but it will all be all right."

"What do you mean?" I gasped, shoulders jerking at the frightening admission "What are you talking about?"

"Your death." Her voice was monotone, but it hit me as though it was a scream. I fell back down to the floor, my heart as heavy as if someone had filled it with lead.

"It is coming then?" I asked, shocked by the wave of sorrow the thought gave me. I had longed for it for so long, after all. I had seen it. I had expected it. Part of me had wanted it the moment I stepped in front of Ryland. I wanted to be with them, with my mate and my children.

"Yes," she whispered. Her voice was so close now I was positive that, if I turned, I would see her. There was nothing but white. "Sooner than you think, but I need you to do something for me first."

"What?" I asked, the question surprising me as I looked up, still expecting to see her.

Instead, I came face-to-face with a girl I had never seen before: blonde hair to her waist, green eyes, and a button nose that was nearly identical to Jaromir's. She even appeared to be about his age.

"You must stop this child," the voice gasped as the girl stood still, looking like a doll in a shop window.

Staring at the child, I waited for answers, not knowing who the mysterious girl was, part of me not wanting to find out.

"This child is coming to kill someone who is needed. You must stop that from happening."

"How can I stop an assassin if I can barely move?" I asked in desperation, watching the child vanish into the smoke of memory.

"You will fight, you will see," her voice came from right behind me, her breath hot against my neck and I turned, expecting the white space of the sight.

But the white was now occupied with a woman I knew well. Older, different, but the same.

Joclyn stood before me, wisdom in her eyes from hundreds of years that had come and gone without either of us seeing them.

"Hello, Uncle," she whispered. "Long time no see."

My eyes narrowed at the phrase she had used so many times with me. I opened my mouth to ask who she was, what had happened, but she smiled before her bright laugh echoed around me as she began to fade.

"When the child comes, you will know," she whispered before she was swallowed by the white, leaving me staring into the blanket of brilliance, the light wrapping around me so tightly it was all I saw. It was all there was, until the sights played again, filling me with everything that had happened in the fifteen hundred years of my existence. My own pain and anguish returned until the sight was gone, and I was left huddling on the floor, a panicked Ryland screaming for some form of assistance, and a few words embedded inside of me, whispering to my soul...

"I love you, Uncle."

CHAPTER 18
OVAILIA

W yn moved like she was possessed, her joints jerking in weird directions as her body relentlessly pushed her forward. I walked behind her at a safe distance, enjoying her struggle, enjoying seeing her reduced to such a pathetic mass.

I smiled wickedly, throwing my hair to the side as Wynifred stumbled over her own feet, her body lunging into the white stone building we were walking next to.

The crack of skull against stone resonated through the empty city, her head impacting into the wall before she slid down to the ground in a pathetic heap, a bright red streak following her.

"Oh, dear," I sighed, my voice dripping with false sympathy. "Are you okay? That looks like it hurt."

Her eyes swung toward me with all the wide-eyed horror I would expect from someone in this situation. The horrified glance was made all the more real by the fact that she had no other choice but to give in to me.

Her mouth opened wide, and for a brief moment, I

thought she was going to scream again, but she simply stared, odd gurgling noises seeping from her throat.

"Pathetic." Chuckling acidly at the withered girl below me, I took another step, pressing the point of my high-heeled boot into her side with an aggressive swing, causing her eyes to grow wider. "I'm sorry. What was that? You say you are okay..." I dug deeper with my toe, watching her writhe as it pressed against the ridges of her rib cage.

Broken sobs leaked out with a pathetic growl from somewhere deep inside her chest.

"Don't you think we should get moving?"

Her mouth snapped shut in one quick movement, her teeth clicking together as tears leaked from her eyes.

"Get up," I growled through my grin.

Wyn flinched at the sound, but she didn't move; she shivered as if she was cold. I knew better, though, especially in this heat. She was still fighting him, and I was losing my patience.

"Get up," I snapped as my magic rushed from me, spinning around her and picking her up off the ground.

A soft scream of fear seeped from her mouth as I slammed her against the wall; her rag doll body rattled against the hard stone as I slammed her into it again and again.

Laughing, I watched her bounce, reveling in the soft sound of her cries, before dropping her again, her body collapsing in a twisted heap.

"Get up." This time, she didn't wait, her pathetic sobs echoing disgustingly as she lifted herself.

Snarling, I turned away from her, my eyes darting down the street to the tall spires of the cathedral. Long shadows clawing over us as the sun fully set.

"Come, Wynifred," I called behind me as the sound of

her dragging steps moved closer. "We have a wedding to get back to."

I wish it was that simple: a job well done, a bonding, and the feast that would follow. However, once the sun went down, this place would become a labyrinth of Vilỳ. We needed to get back before that happened. I didn't want to deprive my father of his prize, after all.

I pulled Wyn's hand out from where she had cradled it against her chest; the wrist was slick with the red blood that oozed out of the open wound in her palm, the color even brighter in the light of the quickly fading day.

She gasped and attempted to pull away. But I held on, malice spreading through my wide grin as I watched her fear grow into something beautiful. Grabbing the blade that protruded from her palm, I twisted it further into her hand, ripping the already ragged flesh apart.

She screamed and I clasped my hand, sticky with her blood, over her mouth, leaving just the sound of my deep laugh in the alley.

The blade had passed through the same place barely months before, but then, she had gone into a dream controlled by Cail. Then, it had been a walk in the park. Now, she was on her own, trapped in the mind of my father, trapped in his control.

"We should get moving," I soothed with threatening grace.

With a strangled sob, she pushed herself up, her good hand gripped against the wall, against the ground, and then reached for me as she tried to find a balance between the uncontrollable movements of her joints.

"Don't touch me," I snarled and stepped away, letting her stumble into an upright position, as though she'd had one too many to drink. "Let's go."

Wyn's eyes glossed over, her body straightening as someone flipped a switch. Her movements, while still jagged, became a bit more fluid. She was giving in bit by bit.

Following her through another alley, the cathedral fell away from view before we emerged on a small side street that, for whatever reason, looked more untouched than the rest of them. There wasn't quite as much blood here, and the trash and debris had been moved aside into what looked like tiny, little piles, like someone was taking care of it, cleaning it. The idea was ridiculous.

"Zdechnout," I whispered as a poisoned Vilỳ flew toward me.

The tiny thing dropped to the ground with a thud.

Vilỳs used to be the smartest creatures among us, wise beings that would converse about philosophy for hours. Now they were vermin, tortured until their minds had broken. Now they couldn't even string two words together.

"Zdechnout," I said more loudly this time, laughing as the winged monsters that had hidden themselves through the street retreated, hiding themselves in fear, leaving us standing alone. Just one more hurdle until we reached our destination.

"Thhhh ... Rrrrr ..."

It took me a minute to realize Wyn was actually trying to say something and wasn't drowning in a pool of her own saliva.

Her tangled body faced the high tower, staring at something I couldn't quite see with a mixture of dread and excitement.

Her hand shook as it lifted, one jagged finger pointing to the high dividing wall that had been built sometime in the 1500s. But it wasn't the wall she was pointing at; it was the tower.

"What is it, little puppet?" I snapped, running my fingers through her hair as I stepped around her, taunting her, watching the fear in her eyes increase as the reality of what was about to happen settled into her soul. "Don't worry; I won't hurt anyone. I'll be nice."

I said the words with a smile, grabbing the jagged stone again and twisting it, a strange hissing noise dripping from her lips. The musical tone of my phone broke through my laugh as I dropped her hand, and the Vil̇ys around us perked to attention before shrinking back again in fear.

"Father," I gasped as I put the phone to my ear, my shoulders tensing for what could come.

"Where are you?"

"In a street, near the cathedral—"

"Can you see the bell tower?" he asked, interrupting me abruptly with his hasty question.

"Yes." My focus snapped to it, my eyes narrowing in instant curiosity. "We are right below it."

"Good." Even through the phone, the swirl of his devious voice wound through me pleasurably. "I'm not getting much; she is still trying to block me. But the secret is in the bell tower. Somewhere above it, some kind of white space."

"A white space?" I asked, thoroughly confused now.

I stared at the bell tower, trying to see through the darkening sky. If I was supposed to find some magical white line, I had better hurry. In minutes, it would disappear along with the sun.

"Yes, it looks like it is a tear in whatever Ilyan created. You need to go through there." He didn't wait for confirmation; he merely hung up.

Wynifred's body jerked violently as he reconnected

with her in an attempt to leech more information out of her.

"Don't worry," I soothed, patting her head like a dog. "It will all be over soon, Wynifred. You are going to help me get inside this dratted fortress. Show me where they are keeping all those lovely *Chosen*. Help me give them a little gift, and then we can be on our way, back to your new mate. I am sure you are as excited to complete a bond with Edmund as I am to see it."

She screamed again with a wail of pain and fear.

Spinning to face her, my wide hand collided with her face in a loud thud that sent her spinning to the ground, the scream silenced into the low whimpers of her tears.

"Shut up!" I hissed as I kicked her away from me. "Shut up!"

I expected her to cower, to move back into compliance, but her screams continued, the sound loud as she pushed herself up like a dog. Running along the asphalt with jerky motions that were both haunting and frightening as she raced away from me.

My eager anticipation vanished into fear as I sent a stream of magic toward her, and missed.

With one jump, her body was a child's paper airplane, up and down, rolling awkwardly as if she had been thrown off a cliff in reverse.

"Wynifred!" I shouted as my magic streamed after her, attack after attack missing as she tumbled through the air before disappearing into the white line I had missed before, the line I probably would have missed if it wasn't for Wyn's little escapade.

When my phone rang again, I answered it without hesitation, a smile quickly widening on my face.

"She went into the cathedral—l"

"Without you?" He began to scream, to rage, but I cut him off.

"Don't worry; I'll get her back. She showed me right where to go."

His response was a snarl, "Then go."

With one sharp click, the phones disconnected, and I took off into the air, soaring right for the white line Wynifred had shown me, my shield tight as I pushed through the tiny opening and into an asylum that we never would have found otherwise.

The second I came in contact with the barrier, it was as though I had been hit by a truck. I couldn't breathe. The strain was so great I wondered if it was nothing more than a Stutter gone wrong.

I tried to gasp for breath, fear growing when it did not come. The weight increased until I was forced out to the other side, my body hurtling end over end toward the ground.

With a snap of fright, I checked my shield, verifying my body was shrouded, only to stare at the spinning world, the ground moving too close for me to truly be able to land safely.

In a rush of fear, my magic pulsed, sending me back into the air, my hair flying as I landed on the roof of the familiar bell tower in what I hoped to be silence, even though it was anything but graceful.

Thank goodness no one had seen.

Regretting my choice in shoes, I looked over the packed courtyard below me, hunting for any sign of Wyn. She was long gone.

On her way to Ilyan. To help. I had minutes before he would know I was here.

Men, women, and even a few children moved through

214

the open square like ants, their movements disjointed, panicked even. Fingers were pointed toward the building that still gushed smoke from the massive hole in the roof.

It was pathetic. If one simple explosion could work them up to that level of hysteria, how could they even hope to master themselves during a war? This was going to be easy.

One jump and I soared down into the courtyard, my wind gentle enough that, unless someone was really paying attention, they wouldn't even notice anything beyond a light breeze. Careful to keep my shoes silent this time, I straightened, the tense exhilaration of what was to come heightening through me.

"I knew he was right. No one should act like that ..."

"But if she can't even control her magic ..."

"Did you hear what Ilyan ...?"

"I saw the smoke. That was no ordinary magic."

Snippets of conversation bounced around me as I moved toward the place I had agreed to meet Sain. The frightened voices pulled me right into what had happened, right into the possibilities of what I had walked into. Listening to them, watching their mannerisms, it didn't take a fool to put things together. Sain had done his job better than I expected.

My soul danced, a smile spreading over my face as I leaned against the wall, taking in as much information as I could, each word a vital clue toward my father's plan.

Suddenly, it was very clear I was going to take much more from this trip than the destruction of Ilyan's army.

In a way, I was sad I had missed whatever show Joclyn had put on.

Crazy Queen Joclyn.

That was the single downside to all of this.

Shaking my hair down my back with the thought, I lifted my chin with excitement just as Sain sidled up beside me so closely I was afraid he would run into me.

The fool.

"Watch where you step or lose your feet," I warned with a hiss, my voice clear even though I was still hidden from view.

Sain jumped at the warning, the motion slow and controlled, before he took a step away from where my voice had come, toward one of Ilyan's men who was making a beeline for him.

"Stay close," he growled at me as he stepped toward the man, his demeanor changing so abruptly from what I had seen less than half an hour ago that I did a double take, staring at him in disbelief.

He stood tall, his eyes wide, his jaw set.

When he had stood before my father and I, he had been a weakling, a pathetic bug that wasn't even worth the squish. Right then, he was powerful, commanding. He was something I had never seen before.

My heart thumped as I watched him, my magic stretching toward him in a type of needy hunger I had felt days ago when we had stood in the snow, and he had talked about Joclyn's disposability.

This was the same man from then, but not the one my father had seen.

I stared, trying to understand exactly who this man was and how deep whatever game he was playing went.

"Sain!" the man called as he reached him, his voice eager as several others turned toward the exchange. "The Queen... is she all right? Have you heard anything?"

Sain shook his head as if he was about to deliver the

news of a death, his eyes downcast, even though his shoulders remained straight and taut.

"It is the end; I'm afraid," he sighed, his voice breaking with what I was positive was feigned emotion. "I am going to be with her now. All that can be done is to pray to the Well of Imdalind that all will be well. Excuse me." Sain bowed gently to the heartbroken man before he stepped to the side, his posture clear as he walked through the hordes like a God, the former sheep parting before him like waves in the Bible.

With a start, I realized I hadn't moved. I stood still, my heart thundering in my chest in disbelief, in what I was refusing to accept as awe. I moved then, my feet tapping loudly as I attempted to catch up to my charge, realizing for the first time how much power this man really held.

People continued to call out to him as we passed, desperate for information. Most of the time, he would wave them off, a few muddled replies passed back and forth on occasion.

"It takes strength to be a Drak. We can only pray now," he continued to say on repeat, the redundancy making it clear he was trying to get through them as quickly as possible. Otherwise, I was in no doubt we would be there all night. His pride wasn't something he had ever been able to hide, and I was realizing with a start that he wasn't holding back here.

Not anymore.

"Only those who are chosen can hold a Drak's power," he repeated as we finally broke through and turned the corner into a long hallway, the familiar vestibule the same as it had been hundreds of years before: brick and open casements, plain and simple. Monks quarters were never ornate.

"Here," he announced, waving to the side even as he continued moving. "The first three doors here."

Fortunately, it seemed everyone had congregated on the patio, so the hallway before us was barren and forgotten.

At least it would make my job easier.

With one flash of magic, I let my shield fall away, shimmering to the ground like some elegant gown, revealing my tall frame.

I was going to enjoy this...

"Where's Wyn?" Sain asked from halfway down the hall, his worry catching me off guard. It was so different from what I had seen in the courtyard a few minutes ago. His mask was back on, it seemed. Everything about him was starting to make sense.

"Dear Wyn got away." The acidic honey dripped from my voice, burning away any romantic ideas he might have had. "Don't worry; we will find her as soon as we are finished here."

I smiled while he cowered, and with one click of my heels against stone, I moved toward the low voices that were filtering through the heavy doors. Their mumbles filled with curiosity and worry.

We didn't hesitate. I didn't even look at Sain before we walked into the room, the large barracks I briefly remembered as a child now lined with beds and filthy people I was moments from killing.

I smiled at them as their eyes widened in shock and awe at our sudden appearance. Men sat up a little straighter as they saw me, women straightening blankets and flattening tangles of hair. My smile grew at their insecurities, at how instantly they began to worship me.

It was a blessing to them to be able to see me and Sain before I was to end each and every one of their lives. I would have, too, if the Black Water hadn't erupted within me. If the door hadn't slammed shut, trapping me in with Sain's scream, the agony matching my own as a sight embraced me—embraced us. The vision of the future, past, and present was so powerful I had no idea where it had come from or what was going on.

It was all I could do not to scream as a kaleidoscope of images barraged me, sending me to the ground in pain. My own scream echoed in my ears. Except, it wasn't just my scream. It wasn't just Sain's ...

There was another.

One that was much clearer, one that was full of more pain and agony than either of ours. Even without seeing, I knew who it was because I knew who the sight was coming from, and I knew what had happened.

Joclyn's magic.

It was more powerful than I had ever assumed.

And she was taking us all down with her.

CHAPTER 19
OVAILIA

My screams echoed loud and hollow in my ears as the sights came. One after another, they flashed with violent aggression, showing me things I had heard rumors of and I had heard my father speculate about. Things I had killed people over in an attempt to discover.

And now, I saw them all, flashing before me in strobes of color and light: burning homes, hushed conversations, the slow twisted murder of a man. And through it all, pain ripped through me as though I was being ripped limb from limb. As though someone was inside of me, digging around.

In a flash of red, the barrier over the city exploded into fragments of light and color, a second later the vision shifted revealing Edmund and Joclyn walking down a beach, laughing in a joy I could not understand. Then there was a scream, and Ryland stood before me with a child in his arms while Sain laughed in the corner of a cave, madness clear in his eyes.

Flashes continued as I screamed, as I tried to escape.

And then it was all gone.

The visions, the sounds, the pain.

It was all gone except for a blinding white light that left me standing in a white room. The makeshift hospital, Sain, the mission, the agony of my body—it was all forgotten.

"Hello, Ovailia," a calm, female voice rang through the white as if it was inside of me. I was confident it was familiar, yet I couldn't place it.

Lurching at the sound, I tried to twist to see what was here, but I barely moved. Even what little movement I could force provided me with the same view—the same, blinding white light.

There was nothing save for white. No one save for myself.

"I'm surprised to see you here, but then, with who your father is, I am not so surprised."

"Hello?" My voice shook, the vibration of it so heavy it disgusted me. My lips curled as I attempted to move, finding myself even more restrained than before. "Who's there?"

"I am here."

I could have punched someone with the redundancy of the answer. "And who are you?"

"I am a Drak. You are not." The voice came without hesitation, but this time, it was heavy, angry, suffocating. It reminded me so much of the anger of my father, of the violence that would follow. I cringed against it, my spine curling together as I braced for whatever was coming.

"I am ..." I started, not quite certain how to finish the sentence, the uncharacteristic fear making it hard to form thoughts.

"A Drak? Oh no. You pretend to be, but you are not. You are not stable." The tempo of the voice increased, and I cringed, hating how childlike and vulnerable I felt in this place, how something in the voice was bringing that out in me. "You would do well to fix that … before it ends you."

"Who are you?" I asked again, genuine fear now shaking through me.

"I will not permit you this. You are not a Drak." With those last few words, the sight shifted, and the white world I had been trapped in fell away, sucked into a black void and replaced by a golden glow I didn't recognize, the same images I had seen before flashing again.

The pain rushed back as the sights began, as everything I had seen played before me. The same scream came from my mouth, the same pain wracking my body. Except, everything was playing in rewind.

Edmund and Joclyn walked backward over the beach. Blood rising from rocks like rain. The massive barrier snapped back around the city like a glove.

The images were not only moving backward; they were being sucked from my mind. They were being drained from me, as if I had never seen them, drained from the world as if they never were.

The scream increased as the pain in my head did. Whatever was happening to me was turning me into a sniveling fool. Even when my father controlled me through the Black Water, the pain had never been this severe, this debilitating.

No matter how much I tried to fight it, nothing could take the weight off. Nothing could free me from the prison I was trapped in.

My mouth opened wider as the scream grew an octave, the sound more musical than it should have been for the amount of pain it represented. I listened to the sound, vaguely aware of the beauty behind it until it began to change, to swell and condense into words. Words I under-stood, even if I couldn't control them.

"The gift of future has been restored," I said, keenly aware I was not the only one talking. I could hear Sain's voice right alongside mine, which meant the sharp scream I was positive belonged to Joclyn was echoing the exact same thing. "The magic was spread too wide but has been returned. The son will rise, the son will fall, and all the blood will cease to flow. The time is now. It grows too late. Kill the fool before the slate. Love no longer seeks revenge. Your power has come to an end."

I cringed as it continued, a million hidden meanings seeping from behind my lips as my mind tried to make sense of it, but before I could, it was all erased and the barracks drifted back into view.

The voices of dozens of confused and frightened Chosen rumbled like bees in my ears, the smell of rosewood and antiseptic making my head spin as I tried to stand. I fought through the ache that rampaged my body, knowing I couldn't stay here if I wanted to finish my task. I tried to look as elegant and frightening as I always did, but these people had no idea who I was. Even though they had reveled in me at my first appearance, they had just seen both Sain and I collapse to the ground.

They all looked at me with the fear I had come to expect, but this wasn't based on the fear of death. It was based on the fear of confusion. I would have to change that.

I needed to take control of my one clear asset first.

The sharp clack of my heels echoed through the large room as I walked toward Sain who was still lying on the ground, curled into a ball like a despicable child.

"Get up," I growled, my foot moving swiftly as I rolled

him over, the man flopping onto his back like a lifeless puppet. "You're pathetic."

"They know," he said furiously as he glared at the ceiling. "I needed more time. But they know."

"They know what?" I snapped, my lips curling as I watched him, waiting for something more, but he lay there, his eyes grim as he stared straight ahead. "What happened to the powerful man in the courtyard? You're pathetic."

His spine straightened before I turned away from his pitiful display, unsurprised to see all eyes on me. I was going to have to play this a different way.

Smiling sweetly, I took a few steps toward one of the girls closest to me. She was young, perhaps not any older than her mid-twenties. Her face had been scarred and ravaged by my father's wonderful creations; the deep cuts hadn't even started to heal, thanks to the poison in them.

"Hello," I said sweetly, careful to put as much honey in my voice as I could. I was convinced I had overdone it by the look of even further confusion the woman gave me. "Sorry about all that. It seems your queen summoned Sain and I into a sight. Her magic has been a bit out of control lately. It affects all Draks when it does that."

"You're a Drak?"

"Who are you?"

"Is the queen okay?"

"What is happening?"

The questions came in a barrage, words crowding around me as I stood.

"I am one of the first," I said, the lie comfortable against my tongue. "I hold the Drak magic within me."

I will not permit you this. You are not a Drak. The voice ran through me, the same one from the sight, and I flinched, the smile slipping from my face as a fear I didn't quite

224

apprehend seeped through me. My memory tried to pull at the sight in an attempt to understand, but there was nothing there.

"You saw."

I jumped at the voice so deep, that I spun in fear, my eyes wide as I came face-to-face with the same powerful man I had seen in the courtyard.

Sain's eyes were hard, his jaw stiff, a power I had never felt from him before flowing off him. But now I felt it, warm and wanted.

"You saw the sight," he repeated, the strength in his voice growing.

"Yes." It was the only word I could get out, but it was enough.

His eyes narrowed before he smiled. The grin was wide and beautiful.

"Perfect," he gasped, his joy confusing me. "You'll work perfectly."

"Sain?" I asked as he stepped away from me to face the confused people who were still intently focused on us. But he just shook his head. Now was clearly not the time.

"Is she a Drak, Sain? I thought you were the only one of the first?"

"No, she is not a first, but she is special. Ilyan sent her to help you. She has found something that can cure you even faster, help your magic grow." The once again pious man walked through the beds like a God.

"How?" she asked, the admonition in her voice evident.

"Sain, darling," I beckoned to him, his back straightened as the room of confused Chosen looked between us. My magic continued to move toward him, the memory of the man I was bonded to so strong I was starting to have trouble breathing.

"Yes, my Ovi," he whispered seductively, stepping closer to me than he had since the night of our bonding, and even though his hands did not move to touch me, his distance still secure, our magic had completely wrapped around one another in a fusion of power that was dancing a very dangerous tango.

"Am I of your kind?"

"You are part of me," he whispered.

I hadn't expected that.

"We need to leave," he hissed, his strong voice low enough that I was positive only I had heard him. "Every Drak was pulled into that sight. They know what I've done."

"What have you done?" I asked, a small spark of elation twisting through me, the danger that surrounded us making it grow.

"You will know soon enough," he said through his smile. "You are going to help me."

Reaching forward, his hand gripped mine, his magic flooding me in a cold bath that sent a shiver up my spine. His magic. It was so different. So powerful.

"We have to leave here."

"Leave?" The elation drained from my body as my agitation skyrocketed.

"Yes. Now."

"I will leave when my job is done," I corrected him, dropping my hand from his in anger. "Your place is here."

"Not anymore, Ovi, and if you and your father want use of my sight, we are both getting out of here *now*. She wants to take it, I only barely escaped. Unless we move now, I will be of no use to anyone."

He had barely finished speaking before his eyes plunged to the color of sight I had seen so many times before, sight I had always been told was only possible with Black Water, and yet, he stood before me, a mug or pitcher nowhere to be found.

Something serious was going on, and I had no idea what, which agitated me more.

"Your plan will work. Wynifred is gone to us. We must move."

I didn't need to ask how he knew what I was planning, how he knew my concern over the loose end I had released inside of Ilyan's confines. I had seen the black of his eyes, and if he said I would succeed, then I would not doubt it.

My smile stretched.

"Wait for me outside," I instructed.

His own disreputable smile matched mine before he swept from my side, departing through the solid door without a second glance, leaving me, again, wondering exactly who he was.

I watched the door close before turning back to the scatter of people whose eyes were still focused on me, although fear had begun to take the place of curiosity.

Not that it mattered, anyway. In no more than a few short minutes, all anyone would hear was their screams.

CHAPTER 20
WYN

"Mommy?"

I had been here before, I realized. I had been in this white, shapeless space. I had been in this place where my body was nothing and everything.

How had I gotten here?

I remembered running away from the cathedral in an attempt to save my friend, to save myself, to save my daughter. Then, I remembered running into Sain... and then there was nothing.

Nothing but hate and a swirling mix of grey streets and a broken city. I remembered Edmund's greasy smile as I walked toward him, unable to control it, unable to stop. The shard in my pocket, the thing I had left the safety of Ilyan's cage for, had betrayed me.

Sain had betrayed me.

My scream had reverberated in my ears as the painful pressure of a stab spread from the center of my hand; then there was this familiar space of nothing and everything, of nobody and everyone. I was floating amongst it, part of it.

"Mommy?" The voice came again, eagerness I didn't

recognize pulling through it. "I think she can hear me this time!"

A garbled voice I couldn't quite make out cut through the fog in answer, the sounds oddly distorted as they ran over me.

"Okay," Rosaline's little voice squeaked. "Mommy, open your eyes. I'm here."

Eyes.

I didn't have eyes. I was nothing... wait. This was the same as before, with Ryland and Sain ...

Like a battering ram, it hit me—the memory of that moment, of Sain telling me to find my body, of promising I really existed, that this comforting mist of nothing wasn't me.

I wasn't me.

But that voice...

That beautiful voice...

It was real.

And if I was real, if this was real ...

I opened my eyes.

I opened my eyes to the dark grey stare of my daughter, to her little, upturned nose, to the dimple that sprouted on the right side of her face when she smiled, to the curtain of dark hair that fell around her cherub face.

She looked at me with this amazed shock, with so much happiness flowing through her that the last memory I had of her meant nothing, and this happy, little girl, this girl with the dark eyes so expressive they took your breath away, was all there ever was. Everything else was a cruel nightmare.

"Rosaline?" The single word broke away from my shock, soaring from behind the mind-numbing disbelief that had filled me.

"Mommy!" she screamed with tears running down her face, long streams of salt water that ran over my cheek and pooled in my hair as she fell on top of me. The lanky strings of her arms wrapped around me in a familiar embrace I had never thought I would feel again.

"Rosaline!"

I couldn't think beyond the numbing happiness that had overtaken my body, the way my heart swelled and throbbed and ached and screamed, and every emotion and every fear and every horror flew out of me like a thousand blood-soaked birds.

The guilt of failing my daughter, the fear of never seeing her again. The pain of loss. The agony of a love never returned.

It all fell away.

She was right there, in my arms.

And none of those things mattered anymore.

"Rosy," I sobbed. "My darling girl." I wasn't even convinced the words were distinguishable from my cries. Neither of us cared.

Rosaline sobbed harder, pressing her face into my neck in the burrowing motion that was so her. "I'm so glad you can see me this time!"

"This time?"

"Yes, when you were here before ... I tried ... You couldn't see ... But now you are here!" She pulled away then, smiling through her tears with the same joyful light I had always loved.

I fought the need to pull her back into me. The elated weight in my heart was so unfamiliar I didn't know how to handle it. It was going to explode out of me. In some ways, I wouldn't have stopped it. That way, Rosy could feel it, too. Looking in her eyes, I was positive she already could.

She smiled bigger, her little hand pressing against my cheeks as she leaned into me, kissing me on the nose as she always had.

"Is this real?"

Rosy's face fell, her brow furrowing as she pursed her lip in the five-year-old pout I had seen millions of other children do before and after her. My soul soared watching it line her face.

"That's a difficult question." The reply came from beside me, the adult, masculine voice even more familiar to me than that of the child who was sitting on my lap. After all, his held centuries of familiarity, centuries of time together before everything had shifted. Then, after Rosy, after me, it had changed, and he had never been the same.

Yet here, sitting beside me, he was the same.

"Cail." It was more of a gasp than a word.

"Hey, sis." He smiled, moving from where he stood in the oddly distorted forest to sit beside us, leaves crunching, twigs snapping at his movement. "It's been a while."

He was just as he always was, my foolhardy and mischievous best friend who had practically raised me. The anger in his eyes was gone; that twisted smile melting back into the impish scowl he had always reserved for me.

"Cail," I said again, fully aware I was caught on repeat. My eyes flashed between him and Rosy, the latter's smile increasing with each glance, her tiny thumb continuing to trace circles over my cheek.

"Wynifred," Cail said with a laugh, picking up a twig from the ground, the mutilated thing vanishing into thick tendrils of smoke at his touch.

"Am I dead?" I asked, unabashed, the solitary logical answer falling into place with a jolt of adrenaline.

Normally, the thought would bring fear, but there,

surrounded by my family, it didn't seem like such a bad ending.

Cail smiled, however, his head pulling into a small nod. "No."

"Then how ...?"

"You were here before with Sain and Ryland ..." He didn't even finish the thought; he let it hang as Rosaline leaned into my chest, wrapping her body around me like a little monkey. "We were here, too."

"The blade." My voice was hollow and monotone, a weird emptiness opening through my chest.

"Yes." His voice was as hard.

"I'm inside of the blade again."

"Well, your soul is, yes," Cail provided, his voice still a harsh line of pain. "Your body is another story."

My body.

My body that was being forced to walk toward Edmund, the man who had sought control of my magic since the day the fire awakened. The man and his terrible daughter who had looked at me with eager grins, who didn't even flinch when I screamed. They smiled, exactly as they always had: twisted, vile, malevolent.

I didn't need any other explanation.

I knew.

I knew because I had seen Ryland under the same kind of control, seen him turned into a puppet, controlled by the same piece of blade that had brought me here last time, the same piece I had pulled from Ryland's heart. The same blade sitting in my pocket.

And Sain knew.

He had seen where I had gotten the blade. He told me to run, and I had trusted him, but I had seen him standing in that street, right by Edmund with that same, haunting, out-of-place smile as before.

I should have known better. He was working for Edmund…

"What is he doing?" I asked, uncertain if I was referring to Sain or to Edmund—not that it mattered anymore.

"Walking around the cathedral, trying to make you show him the way inside." It was Rosy who answered, her body not so much as moving from where she lay against me. However, her voice had lost all of the excitement, dragging in a kind of exhaustion that sent the mother in me into high alert.

"Rosy?" I asked, but she didn't so much as move.

"She's fighting his control," Cail supplied, his voice awed as he leaned over to me, his hand soft as he ran his hand over the crown of her head. "She's disrupting his connection."

I looked between the two of them when a sharp pain shot through my hand.

"You can feel it, can't you? Where the blade is?" Cail asked as he snapped another twig into smoke.

I nodded, confusion still rampaging over what exactly I was going through.

"That's how he controlled Ryland. You know this. I was the one who impaled you with the blade the first time, after all." Another snap of a twig, his fists tight around the two pieces in his hand. I didn't need to look at his face, at the way his brow furrowed, to see his temper rising.

Hundreds of years ago, I would have calmed him. I would have shielded his heart. Right then I sat, not convinced of what I was looking at or even which Cail I was dealing with.

The thought slapped me in the chest, the similarities

painful. He had broken his mind when he bound the curse, just as mine was bound. Each of us, essentially two different people trapped inside a whole, every part fighting for space.

Even Rosy, in a way, was shattered into many: a child, a woman, an immortal trapped in a forever, having to live with what had been done to her.

My hold on her tightened again at the thought, but this time, she grunted, the stress finally getting to her.

"So he's controlling me the same way."

"Well ..." Cail answered, a small smile playing around his lips, "he's trying. Rosy is very good at stopping him. He is not a fan of her."

"It's my soul," she answered, her voice the same exhausted sigh as before. "He used my soul to make the blade. It's all of me. Everyone else is part of me—my soul, my blood. He can control it because he is my grandfather, because a tiny part of him is here, too. But I can stop him. Stop him from hurting my family—Uncle Cail, Uncle Ryland, Aunt Joclyn. All but Sain. Sain controls me. I don't like him here. That's why I couldn't see you before. But now you are here!" she finished happily before she collapsed on me again, her weight comforting against me.

"Now I am here," I whispered, the palm of my hand running over the crown of her head with a comforting weight that even she seemed to respond to. I was enjoying having her against me, enjoying the ability to run my fingers through her hair. To smell her.

"Where did you find the blade?" Cail asked after a moment, his voice tender as he pulled me away from the partial nirvana I had found.

"Inside of Ryland," I whispered, my heart tensing with

the fear that inhibited the memory. "I could hear Rosy call for me."

"So one of the six..." He sounded like he was talking to himself.

"Six?" I asked, not following what he was saying.

"Yes." His dark eyes pierced mine as I met his gaze, the intensity of them frightening. "I'm assuming you want to release us."

"Well, that's the plan, yes."

"Then you will need all of the fragments of the Souls Blade. You have to put it back together."

"You sound like you are sending me on some epic video game quest." I could barely keep the laugh in.

"Maybe I am." His deep chuckle bounced around the smoke trees that surrounded us, sending the distorted trunks into some kind of belly dance.

"We're inside," Rosy whispered from where she lay on top of me, her tiny proclamation pulling me out of my musing. "I'm trying to find Ilyan or Ryland so they can stop me."

"How long do we have?" Cail asked, his body rising above us as the trees distorted and swayed with the movement.

I didn't have long.

I tried to keep my pain inside, but it wasn't working. Rosy was tensing, her heart thundering against mine, her tiny fingers gripping my clothes as she too realized I would have to go.

"Where are the blades? Where are the other pieces?" I asked, quickly.

"You have Ryland's. The other ones I know of are inside Ovailia and Sain. There used to be one in me, but I have no idea what he would have done with it. And there is another that went missing about the same time you and Thom left that compound. So if you don't know where it is..." He faded off, obviously not wanting to say anything in front of Rosy, not that I blamed him. But it also wasn't like I could go up and ask Thom if he knew where a shard of our daughter's soul was.

I had to find another way.

I nodded in understanding, trying to ignore the pain that was steadily building in my chest, when Rosy screamed, her tiny body lifting off mine for the first time to look at me, her eyes mad and horrified.

"Rosaline?" I asked, too scared to hear the answer.

"You have to fight him, too, now, Mommy. You have to go."

"But I—"

"You have to go," she sobbed, her eyes glistening with so many tears she probably couldn't see through them. "You have to save Daddy."

I could barely breathe.

Daddy.

"Thom?" I asked, pushing the long strands of hair out of her face. "What's wrong with Daddy, darling?"

Rosaline bit her lip as she looked at me, her eyes so wide that it reminded me of those last moments. A sharp pain rocked through my chest as I fought back the horror, fought back the scream, and braced myself for the plea of help that would come from her blood-soaked body.

But it was just my little girl, my child wrapped in my arms, my child as innocent as Thom and I had tried to keep her until the end.

"Honey," I tried again, "what's wrong with Daddy?"

"Grandpa is trying to make you kill him," she gasped,

her eyes refocusing on me. "You have to save him. You have to go."

I looked from her to Cail in confusion. For once, Cail looked as confused as I was. However, he wasn't looking at me; he was looking at her, the little girl who clung to me, her hands wrapped around my arms so tightly she was most likely going to leave marks.

"Can you get her out of here?" Cail asked her. "Will he stop you?"

"He can try," she said, her face turning up in the same mischievous grin Cail always had. I had forgotten how much she had always adored and idolized him until that moment. "No one can stop me anymore." She smiled at him, a defiance I had never seen in her sparkling behind her eyes. It was a look I had seen a million times before, but not in her or Cail. I had seen it in me. It was something that even my brother did not miss.

"She is your daughter, Wyn."

"I know." I didn't think I could get any more than those two delighted words past the rock in my throat.

Rosy looked back at me, the power in her eyes mounting as she pressed her hand to my cheek, her lips soft as she kissed my nose again.

"You won't be able to come back here. I'll keep fighting him, but you have to fight now, too. Just remember what's real." It seemed like such an adult thing to say, and it caught me off guard.

I looked from her to Cail in some hope of an answer, but neither said a word. They looked at me with a combination of fear and support.

"I love you, Mommy."

"I love you, too, darling."

"Say hello to Daddy for me."

"Go kick his ass, Wyn."

And then they were gone.

The calm of the forest was gone. The comfort of her touch was gone. The companionship of my brother was gone. And I was left staring at the same war torn world as before, when I had walked toward Edmund without control. Except, I couldn't see straight, everything shifting. Everything faded in and out of focus as though they were bathed in a heavy curtain of smoke.

I was surrounded by it, surrounded by this uncomfortable heaviness that made it hard to think, everything fluctuating before me as though I had drunk far too much Slivovica. It was too much.

It was darkness, and confusion, and a screaming that never stopped.

I didn't know where it was coming from or why. For all I knew, it was coming from me, that the haunting, somewhat musical, sounds of terror were mine.

The disorientation was terrifying.

I tried to focus, tried to make sense of it as my shifting vision turned to a door I knew all too well, a door that swung open to reveal a man I had hovered over for months, a man I had been forced to watch slowly die.

"You have to save Daddy!" Rosy's shout echoed through me as if she was standing right beside me. "Fight him!"

The walls shivered as I took a step forward, my motions uncontrolled, the forceful movements jutting through me as my hand rose toward Thom.

"You have to save Daddy!"

No!

The word was a tiny spark inside my head as the magic grew, the powerful heat of it triggering a knowledge and a control that surprised me. My magic, my soul, they were connected. I pressed against it, grabbed at my power, forcing it back under my control.

The room shook so badly that, for all I knew, the earth had begun to shake, the earth had turned to liquid.

No!

The call was a shout inside my mind, a determination to keep fighting. It was then that I realized the desperate call was not mine, but that of another. One who was very quickly losing control.

Edmund.

No! It came again.

This time, I laughed.

I laughed as the shaking surrounded me, as the world came into focus, as I ran from Thom, everything drifting from black to grey until there was only black.

CHAPTER 21

ILYAN

I had spent the last thousand years avoiding this never-ending pain, ever since the black water had licked against my chest. The pain had gotten worse with each burn, with each drop of black water against my skin. The palm I had burned getting the water into Joclyn in a moment of life or death, the welt on my arm from trying to save her, each one had branded me. Now they burned, they ripped me apart as I followed it, as I let it devour me.

I followed the burn as I held Joclyn against me, her panic moving through me, her heart beating against mine. A burning force spread to every inch of me, tensing my muscles, tightening in my stomach. It grew until it was all I could feel, not just mine, but hers, as well.

The pain was us.

The magic was us.

It was everywhere.

And then it was gone.

Gone in one numbing blast, leaving me with the shadow of the Black Water and the familiar warmth of Joclyn's magic against my soul.

There was nothing else. No screams. No panic from my brother. I couldn't even physically feel Joclyn where I held her against me.

Heart thundering in my chest, I opened my eyes, expecting to see the calm silver of hers, expecting this nightmare she had been trapped in for the last few hours to be gone, for everything to be okay.

She wasn't there. Nothing was there.

I spun on the spot, desperate to find her, to find anything that would clue me in to what had happened. Nothing was there.

Just a blank stretch of nothing.

"Joclyn!" My magic stretched away from me in a frantic need to find my mate, my hands grasping through the nothing as though her sleeping body would be hidden beyond what I could see.

Nothing.

"Joclyn!"

No answer.

Just the painful pulse of my heart in my ears.

"Joclyn?" I called again, trying to follow the pull of her magic, trying to find her. Still, nothing. Nothing to follow, just the usual pull coming from somewhere deep inside of me. The immense wall of her power, so strong I couldn't even feel my own anymore.

She was all there was.

"Joclyn," I gasped as I collapsed to my knees, the demands of her magic so intense I was certain I would be strangled by it.

"Hello." A child's voice blossomed out of the white nothing like a gentle lullaby, jolting me out of my alarm as the weight of Joclyn's magic restrained me.

"Joclyn?" I asked hesitantly even though I knew it

wasn't her. It wasn't her voice, even if it was familiar.

"Hello." The warmth of Joclyn's magic pulled at me as the child spoke, an unfamiliar heat moving alongside it, moving through it like a shadow.

"Hello?" I looked up, hoping to see the child or some other creature standing before me. But there was nothing.

"Hello."

With a start, I realized the voice was seeping through me from the unfamiliar magic I had felt a moment before, a magic so close to Joclyn's that I couldn't tell the difference. The two powers spiraled throughout me as if they were somehow connected.

"Who is there?" I asked, my focus more on the magic as it enveloped me, paying attention to the way it moved, searching for clues as to who was talking or even what was happening.

"I'm here," the little girl said with a laugh, the sound similar to Christmas bells.

"And where is here?" I was tense, the fear and uncertainty coming back, despite the fact I could still feel Joclyn's magic calming me.

The lack of control and understanding I was experiencing made the emotions worse. I had been in situations of life or death before. I had been moments away from death. But even in those traumatizing moments, I still had control over my life, I could choose to live, choose to die, choose to fight, choose to give in.

Here, I had none of those options.

I could only focus on trying to figure out what had happened. On where I was.

My gut was telling me that, by following the water into

Joclyn's power, this was a sight, but I had seen her sights before, and they were not like this. I had connected with her mind before, and it was not like this.

"You know where you are," the voice came again with a laugh, the childlike game winding up my spine in agitation. "You were just thinking about it."

I cringed at the intonation, and Joclyn's magic flared within me at what was said, her own fear increasing alongside mine.

"You can hear ...?" It wasn't possible. Only Joclyn could tap into my mind, and then it was because of the way our souls had fused. This voice, however, was not hers. "Joclyn?" I spun on the spot, searching from end to end of the void to find who was speaking and understand what was going on.

"Joclyn!"

I could feel her magic. I could feel it swell as I said her name, the warmth of it seeping into my bones, wrapping around me in a comforting weight.

I gasped at the intimate touch, my eyes closing as my heart rate pulsed in excitement, each throb promising me she was right there, so close I could feel her skin against mine.

Opening my eyes, I expected the lights that were so common for us to appear among the void of white, but there was nothing. Just a powerful sensation that she was right there, standing beside me.

My magic pulled me toward her.

"I am not Joclyn, but I know her very well."

"How do you know her?" I asked, the simple phrase not making any sense. "Where is she? May I see her?" I kept my voice low as I continued to look into the nothing, my heart rate accelerating even as I tried to keep myself calm, to speak to this mysterious thing as I would a child. Regardless, something deep inside whispered to me that whatever I was facing was not the child they were masquerading as.

"No. She is not here anymore. I took her somewhere else."

"Where?" With a start of fear, the word erupted, long, hollow sounds stretching away from me.

I cringed, tensing as that strange magic increased inside me, the waves of it moving through me, blending with Joclyn's as the sound of the laugh deepened, heightened.

"She loved you very much, you know." All signs of the game she had been playing were lost in the heaviness of her voice, the sound of the echoed laugh running over it.

"Loved?" Fear and anger erupted with the single word as the laugh continued to resonate, as if someone had bumped a gramophone, the sound coming again and again.

I could feel my temper rise to dangerous levels, my anger increasing until Joclyn's magic swelled again. The warmth of it wrapped around me so tightly it was all I could focus on, and the weight of my anger seeped away with it, the sound of the laugh fading to shadows until it was just me and the heavy familiarity of Joclyn's magic pulling at my mind and soul.

The weight of her pressed against my chest, laying over my arms. Just as she was in the world I had come from, before I had been pulled into this place.

I stopped. The knot in my stomach spun abruptly at the revelation that was whipping me around. I had dismissed it so easily before, but there was nothing else ...

"You are thinking about it again," the child reiterated. My mind focused back on that room, on the girl I held.

"About where you are. About what this is. Have you figured it out yet?"

"This is a sight."

She laughed at my revelation, the joyful sound making it clear I was right.

"Yes." The laugh dripped off her voice. "This is where sights live, where they are created. This is a sight before it is seen, when it is full of possibilities and futures. This is the very base of Drak magic. This is where everything begins and ends."

"But there is nothing here," I gasped, knowing how ridiculous it sounded, I knew magic better than any, after all. But this, this did not feel like magic. I felt no power. I felt no strength. It was only the empty space of my mind.

"Possibility is here. Dreams are here. Would you like to see your beginning or ending?"

I didn't even have a chance to respond before her laugh rebounded, the sound loud and haunting. The white void I was trapped in shifted and spun as I watched, my mind aching with the change, with the force and power of the magic I was being subjected to.

With wide eyes, I watched the white meld into vibrant colors and shapes. My heart tensed at what I was about to see before the image landed on a room I knew all too well.

My parents' bedroom.

"Your beginning first, I think," the child's voice whispered, her voice mellow as the mysterious magic within me spread. The light, joyful nature of it seeped away my fear as I looked in on a room I had been in thousands of times before.

It was my own space within Imdalind now, but it hadn't looked like this for centuries. The wide bed took up much of the massive room, ancient furnishings cluttering the space. It was in this room that I had held Ovailia for the first time—her, a tiny infant; me, an adult.

Shocked, I looked as my mother lay in that same bed. Her blonde hair was wound in a long braid, the golden ribbon woven through the intricate weave. The length flowed over the bed, wrapped with my father's, the délka vedení královsk intertwined. Just as they did with Joclyn and me, I realized with a start.

My father sat nestled against my mother, his dark hair longer, his face softer, his eyes smiling. I didn't think I had ever seen so much joy in his eyes. I didn't think I had ever seen my mother so happy as I did right then, as they sat in that bed, holding an infant in their arms.

I watched the scene before me, I watched the father of my childhood memories. I had almost forgotten that smile, forgotten the way his eyes lit up when he smiled. I had forgotten how he used to love, that he used to know how.

"Give him the stone, darling," my mother whispered.

Father smiled at her before he kissed her, the longing apparent as she laughed, before pulling away with the same joy in his eyes.

Smiling, he placed a small, white stone against the hand of the child. The tiny, white bead turned a violent shade of blue the second it made contact with my skin.

My parents looked at the transition in awe. Mother gasped before she laughed while Father's smile expanded in awe.

The tiny birthstones usually took time to change, took time to connect with the infantile magic, time to pull it to that one spot. This time, it was instantaneous.

"You began there," the voice came again as the image of my parents faded back to the void.

My head spun with the strength of Joclyn's magic, the force of it like a confirmation.

"So this is what she is? It's amazing. *She's* amazing." Awe dripped from me at the remarkable reality I was facing, the void seeming to be more than the empty nothing I had taken it to be. "How am I seeing this?"

"You hold the water in your body, more than any other who does not bear my blood. You have been burned for the one who speaks to your soul, for the one who came to change it all. You have survived its pain and bonded yourself to the one the mud has chosen to guide my kind. You are powerful, Ilyan Krul. I will allow you to see." The childlike quality of the voice had deepened. The laugh that lived behind the words shifted to a darkness that wound through me, becoming an aged wisdom it hadn't portrayed before.

I spun on the spot, searching again for the owner. Still, there was nothing.

"So I am Drak now?" I questioned, the words feeling heavy and impossible. My mind still moved over what I was surrounded by in a wave, a desperation to understand gripping me.

"I have shown you your beginning, but it is no more than part of the story, you know. So much of what you have seen has been broken by one who should not be among us. You wish to see sight. You wish to know? I will show you what is true. I will show you what you should have seen. It all ends *before* it begins."

The deep rumble of her voice intensified as the magic did, melding with Joclyn's so perfectly they seemed to be one. My magic pulled at me as if they were.

"Joclyn?" I asked the space, my voice hollow as her magic responded, as the voice continued to meld into one I knew all too well. One I loved.

"This is sight."

I turned at Joclyn's voice, expecting to see her behind me, panicked about what I would face and unprepared for what came, instead.

For what I was plunged into.

CHAPTER 22
ILYAN

W ithout the slightest warning, I was plunged back into the maelstrom of light and sound. My head spun violently as my magic swelled, Joclyn's right alongside it. With a twist of my stomach, the void filled with images that moved so fast I could barely focus on them. I knew that, with each image, with each flash of past and future, what I saw would be permanently embedded into me, stored within my memory.

With a jolt of fear, Sain screamed in my mind, a young Dramin cowering below him, as the man held the boy against the wall of an alley.

A flash filtered to that of Edmund standing over Ovailia as he cut down her back, the flesh ripping open as she screamed and begged for mercy.

Wyn disrupted the scene, the girl barely a child as she sat, playing a game of marbles, simply to erupt in anger, her rage engulfing her in flames. Massive balls of fire soared around her before submerging her body, her skin burning away from the bone and creating something darker than I had ever assumed her to hide within her.

Her screams lingered in my ears as the image shifted to the French countryside where Joclyn walked by the house I had built for her so long ago. Her hair blew in the wind as she looked out at the waves, tears streaming down her cheeks.

My heart rate intensified at the image of my beautiful mate, alone, before it faded to me as an adult, teaching my brother Markus the traditional marriage braid. His smile was wide at his fortune, at being safe from our father, at what the following night would hold for him. That precious image shifted to his murder days later, that heartbreaking moment a flash of color in my mind. The haunting echo of Edmund's laugh rippled through me before I was plunged into the belly of Imdalind, into the tunnels I had blocked many years before, right to the deep wells of the earth.

Sain, my grandmother, the first of the Trpaslíks, and the first of the Vilý gasped for air at the side of the wide well of Imdalind. The Vilý wriggled as it coughed and sputtered for air, its bright blue wings unfurling from the sticky muck like a hatchling. With a scream, its sphinx-like face twisted as it awakened from whatever life it knew before.

One after another, they came, images of past, present, and future wound together so tightly my head swelled with the information, with the emotion carried on the back of them. I could barely process, could barely think. The throbbing ache swelled before the calm voice of the child came again, the voice high and haunting as it cut into the images bombarding me.

"This is sight as Joclyn knows it. You will know it too, so that you can help her carry it."

Joclyn's magic wound around my soul as the visions continued to slow. Like slides in a movie, they came and left, slowing until I was staring at myself from a time long before.

"This is sight," Joclyn's voice filled me, her magic pressing against me as I searched for her, unable to see anything except what the vision was showing me. "This is true."

Everything moved in overdrive, my soul frozen in fear as I watched myself walk down the hall of the main hall in the middle of Imdalind, right to the first pool of sight that the Draks had used for centuries.

It was the exact scene from hundreds of years before, Sain surrounded by Draks, their bodies still as they stood, enveloped in capes. He walked around the pool to greet me, everything silent as he spoke at a speed I could not comprehend, leaving the 'me' of the past alone by the pool's edge as I stripped off my shirt. Water rose up before me like a pillar, eating away my flesh as it connected with my magic.

"This is the end," the child whispered as the sight I had seen a hundred times before swelled within me, my heart ready to see Joclyn, to see what I had committed to memory so long before. To see that moment when I knew she would be mine.

But it wasn't.

It wasn't anything like I had been shown before. The words were the same, but the images, the meaning.

Everything was different.

And in one moment I knew that everything I had been working towards, everything I had expected, was shattered.

"There is one among us..." The familiar words were spoken in the unified voice of the Drak, the sound hollow and familiar.

The sight pulled me away from the massive cave, away

from the water, and into a world that was full of terrifying screams.

"...who seeks to change the magic, someone who seeks to kill the magic."

Screams filled me as I watched a destruction I had seen before. Instead of the dangers, instead of my father's laugh, I saw him. I saw him stand as he ordered the deaths of hundreds, Sain cowering by his side, his hands and feet in shackles.

My heart ached as the blood flowed, my father's laugh matching the voice of the Drak in perfect harmony.

"He seeks to kill the magic for his own personal gain. We see him as he fights, as he sheds the blood of us, as he sheds the blood of others. We see him as he stops the reign of magic, as he stops the time of ours."

The voices of the Drak faded away as the sight shifted. My father walked into the same hall of sight I had seen moments before, his face sallow and grey as his hands writhed, eyes wide with fear.

I watched him kneel before Sain, the old Drak grinning as he placed his hand on my father's head, the depth of his voice shocking.

"*You must kill them all, Edmund. All of the Chosen. The sight is clear.*"

"*There must be another way!*" my father sobbed, his whole body convulsing as he fell to the ground, the sight shifting as he fell.

Timothy ran over my sight, his squat frame tearing into a large forest clearing that was filled with an army. Thousands stood at the ready, bathed in ribbons of sun. It would have been beautiful if not for the reason they were there.

Edmund smiled as Timothy approached him, his face strained as he ordered the army out, as the sight shifted to the screams of hundreds of children, hundreds of Chosen massacred before my eyes. Vilỳs were captured, wings ripped from their bodies before they were thrown into a burlap sack.

I tried to scream, tried to run from the changes in the sight, but I couldn't move. I was forced to watch as the scene kept me trapped in a reality I wasn't ready to face.

"You, I'll save for last," Timothy hissed as he grabbed the blue Vilỳ I had seen born from the mud, his face defiant as he threw him into an oversized birdcage, locking the door with one flick of his magic.

"Is this now?" The echo of my own voice rippled throughout the sight, the sound distorted as it traveled from the past, reverberating throughout the sight as it shifted again.

"The time is now, My Lord," the Drak responded, their voice hollow as it shifted violently across the painful image I was faced with. "You alone will be brave enough to fight him. Where others will lose their lives, you will prevail."

Everything in me twisted uncomfortably as the sight faded to black, the dim light of a dungeon I had seen many times before coming into focus. Crude shapes of what I could assume were people drifted in and out of focus, and over it all, the deep, heavy words of a Drak flowed freely, the voice dead and monotone.

"The child is the key. If she lives, then the first of the Chosen is defeated. If she dies, then he prevails. Through her line comes the Silnỳ as seen before. Take her to the tallest spire and take flight. The time is now."

If I could focus beyond the sight, focus beyond what was before me, there was no doubt I would be crying.

One after another, the sights came, images flashing

from the beginning to the end of time as everything sped up.

Edmund, ordering the death of thousands. Edmund, wooing woman after woman as he took their magic, leaving orphans behind. Myself as I fought him, trying desperately to defeat him, to stop the reign of death he had unfurled on our kind.

The mumbling voice of the Drak echoed during the sights, the tempo of the sound increasing as it mutated into the distorted words I had heard before.

"In a time far ahead, near the end of the world, in a time when everything is changing and everything is new ..."

The images I saw shifted to things that were now so commonplace the wonderment I had felt the first time flitted away, leaving me confused as I watched cars, airplanes, and toasters.

"There will come a child."

In an instant, the image shifted. This time, I recognized it as what I had seen before, the image of the same woman being handed an infant, a beautiful baby girl who, even in sight, pulled at my heart.

"A child, an infant, a child whom we see. We see her when she's born. We see her when she's grown. We see her now, and we see her then."

The images were the same as I watched Joclyn's childhood, as I watched her grow. I watched her find joy. I watched her find her smile. I smiled, too.

"She is of the Chosen. Marked by the sign of the creature of fire, she has smoke in her eyes. A Chosen Child just for you."

These images were all familiar to me now: this love, this connection, this powerful magic we shared. I could feel it wrap itself around me. It all enveloped me as I saw our first kiss, flashes of magic I now understood and had already experienced.

"For in this child is power, power beyond belief. She is the most powerful. She will be the Silný, the one who protects us all."

Images twisted as I watched, subtle changes infecting the sights. I had noticed them, but none so apparent as when I saw Joclyn and I leaning up against a wall in the ruins of Rioseco, a battle unfolding around us. Flames surrounded us as we stood in each other's arms, blood seeping from a wound in her stomach and the long, golden ribbon trailing from the braids in our hair.

The délka vedení královsk.

"This is truth," the child's voice came right on cue, the tone deep and terrifying as the reality of what I was watching hit me hard in the gut.

I had lived this. But what was more, when I had seen this the first time, it had been different. It had been a different wall, a different battle. Sain had changed it.

"This is truth," the child said again, her voice boring into me as I stared, my mind numb as the truth was made clear to me.

My heart beat in a painful heaviness as the sight continued to unfold, the images broken as the prophecy cut through my focus. The words that had been Sain's now blended with that of the child, the chimes of her voice a haunting melody.

"You will love her," they said together, "but you cannot have her. You will protect her, but you will fail."

I cringed as the voice of Sain and the woman blended in and out with those of the Drak, rising and falling as the anxiety built. My muscles uncoiled in fear of what I was about to see: the image of Joclyn's death, the heartbreak that had haunted me for hundreds of years.

"This is truth," the child spoke over the prophecy of the Drak, her voice loud in my ears. "This is the end."

I thought I had been scared before, thought I had been ready for what was coming, but not anymore.

With those few words, a dread I had never experienced gripped me, the deep monotone of Sain's voice increasing the fear.

"The one bred to die."

It wasn't me who was screaming. It wasn't me who was mourning. It wasn't her body in my arms. It wasn't.

Not anymore.

Joclyn screamed in panic and pain as Ryland lifted her over his shoulder, his face streaming with tears as he walked away from something I could not see. Ovailia's laugh reverberated in my head as the cave formed around the scene, the broken rocks shifting as everything fell, as everything broke apart.

Underneath it all, I lay, spread out over the rocks, blood seeping from my body like a river, a crimson stain spreading over the grey stone I lay on.

The grey stone I had died on.

"What?" I heard my voice breaking in the sight, the echo of the past having a whole different meaning, given what I was now looking at, given the horrors of a future I now faced.

I could feel the voices of the Drak run over me, could feel the sight come to an end, but I couldn't look away from the image of my death.

I couldn't look away from the blood.

Pain I didn't fully understand drenched me in a force that sent a crippling ache over my chest. The ache grew as the vision faded away, leaving me gasping in the void, my hands clenching my hair.

"This is sight," the haunting sounds of the child's voice moved around the white void I had returned to.

"No!" I screamed, the volume of my voice reverberating with pressurized power. "No!"

"You have been born for something different than you assumed."

"What do you mean? What is this?" I yelled into the nothingness, spinning in place as I tried to find the owner. My magic stretched away from me in an attempt to find Joclyn. Nothing was there. Even though I had the distinct impression Joclyn was close, I still could not see her. I could not see anyone who could be speaking to me.

As before, it was empty.

"Everything you have been told is a lie. I have shown you truth."

My chest tightened painfully as she spoke, the dread and fear running through me, keeping a tight grip on my heart.

"Your life, your death, how you die, how you live, why you have the magic you do—"

"I won't accept this!"

"It was all a lie." The voice was a hiss now, and I could barely focus through the dread, through the anxiety that had taken control.

"No!" I yelled, my anger truly out of control now. "I won't let it be."

"Why do you say that?" the voice came again.

I spun toward it, this time coming face-to-face with a child. A little girl with bright blue eyes and dark curls down to her waist stood before me as if she had always been there, her head cocked to the side, as if I was the most interesting thing she had ever seen.

"You will die," she said, her voice light and calm, more reminiscent of how someone discussed food than the death of a loved one.

"Then I will die," I fumed, staring at the little girl with more anger than a child her age should ever see. "But I will not accept that I was born for something other than to protect the one I love. I will not die there. I will not fail."

"Is that all?" the girl said with a smile, her curls bobbing as she took a step closer to me. "You will protect her, Ilyan Krul—of that, the sight is clear.. It is your choice if you continue to stand by her, if you continue on the path of what is true. Or if you chose to find your own."

"Find my own path?" I gasped, not understanding what she meant. I had seen my death. There was no other option.

"There is always another choice in this life. There is always a chance to fix what was broken. Nothing is set in stone." She said with a smile, her nose wrinkling familiarly. "Would you choose to protect her, even if you knew it ended in your death?"

"But what if I can change it?"

"What if you can?" she said, that mischievous smile pulling at something deep inside me. "There is no promise of that. Make the choice, we will have to see what comes after. It is only after the choice is made that the path is known."

I looked around the space, at the void of possibility and dreams, or so she had said. But right then, it all made sense.

"Will you protect her?" she asked again.

"I will." The answer came without hesitation, the strong presence of her magic within me seeming to warm at the simple declaration, my heart beating right alongside. "I love her. I love her more than I have any other, and that love ... I will fight for her no matter what comes our way. I will stand by her, no matter what demons she faces, for she is of my heart, and I am of hers. I will protect her until my blood spills over those rocks as I take my last breath, and I will treasure every moment I have with her. No matter what comes."

I spoke to the child as I would to an enemy, my voice heavy and deep as my heart opened up, as I spilled out every emotion and desire and fear. As I let this tiny child see me.

"That is what I was hoping you would say." She smiled as the love and magic continued to swell inside of me. Her grin was wide as if I had said something more than what was in my heart.

"Does Joclyn know of this change?" I asked with trepidation, my heart thundering inside my chest with the truth of what this revelation could mean and what I did not want Joclyn to worry over. I would always be by her side. I didn't want to give her any reason to doubt it would ever change.

"You are true, Ilyan Krul."

My question lingered between us as the void faded back to the black, back to the flashes of sight which moved so fast I could barely see them. One vision blended into the next as my head throbbed, my body aching as if someone was pulling me into a Stutter without warning.

Gasping at what I was seeing, my mouth opened in the same wide scream of before. A deep, hollow voice echoed in my mind against the agony my scream held, against the fear that had debilitated me.

"The magic has been returned," the voice began, the scream fading to nothing as my own voice joined it, the dead, hollow tones foreign and frightening. "The son will rise, the son will fall, and all the blood will cease to flow. The time is now. It grows too late. Kill the fool before the slate. Love no longer seeks revenge. You will seek the end to end."

I gasped as the words finished, as the black of the world and the depth of the sight faded back into my room and everything erupted in noise and panic.

Dramin lay on the floor, mumbling about sight and white rooms. A panicked Ryland hovered over him. Jaromir sat, crying in the corner, looking around at each of us as though we were possessed, something I was confident was very possible given what had happened.

The weight I had been missing dropped into my arms as Joclyn's magic ebbed away, the flow of it lessening as I returned to reality, returned to her sleeping body that still lay against me.

"Joclyn?" I asked, my fears moving a million miles an hour in an attempt to understand what was going on. Everything felt like a distorted dream on this side.

She lay there, unmoving, as Dramin's mumbling slowed, the frantic shout from Ryland growing louder and louder.

"Ilyan!" he practically shouted, pulling my focus from Joclyn. Fear was etched so deeply on his face I was certain the lines would never fade. "What happened? Are you okay?"

"I don't know," I said in a panic, hating the lack of control I had. Hating that I couldn't give him more of an answer. The truth of what I had seen and what I was now facing was a confusing mess within me.

"We need to go."

Joclyn's voice erupted before me, the tone as deep as

what I had heard in the sight moments before.

Heart racing, I looked down, part of me expecting everything to be normal, but her eyes were still as black as they had been before, her face as blank.

"We cannot wait," she said as she sat up in my lap, her hand soft against my bare chest, her black eyes staring into me with a terror I never thought I would experience while looking at the woman I loved.

Ryland froze in panic where he knelt on the floor, an equally as shocked Dramin looked from me to Joclyn in terrifying wonder.

"Jos?" Ryland asked, his voice shaking as he stared at the girl who looked like she belonged in a horror movie.

"Ilyan," Joclyn spoke to me as if no one else was in the room, no one else had spoken. "We must go ... before it is too late."

"Go where?" I could barely get the words out. "Joclyn?"

"Ilyan," she said again, her voice bleeding into a deep panic as the black faded from her eyes, leaving me staring at the beautiful silver. "Ovailia is here. We need to stop her. We need to stop them both."

She had barely spoken before the cathedral erupted in screams, before the pained shouts of hundreds of dying people seeped through the walls and into me.

"Get them away from the door," she whispered, and then she was gone, vanished into the air with the tiniest of pops. The sound ricocheted in my ears as Dramin and Ryland looked at me, their faces full of the same awe and confusion I felt.

I didn't know what else to do. I jumped from the bed, following the pulse of her magic, following the screams, and rushing after her.

No matter where it took me.

CHAPTER 23
JOCLYN

R ibbons of time zoomed through the space of the Stutter in bright, colorful strips that finally made sense.

All of it made sense.

I had stood with the blood soaked future of me as every possibility, every future filled me. That's what this was, every moment. And I was moving through them.

I didn't stop to stare, however, my focus was solely on what was ahead, on the room that opened up at the end of the tunnel, the space growing brighter as I moved closer. The sound of their screams resonated through the tunnel of sight, the smell of death and smoke hitting against me like a wall.

A jolt of pressure rippled up my spine, the once peaceful hospital emerging around me as the Stutter fell away to a room engulfed in flames of red and orange, painful tongues of fire lapping against the people as they screamed, as death tried to take them.

The powerful shield I had covered myself with was barely enough to keep the fire from consuming me.

The heat was suffocating, their screams deafening as smoke filled my nostrils. The people around me were burning, screaming for help as I raced to the door that was obviously locked in place by a powerful spell. Some of the Chosen were clustered around it, clawing at the only exit in desperation.

"Move!" I screamed through the flames, not even giving them a chance to hear my command before my hand pressed against the air in front of me, sweeping them to the side in one quick motion.

Screams of surprise mixed with their panic. My heart raced as my magic flexed in a powerful jolt, the true strength of my Drak magic wrapping them in a shield as I held them in place.

My heart roared in a thunder, my magic a whirlwind as it spun around me, gaining momentum and power before I pressed my other hand in the air. Sparks of green and grey broke off from the whirlwind I was surrounded by, slamming into the wooden door.

The pulse was weaker than I knew would be needed to break through whatever was holding the door in place, but strong enough to seep into the oak, lighting the hallway opposite and giving enough warning to those on the other side to move away.

I hoped it was enough, that Ilyan had taken my command to heart and that he wasn't still sitting on our bed in confusion. I didn't have time to wait. I didn't have time to check. People were dying.

My magic swirled as my hair whipped over my face, the long, golden ribbon dancing gracefully through smoke and ash.

Terror soaked into me, the emotion fueling me as I

pressed my hand toward the door and released the powerful jets of magic in one quick flux.

With a boom like a gun the magic moved away in a violent ribbon of the brightest red. The attack smashed against the door in a blast that shook the cathedral. The heavy oak door shattered, splinters flying through the air as the rafters shook, tiny pieces of roof falling down on top of us.

Screams erupted from the flames as they fled from the burning hell, their movements broken and pained as they fought through the agony that consumed them.

I didn't know if I was exhausted or not. I couldn't tell. I felt the adrenaline, I heard my magic whisper to me what needed to be done next.

With the door gone Skříteks streamed in, trying in vain to rescue those who were left, who were still trapped, only to have their screams join the others as the fire engulfed them, too.

"Everything is burning beyond my control. We need rain," I whispered, my own voice echoing what was inside of me. The depth of it calmed and relaxed me as I lifted my hands to the sky, my magic swelling in a swirl of power that pressed against my skin, waiting to erupt.

With a howl of exertion, I clapped my hands and the power left me, rushing across the space in a wave. It pushed against the flames, the tongues of heat swaying like trees in the wind. A rumble of thunder shook the air as a bolt of lightning erupted from me, moving out of my skin as a cloud of smoke of the deepest purple erupted in billows that smothered the fire, suffocating it.

Jaw clenching, I watched it spread, panic moving over those who were left in the fire, their pain and agony mixed with an undeniable fear of what was happening, what I was doing to them.

Closing my eyes, I focused on my power as it pressed against the heat, as it swallowed the destructive force of the magical flame only to have it press back in a tug of war of dominance and destruction.

"Not today," I snarled, the Drak magic swarming my blood, boiling out of me in a powerful surge that migrated around the flame, engulfing it. Moving it into me.

Letting it become part of me.

I took it all, the fire falling away until there was only the deep purple of my magic left.

Screams of terror faded to nothing more than pained sobs as I stood there, breathing deeply, and spread my magic through the fog, my body calming as I connected to each of their powers, to their magic, and I felt them calm, felt them heal.

Skin knit back together, lungs healed from the boils that burned through them, hair regrew, hearts began to beat. One by one, I healed them. I undid what Ovailia had done.

The smoke faded back into the nothing between worlds as it drifted back into me, leaving me standing as a lone pillar amongst the destruction.

"Joclyn?" An echo of a voice ran over me, the same word coming to me on repeat as my sight pulled it into me.

"Joclyn?" Again it came, loud and clear, as Ilyan ran into the room, Ryland at his heels. Both men looked frightened as they moved through what was left of the door and into the graveyard of charred mattresses, burned blankets, and twisted bed frames. And through it all, perfectly healed Chosen, wide eyes as they stared at me.

Ilyan's magic pressed into me as he ran toward me, his eyes panicked and desperate. His magic enveloped me in swirls of comforting warmth, his usual need to know if I was safe coming on strong.

I sighed, letting the warmth connect to mine, filling in the gaps I hadn't realized were there before. My perfect match.

"Ilyan."

Ilyan pulled me against him, the heavy tempo of his heart echoing through me. I had never felt his heart beat so fast before, never felt fear vibrate through his soul so heavily.

I clung to him without question, letting my magic move into him, soothing away the panic that had gripped him.

'I'm okay, Ilyan,' I whispered into his mind, letting the words calm him along with the magic. His magic pressed further into me, searching for something.

"Ilyan?" With a painful beat of my heart, I looked up at him, my own shocked trepidation budding right alongside his. "What is it?"

"It's changed," he whispered.

"What's changed?" My brow furrowed in confusion as his magic continued to move into me, the heavy weight of it pressing against me as he checked me for injuries—no, I realized with a start, as he checked that I was me.

"Your magic, it's different."

He didn't look away, his eyes focused intently on me, his hands drifting from my back to hover above my arms, the fingers caressing the air above, as if he was afraid to break me, afraid to make contact.

"Different?"

"Your power," An electric pulse moved in the air that separated us. My skin was alive with energy, magic prickling with an eager need for his touch. "It's different. But the same."

"You're ... You're not making any sense."

"You can't feel it, can you?"

"Feel what?"

He tensed as I did, his fear seeping into me, his confusion increasing right alongside mine.

"Your magic," Ilyan whispered, "It feels the same... as what I felt in the child... in the sight."

"What sight?" I asked, already knowing the answer. I knew in the loud whispers of my magic, the way the Drak magic flared and showed me exactly what I asked of it: Ilyan standing in a white space, speaking to a dark-haired, little girl I had never seen before. Ilyan screaming, Ilyan with black eyes.

"You saw," I gasped, my eyes fading as the sight left me. "You were in the sight."

"Yes. When I tried to pull you out ... I saw ..." Ilyan froze beside me, eyes locked with mine, hands still hovering inches above my arms, the electricity rumbling between us. "What you are."

"And what am I?" My voice shook as he smiled, as the trepidation left him, melting into the deep awe he always held for me.

"A Drak. A true Drak. I can feel that now." I calmed at his confirmation, my soul rumbling with the knowledge that he felt what was so clear to me. He placed his hands against my skin, and our magic connected as it had done so many times before. Except, this time, for the first time since our bonding, our magic *truly* connected.

The lights of before were nothing compared to what now surrounded us. Lost in a universe of starlight and color, our magic moved and danced through the air in a carousel of energy. Together, our magic surged. The magic of the earth, the magic I had absorbed, the magic traveling on the wind around us: it all sparkled in a powerful surge that rose up like a wall.

With a mixture of fear and awe, the shadows of sight flashed in muted color before everything around us faded, leaving us standing in the middle of the ash-filled room, Ryland and the others staring at us with wide eyes.

"I guess I don't have to worry if it's you or not," Ilyan mused from beside me, a laugh hidden underneath his deep accent. "I don't think I could do that with anyone else." Ilyan looked at me with all the depth of the love I had seen so many times before, his body warm as he held me against him, his hands wrapped tightly around me.

I stood still as I watched him, my heart pulsing in anticipation and need. My fingers dug into his back with desperation for what was to come.

He smiled with that same coy look he always gave me before he kissed me, before his lips connected with mine and swept my heart and soul into him. The touch of his lips made it hard to breathe, something I wasn't really regretting right then.

"Well, that was new," Ryland interrupted with a snap, his face grim as he walked over to us. The elation seeped from my face as quickly as if I had been slapped. "We've got a problem, Ilyan. So, if you wouldn't mind waiting until later to finish this ..." His voice trailed off as he gestured to us, the smile on his lips not matching the hard light in his eyes.

"How many did we lose?" Ilyan asked, still holding me against him.

My heart plunged right to my toes.

"At least ten. I won't know definitely until Etma and the other healers are able to tend to them all, but *that's* not the problem," Ryland sighed, his eyes darting to mine for a second before returning to Ilyan, the tension building into a tight knot in my spine. "One of the survivors said that Sain was here as well, with a blonde woman they didn't know …"

"It was Ovailia." I answered gravely, a flash of sight erupting before me as I spoke, the same image of her running through the streets of Prague, overlaying the room.

"Where is she?" Ryland snarled, his anger seeping off him before he turned away from us, ordering one of the Skříteks to find her with a bark so loud several people jumped to attention, obviously surprised the order had come from him.

"Ry, she's gone." The hollow of my voice reverberated through my head as my eyes faded to black, the sight fluctuating as it pulled me farther in. Blood-covered hands were all I could see before it shifted, pulling out to Edmund's laughing face.

A jolt moved up my spine as his smile widened, as he wiped a blood-soaked hand against his brow, the laugh still ringing around me. I watched the vision, tension moving through me over what would come next. Instead, it faded, leaving me staring at the red of foresight before Ryland and Ilyan snapped back into focus.

Ryland stood in shocked silence before me.

"You won't find her here," I told him. "She's already outside the city."

Ryland's jaw tightened with a snap, anger clouding his eyes in a dangerous warning that I felt the need to move away from.

"Crap. That will make this next part worse, they were talking about Wyn, talking about needing to meet up with her before they left. Needing to find her in time for a bonding …" He stopped mid-sentence, and I didn't blame him. I felt like I had been punched in the gut, my lungs constricted so painfully that I wasn't convinced I would be able to force the air in.

"No." As it was, I could barely get the single word out.

"You are telling me that Wynifred is working for my father, as well?" Ilyan's voice was a rumble of feral warning, his muscles tensing underneath me as his magic quivered with an anger I wasn't positive I had ever felt before.

"From what we are hearing." Ryland shuffled his feet, a tick I had seen so often I already knew what was coming. I could feel his discomfort rolling off him.

"What is it, Ry?" I asked.

His eyes met mine directly, his jaw so tight I was worried it was glued together. "We still can't find Wynifred, and Etma has informed me that she was seen in the court-yard a few hours ago before the cathedral collapsed. A few people saw her attack Risha—"

"Risha!" Ilyan yelled, his distress understandable. "What happened?"

"Etma says she is unresponsive but stable. She thinks Risha was knocked out." Ryland's voice cracked and broke as he spoke, his worry seeping through in waves of appre-hension.

Wyn and I had joked for months about his supposed crush on Ilyan's second, but I didn't think I had realized until that moment exactly how deep his emotions were.

That it was more than a crush.

"Do you need to go to her?" Ilyan asked, his voice caught between worry for his brother and worry for his people, his thoughts for them moving just as fast.

"No," Ryland said, his curls bouncing as he shook his head. I had a feeling he was trying to put on a brave face. "There is nothing I can do for her now. I will be more help here. We need to find Wyn, or at least try, before she attacks someone else."

"She attacked me, too," I announced. The memory of those moments before the sight had taken me pulled at my soul uncomfortably. Those vivid pieces of sight I was granted twisted inside of me. "I was trying to take that blade from her."

"What blade?" Ryland asked, the worry from before lost in the hardness of his voice. The intensity of it made me wonder if he already knew what I was about to say.

"She has a piece of the Soul's Blade."

"The Soul's Blade? How did she get that?" If I had thought Ilyan was teetering close to destruction before, it was nothing to now, nothing to the explosive way his magic roared through him, through me. Nothing to the feral growl that escaped his chest.

"I saw it in a sight. I saw her remove it ..." I stopped, my eyes flashing to Ryland, my memory pushing everything together in one, big clump. "She got it from inside of you."

Ilyan turned toward us as if he had lost his footing, his hair fanning out, eyes wide, jaw tight. If I wasn't as connected to the man as I was, I probably would have stepped away. As it was, I held still, facing the two brothers as differing levels of anger and confusion overtook them.

"She removed it from inside of me?"

"When?" Ilyan snapped, his anger rising as he turned on his brother.

Ryland winced at the tone, and a raw fear ripped down my spine. Pushing the emotion away, I stepped toward my mate, letting my magic flood him as I wrapped my hand around his.

"It was the room above the clock ... before we came here."

With those few words, my Drak magic flared, pulling me into that moment of Wyn kneeling before Ryland's unconscious body. A voice erupted around her, the pained sobs of a child causing her to flinch the same way she had before. Her whole body rocked violently as the sight fluctuated, a child taking her place. The same little girl I had seen in the alley sitting right where she had, the same blade resting in her hands, the same blood covering them.

"Mommy?" The child's voice cut through me, her eyes haunting as they turned toward me, pulling me out of the sight with a start, my chest heaving.

"Rosaline." I jumped at Ilyan's voice, his hands feeling like a dead weight against mine.

"Did you see?" I asked him.

"Yes. The blade is made from her soul," Ilyan said with a nod, my question lingering unanswered between us. "She must think she can free her daughter somehow."

"She is a fool," Ryland hissed from beside us. "My father used that blade to control me, to torture Joclyn, to kill her brother. What does she think is going to happen to her? That Edmund somehow won't take control? The second he knows she has it ..." Ryland's voice faded away, his eyes bright as they snapped right to his brother. "They spoke about getting her back to Edmund. He already has her."

"If Edmund has her, he also has her magic." Ilyan straightened his shoulders as he rose up to his full height, the power in his eyes emanating around us. "I have no way of knowing that they aren't all outside of our reach. Chances are that the three of them are already past the barrier, but we must let the guards know. We may still have a chance to find Wyn. We *have* to find her, and remove the blade. Ryland, you are my second now."

Ilyan placed his hand on his brother's shoulder, and

Ryland straightened under the weight, his eyes wide in shock. "Take control of this situation. Get people looking. Let everyone know the change in Sain, what has happened, and get as many people searching for Wynifred as possible. Let them know she is dangerous and not to approach either her or Sain on their own. They need to come right to me."

"Dangerous," I repeated the word, knowing it wasn't that far off, not after what happened in the cathedral.

I looked toward my hand, expecting my flesh to be falling off the bone again.

"Normally, I wouldn't consider her as such, but given the situation ..." Ilyan paused, his focus shifting between Ryland and I. "If she doesn't have control of her magic, then we could very well all be dead by morning. Find her, Ryland."

"Yes, my lord," Ryland gasped, his voice seeming to be stuck in his throat.

"Ry," Ilyan sighed, his tone clipped as he pinched the bridge of his nose again. "I am still your brother, and if you call me 'my lord' one more time, I will beat you up like the mortals do—boxing or whatever they call it. Heaven knows you need more of that in your life."

Ryland nodded before moving away, winding his way through the few Skřiteks who remained, beckoning them away, his hands moving fast as he began issuing orders.

Everyone exited the room, running to their new tasks as Ryland tried his best to appear strong as Ilyan pulled me out of the room, running past the Skřiteks who looked at us with curious eyes. We raced down the hall toward the one place we all knew Wyn to be when my feet went out of from under me, the faintest clink of glass echoing over stone as whatever I slipped on sped away.

"Are you okay?" Ilyan clung to my hand for dear life, his

heart rate accelerating in a panic deeper than what I would expect from a little fall.

"I'm fine," I whispered, my magic already pulling me back to whatever I had stepped on. My magic whispered louder with each step, my Drak power screaming.

It was a vial, a tiny glass thing filled with swirling green fluid that was dangerously close to leaking out thanks to a large crack along the side.

"Ilyan," I called, my voice strangely hollow as my magic pulled. My fingers were inches away from picking up the thing when sight pulled into me. One simple image of Ovailia dropping the same green fluid onto Thom's skin was all I needed to see.

"Mi lasko?" Ilyan's voice pulled me out of the sight with the force of a gun, his fear escalating as I looked up to him, my eyes wide before I pointed down to the vial below us where the green was now spreading out and over the floor like syrup.

"Don't touch it," I instructed, my voice shaking. "It's what Ovailia used to hurt Thom. It's what she was going to use on all of them."

His eyes grew wider as I looked at him.

My sight pulled me forward, flashes of images I could barely make out, before Ilyan came back into focus.

My lips spread into a wide smile. "I think I can use it to save him."

CHAPTER 24
OVAILIA

S ain's ragged breathing echoed through the stone hallway, grating on my nerves. I recoiled at the sound, at the way his feet dragged against the stone, the way they always had when he walked.

His left leg was slightly turned, dragging like he couldn't quite lift it off the ground. This time, however, the scrape seemed to be a little bit more pronounced, the drag a little bit longer.

But after what I had just seen; I no longer thought any of him was real.

My heartbeat increased to match the sounds, unfamiliar fear rising up in me as I second-guessed my decision to bring him here; but after his cover had been blown in the cathedral, what choice did I have?

Perhaps I should have just killed him along with all the other Chosen back at Ilyan's now foiled safe house. Except after what I saw in him, the man I saw... I couldn't.

He had shown me who he truly was.

And all that he had done.

And I liked it. I liked him.

My lip curled, heart tensing as I turned to face him, pulling us to a stop right before the corridor that would take us to my father's chambers. Sain's broken gait slid to a stop after mine, his shallow breathing stopping as though he had turned it off.

He probably had.

"What are you?" I hissed into the silence, still staring ahead.

"I am a Drak." Even though it was a whisper, his voice had changed, that firm command tingling its way up my spine. The tap of his shoes resonated as he moved closer, his steps firm. Stable. "I am the first of my kind. What are you?"

His voice was a hiss in my ear as his hand moved over my hair, his fingers soft as they ran down the long strands, his knuckles tracing down my spine. My magic certainly pulled at the touch, his own connecting with mine in a dark cold.

Shivering, I pulled away to face the man who, as I had seen in the cathedral, looked neither weak nor old. He stared at me with that confidence and power that threatened to pull me to my knees. My magic pulled toward him as if it could sense the change, as if it hungered for the strength he held.

"You didn't answer my question." His voice was a low rumble of power as he closed the gap I had left between us.

Heart racing with each step he took, my mind begged me to attack him, to end this. My magic however, was keenly aware of the powerful change in him. I hungered for him.

"What are *you*?" he parroted back to me. He was now so close to me that all I could see was the deep green of his eyes. "Are you your father's pet?"

"I am not his pet," I barked, the anger finally plowing through the desire.

"No? So you are his servant, then?" He spoke slowly as he moved even closer, a smile creeping around his lips as he pressed himself against me. His hand rough against my hip.

"No."

"So, you are like all the other Chosen. You are his slave."

This time, I erupted, my anger boiling right to the surface as I rushed him. My skin heated against his as I wrapped my hand around his neck, pushing him into the rough, stone wall we stood beside with a jolt. His eyes widened in shock at the force, his smile still a grating insinuation as he looked down at me, not a drop of fear lining his face.

Bastard.

Clenching my teeth together, I pressed him against the wall again, slamming his head against the stone.

"I am not his servant," I hissed, my anger boiling as he continued to smile.

"Then what are you? Because you seem like his slave. You do his dirty work. You take the punishments for each failure without question. You dote on him, and he what? Spits on you? Slices down that beautiful back of yours?"

Without warning, his hand snaked around me, his fingers soft as they moved under my shirt and up my spine, tracing the ragged scar. His magic was a deep rumble as it moved into me, pressing into my core. I sighed at the caress, my magic reacting with a powerful flare.

Attempting to focus, I stared at him, the glare fading as the Black Water within me reacted to his magic. The poison pressed against my spine as it tried to connect with the man who controlled it.

"So that is how you can see. He put the water inside of

you ... Beautiful." His eyes grew wide and greedy as his hand fanned over my back, the cold spreading over me.

I could have sunk into him. Let him take me. I would willingly let him do anything to me... No! What was I thinking?

I pulled away from him, heart thundering in my chest, back straight, as I tried to decide if I should attack him or not. It would be easier to turn him into my father and be done with it. But I couldn't think, the pressure in my chest increased with either option.

"So, a servant," he mused, and my gut twisted at the insinuation. "But more than that, you are a science experiment, as well. He doesn't value your existence at all."

"Don't spread such lies, Sain!" I hissed, my magic seeping from my fingers to spark against the stone in railroad tracks of lightning.

"You are worth so much more than that," Sain whispered, ignoring the warning of my magic, his smile distorting his face as he grinned. "So much more."

"No!"

Sain's eyes widened at my shout, his focus leaving me for no more than a second as he looked to the hall behind us. Warning was clear on his face before he stepped away, his back arching into the familiar cower, his shoulders hunching, his foot turning in.

The powerful man I had stood in front of a moment before wilted into the disguise, one that fooled me for centuries. Sain, I realized with a start, was more than a man giving false sights, more than a man manipulating the leaders on either side of this war, more than some pathetic game played by a pathetic man.

He *was* power.

Sain looked up at me as the loud, hollow noise of footsteps echoed through the hall behind us, the sound mounting as one of my father's guards came to investigate the noise.

"Ovi," Sain whispered, his voice deep and strong as he looked up at me from his folded position. "The water within you is strong, as strong as you are. No one else could hold that and use it like you have, like you can. He doesn't see that. He doesn't value that. He doesn't care. But I see what you truly are. I see what you can become. I see your strength. Be alert, Ovi. No matter what you say, he will only use you. Don't let him. I know another way."

Frozen in place, I stared at him as the rhythm of the steps behind me ripped against my pulse. Sain had barely ceased to speak when he collapsed to the ground in body-seizing sobs.

"Ovailia!" Damek's voice cut through the cries unexpectedly, my spine jerking as I turned toward him, scowl already in place. It was easy with him, even with all of the confusion over what I had just witnessed. Over what Sain had just said.

Damek withdrew under my gaze, his eyes wide with fear as the sound of Sain's forced sobs continued to ring around us. I couldn't help smiling at the fear that crossed over Damek's face. At least I knew I could still make people wilt before me.

"How many times have I told you," I snarled, the fear on his face increasing as I stepped toward him, "not to call me that?"

"Yes, my lady." He cowered, his back moving into a curve so low I was certain he had been practicing.

"I'll be a good servant," Sain sobbed, the words so clear through his cries that I knew what his intentions were. I knew what he was trying to do. More than that, I knew what *I* had to do.

What I wanted to do.

I could only pray to the mud that it didn't end in my death.

Sain's twisted game weaved around me as I stepped toward him, kicking the point of my heel into his ribs with such force that I was confident I heard something crack.

His pain screamed against the rock and ricocheted back to me even louder than before.

"I'll be good. Trust me. Trust me."

"Pick him up," I ordered Damek, the poor man who still cowered behind me like the mongrel he was. "I am certain my father is expecting us."

Damek nodded before he walked over to the old man, his magic surging powerfully as Sain jumped and screamed in pain, his body writhing with whatever the sadistic man was doing to him. Expectantly, my heart jerked, an unfamiliar knot in my stomach springing to life at the sound, a remorse I never thought I would feel digging into me.

I tried to ignore it, but with each of Sain's screams it strengthened, until I was sure that I would kill Damek and run if I had to endure another moment of his games.

"Damek, don't play with the food," I spat, trying to hide the shake in my voice, but Damek heard anyway, his eyes a thin line as he turned to face me, the lapse in judgment unmissed.

"I'm not the only one who's playing with him, it seems."

Eyes narrowing in warning he stood before me, even though, this time, he did not recoil. The twist in my stomach intensified.

"I don't like having to constantly remind you of your

role with me, Damek," I hissed, my voice a hard line as I pushed the emotion away, spitting his name out like acid. "You do what I say. You listen to what I ask."

"No offense, *my lady*"—his words were as hard as my own, his eyes digging into me as he took a step closer— "but I am your father's guard, not yours."

Damek smiled wide and greasy as he moved away, dragging Sain behind him. His voice was loud as he howled in what I assumed was genuine pain. That was, until he looked up at me, his eyes wide and strong even as he cried.

Tension bound me as my magic stretched to him, as his eyes locked me in place. The words he had said before echoed through me with the force of a drum. *"Trust me!"*

Sain's sobs returned in full force as we turned the corner that led to my father's quarters. The hall was as destroyed and disheveled as it had been for the last few months; Ilyan's former belongings were thrown about, piled in ripped and broken heaps of rubbish, smears of blood and who knew what else splattered over them.

Entering into my father's quarters, however, the destruction from before was gone. The sterile space was even more frightening after the hall we had left.

Here, everything was in its place, everything the way he liked it. From the perfectly made bed to the tables covered with trinkets collected from his kills to the little girl who cried in the corner. My heart seized at the image, this one unfamiliar for the perfection he always demanded. The child looked up at me as we entered, her eyes wide and full of confusion and betrayal, her life meaning little more than the rags she wore. The shards of fabric drenched in bright red blood that I was sure was her own.

The reality of what I had walked into became frighteningly clear.

Sain's sob silenced as the tense weight of fear moved over both of us, Damek continuing to drag him over the floor behind him as if he had forgotten he was there.

"Master!" Damek yelled as he ran into the room, his pride seeping off him. "I found her lurking in the halls."

"Wonderful," Edmund's voice resonated from the bathroom where the sound of running water seeped from behind the wide door, the dark crack of the entry looming.

The door behind me closed with a snap, the guards that leaned against each wall shifting their placement as if on orders. The broad man who had been so kind to me the other day inconspicuously stepped before the door we had come in through. His face was grim as his eyes met mine, his lips a tight line.

The water from the bathroom stopped, and my father emerged from behind the door like a shadow, his hands still wet.

"Wonderful," he repeated as he extended his hands out, letting Míra dry them off while his eyes focused on me, digging into me.

I fought the need to step away. Fought the need to run. The intensity of his stare grew with each beat of my heart that passed, each low draw of air.

He smiled, patting Míra on the head roughly, her back arching painfully at the pressure. A small sob seeped from her as she fell to the ground, her body folding into itself. He didn't even seem to notice; he just looked at me, his steps slow and calculated as he moved closer, a wide smile spreading over his face.

In the hall, Sain had smiled at me, but his was not like this. Sain's smile was in power and strength. Edmund's was in eagerness for what he was about to do, for the blood he was about to spill. It was a look I hadn't seen directed at me for hundreds of years. My back ached with the memory, my heart tensing with apprehension so intense I had forgotten such an emotion was possible.

"I'm surprised to see you, Ovailia," Edmund cooed, his voice low and deep, the rumble of it infecting me. "I thought for sure you would have defected back to your brother after your failure."

"Father," I gasped, unable to hide the shake in my voice anymore, unable to keep the fear at bay. "I would never do that. You are my master. I am loyal only to you." As I said the words, I stepped closer to him in desperation. However, even as I said them, I was no longer convinced they were true. I was no longer convinced I would give my life up to this man.

Sain's sobs grew louder as I cowered before my father, the words 'pet' and 'servant' resounding in my ears.

Edmund's face fell, his focus falling on the imp for the first time. His eyes narrowed in an anger that trickled through the room like poison, Míra and Damek stepping away in preparation.

"I'll be good," Sain sobbed as Edmund came to a stop inches from me. "A good pet."

"I see you brought Sain back." He turned back to me, the back of his fingers running down my bare arm, leaving trails like ice against my skin.

I couldn't help it; I shivered.

I wasn't the only one. Míra shrank back at the movement, the guards tensing, even Sain quieted.

The color and emotion in my father's eyes were dead as he stared at me, the gentle touch of his fingers against my skin becoming a tight vise around my arm. A sob seeped from behind my lips as the bite of his nails pressed into me.

"Where. Is. My. Bride?" He spat each word in my face,

the grip of his nails against my forearm increasing, the sharp points digging into me, breaking the skin.

"I lost track of her," I hissed out through the pain, trying my hardest to stand up straight before my father, to show him I could take it, but finding it hard when I knew what was coming. "I tried to find her ... but we had to run ... Something happened ... They knew we were there." The words came out in strained gasps, my chest heaving as his fingers pressed into me, spreading the tiny cuts in my skin apart, causing blood to flow down my arm in hot rivers, pooling against my wrist and in my palm.

"What happened, Ovailia?" he growled, leaning in to press his face against mine, his breath hot in my ear. "What could have possibly happened that would make you think you could just leave her there."

"There was a sight," I gasped in desperation as Sain's cries faded to nothing.

The muscles in my back reacted as his free hand wrapped around the loose fabric of my shirt, the sheer purple cloth pulling against my abdomen before he ripped it from my body. His hand moving immediately to claw into the scar that lined my spine.

Hot, wet rivers moved down my cheeks as I cried, their heat matching the blood that coursed down my arm. I tried to move away from him, but he held me in place, leaving me staring straight ahead into the bathroom he had come from, the floor red with blood, a limp hand laying across the tiles.

So it wasn't her blood then.

"What sight?" Edmund's voice was deep in my ear as his fingers pressed harder against the tip of the scar.

I opened my mouth, ready to tell him everything, what I had seen, how we had killed all of the Chosen. It was right there on the tip of my tongue, my heart thundering in desperation to get it all out, my chest heaving in a dread of what would come if I did not.

But there was nothing to tell him, nothing I remembered. Nothing except a white room and a voice that echoed in my head, screaming at me, screaming through me.

"I will not permit you this. You are not a Drak." The words were not mine, but they came, anyway. They came through me, and my father's eyes widened in anger, my nerves twisting with the reality of what I had said. Of what had happened to me.

"What?" My father's voice roared as his blood-covered hand wrapped around my hair. "You have no right to this! To tell me I am not a Drak! And you are? I made you what you are, you filthy, little half breed!" He spat the words as he threw me to the ground, my feet slipping in pools of my own blood as I fell. "I am the first of the Chosen. I hold all of the magic!"

His voice was a roar and a rumble as I lay on the floor, my breath coming in desperate inhales of anxiety, of fear I was quickly accepting as normal. Emotions swelled as his foot pressed against my calf, the heavy weight increasing as he held me in place, as he pressed down, as the bone snapped underneath him, as his laugh boomed.

I screamed at the break. I couldn't help it. I couldn't stop the sound. It bled from me like a white flag; except, I knew this was a white flag Edmund would never accept. He reveled in the pain, loved the sound of punishment well met. With that one scream, I gave him what he wanted, but also the promise that more would be coming.

He fell on top of me as my scream reduced to a sob, the bulk of him sitting against my hips, holding me in place. I could already feel my magic working to repair the break in my leg, but it was pointless. More would come. I couldn't stop it.

I had walked into this.

"What am I!" he screamed, the parallels of his chosen question a cruel joke. I tried to fight against the weight, simply to have it increase; his barrel of a chest pressed against my bare back. "Am I a Drak?"

"Yes!" I screamed through the sobs, as his hand wound around my wrist, the weight against the joint intensifying as he bent it backward, the tendons straining with the unnatural movement.

"Are you a Drak?" he yelled as the tendons snapped when he pressed back even more.

My scream broke through the hiss of his anger and everyone around us stepped away.

"Answer me!" he screamed again with more force, more ripping, more blood moving over my skin.

"Yes!" I could barely get the word out from above the pain.

He dropped my wrist with a laugh, moving away from me. I wasn't dumb enough to think for a second that would be the end.

My eyes snapped open, a desperate part of my brain trying to formulate an escape plan, as I gazed into the dark green of Sain's eyes. His focus did not deviate from mine, the intensity of his gaze freezing me in place. He should be cowering. He should be in pain, but he looked at me with a smile, his eyes flashing from black to green again before his voice drifted over to me.

"I know another way." Sain's voice was an unheard whisper, the repeated promise stuck inside of me as my father wrapped his hand around the ankle of the already broken leg.

With one yank, the bone separated, my desperate scream drowning out Sain's whispered words. I slid across the floor and back over the pool of my own blood.

"You cost me the fire magic, Ovailia," he hissed as he dropped me in the middle of the floor, the rhythmic grinding of metal against stone flinching through me as he sharpened a knife. "You cost me a mate. Imagine the magic we could have created."

"I'm sorry," I sobbed, knowing the words would never be enough, knowing he didn't care anymore.

"Yes," he barked, the sound of stone and metal stopping as he stood beside me, his bloodstained shoes inches from my face. "So I have heard. Again and again. *You are sorry.*" He sighed, the sound beating into me as he crouched down, the blade swinging before my eyes, reflecting the light of the room against me as he twirled it. "I'm getting tired of your excuses."

I flinched, expecting the knife to make contact, expecting a gash against my cheek, against my arm, against my back. I waited for it, but it never came. He knelt there beside me, the knife twirling between us in warning.

"I made a decision. I am going to send Míra to do the job you could not. I will send her into the cathedral to kill them all. It will be her first, real task, and because of that I'd like to offer you a deal." He paused, but all I could do was sob.

I couldn't find the words in me to formulate any kind of response. He just laughed, the sound deep and hollow as it resonated through the silence. He finally stood, his steps vibrating through where I lay on the cold, stone floor.

"If she survives, if she succeeds, then I will let you live," he paused, everything tensing as the sound of my sobs increased. I knew him too well to believe it was that easy, that I would get out of this unscathed, if not alive. "If she fails, you die. That is, of course, if you survive this."

He had barely spoken before I felt the icy chill of the knife, the sharp point pressing against the base of my spine.

I screamed before I felt the pain, before I felt the cut, knowing what was coming. The sound of my scream, of my pain, mounted as the blade sliced through me, splitting open the scar he had made centuries before, opening up the flesh all the way down my back. I felt the cold of the knife, felt the heat of my blood, and felt the burn of the water as it was released from its prison. Regardless of all that, all I could hear was the scream of my pain and the sound of his laugh. All I could feel was the grip of his servants as they rushed to hold me down.

"You are not a Drak."

CHAPTER 25
OVAILIA

I didn't know if it was the pain or the sound of my own scream that pulled me out of the black of my unconsciousness, but now that I was out of the blissful, pain-free prison, I wanted to go back.

Everything hurt. Everything ached and throbbed and burned; pressing against me, trapping me in place. I tried to move, but every shift of my weight brought more agony.

"Shut up!" a voice hissed in my ear, the tone so low that I didn't recognize it. "If you keep screaming like that, they are going to come back here, and neither of us really needs that right now. We aren't ready yet." Cold hands pressed against my back, the agonizing pain increasing before his magic moved into me, a wave of ice that flooded me in moments, numbing the pain and leaving me heaving, face down on a bed, warm rivers running over my skin, making it obvious I was still bleeding.

His magic took control, my own moving right alongside his, feeling every broken bone, every ripped muscle, everything my father had done to me. I was very glad I had blacked out early on.

"Good," Sain whispered.

My eyes fluttered open to a dimly lit room, everything cast in shadows so deep I couldn't really make anything out. Even the man who sat beside me on a bed I recognized as my own was covered in shadow. Although, why we were here and not in my father's preferred dungeon, I had no idea. It wasn't like him to keep people comfortable when he was torturing them.

"I don't want to keep putting you back together. You are of no use to me broken."

I cringed at the phrasing, so similar to what my father had spat at me before. Although the hatred in Edmund's voice was missing from Sain's, the inflection was still there, and I cringed, hating how weak and out of control I felt.

Somewhere in the back of my mind, I knew I should be scared, knew I should try to formulate a way to get out of this situation, to make it to Ilyan. I had done it before. However, I highly doubted he would forgive me this time, that he would give me sanctuary.

Not after everything I had done.

Even if I could escape, I would simply be walking from one death sentence to another. At least I knew that death at the hands of my elder brother would be pain free.

"What use am I to you, Sain?" I asked, each word sending pain over my spine, each word shaking out as I pushed past the agony to deliver them.

I expected a harsh rebuttal, expected some form of punishment for my retort. To my surprise, however, he laughed, the sound deep and rich as he rose from the bed. His magic left me as he walked away, and my body rippled with pain that I tried my best to ignore, my teeth clenched in stubborn defiance.

With a heaving sigh, he collapsed on a large, overstuffed chair I kept in the corner, his face and body cast in long, dark shadows, the blue and black moving over him like bars. The effect made him look like a villain in a movie.

"Well, good morning to you, too, gorgeous."

My heart tensed excruciatingly inside my chest as I tried to understand what I had been thrown into and wishing in vain I could at least move.

"What do you want, Sain?" I tried to say the words with as much warning and venom as I usually held, something I was marginally successful at.

"I want you to heal. I want you to survive what your father has done to you." He spoke slowly, the same depth permeating his voice, the same powerful undertow still weaving its way through it. Still, I hadn't expected that answer.

I also wouldn't believe him. "What do *you* want of me?"

Sain sat still, his face covered in black shadows as the silence stretched between us, his fingers twirling something in his hand, the shape of it long and dark. He then leaned forward, his face slowly moving into the dim blue light as he rested his chin on his fingertips, the depth of his eyes absorbing me.

"You were my mate for hundreds of years, Ovailia," he sighed, his voice calm despite the unchanging intensity of his eyes. "Is it so hard to believe I still care for you?"

I cringed. "Cut the crap, Sain. I don't know what you are up to—"

"You're right." He smiled, the grin menacing, the intensity of his glare rippling through me. "You don't, but you will."

Grinding my teeth, I found myself wishing beyond anything that I could rush him, attack him, do anything to hurt him, to make him spill whatever precious secrets he had been hiding from us for centuries. However, I was trapped, staring at him.

His smile widened before he rose from the chair, his eyes undeviating from mine as he stepped closer.

"Do you know what I am?" His voice was low as he sat down on the bed behind me, out of sight, causing my body to ache as the bed shifted underneath me. "You asked me that question before. I was wondering ... Do you know *what* I am?"

"You are a Drak," I hissed, anger rising from the loss of what little power I had held in the situation.

"What kind of a Drak?" His voice was soft and so close I was convinced he was leaning into me.

"The first." My heart raced as the bed shifted again, my muscles tight as he leaned over me, his arm and hand holding me in place.

"Oh, I am more than the first. I am the first, the last, and the only, something you couldn't possibly understand."

I froze, focusing on where his hand leaned against my side, my eyes wide as I searched in vain for some shadow, some sign of what he was doing. There was only darkness. There was only silence. I couldn't even hear his breathing.

"But I don't think that was really what you were asking, was it?" he asked.

I couldn't even bring myself to say anything as I lay underneath this stranger. His magic pulsed against me in that familiar need I had felt so many times before, the fingerprint of his power so different I didn't recognize it, despite knowing it was him.

"You wanted to know *who* I am." He was closer still, his warm exhale moved over me, fluttering through the loose strands of my hair, tickling my neck. I shivered, something he enjoyed judging by the laugh, the soft, airy chuckle that moved over my skin. "You want to know who you saw in the cathedral... in Imdalind. You know I am up to something, and you want to know what it is. You want to be close to this power."

"Yes." The word was more of a sob as he pressed himself against me, his chest lying on top of my back as the weight smothered me in an agonizing heaviness that awakened every pain he had so recently taken away.

"You must want to know very badly," he mused, moving his free hand to push the loose hair out of my face, his touch gentle.

I tried to wiggle, tried to move so I could see him, but it was no use. I was trapped underneath him, forced to stare at the shadows before me.

"Your father was right there, after all. Two words and you could have told him, told him everything..."

My heart beat faster at the realization, something I was certain he noticed with how closely he was plastered against me.

"But you didn't. You know I am right. Pet. Servant. Slave. He cares for nothing. Just as I intended. Look at what he has done to you. He has done it before you know."

"What are you—"

"Your father removed your spine, you know."

I froze as Sain cut off my confusion, the question I had been about to ask lost in the shock of the words he had spoken, the painful reality shifting over me.

"I watched him rip it from your body, squeezing the bones as the Black Water dripped from it, burning you ... Here," he informed as his hand pressed into my upper thigh with a spark of cold. My body cringed in pain at the touch, at the way the fire shot through my blood. "And here." He pressed again, this time on my back, and this time, I screamed, the sound loud and abrupt as fire shot from the welt and into my body, hot and aggressive, like a jolt of electricity.

Sain clamped his hand over my mouth with an abrupt desperation, his fingertips digging into my face as he hissed in my ear, "Shut up!" The scream stopped, even though the pain continued to intensify. "You are not healed enough for them to come yet."

He froze over me as the scream dwindled to nothing, the sound of footsteps a hollow beat in the hall beyond the door, stopping right outside of it. I could hear the guard breathing, could feel his impatience seep through the door.

This room was as much a prison as the dungeons below, I realized. It didn't matter where Edmund put us; we were still trapped, and I was still incapacitated. My fate, I realized with a jolt, was entirely in Sain's hands.

Slowly, Sain's grip against my mouth lessened as the guard moved away.

"What do you want from me?" I huffed the moment I knew it was safe, my voice pained and broken as I forced it out.

"I need your help."

I froze. He could have said he wished me to be his bride, and I would have been less shocked by the response.

"How can you need my help? You have all the power you need. You've been playing us all along."

His weight finally left me as he jumped over my back, the movement light as he twisted into my line of sight.

"Not just you, gorgeous." His magic flared as the massive chair slid across the floor without so much as a sound, his weight falling into it as it glided underneath him. "I've been playing everyone. I'm sure you've noticed. You're smart so I know you have. That's why you didn't turn me in. You like it. You like me." As he sat back in the chair he sent the shadows flickering away from him. As though they were scared of him. "That's why I let you see me."

"What are you doing?"

"Orchestrating," he said, his voice calm as he leaned forward, the playful glint in his eyes deepening, pulling me into them. "It's like I told your father before... It's like a perfectly planned game of chess... Oh! What did I say again?" He closed his eyes softly, his face calm and serene for the briefest moment before it melted to a blank slate, his eyes open with the encompassing blackness I had seen so many times before. "Two men stand; one will fall. Blood will drip. The game is played, and those with the most pawns will take the stage. Take your man and play the game, but be careful where your trust is laid." His eyes faded back to green as the words seeped into the darkness surrounding us.

The memory of that moment dug into me, frightening me.

"Hmm," he mused, more to himself than to me. "It seems that sight has changed. I guess we must play to match." He looked off into the dark for a moment before his focus snapped right back to me, the sight repeating on his lips in a low hiss I could barely make out.

"Be careful where your trust is laid, Ovailia," he whispered, the chair flying back into place as he stood, hovering over me like an oppressive bat. "I need your help. Will you help me?"

My eyes were hard as I looked into the man who, I realized, had more faces than my father. No, he had more pawns in the game. He was more than the king my father perceived himself as. He was the queen, and the game was in his hands. Just as his sight had said.

"How can I trust you?"

I had expected the question to startle him, but he smiled. The wide grin stretched his face awkwardly as he leaned away and pulled that same long pen from his pocket, twisting it in front of me. The deep red of the surface caught what little light was in the room, glinting purple. It wasn't a pen. It was a Soul's Blade.

"I pulled this from you when I was stitching your spine back together. It wasn't all in one piece like this. I had to find them all—all the little splinters he had spread through your body: some against your ribs, some fusing your spine together to keep the Black Water in place, one right through your heart. I pulled them out, one by one, and put them back together—"

"Why do you have that?" Fear gripped me as I stared at the vile thing my father had used against me time and time again. The magic was dangerous. It shouldn't be here.

"Don't worry." He folded the shard of Soul's Blade in his hand like a switchblade, his voice dripping with irritation, obviously understanding the panic on my face. "He can't control me. My magic is too strong for him to even try. I need the blade just as I need you."

I jerked away, not from the proximity, not from the fear of what he was saying, but from the actual meaning of what he had just said.

"I want you," he soothed, the tempo of his voice changing with those few words, the melody calming, like a song. "Can you trust me?"

His voice wrapped around me, his hand continuing to trail up and down my bare back in a calm rhythm, his magic moving into me, swirling around my own. Playing with it. I could feel it try to connect with mine. I wanted it to.

"Yes."

"I trust you, Ovi," he whispered as he leaned down to me, his lips soft against the hollow of my ear, his voice soft as he whispered to me. "I want you."

I shivered as his magic surged before pulling back. His touch, his soothing rhythm abandoned me, leaving me wanting.

"I want you, Sain," I gasped, part of me hungry for his touch, part of me confused as to what I was even saying. "I want to help you."

"Good, because now I need you to scream."

Instantly, the calm I had felt left. The gentleness of his voice was gone, and the beauty of his eyes had faded back to that dark warning, back to the greed and power I now knew was truly him.

"No!" I gasped in desperation, my heart rate accelerating with the pain I already knew was coming.

"Sorry, Ovi, but it is for the greater good. I promise it will be worth it."

I had barely heard the words when his hand pressed against my back, pressed against the base of my spine that was still trying to fuse itself back together. His grip was rough as he dug into me, as he snapped the fragile bones in two.

The scream erupted in a violent ripple, echoing in my head as the pain engulfed me. One vertebrae after another snapped as his hand moved up my back. The scream escalated until a shout reverberated down the hall, the deep anger of my father's voice mixed with them.

"I trust you, Ovailia. You will heal in time, so make sure you don't let me down," Sain whispered as he moved away, leaving me writhing in agony as he went back to the chair, curling himself in a ball, his eyes fading to black as he cried and muttered to himself.

I watched the change through my pain, my screams subsiding as the door smashed open, a beam of bright light painting the room yellow as my father, Míra, and at least five other guards streamed into the space.

"Shut her up!" my father screamed.

Míra jumped into action as she vaulted onto the bed, straddling me as her tiny hands clamped over my mouth, pulling my head back roughly in a move obviously meant to strangle me.

I gasped for air, the scream ending as the girl's magic moved into me, numbing through me before freezing me in place, my muscles and tendons and bones outside my control.

My heart beat in fear as she let me go, my face slamming into the bed with a rough smack, my body no longer responding to the signals I was sending to it. I was forced to lie lifeless on the bed and watch everyone in front of me.

"Play the game ... Play the game ..." Sain repeated in a low mumble from the chair, no one so much as paying him attention. But I watched him, waiting for some hint as to what he was going to do. As to what he wanted me to do.

"Nicely done, child," Edmund mused, his voice deep and dark as he stood over me. His hand was rough as he grabbed my hair and pushed and pulled my head from side to side. "You are learning."

"Play the game ... Play the game ..." Sain repeated, his voice rising louder as he finally pulled Edmund's attention away from me. The pride and joy in my father's demeanor left.

"This one, on the other hand ..." In three quick steps, my father was on him.

Sain's actions grew more desperate and pained with each tap of my father's shoes against the stone. The moment Edmund reached the old man, his head turned, his eyes black as he continued to mumble. The look froze Edmund in place, his shoulders pulling into a square as he laughed, the sound deep and low as Sain repeated the same phrase again.

"Damek!" Edmund's voice was loud as one of the shadowed figures pulled to the front, the scars that littered the man's face more obvious in the bright light from the hall. "Go and get me a mug. It seems I have more use for this one than I thought."

"Play the game ..." Sain repeated, his voice moving into a slow lull as the black faded, the green eyes downcast and broken as he looked around in fear to those who now surrounded him. His hands pulled into his chest in a move that I used to interpret as fear, as a broken man who was made to bend. "Edmund!"

"Sain." Edmund scowled as if Sain's shout of feigned terror was nothing more than a greeting. "You saw something."

Sain moved farther away as Edmund took a step closer, his hand moving to claw at the chair in a desperate need to escape.

"Y-yes..."

"What did you see?"

Sain visibly shook under the weight of Edmund's question while my heart, the single thing in my body that could move, thundered. Fear and pleasure mixed together in a weird blend of emotion as I watched Sain perform, and understood what was going on. What he had been doing all along.

"The girl ..." Sain gasped, his voice shaking as he raised a finger toward Míra. The girl stepped back in shock as Sain looked at her, his eyes flashing black for no more than a moment before he looked back to Edmund, his body shaking so badly it looked to be convulsing. "I saw her ..."

"You saw her *what*?" Edmund asked, his voice mixed between a gentle nudge and a snap.

Sain twitched at the inflection as if he was a wounded animal, the motions so similar to what I had watched him do for centuries while he was my father's captive that I felt myself surrender to him.

I was in awe of him.

"I saw her ... in Prague ... I know how to get her into the cathedral."

"Wonderful."

CHAPTER 26

WYN

"Wake up!" Her little voice was clear as she yelled in my ear as she had when she was alive, running into Thom's and my bedroom and jumping on the bed every morning. "Wake up!"

I could feel the bounce of the bed, the rhythmic motion moving over me like blankets being pulled down. I almost expected Thom's arm to wind around me, for him to pull me into him as he nuzzled my ear in an attempt to gross her out and scare her off.

"Wake up, Mommy! Hurry!" Her voice was more frantic now. She must be hungry. Maybe I could convince Thom to make her pancakes.

The bed kept jostling, all there was was the rhythmic movement of the blankets being pulled over my shoulders, over my head, and then back again. I wanted to tell Rosy to stop pulling at them, but the words wouldn't come. In and out, they moved, the blankets extraordinarily cold and wet, so much colder and wetter than I remembered.

"Wake up, Wyn!" This time, the voice wasn't Rosy's; it was Cail's. The shout was loud and abrupt in my ear as it

301

pulled me back into the reality of a red-tinted world. My eyes opened to wet cobbles and the blood red water of the Vltava lapping over my body as the tide rose, inches away from sweeping me away.

"What the hell?" I hissed, half asleep as I scuttled away from the waves that were trying to drag me under.

I placed my hands against the soaked cobbles, and nearly screamed at the pain that shot up my arm from my left hand, from the bright red blade that was still impaled through my palm. One, blood-soaked point emerged on either side of the destroyed skin.

It was then that I screamed.

Loud and frightening, my pain echoed around the old buildings, off the cracked windows and the abandoned cars. It moved away from me in a wave that, with one hiss, one shriek from a hidden Vilỳ, I knew was a mistake.

I swore. Loudly. After all, what did it matter if I was loud, I had already called every Vilỳ in a half mile right to me.

My joints ached as I attempted to pull myself up, legs shaking, chest heaving as I fell over my own feet, scuttling over the wet road like an injured animal. The world spun as I propelled myself forward, one foot landing in front of the other in a desperate need to escape the fanged creature, as well as any others that would follow.

And they would.

I raced away from the river, praying I was going the right direction, something that was nearly impossible with the kaleidoscope I was running through. My legs twitched as I tripped over them, the unbalanced steps sending me into walls and crashing against cars. The sound of each bang, each sob echoed through the street, creating the perfect path for the little beasts to find me.

I was going to get myself killed.

Snarled screams of the Vilÿ echoed through the street behind me, their gnashing teeth and beating wings echoing in my ears. They were getting closer. I was screwed. I was so freaking screwed.

Swinging my uninjured hand behind me like a baton, I tried to bring my magic up, ready to drop the filthy thing out of the sky before any more came. But, nothing happened. No flame, not even a spark. My magic was no more than a low buzz under my skin, congregated around the blade.

As if it was stopping it.

I needed to get it out, not that I could just stop and do that while I was running for my life.

I needed to get creative.

Dodging into an alley, my heart thundered as I leaned against the wall, listening, waiting for the thing to follow me, knowing it wasn't far behind.

With a hiss and a snarl, a Vilÿ came around the corner. I reached for it, wrapping my fingers around its neck and slamming it into the wall. My whole body shook as I held it there, staring into its dead eyes as it gnashed and fought me. Its little claws scraped against the hand that held it captive, but I didn't so much as flinch. Those tiny pinpricks of pain were nothing compared to the agony shooting up my arm.

"I remember you things when you were annoying little peacemakers," I spat, part of me wondering if he could even hear me. "*We must love everyone. Do not judge based on what you see.* The hippies would have loved you. You were almost as bad as the Drak."

It continued to snarl as it fought against my hold; even in my weakened state, it had no hope. I pressed harder, flattening my hand against it as I held it there. Slowly, it stopped trying to fight me, the sharp point of its claws digging into me less and less.

"I'm sorry," I whispered as its head fell to the side, wings sagging as I let it drop, lifeless, to the ground.

One, I could choke. Two hundred... ha. I needed to get out of here. I needed to get the damn blade out of my hand. To do that, I needed to hide. Not that it would make any difference with Vilÿs, but it would be better than going out into the middle of the street and waving my arms around.

Dragging my feet against the garbage-strewn floor of the alley, I clung to broken bits of mattresses, chairs, and the wall as I made my way to a large dumpster, the massive thing taking up most of the space of the dingy thoroughfare and providing me with the perfect cover.

Hissing in pain, I slid down the wall, sitting behind the dumpster, as everything that had happened from the last little while slammed into me. Attacking my best friend, to Sain, and then Sain standing beside Edmund, and Rosy and Cail, and Thom ...

"Thom," I said aloud, the frightening memory swimming through my mind—that moment as I fought against Edmund's control in a desperate attempt to stop myself from killing him.

No, to stop Edmund from killing him.

I had thought I was strong enough to face the demons the blade awakened, to save my daughter. But, Edmund was stronger. The blade was stronger. This dangerous thing had better not end in Thom's death.

I needed to get there in order to make sure he was okay, to give this dratted thing to Ilyan before something worse happened. I only hoped he could destroy it.

My arm exploded in a jolt of pain as I looked down at

my hand, at the blade and the dried blood that clung to it like a scab.

Closing my eyes, my other hand wrapped firmly around the end, the rock slick with dried blood, warm and uncomfortable to the touch. I breathed, part of me praying I didn't go into cardiac arrest. It would be like a band-aid, or so I said in my head. I guessed the analogy would be correct if the band-aid was made of massive leeches, barbed wire, and duct tape.

"Five, four, three ..." I didn't wait, just pulled, the action rough and quick as the thing dislodged from my hand with a loud, wet smack.

Every muscle stiffened in mind-numbing pain. It took all my willpower to keep the scream inside, to keep the agonizing pain hidden, and keep me safe from any other magical flying rats that were about.

I slammed myself against the stone wall, a new pain erupting through my skull at the impact, but even that pain was not enough to compete with what now ripped through me.

My hand burned, the hole of the blade that was no bigger than a pen spreading and widening as the flesh burned, as it curled and died. Stomach spinning, I heaved, the smell of blood and vomit so strong I could barely breathe through it.

Balling up the hem of my shirt as best I could, I pressed it against my hand in an effort to stop the bleeding that was now flooding from the golf ball-sized hole in the center. I still couldn't feel my magic. Nothing rushed to my hand in a mad attempt to stop the blood flow.

If I stayed here much longer, I would bleed out.

I had to move.

I had to fight my way back to the cathedral. I had to find Ilyan before it was too late.

Shaking, I attempted to place the shard of blade in my pocket, trying to focus on a world that was spinning and shifting before me. Everything shook. *I* shook as my body moved into what I was convinced was shock.

I leaned against the wall as I forced myself to stand, my eyes wide as I stumbled down the alley, part of me praying Ilyan would magically be standing at the top of the street.

No one was there.

At least there weren't any rabid Vilẏs, I supposed.

Using the wall as support, I moved back down the alley, my eyes darting in every direction as I tried to get my bearings, praying I was on the right side of the river, praying I was close to the cathedral.

I was on Latenska, the long street that moved over the river and stretched into Old Town, which was less than half a mile from where I needed to be. I hoped I could get there in time, or Jos would probably find me in a few days, face down in a pool of my own blood, surrounded by Styx lyrics.

I ran, my good hand clawing at corners and windowsills as I stumbled, keeping my pace as fast as I could given that my legs still weren't working right, and the added pain in my hand was making it hard to see straight, hard to think.

Everything ached, each step getting harder to think through. Of course, that might be due to the amount of blood I was losing. It snaked over my fingers, dripping onto the ground in a rhythm that was perfectly matched to the frantic pace of my heart.

I supposed I should calm down.

"Who needs blood?" I asked aloud, the words slurred as I turned a corner, the wide foyer of the cathedral opening up before me. The cathedral beyond the massive space was broken and smoldering as though it had been destroyed, as though they had been attacked. Staring at it, my mind struggled to focus on what I was seeing, trying again to recall what had happened. Ilyan's barrier made everything look abandoned from this side, but that level of destruction was a little excessive.

The last few feet to the cathedral seemed as long as a football field, the golden gate broken and looming so that it looked more like a gateway to Hell than to safety.

With all I had done in this life, I would certainly deserve that.

"Ilyan," I gasped, my voice broken as I took another step, my stomach spinning as much as my head was. Everything before me fell apart, black looming in and making it hard to see. "Ilyan," I gasped again, my broken legs twisting underneath me as I spun on the spot, collapsing as the world continued to twirl.

My head made contact with the heavy cobbles of the courtyard with a slap, the plea reverberating in the cave of my mind, the simple word mixing with a scream that flooded the air.

I wanted to tell whoever was screaming to shut up; they were just going to attract the Vilÿs. I couldn't get the words out. Staring ahead, shoes moved toward me, voices pulling through the screams in a weird echo I didn't understand.

"Wyn?" The voice resonated through my head like a bass drum, the same word coming again and again as the fear in the name increased. Maybe they could get whoever was screaming to shut up. "Wyn!"

"Help," I said, my desperate pleas barely above a whisper. "My hand. Help. Heal it." I wasn't confident they had heard me above the scream that wouldn't stop. I couldn't focus enough to know anymore.

Pain throbbed through my head as wide hands lifted me, then bouncy black curls came into view, the familiarity of them seizing through me in a wave of dread.

Edmund.

No. It couldn't be. He couldn't be here. He couldn't be.

It was then the screaming stopped, the terror taking its place. Blood sprayed everywhere as I flailed, nonsense spewing out of my mouth as I tried to get away from him, to fight. Screw fixing my hand, I would die trying to escape him if I had to. I would rather die than go through what Edmund had planned for me.

"No!" I screamed, "I won't marry you! No! Let me go! No!"

The calm heat of a power I didn't recognize flooded me, moving right to my hand, right to my heart as it calmed me, as it cauterized the wound in an obviously desperate attempt to stop the bleeding, to stop the hole from growing.

"Geez, Wyn," Ryland gasped as I stopped fighting, his voice breaking through my horror in that same weird echo I had heard before. "I didn't know you thought of me that way. I'm flattered, but I'm not interested."

"Ryland?" I gasped, turning to face the boy who carried me, but he didn't even look at me. He held me against him, his jaw tight, eyes focused ahead.

"At your service." His voice was chipper, but even I could tell he was putting it on, something dark edging beneath him, like he was trying to hide something. "We've been looking for you."

I didn't know what to say, my body felt very heavy and foreign as I lay in his arms, my magic slowly coming back to life as his filled me. Something, considering the way his brow furrowed, he was not happy about.

"Ryland?" I asked, confusion and fear rising up in me, barely able to get the one word out.

"Ilyan says I am to treat you like an enemy, Wyn."

I froze, so much for safety. By the mud, what had I done? I swallowed, looking away from the boy to the cathedral, to the barrier.

"Why?" I asked, my mind panicking over whether or not it would even let us through.

"You attacked Joclyn, Wyn. You attacked Risha." His muscles constricted at the last name, and the dread I was feeling dipped into me painfully. No wonder he didn't want to be helping me right now. "And last anyone heard, you were going to be marrying Edmund, which seems to be hauntingly accurate given what you were yelling at me ... I mean ... I do look awfully similar to my father—"

"I have a reason ..." I could barely get the words out, the selfish, pathetic nature of my excuse grating on me.

"A reason for marrying my father? I don't want you as my stepmother, and neither does Ilyan."

"No! I obviously don't want that, Ry! I mean, for attacking ..." I felt like I had been hit in the chest... or maybe stabbed in the hand. After everything, trying to pass off my selfishness as a *reason* for attacking my best friend was pretty pathetic. I guessed Ilyan had a right to tout me as dangerous.

Maybe I was.

No, I knew I was.

"We know about the blade," Ryland said, pulling me out of my quickly building panic with a growl. "And you should know better."

"Says the boy who attacked his mate *and* his best friend when under the control of his father—"

"That's different."

"How?" I spat, my temper quickly rising to a dangerous level, the heat of my magic rising to match.

I could still feel Ryland's magic as it attempted to heal my hand. I knew he felt that, felt the heat, felt the warning. It was something he obviously didn't miss.

"First, they were the same person," he barked as he turned his head toward me, his eyes narrowing in obvious irritation. "And second ..." He stopped in place, his arms tense as he halted barely steps away from the barrier, steps away from what my head had interpreted as safety. But he didn't move. He froze, glaring at the barrier with a jaw so tight I was concerned for a minute that it would snap off.

I knew why he had stopped, he knew as well as I did that the situations were pretty much the same.

Minus the whole marriage thing. *Ew.*

"I'm not going to attack anyone, Ry," I whispered, knowing exactly where his mind was. "I'm not working for Edmund."

"I know that, and I'm pretty sure Ilyan knows that. But I can't disobey orders, either." The same fear as before moved through his voice, heavy and broken, everything tensing.

"You're not going to kill me, are you?" My magic flared in preparation.

I knew I was still weak, but I could hope I had enough energy to take on Ryland. I doubted it, and I didn't want to. But I wasn't going to go down without a fight.

"No, Wyn. Don't be ridiculous," he groaned, his voice making it obvious he was trying to make it light-hearted, even though there was something else there, something that made my muscles tense. "Can you stand?"

I nodded in answer, regardless of being convinced whether I could or not. Standing, I could probably do;

although, if I would be completely vertical was still a matter of debate.

Walking, however, I knew was not going to happen, and judging by the way the nerves on the left side of my body were jumping around, I was beginning to wonder if walking in a straight line was ever going to happen again.

I would never pass a sobriety test. Flying would be interesting, though.

With a deep exhale, Ryland set me back down on the ground, his motions careful as he made certain I could at least hold my weight before he let go, his magic leaving as soon as we lost skin contact.

I gasped as the powerful numbing balm of his magic left, the pain flooding right back through me. It jabbed through my arm and erupted in my head like a billion, little bombs all going off at once.

Tensing in pain, I fell to my knees, my body deciding not to hold my weight at all. Figures. Everything spun and seized, my stomach churning angrily as the pain threatened to do me in, everything vibrating as my stomach turned and twisted in a viable threat.

"Are you okay?" Ryland asked as he fell down beside me, his hand strong on my back.

Focusing on my breathing, I tried desperately to find something to stare at. If only the world would stop shifting and duplicating. Even Ryland was caught in some odd vortex of clones.

"I think so," I said, looking at one of the five Ryland's to choose from and hoping it was the right one. For all I knew, I was staring far off to the left.

"I'll take that as no," he grumbled. "I don't have any other choice, Wyn. Ilyan barred you from the barrier. Even if I try, it won't work. You are going to have to wait here. Can you hold on?"

I nodded numbly, still not quite certain if I was looking at the right Ryland.

My heart pulsed painfully as he turned from me without another word, his body swallowed by the liquid air that surrounded the cathedral. Everything became wobbly, confusing my already twisted brain more.

I didn't dare move as I focused on the spot he had vanished through, knowing he could see me on the other side. Chances were high that he was watching me. Chances were even higher that he wasn't alone.

I sat, staring at the cathedral, the distorted damage hard to make out with the way everything was shifting. For a moment, it looked like one of the main walls was about to fall in. Thank goodness it was the false reality created by Ilyan's shield.

I knew Joclyn and I had done some damage with whatever had happened before, but I would seriously be dead if it was that much. That alone would be more of a reason for Ilyan to put me on an 'armed and possibly dangerous' list.

The air moved as though it was a mirage, my heart rate accelerating in fear of exactly who was coming through and what I could be facing. It had been such a relief when Ryland had found me, and granted, the whole stopping-my-bleeding-before-I-died thing was awesome, but I suddenly found myself wishing I had bled out.

Edmund was a terrifying master, but Ilyan brought out a whole different kind of fear, one that made you simultaneously feel guilt and an unquestionable desire to be better.

It was irritating.

The man himself came through first, his hair a tousled mess, face covered in ash and soot. I looked up at him from where I cowered on the ground, my heart immediately moving into overdrive.

Something had happened, something more than me attacking Jos, something more than me being controlled by Edmund. The image of Thom in that bed, the magic sparking between my fingers, flashed before me, and I winced. I didn't dare ask, seeing the remains of a war on his face, seeing the anger creased in his forehead and his downturned lips. I already knew it was bad.

"We need to have a chat, you and I," Ilyan said, his voice a deep, oozing rumble as the air behind him continued to move, Joclyn and Ryland following him through the barrier.

I didn't even look at them. I knew better than to look away from the powerhouse I was faced with.

My heart was rampaging inside of me, everything twisting violently and increasing the pain I was stuck with. Nodding numbly in response, Ilyan squatted down in front of me, his tall frame folding elegantly despite the lankiness of him.

"Give it to me." His voice was harsh as he extended his hand toward me, palm up.

I hesitated even though I knew I needed to give it to him. It was why I had come here. I shouldn't have it. If I had learned anything in the last two hundred years, it was that.

My lips pressed into a tight line as I shifted my weight, fidgeting with my pocket in an attempt to remove the blade from where I had stowed it. My heart rate increased the closer my fingers got, the sound rumbling in my ears as Rosaline's cries intensified louder and louder and ...

Mommy!

Tears rolling down my face, I forced the thing from my pocket, trying to ignore the way she cried for me. The sound ripped into me as I extended the blade toward the man who had saved my life on more than one occasion, and I was quite certain he was going to do so again.

"Ryland," Ilyan said, his focus solely on the blood red shard of the blade I extended toward him, his lip curled in what was unmistaken disgust.

The boy stepped forward, curls bobbing as he handed Ilyan a small, metal box, the top of which opened on its own. Ilyan extended the empty vessel toward me, his intent clear.

Without question, I dropped the blade into the case, the sound of the screams and cries that came from the blade growing more panicked as the lid closed, Ilyan's magic sealing it in place. Then there was only an indefinable calm that stretched over me.

"What were you thinking?" Ilyan's voice was as firm as the lines in his face, the look in his eyes compressing into my shoulders as, for the first time, I looked away.

"She's my daughter, Ilyan," I gasped, hot tears moving down my cheeks. "I can't abandon her."

"She's my niece. She's my blood as well as yours." Ilyan sighed, my focus drifting to him, drawn to the calmness of his voice, to the soft hand that extended toward me. "Did you truly think I would abandon her as well?"

All I could do was stare at him, stare at the tears that welled in his eyes, stare at the gesture of his hand before me. My heart thundered heavily in my chest as I tried to vet what he had said, the guilt ripping me apart.

"I've been a fool." I whispered, he pressed his lips into a tight line, pinching the bridge of his nose as he shook his head. "I'm so sorry."

"Give me your hand, Wynifred."

Swallowing, I did as I was told, placing my uninjured hand in his palm, just to have him smile and drop it, picking up the other without question. Then his magic seeped into me as he began to heal it.

"I know you better than to think you would defect to my father, let alone marry him," Ilyan sighed, his smile fading back into the hard line I had expected. "But do something like this one more time, Wynifred, and you *will* force my hand."

I looked at him, his hand a vise around mine, his magic throbbing through me with a powerful flood of energy I knew was more in warning than in healing.

I stared at him for one moment, knowing I needed to trust him. I needed to trust myself.

And I nodded.

CHAPTER 27

JOCLYN

He was singing as his fingers moved through the wet strands of my hair. His magic moved through me with each touch, the sparks of him blending with mine more perfectly than they ever had.

It wasn't just here either. It was in our Tŏuha, where we had spent hours tangled up in each other, and it was in the shower before as he kissed me, our bodies flush against each other.

It had been different since I had emerged from that sight. Different. But better.

"Much better," Ilyan whispered, his fingers soft as they lifted and twisted more hair into my braid. He had obviously been listening. "Well, perhaps not better. Just right."

"Like it was always supposed to be that way." I spoke more to myself as I traced a scar that lined the inside of Ilyan's thigh. A fight gone wrong, was all he had told me when I asked, thinking about it now however pulled the sight right to me.

He was in a city, wearing robes that made him look like a prophet, saving a woman from a Trpaslík who clearly had insincere intentions. All I needed was the flash, but my magic gave me all the information, everything filling me as though I had always known. Including the fact that the blade he had been pierced with had been poisoned.

Made sense, it was his only scar that wasn't caused by black water and it looked just as nasty as the one that circled my abdomen. Although, running my finger over it now I was starting to wonder if it would heal all the way.

Like my magic would be able to heal it all the way now.

"I think it will," Ilyan responded, always tuned into me. "I don't know what happened to your magic. But the strength of it..."

"You've never felt anything like it," I finished for him. He had only said the same thing at least a dozen times in the last few hours.

'It hasn't been that much.'

'Yes, it has.' I chuckled at him and kissed the scar on his thigh as he secured the end of my braid with the délka vedení královsk.

His hands moved over the braid to trace the bare skin on my shoulders, on my back. I shivered at his touch and turned, kneeling on the floor as I faced him.

"Don't worry, I've never felt anything like it either," I teased, hands on his thighs as I lifted myself up, dragging my body against his, the warmth of my skin against his turning everything into a boiler long before I reached his lips.

When I did, I captured him hungrily, my nails digging into his thighs as he grabbed me, lifting me to straddle him even as he kissed me, as he nipped at my bottom lip only to trail kisses over my jaw... over my neck... all while his fingers traced the lines on my back.

"If you continue, you are going to ruin my braid." I was barely able to get the words out.

"Then I'll just have to give you another one," his response was a hungry growl, his teeth nipping at my collar bone before he flicked his tongue against the tender ridge of flesh. I jumped, yelping as he held me tighter.

"And then what will you tell Ryland when we are late for his confirmation council?" I didn't want to pull away from him, really I didn't, but we were actually on the clock. Plus our time was already tight thanks to all the extra time in the shower we had spent...

"Why must you be responsible?" he moaned in my ear, still kissing me even as he shimmied out from beneath me.

"My most humble apologies, my lord." I gave him a bow as I stood, and he promptly smacked the bare skin of my backside. Hard.

I yelped and jumped up, hand over the quickly reddening flesh.

"You deserved it for calling me that," he said in that low husky voice of his, pressing a kiss to the tender flesh before he sunk to the floor in the same position I was in, handing me the ratted mass of his délka vedení královsk. "And if you are not careful, I'll do it again."

Oh, he knew better than to threaten me, the tease. Good thing I knew how to get him right back.

"Okay, my lord," I whispered in his ear, biting at his ear before I began to run the brush through his hair and left him quivering and growling between my legs.

He settled down after a minute, helped along by my magic as it ran through him. Little pin pricks as I braided his hair. Something I was slowly getting better at.

"What do you think they did to it?" he said after a

minute and I dropped a strand of the braid. I already knew what he was asking. We had purposefully avoided this until now, and both of our minds had locked it away.

I know. I had checked as much as he had.

"What happened in there?" his voice was a whisper, his hand a firm support on my knee as his magic flooded into me. "How did Wyn's attacking you even unlock that?"

I shrugged, not that he could see that. "I think Wyn was trying to burn away a shield I had up, and ended up burning Sain's shield over my power instead. But that's just a guess. I didn't think to ask."

"Ask? Was there someone in there?" I could have sworn his voice was shaking.

"I saw myself." Luckily I had thought enough about this that I already knew what to say. "But it wasn't me as of now. She was like future-me or something and she clearly knew more than I did, and she was covered in..." I hesitated, the image of the woman flashing in my mind. "Her hands were covered in blood, her head in ash." I swallowed, shaking my head before I went back to braiding. Ilyan said nothing, so I went on.

"She told me how Sain had blocked the Drak power since the beginning. How the mud chose me to carry the true Drak power and she unlocked my sight. Showed me how to use it."

"How do you use it?" My fingers weren't even moving anymore, my hands had fallen, Ilyan's hair and ribbon only partially braided through his hair.

"I just... talk to it. It's always there with everything, and all I have to do is ask. It's like, I always know what's coming, what could be. Every possibility is inside of me." My voice had gone hollow as I sat there, staring into the

319

golden strands of Ilyan's hair as he sat before me, as he stood on a mountain, as he sat in a leather back chair, as he was propped up on green checked pillows I had never seen before.

"Joclyn?" I blinked, every image of the future fading as Ilyan swam back into view, his hands already wrapped around mine. How long had I been gone? He had even finished braiding his hair.

"It's a lot." My voice was still flat, as though I was trapped in sight. "I am sure there are things I can do, that I can see, that I don't even know. Everything just feels..." I stalled out, that calm of the white room, or the everything I had inside of me feeling too big for just one word.

"Limitless," Ilyan said, and I nodded, that one fit. He grinned, the look in his eyes almost making it seem as if he understood.

"You said the sight pulled you in, too?"

He nodded once, his lips pressed together, "Yes. I saw you, too. But not you of the future. You were a child. I didn't recognize you at first. You looked different, and you had blue eyes."

"Blue eyes?' I asked, he smiled in answer, his thumb dragging over the back of my hand and leaving a trail of sparkling magic behind. "So, before you received your mark then."

"Hmmm." Something was digging at me about that, my magic twisting at the nape of my neck as though it was trying to tell me something. "I always thought my eyes would have been green. Like Dramin's. Like Sain's."

At the mention of his name my sight reacted, flaring as it pulled me into sight. I only heard a whisper of Ilyan saying my name, the pressure of his hands against my own increasing before everything was pulled away and into that void again, the burn of sight flooding over me.

"The path diverged." My voice began, showing the image of Ilyan on the floor of that cave, of his lifeless body staring into nothing. The picture was so vibrant, and the connection with him so strong that I already knew there was no way that he wouldn't have seen it that time. My heart tensed, panic flaring, but I didn't have any time to dwell before the sight shifted, the image flickering in and out until it wasn't Ilyan laying on the floor of the cave, but Ovailia. Blood seeped from her mouth as she stared into nothing, water from an underground river I hadn't seen before lapping at her ankles, pulling at her legs as though it would pull her in.

"The choice was made." The image flashed to white again, Ovailia vanishing only to be replaced by Ilyan and I, running through the orchard in the caves of Imdalind. We were obviously older, years older, even though we hadn't aged a day.

We weren't alone. Other bodies flitted through the trees as we chased each other, the laughter flitting through the sight in an echo. Three boys; two blondes, a brunette who was clearly younger than the other two, and a little girl. She looked nearly identical to me. Long dark hair, the same smile. Except her eyes were blue.

Ilyan's blue.

"The future is prepared." My voice continued in the same hollow as the six of us came together, laughing, Ilyan hoisting the little girl onto his shoulders.

"Unless the blood will flow." The image of the happy family faded as if it was melting, replaced by one of Sain. The old man laughed as he stood in the middle of a stone stage, a pile of bones beside him. Ovailia clung to him as the crowd before him kneeled. They watched them shake in fear as they bowed before him as they worshiped him.

"Do not trust her."

Everything vanished as the world was sucked back into existence. I flinched as though I had been slapped, the images of Sain and Ovailia twisting in my stomach. But those weren't the images that had sent my heart into a tango, that had left Ilyan with a tear stained face.

"That was her," he gasped, his voice broken. He didn't have to explain.

It was the orchard. It was the future of a family that until this moment I didn't even think was possible. I had been fighting so hard to keep Ilyan from the fate of his death against the rocks I hadn't even stopped to think what else might be out there.

"Ilyan?" I asked, the flash of his body against the rocks flashing between us, but he shook his head.

"No. It doesn't have to end that way. Not anymore. We know what we are fighting for, now. No more secrets. We are going to fight together." His hands were firm as he pulled me to stand, both of us standing there, the heat of the barrier warming our skin.

He had seen it. One peek into his mind and I knew he had already seen the moment of his death. We were both fighting against it. Fighting for the life we could have, with our children in the orchard.

"Now we get to fight together." I said, lifting myself onto my tiptoes to kiss him. His arm twisted around my waist, my body flush against his as he lifted me and kissed me deeper.

There was more we would have to discuss, more than I had seen that I was sure I would have to rip apart later. But right then, all I cared about was the powerful King that held me. The Skřítek who had claimed me.

"I think we are going to be late," I whispered into his ear, his whole body shuddered beneath me as he growled, the hungry sound rippling through the air as he threw me back down on the bed.

"I know we are."

CHAPTER 28
RYLAND

"Sir! Sir! Can you spare a minute please... please..."
I turned for the third time since coming into the long hall that all the injured had been moved to after Ovailia's attack. The ash covered face peered out from behind the quickly erected bed screen, eyes wide as he waved me over.

"Yes, what is it?" I tried not to sound too frustrated, but it was hard to do seeing as I had come here for a different reason than to answer a million questions. Unfortunately, Ilyan's proclamation to make me his second had clearly gotten here before I did.

'Of course it has. They all know.'

The guy was about my age, his wide eyes scared as I stepped closer. Guess I had been a bit too snappy. Either that or the other rumor about what else I was, was also drifting through the tents.

"Is everything okay?" I clarified, careful to keep my voice calm. The guy's eyes widened more.

"Yes... you're... you're the King's brother right? The second?" It was clear he had no idea who I was, or anything

DAWN OF ASH

about me. I wasn't even sure he knew what a 'second' was. I felt my shoulders relax and I nodded.

"What can I do for you?"

"Can you tell her thank you?" he asked, winding his hands as though he was afraid to be overheard. "The Queen was the one to save us, I saw her. It was... beautiful." He paused, his voice catching as though he was going to cry. Maybe he was, I had seen the true strength of Joclyn's power before, and it was awe inspiring. "They say that she also healed our magic. I've never met her. Can you tell her thank you, tell her I hope to be even a shadow as powerful as her."

I nodded. I wasn't sure why he was so nervous about saying that, but after everything he had been through I guess it made sense. He had nearly died, twice now, I didn't want to know the scars that was going to leave.

"Of course," I clapped my hand on his shoulder, careful to keep my magic away and shielded. His magic may have been centered, but he hadn't been trained. Last thing we wanted was another explosion in here.

'Are we sure? It would finish the job...'

"The Queen is amazing. I am sure you will meet her soon." That time I couldn't help but smile, thinking of the shy girl she had been. The Chosen nodded again, glancing down the tunnel of sheets that were separating the beds before he darted back behind his.

I turned, picking up my pace before I was stopped again, and half-ran through the sheets, the scent of burning hair, blood, and Ditka Leaves flooding the air. This side of the room must be where the more critical cases were. But it was also where the Skřítek healer had told me she was.

'It would make sense. You know what Wyn is capable of.'

I moved into a run, counting the turns and beds before I

hit the last turn, sneakers squeaking against the floor as I faced the last bed in the aisle, and Risha laying under a pile of blankets. The scent of leaves was stronger here, probably tucked in between her blankets.

My heart calmed at seeing her, even though my magic went into overdrive at seeing her. It was screaming against my skin, practically kicking against me in an attempt to reach her. To heal her. Not that I was sure there was much else I could do, she was in good hands. Besides, even standing here I could feel her magic buzz through the air. The sing-song tremble of it was familiar to me now.

'It should be. You had another, you should kill Ilyan and take her back.'

No, I shouldn't. That was in the past. Right then, I was standing before the future, and I was happy about it.

"Are you going to stand there staring at me, or are you going to come sit down and stumble over your words again?" Risha said, eyes still closed as she lay on her pile of pillows, sinking into them as though they were a cloud.

"I wasn't standing... I mean I was staring..." I gave up, her laugh pulling my lips up into a smile as she opened her eyes.

"Or, I guess you could stand there and stumble over your words. That works, too." We stood there, staring and smiling at each other, the pleasant buzzing of her magic in the air growing stronger as she gestured again to the chair.

I probably sat in it a little too fast as it creaked and slid against the floor loudly. Could I just be normal around her for once?

"I'm doing better by the way, just to save you the trouble of asking." She winked at me, although she did gasp and grunt a bit as she pushed herself to sit.

"Are you sure you're okay? You sound like you are practicing to become a cow." There were probably a million other things that I could say to her, but that was what came out instead. Thankfully she laughed.

"Yeah, luckily Wyn didn't hit me with anything too bad. Or, you know, I probably wouldn't be sitting here." She tried to force a smile at that, but I just couldn't join her that time.

My heart rate had already picked up again.

"What did she hit you with?"

"Nothing that they have ever seen. From what Etma thinks, it's a combination of five different spells. Her guess is that she was trying to go easy on me. Which, with how she looked at me I wouldn't doubt. She didn't want to hurt me."

I nodded. "I don't think she wanted to hurt anyone. She was just scared."

Risha looked at me, waiting for me to continue. I couldn't even if I wanted to. Ilyan had commanded that the details about the blade and Rosaline be kept between him and his high commanders, which I guess with how my tongue was instantly tied no longer included Risha.

I would have to talk to him about that, seeing as I had assumed this whole 'second in command' thing would only be until Risha was healed.

"You can't tell me, can you?" Risha's voice was low, but she didn't look upset. If anything her eyes were brighter, the color in her cheeks more flush.

"I can't," I said, and she smiled more, which only made my heart rate explode. There was something about her smile that always made me crazy. I hoped I never lost that feeling. I never wanted to.

"You're not upset?" I leaned in, scooting my chair closer

to her bed, which of course had to happen as loudly as humanly possible.

"Not at all. I'm happy. You deserve this Ryland. You deserve for everyone to see how strong and brave you are, to understand all that you have overcome. You belong by Ilyan's side." Her eyes were shining as she leaned into me, the air between us electric as I leaned in, and grabbed her hand.

"Thank you," my voice caught in my throat, but not from what she had said. But from what I had done.

I had been so careful not to touch her. Not to give my magic the chance to mingle with hers.

I pulled back, but her hand wrapped tightly around mine, her fingers firm as she weaved them through mine, pressing my palm against hers. The warmth of her magic was right there, right against mine, both of us keeping them carefully contained. I could feel it swirl, my own sparking in expectation.

When I had felt Joclyn's magic for the first time everything had exploded in white light. That was partially why I had assumed the sight was wrong, that I was to be her mate and not Ilyan. Why I, oh-so-foolishly, thought I could take his place. But that was with Joclyn, and I had never heard of that happening with anyone else before.

I had no idea what to expect. Or how I would know...

Every muscle in my body was coiled, my heart screaming in need and fear as we sat there, staring at each other. It was as though both of us were waiting for the explosion, for the mind numbing twist of power that you always got when your magic finds its mate. We were both ready for it to happen the second we released the shields that we had placed around ourselves.

"Do you really think that's true?" A female voice

suddenly hissed from the bed next to Risha's. Her hand tensed against mine and we both turned. "She screams for hours and then she magically saves them all on her own?" The female hissed her voice growing lower, her tones piercing as she claimed something she obviously knew to be true. "You heard what Sain said, she's mad, I wouldn't be surprised if she started the fire all on her own. She was screaming up until the moment the fire happened."

'They all know. They all see. Perhaps I will get my way after all.'

My blood was boiling, jaw tight as I moved to stand, but Risha pulled me back down, her hand tightening around mine.

"I can't--" I began, my voice even lower than the woman on the other side of the sheet.

Risha pulled me into her, her eyes on fire as they burned into mine. So close... "You have to. Consider this your first lesson, Ry. Listen, get intel. Never react."

She smiled again, and we both sat back, even though she didn't loosen her grip on my hand. She was right of course. I had lived with my father long enough to know exactly how to react. It wasn't the first time I had heard blatant lies spewed around about my best friend.

It was however the first time I could do anything about it.

I ran my finger over the back of Risha's hand, focusing on her warmth as I tried not to turn into a knight in shining armor.

"But then who put it out?" A second voice hissed on the other side of the sheet after a minute, we were instantly both leaning forward again.

"Ilyan," the first voice returned, obviously smug. "He

can stutter, can't he? Think about it, he stutters in, extinguishes the flames, stutters out and gives her all the credit."

More than one person made a noise of agreement, hushed whispers drifting through the thin cotton separator. I stiffened, even as Risha's hand relaxed in mine, her eyes wide as if she too was contemplating what was just said. I knew why.

"We all heard what Sain said about her," the first female said, voice raised over all the others. "We all saw what happened at that fountain all those months ago."

"And everything else since then," a new voice muttered, more hushed whispers responding.

My magic was in a full boil now, it raged through me as exactly what Sain had done became glaringly clear. Ilyan and Dramin had only touched the surface. He hadn't just controlled her so that people would think she was mad. He had fully discredited her. He had split Ilyan's kingdom.

At the thought, the slimy smile I had seen on a few occasions came to mind, the smile I had disregarded as control, as a slice of the madness Edmund had given to him.

He had played everyone, even me. Even Risha who was nodding towards the voices. As if she agreed.

"You might be onto something." Another voice, and then more whispers.

"Didn't she attack Wyn and tear down the cathedral right before that too?" a man said, his voice familiar. The same boy I had just talked to before finding Risha. No wonder he had been looking up and down the aisles. He didn't want to be overheard

"That's what I heard." The first voice again. "Wynifred ran out of the city to try to escape her. I heard someone say that they heard someone else who saw Wyn run--- The Queen tried to kill her..."

I stood up, the chair clattering to the ground in a loud bang as Risha's hand slid from mine. I didn't even care, my magic was too angry. I was too angry.

I mumbled an apology to Risha before I tore from her tiny make-shift room, to the bare hall between beds and the five faces that were peeking out from the bed right beside.

Their eyes widened as they saw me, saw the anger. But it was that same boy that I looked at, his wide eyes not full of the same fear as the rest of them, but of guilt.

"You saw her save you," I hissed at him, stepping right up to them. None of them moved. "You felt her magic heal you, and now you listen to these lies. Spread the truth."

I stormed down the hall before any of them could respond, although I was sure that more than a few whispered rumors were going to follow me out.

'They will. You are only proving to them what you are.'

"Isn't that the King's crazy brother? He's one to talk."

It took all my strength just to leave, and to not give into my father's laughter.

CHAPTER 29

JOCLYN

I could breathe up here. Even though the lingering smell of smoke saturated the air, I didn't feel quite so confined as I did in the mad house that the cathedral had become.

Everything had become crammed. Crammed and crazy.

Everyone was shoved into tents and tiny rooms, living on top of each other as we rebuilt from the attack. Which should have been easy, if it wasn't for the stares and whispers that followed me everywhere. Even watching them from up here I could see them huddled together, the gossip never ending, the arguments that I had come up here to escape continually breaking out.

And here I was thinking it would get easier after I revealed Sain for what he truly was.

'Is that why you left me alone to dispel this mess?' Ilyan asked into my mind. The quick response made it clear he was tuned into me, something that had been a little more common since yesterday.

I couldn't really blame him. I just wished he wasn't

keeping me out of his mind quite as much. That was new, and I didn't like it.

"I don't see it as *dispelling* so much as 'handling' with a greater finesse than I could ever muster." I laughed as I said it, and his own chuckle joined in.

Taking a deep drink from my mug, I closed my eyes and sent him the image of the endless sunset I was surrounded by. '*Besides, Ilyan, it's beautiful up here. You should join me. Leave Ryland to clean up the mess.*'

'*Spoken like a true Queen.*' I couldn't see it, but I could hear the wide smile in Ilyan's voice. The humor in the situation leaked through our connection and filled me like a deep, warm bubble.

I sighed, my heart moving into a familiar rhythm as it thumped to match his, our souls binding together. It was enough to make me leave the safe confines I had closeted myself up in and find him. Almost.

I leaned forward from where I was hiding near the roof of the ancient cathedral, over the old, stonework of the flying buttresses that connected the low spires to the chapel. I could see everything from up here, even beyond the bustling courtyard, beyond the barriers of Ilyan's shield and into the city. The soaring heights of the building lifted me above the world below and gave me that same freedom I had sought after for so many years. After all, it wasn't the first roof of a building I had found sanctuary on. Although the gothic cathedral was stuck in a state of architectural disarray, thanks to the little mishap Wyn and I'd had, this was still secure.

I needed that right now.

I clung to one of the gargoyles as I looked for Ilyan, the stone nose of the beast slick from the ash of the fire.

'*I am queen,*' I whispered back, forcing as much feigned prissiness as I could muster into my voice.

'*You are my queen,*' Ilyan's response came, his voice deep as his magic flooded me, the powerful connection pulling me right to the tall blond-haired man who stood in the middle of the space, his face turned up to where I was hidden, his lips spread into a wide smile. '*My beautiful queen.*'

Giggling like a lunatic, I leaned back in and pressed the mug to my lips again, only to hear Ilyan's chuckle move through me, his love swelling before someone pulled his focus and made him return to one of the many issues that had popped up within the camp. It was something I couldn't avoid much longer.

"Just one more," I said with a sigh, more to myself than anyone else as I refilled my mug.

Dangling my feet over the stone ledge, I made myself comfortable, wishing I could hide up here until everything was over, but I knew that wasn't possible anymore.

I had tried to hide with Wyn at first, but she was confined to Thom and Dramin's room 'until further notice' and I didn't want to be stuck in there any more than she did. Between Thom being stuck in a coma, Wyn being exhausted from emotional onslaught and the fact that Dramin had become even more closeted, mysterious, and sulky after the fire, that room had turned into an angsty prison.

Between that or the roof, I think I had chosen wisely.

With another deep drink from my mug, my Drak power blazed to life, morphing into an image of Ovailia, tears streaming down her face. The shadow of the sight blended over the courtyard below me, the two images intermingling uncomfortably.

My heart rate picked up, the warmth Ilyan had left me with vanishing with one flash of the sight. Without a second thought, I closed my eyes, opening them to the black and letting the sight take hold.

"Show me," I whispered as the sounds of Ovailia's sobs moved over me, rumbling in my ears as she cried. I could see the whites of her eyes through the deep shadow she was surrounded by, panic and fear running through her as blood dripped down her face. My magic prodded the image to move as I tried to look away from what my sight had focused on, trying to find any clue as to what was happening, but it was only darkness, only the shadow of her face, only the sound of her sobs. The scent of her blood washed over me as I watched it drip down her cheek, the iron and salt smelling sweet, but I wasn't sure why.

This wasn't the first time my magic had shown me this moment in time. I had seen it before, only hours before, and even then it was no more than her crying in a dark room. I couldn't tell if it was past or present or even what was happening. The image wasn't clear enough.

With a blink, I banished the sight away, storing it with the others. My heart rate slowly decelerated as the people below me came back into focus. Even though this reality wasn't any more relaxing than what I had seen.

'Did you see any more?' Ilyan asked, making it clear he had seen everything I had, something that was happening consistently since he had been pulled into that sight.

I cringed at his question, part of me desperately wishing I had at least seen something to put his mind at ease, if simply to get him to stop asking me about it.

Don't get me wrong; Ovailia was barely one step from the bottom of the list of 'people I would like to kill,' but she was also my mate's sister. I knew him well enough to understand that, even though he would never say it. I could feel him worry for her. I could feel his need to still protect her somehow. I wished I felt the same.

"It's still dark," I whispered to myself with the slightest hint of a growl, taking a quick drink in an effort to mask my irritation.

'Will it become clearer?' he asked, causing my shoulders to knit together a bit.

'It might,' I sighed, knowing full well my irritation was becoming more obvious. *'Or it could be that the room is dark.'*

I was snotty and I knew it, as did Ilyan. Anyone else might have backed off, but Ilyan chuckled.

'Can you tell your sight to turn on the light?'

Rolling my eyes at his response, I leaned back, resting against the cold stone of the cathedral, fully intending to fall asleep and make some excuse for my disappearance later.

'Draks don't sleep.'

'Thanks for the reminder, darling,' I growled.

His laugh intensified before I gently locked him out of my mind, needing silence for a bit.

Silence and a steaming mug of Black Water.

"Just one more," I said again, refilling it and hating the weird amount of guilt that moved through me.

I shouldn't feel bad about taking a moment to myself, but I did. I vaguely remembered my mom saying something about that once... about responsibility and requirement. Stupid adult-hood. If I could see the path to end this fiasco, it would be worth it.

With a sigh, I pulled the tiny bottle of green fluid out of my pocket, the poisonous contents already transferred to another shatterproof container. After I had found it yesterday, I had known it was the key to healing Thom, but I hadn't gotten any closer to that actually happening. My magic hadn't given me any more clues, even with sitting between him and Wyn for about six hours last night. I got nothing. Then again, I might have been more concerned with fixing the massive hole in Wyn's hand than harnessing whatever juju my magic had a tendency to whisper at me.

Neither task had really been a success.

Six hours and Wyn's hand didn't look any better than it had when she showed up outside the barrier. Whatever that blade had done to Wyn, the hole in her hand was impossible to close. I had a feeling we would have to find her some pretty epic gloves to cover that mess.

"I had a feeling I'd be running into you up here eventually."

I jumped at the voice, Black Water flying all over me at the almighty jerk caused from hearing Ryland's voice so close, and without warning.

"Ry!" I yelled, water dripping over every inch of me. "You scared me!"

"Jos! Wow! I'm sorry!" Ry's eyes widened as he rushed to me. I saw what he was doing no more than a second before he did, the words, the desperate plea for him to stop coming a second too late.

"Stop!" I snapped as he reached out to help, as his hand made contact with the Black Water that covered me, as he yelled out in pain.

The second his skin pressed against the water my head spun, my sight pulling me right into his life, right into what he wanted to know.

The ember burn of my eyes grew darker as images flashed before me: his childhood, his moments with me, the abuse he suffered in the dungeons of Imdalind. I saw it all.

My heart seized at the pain and loss and confusion that dwelled in his heart, at the desperate need for something to be okay, for something in his life to be beautiful.

I watched his memories, his past, as he put a smile on his face, as he continued to fight through the pain of life, through the uncertainty of the hell we were marching into. My own heart seized right alongside his, my own pain and troubles increasing, the depth of my understanding scaring me.

The depth of my own need for that silver lining.

As his desire swelled inside me, the sight changed and shifted, the images becoming fogged as they moved into an unknown future. There was an image of him ageing, wisdom lining his face as hundreds of years moved by him, as the world around him changed, and the life around him changed with it. He was still the same boy, save for the lines that covered his face, evidence of a million smiles and a happy life. His eyes were filled with joy, and in his arms was a beautiful, little boy with dark, curly hair.

Ryland smiled at the child, throwing him into the air as his laugh rippled through my head. The sound was loud and beautiful as it swelled through me before the sight faded, reality shifting back into focus, and the boy who was desperately blowing at the burns on his fingers swam into view.

Shaking my head, I let the dizziness drift away, my magic swelling with whispers and promises as one by one the prophecies of his life left.

"What the hell, Jos?" Ryland yelled, his eyes dangerously dark. "Do you burn people now?"

"No," I said with a roll of my eyes. "But Black Water does, and you should know better. And blowing on them won't help, by the way."

It was probably good I couldn't be mad at him after what I had seen. Instead of the verbal reprimand he probably should have gotten, I just rolled my eyes, wrapping my hand around his fingers, letting my magic soothe him, taking away the Black Water that had moved into him.

"And I should know this why? I mean, my experience with Black Water is *so* extensive." I could tell he was trying to control the anger in him, but obviously failing.

I laughed, something that didn't really sit well, unfortunately.

"Don't worry, Ry. Mine isn't much better." Releasing his hand from mine, I looked at his now healed fingers, my own brand of awe moving through me, nothing was there, just perfectly healed skin. I didn't think that was possible with black water burns, or it wasn't before Sain's block on my magic was removed. I might have to try that on Ilyan's chest or even his palm. I knew he would be grateful not to deal with the endless pain those gave him. "Feel better?"

He nodded at my question, one eyebrow disappearing into his curls quizzically.

I sighed, his look and question obvious.

"Yes, I saw something, and yes, everything will be okay for you. I'm not telling you any more than that."

"And?"

"And you're happy. I'm not telling you any more than that," I repeated through my grin. I already knew I wasn't going to be able to hide it from him for long. I was aware of his skill to get stuff out of me.

"Yeah, yeah," he said, the hint of a smile beginning to form. "You really aren't going to tell me more than that?"

He leaned in, and had the absolute gal to bat his eyelashes at me. I might have melted under that a year ago. Not so much anymore. I was too stubborn, and he knew it.

"No, I'm not telling you any more than that." I half expected him to laugh, but instead the smug smile of his game slipped off his face, disappointment taking over his eyes.

"That's no fair, Jos."

"Ha! Life is a journey meant to be experienced, Ry. What's the fun if I tell you all the stops along the way?"

"I would know where I am going ... I wouldn't run into quite so many walls at the very least," Ryland said, the teenage irritation dripping off him.

It was all I could do to keep the smile off my face, although the attempt to keep the stoic, wise grimace wasn't going too well, either.

"Don't run into walls. That can't be good for your complexion, or your nose for that matter."

"Thanks, Jos." He grumbled, the angst dripping off of him and infecting me. "And stop being all wise and philosophical and stuff. It's weird."

"You're weird." I looked away from him, our familiar banter taking the edge off the turmoil that was playing out below us.

We sat, listening to the whispers of the people below us, watching the line of the red sun slowly move over the city as it disappeared past the horizon.

"You were on a beach," I whispered after a few minutes. His eyes widened as he moved to face me, obviously eager to absorb anything I would give him. "There were other people involved who you may or may not be related to." I wanted so much to share it with him. But I knew now just how fragile my sights were. I didn't know if it was the right choice not to show him, but something in me told me now was not the time. Although, I did seem to be having a lot of sights featuring children lately. "It was a happy scene, Ry."

"Happy." He almost didn't seem to believe it.

"Very. Just don't go thinking I'm infallible, okay? I'm kind of done with that lie being spread around."

"You really aren't going to give me more than that, are you?" he teased.

I shook my head, a smile spreading over my face. "Trust me. It will be better this way, but that fear you feel, that desperation for normality..." I whispered, leaning in as his color faded from his cheeks and I took his hand. "Everyone has it, Ry. Just know it doesn't last forever. Not for any of us. It may take a bit, but everything will come out all right."

I had barely said the words when the violent image of Ilyan's death flooded my vision, overlaying the city roof-scape with the steady flow of Ilyan's blood. I cringed against it, my heart rate picking up to a dangerous level. I was not infallible. I had to remind myself of that too.

But, in the case of that one, I had to find a way to stop it.

"Everything will come out all right," I said again, more to myself that time.

I shifted my body forward in an attempt to seek out Ilyan, as if seeing him would set everything right in my mind and confirm the good that I was desperate for. My magic moved away from me to find him, but instead of streaming to the courtyard I was pulled in a different direction, my mind and magic drifting over the city, winding through the streets as my heart rate increased, dread filling me as the shadow of what I was certain I wouldn't feel again drifted over me.

My mind filled with the images of the dilapidated city, the streets shrouded in the black of night, the ancient beauty of it turned into a dangerous labyrinth I had no interest in entering. That was, until the shadow of magic I was feeling sparked through me, everything tensing as the image of a single, cloaked figure moved through the dark, running from street to street as it had the last time I had felt its magic.

"It's the same." My voice was a hollow monotone as it rumbled through the dusk, the magic winding through me with a deep mockery as every muscle tensed through me.

He was here.

After what he had done, after what people had seen him do, he had come back.

"What's the same?" Ryland asked from beside me.

My focus was so intent on what had unfolded I didn't even answer him.

"Ilyan," I said aloud, fully aware Ryland could hear me. "Sain is in the city. I can feel him on the other side of the river—"

'*Sain!*' Ilyan's voice erupted loudly, his body running into the center of the courtyard as he looked up to me. '*Why would he come back?*'

He asked the question, although the answer was so clear I almost hated having to say it. Sain had been doing much more than spreading rumors; I was confident of that. And if you took the time to play a game, you didn't walk back into your enemy's territory without a motive.

"It's a trap."

There was no doubt. However, we couldn't let him get away, either. It was a game of the worst sort, but at least we weren't going into it unaware. If we played our cards right, we could have the upper hand.

'*How many does he have? Can you tell what he's planning?*'

"I'll find out. You get a team together. As many as you can." I looked at Ilyan as his mind followed mine. His eyes were hard, his jaw straight as he nodded in confirmation.

"Can I be part of this conversation, too?" Ryland groaned from beside me, his weight shifting as he moved to stand. "I'm Ilyan's second. Doesn't that count for something?"

"Stop being a baby," I growled, not even paying him attention as I closed my eyes, focusing my magic on what I assumed was Sain running through the streets and moving out from there. I scoured everything as I looked for any other trace of magic, for anything that would tip me off to what he was planning. There was nothing. I moved through every street in the city, every building, but it was empty except for the Vilÿs that lay in hiding.

"There's nothing." My voice was dead, the shock still rumbling through me uncomfortably.

I wasn't certain how that was possible. Why would he come back if not for a trap?

"I hate that you guys do that." I wasn't certain if Ryland was laughing or growling.

'Nothing anywhere?'

I didn't blame Ilyan for questioning.

"No, I can't find anything. Doesn't mean he isn't up to something, though. It's up to you if we want to go in blind or not."

I looked to Ryland then, who was now so irate at being left out of the conversation I half expected steam to start issuing from his ears.

"Care to fill me in?" he snarled from behind clenched teeth, obviously trying his hardest to stay cool.

"Sain is in the city," I repeated. "He's alone."

Even Ryland didn't seem to believe that little bit of information judging by the way his eyes narrowed.

"Why would he come back?"

"Exactly," I said, a finger wagging at him as he stepped

back in obvious discomfort. "I say we go and leave the team on ready in case we need them."

Ryland looked at me with even more confusion than before, clearly trying to follow along. "Go where?"

I guessed I probably should have mentioned that last part wasn't for him.

'Sounds good. I'll meet you in the dark.'

Ilyan's voice faded, the directions clear as I turned toward Ryland, his eyes now so wide, his temper so high I had a feeling trying to explain anything was going to be a fool's errand.

Ask questions and seek apologies later, I supposed.

"I'm really sorry for what's about to happen," I whispered, my hand gripping tightly around his waist as my magic plunged into him, the energy flaring as I pulled him into the Stutter with me, his scream loud in my ears.

CHAPTER 30
JOCLYN

"Never do that again!" Ryland's voice echoed around us the moment we reemerged on a dingy street in Old Town, his body collapsing against a wall that hadn't been there a moment ago.

Crinkling my nose against the smell of a million dead fish, I shot Ryland a look. The poor boy heaved as he clung to the wall beside him. Obviously Stutters did not agree with him. It's not like I was much better after my first, but then, Ilyan had knocked himself unconscious for several days, so I mean, maybe it wasn't that much better. I wasn't even sure why I had thought I could drag him through in the first place. I was beginning to wonder exactly how much power I had regained from Sain's control. My magic just kept surprising me, the power felt daunting at times.

"Try to keep it down," I hissed as I glared through the dark.

"You say that like you didn't try to kill me."

I rolled my eyes at him before I walked away, the sounds of his gasping lessening with each step I took.

My magic moved in a rush as I pushed it through the

streets, attempting to find where Sain had gone, but there was nothing: no trace of his magic, no image of a cloaked figure running through the dark. It was no more than a dark world, ribbons of deep red seeping through the gaps in the buildings as the sun set and plunged the shadowed world into a dangerous territory. We couldn't be out here long.

'Ilyan?' I called to him, my breathing picking up alongside my anxiety. *'Where are you?'*

'A few streets over.' The reply came automatically, and my magic pulled right to him as he raced towards us, searching.

'It's too quiet.' My voice was clipped, the sound opposite of the heavy beat of my heart in my ears.

I took another step closer to the end of the street, the wide intersection seeming too perfect for the situation we were up against. My heart throbbed in my chest, almost expecting to find someone hidden around the corner, waiting to attack.

Closing my eyes, I pressed my back against the bricks of the building and let my magic pull away from me again. With a slow exhale, my mind's eye opened to the streets that surrounded us, pulling through the empty ruins as I searched, knowing he should be close.

Still, nothing.

But I had seen him.

Turning back to the dark shadows of the street behind me, Ilyan jumped from the rooftops to land before me.

"I don't like this," Ilyan hissed, his eyes darting down the street behind me.

"'Kay, I think I survived that ..." Ryland gasped as he came up behind us, his body still visibly shaking, even though he was trying to act all macho. "But never again, Jos. I'm still not completely convinced I haven't died."

"Ryland?" Ilyan asked, his back tensing a bit underneath me. "How did you get here?"

"Jos brought me. Didn't she tell you through her wicked mumbo-jumbo telecommunications radio thing you have going on?" he said with a glare between the two of us.

"No, she didn't." The corner of Ilyan's mouth twitched as he looked down at me. "And you didn't pass out for days. I guess I did choose wisely."

"Yeah, I know you did." I grinned, standing on my tiptoes to kiss him. Fire spread over my skin as my lips made contact with his. I kissed him deeply, moaning a bit when he pulled me into him. Part of me knew I should pull away, at least before the crazy lights showed up. Those didn't really seem Vilỳ safe.

"If you are going to drag me along, can you at least keep this down to a minimum?" Ryland snarled, disgust evident in his voice. "We are supposed to be on a mission, not a make out session."

"Oh, I quite agree," another voice broke through the darkness around us, a snake that wound through my spine and froze me in place. The tones of the voice were unfamiliar and foreign, yet, I knew who it was.

I knew before he stepped out of the shadows, the hood low over his face. I knew before he smiled at us, the wide grin cutting through a face that was different than I had ever seen.

I could see him there, but his magic was gone.

Ryland stiffened as he turned, both he and Ilyan moving to stand in front of me like my own personal bodyguards. I rolled my eyes at them and barged my way between them to face my father.

He smiled, standing straighter and taller than I had ever seen him.

"Sain," I whispered as he finally removed the hood, his smile spreading as eyes as black as the night looked into us, the color fading back to their normal green with one blink.

"Oh, come now," he cooed, his voice as unrecognizable as the person before us was, and judging by the anguished tension that had wound through Ilyan, it was unfamiliar for him, too. "I think I deserve a more formal greeting than that."

"Deserve may be the wrong word there, *Father*." I spat out the last word like it was poison, part of me expecting him to flinch or howl in anger. However, his smile deepened, his steps hollow as he continued forward, step after step grating against me.

"Oh, no, child." His voice was soothing, if the threat behind his words wasn't so clear, I might have believed the lie he was trying to weave. "Deserve is *exactly* the right word because I deserve what is about to happen to me, just as you deserve what is about to happen to you. I have been working toward this since before any of you were born. It's fitting that you would be here to see it to its end."

"What have you done, Sain?" Ilyan plastered himself against me, his feral snarl erupting through the dark in warning. Sain, however, took one more step forward, obviously unfazed. But worse, he was also unafraid.

"Done?" Sain asked with a laugh.

Ryland slowly stepped back, away from the man and closer to where Ilyan and I stood.

"I have done nothing. I was not the one to kill your mother. I was not the one to start this war. I have merely given—eh—helpful guidance along the way." He flipped his hand to the side, the movement so casual you would assume he was discussing anything other than the orchestrated destruction of an entire race of people.

My blood boiled with every word he spoke, as I looked into the reality of what—no, of who—we were truly facing. "It's all a game to you."

"Oh, yes. One of the best sort. And you all have been playing without even knowing."

"You've used everyone. You used me..." Ryland growled, his feet shifting as if he was debating whether or not to attack Sain right away. I wrapped my hand around his wrist, pulling him back so he didn't do something foolish.

"Used is a harsh word, Ryland. I used no one. I only helped them see their true potential, helped them understand what they were really meant for, even if they didn't see it themselves—"

The true reality of what he had done became frighteningly clear. This was more than spreading rumors about my magic. This was more than controlling the magic of the Draks. Looking at this stranger, it was clear that his motives went deeper than just some stupid prideful games to regain his crown.

"Well," Sain's eyes narrowed as he took yet another step forward. "I guess I have done *something*." His smiled stretched wide as he froze before us, his magic slowly starting to awaken. The same, powerful strain I had felt running through the city before emanating from him like a poisonous fog, sticking in the air as though it was attempting to strangle us. His smile rose as his magic did, the darkened street behind him illuminating as the forgotten streetlights blazed to life, blanketing us in a flickering yellow bath.

Our shadows stretched and swayed over the blood soaked street as the lights flared, swallowing the dark until it showed us what he wanted us to see.

Until it showed us what he had 'done'.

A pile of lifeless corpses, their clothes still wet with blood, their faces gaunt as they stared at nothing. Their hands were posed as if they were still trying to attack whatever had destroyed them, as if the magic inside of them was still trying to get out, still trying to save them.

But there was nothing except death.

"I did this." He smiled, proud of his handiwork, as if the life he had destroyed was more beautiful than the life that had been. I didn't even care if they were Edmund's men; it still made my stomach turn. "Edmund sent me with 'fifty of his strongest' on a mission to kill you. I made him believe I could use my sight to sneak them into the cathedral to draw you out, something that was obviously not too hard. However, I didn't need them to complete *my* task. But Edmund needn't know that."

"You're a monster!" Ilyan erupted as he stepped around me, the rough edge of his magic cutting through me as he stepped forward. I lunged for Ilyan as his brother did, both of our magic flooding into the King in a desperate attempt to quell his temper.

Sain, on the other hand, stood still, that disturbing smile still in place while he watched us, laughing.

'Ilyan,' I spoke into his mind, my hand wrapping around his neck as I pulled him toward me, Ryland stepping between us and Sain protectively. *'Calm down, my love. I am here. Do not rise to what he is doing. We know his game. If we want to survive this, we need to play it with him.'*

Ilyan's widened eyes darted toward me as his thoughts flooded me. The temper in his anger made it hard for him to focus. I had never seen him like this.

As I looked at him, fear looked back at me. Dangerous anger that rumbled through me in a warning that went unheeded. Keeping my magic inside of him, I let it soothe him. This side of him was frightening, but my love wouldn't change. It only grew, my connection with him expanding alongside.

'I'm here. Now it's my turn,' I whispered to him before I turned away, my hand not leaving his as I faced my father, my real father, for the first time in my life.

My jaw was tight as I narrowed my eyes at the man who had reduced me to anger-fueled hysterics so many times before. Now, I was only left with a ripple of annoyance.

This was a villain I had faced many times before, a villain who had walked out of the shadows to show his true colors.

"Well, Joclyn," Sain said with a growl, "it seems you have finally come into your own... Would you like to test the limits of that magic of yours? Test it against someone who can actually match you?"

He didn't give me any warning before he attacked. His eyes moved to the black sheen of sight as his attack sprang forward in a stream of silk that slithered through the air, moving right toward where I stood as it doubled in size.

Sending a counterattack right into it, I screamed with exertion, only to watch Sain's magic devour my defense. The weaving ribbon of power shimmered with light as it absorbed the power.

I jumped to the side, Ryland and Ilyan following suit as the attack sped past us, impacting the road where we had just stood. I screamed in frustration, scuttling in an attempt to get away from whatever was coming. Before I had moved more than a few inches, the street before my face exploded, attack after attack following as I was forced back. I moved as fast as I could, hissing in pain as magical residue and burning rocks fell over me.

"Joclyn!" The street erupted in green as Ilyan ran to me,

his attack streaming toward my father only to fall to the ground in a shower of sparks as Sain snapped his fingers.

"No, no, I don't think so." The hiss in Sain's voice increased, the dangerous ripple of his warning echoing through the street. "This fight is between my daughter and me. But don't worry, *my lord,* I will keep you and your brother busy."

Ilyan screamed as Sain threw him into one of the buildings that surrounded us without so much of a twitch of his fingers.

"Ilyan!" I jumped to my feet, turning to face my father whose eyes were still shrouded in black, his white teeth flashing in a menacing grin.

"I doubt you can stop my power, Ilyan. If I say she is mine, she is mine. Besides, I have a much bigger job for you."

I stood still, my heart longing to run to my mate, but knowing that I wouldn't get more than a step before Sain would attack. We had all underestimated him.

Maybe we had underestimated me, too.

"No more games, Sain," I growled, narrowing my eyes at him.

"Oh, I don't think so, Joclyn. We still have many games to play, so why don't we play the best one right now?" His eyes dug into me as he tapped his toe, the hollow sound of his shoe against the street echoing menacingly. I jerked at each tap, the sound growing, shaking painfully through my bones. I looked around the alley in a panic, not knowing what to expect when the carelessly thrown away corpses in the pile behind him began to twitch, began to move.

Horror filled me. Sain's menacing smile was forgotten as I looked away from the demon, staring at the lifeless flesh that convulsed in harmony with the tap of his shoes.

With each beat they twitched as though they were being pulled on a string, with each beat Ilyan and Ryland moved closer ready to protect us from whatever was about to emerge from within the pile.

Then the remaining pile itself began to disband, one body after another rising from the dead, their heads lolling to the side as legs jerked and twitched below them, pulling them toward us.

"Beautiful," Sain whispered without even looking away from where we stood, our focus glued to what was happening. "It's something Edmund never mastered, no matter how hard he tried. Him and all those beating hearts he devoured, he never understood the full depth of that type of magic. Keep the magic alive and you can use it. You can mold it into whatever you want."

I could feel Ilyan shake in fear beside me, his thoughts moving into overdrive as he tried to understand what he was seeing, tried to understand what was happening, tried to understand how this was possible.

'Magic this powerful shouldn't be possible.'

The way Sain looked at us made it clear that magic this powerful *was* possible. Magic this powerful was in him.

And if it was in him, then it was in me, as well.

'Don't forget that, Joclyn. You must defeat him.'

'I will.'

"Go get 'em, boys," Sain sneered as he stepped forward, his magic sparking as it pushed Ryland and Ilyan away from me, their bodies soaring through the air as he separated us.

I screamed, reaching for Ilyan, realizing too late that no matter how hard my magic tried to reach him, I couldn't. A wall lay between us, keeping me from him. Keeping him from me.

I was trapped, facing my father as Ryland and Ilyan were stuck facing the monsters of Sain's creation. I could hear their screams, feel Ilyan's fear. But my magic couldn't reach him. I couldn't pull him back to me.

'Joclyn,' Ilyan yelled as the disjointed corpses reached him, as he and Ryland screamed and fought a wall of monsters.

"Ilyan ..." They were outnumbered. I had to hurry.

"How sweet, I sure hope you get to see each other again." Sain looked at me, the warning of his smile increasing as his eyes dipped to black. "Now, let's see if you are as powerful as the sight predicted you to be."

Violent spells streamed toward me, his body moving fast as he continued to look at me with black eyes, his hands barely moving.

I moved without question, dodging, countering, hands flailing as I tried to deter him, but they kept coming, powerful enough forces that in the end I just threw up both hands, a wall flying from me in a desperate attempt to do away with his endless onslaught.

Everything vanished, leaving us with the colorful wisps of his attacks, the swirling smoke trapped inside the globe as he circled me.

"There is one among us who seeks to change the magic." Sain's words swirled in darkness as he repeated the prophecy, the verses sounding even darker as they were spoken by the one I now realized they were referring too. *"Someone who seeks to kill the magic. He seeks to kill the magic for his own personal gain. We see him as he fights, as he sheds the blood of us, as he sheds the blood of others. We see him as he stops the reign of magic, as he stops the time of ours."*

He smiled, an attack flying toward me as the smoke fell to the ground, the lingering smell of sulfur and death strong in my nose. "Do you see now, child? Do you see what is to happen?"

"It was your sight, Father. But that was not all it said. *She is the most powerful. She will be The Silný, the one who protects us all.*" I snapped as I attacked him again, his eyes wide as the violent stream of magic narrowly missed him, fear glossing over his eyes for just a moment before the smile returned, the glare enough to make anyone flinch. I stood still. "Do you doubt it now?"

His eyes snapped back to black, digging into me as he smiled.

A ribbon of yellow flew toward me, and I swung out of the way, only to be hit by a jolt of attack, a powerful wave jerking through my spine, freezing me in place.

"I doubt nothing that is based in truth," he mused as he stepped toward me, grinning as the same black smoke I had seen before twisted around his fingers. "Sight, however, is not based on such ridiculous atrocities."

He fired again, another attack surging through my body as I screamed. Ilyan's yell of fear echoed in my head as he tried again to break through the barrier to reach me, but the barrier didn't so much as budge. No matter what attack Ilyan threw at it, the sound of Sain's laugh ripped through me as his eyes faded from black to green.

"You say your power is free, Joclyn, and I can feel that. Yet you do not use it. You are going to make your death the easiest one yet." He sighed, his magic leaving me as I fell to the ground in a gasping heap.

Ilyan's shout continued to rip through me, his worry filling my mind. "I guess I shouldn't complain, once you are gone, everything else will fall into place. You are the last thorn in my side."

'*Fight him, Joclyn.*' Ilyan's voice filled me as I looked up at my father, looked up at that sly smile, the hatred I felt for him flowing, Ilyan's magic swelling in me as I pushed myself to standing, my jaw tight as I faced him.

"I knew you weren't worthy of the magic the mud gave you. No one is. No one but me."

His eyes faded to black as he moved, the attacks coming again in a torrent that I was only barely able to dodge.

"Pathetic," he barked, his magic shot right to where I was about to roll to, hitting against a small pile of trash and sending it into flames, as though he knew where I was going to go. *Because he does*, I realized with a start.

You say your power is free... yet you do not use it.

With a blink, my eyes plunged to black of sight, my magic swelling as the vision overlaid reality in a seamless prophecy. Sain moved from point A to point B moments before he actually did, and this time, I was ready—my magic was ready.

With one surge, I attacked. With one surge, I hit him.

"Wonderful," Sain crowed the moment I glanced at him, my heart thundering in my chest while the reality of what was about to happen increased. "Don't hold back now. I want to feel justified when I kill you."

"If I let you." I attacked as he did, streams of color and magic, walls of fire and smoke.

The shadows of two realities were moving one right after another, my magic moving to mimic what he was doing, what he was going to do, just as he did to me. He stuttered effortlessly from inside of the dome, his body disappearing and reappearing so fast that if I hadn't been paying attention I would have missed it. But instead, I turned, deflecting his attack as he moved back to where he started, his grin wide.

"Good," he sneered, "but it takes more than seeing to know what to do."

His smile spread before his attacks began again, the complicated motions increasing as Ilyan's screams of fear and pain echoed through the dome.

I turned toward Ilyan's shout, toward his pain in a need to help him. That one move, one misstep and I failed to dodge Sain's attack as it moved into me. A burn moving through my body like water on ice. I gasped at the sensation, turning back to him as I stumbled back, my attack moving toward him in a pathetic attempt to counter.

He only laughed as he sidestepped, another attack moving toward me as a shadow of myself appeared behind him. I watched the movement of my future self, not sure I had the strength, but followed unquestioningly as I stuttered from one point to another. I appeared behind him as I did in sight, my hand moving forward, ready to attack as he turned, an attack of his own moving right into my gut. His magic flared as he, too, stuttered. This time, he moved away from me, leaving me standing, heaving as my magic tried to dispel the pain.

As my magic began to fade.

"Joclyn!" Ilyan screamed. His magic moved through me as his own pain filled me, the sounds of magic attacking the barrier rumbling around us.

"Oh no," Sain tsked, the sound reverberating as I watched him through watering eyes. "You were doing so well, too. You just forgot one thing: sight is a guide, not a road map. In fact, didn't you say that a few minutes ago?"

He attacked again, magic slamming into me and throwing me into the air and against his barrier. I slid down the surface like an egg, crumbling against the ground with a moan.

"Don't trust it," Sain growled as he walked toward me, the sound of Ilyan's fist against the barrier a loud hollow pressure inside my head.

"Joclyn!"

I knew I was done for. Judging by Sain's smile, he knew it, too. He wasn't going to hold back. I could hear Ilyan and Ryland as they fought in vain, their mad attempt to defeat an undead foe ending at nothing.

We were cornered.

Squaring my shoulders, my heart beating as I stared at my father, trying to pull through Sain's attack to gain enough power to attack just once. I wasn't going to go down without a fight.

It couldn't end like this.

It wasn't supposed to.

"What?" Sain sneered, his magic pushing against me. "Aren't you going to beg?"

"Girls don't beg." The voice came from behind me, loud, angry, and stronger than I was certain anyone else could manage at the moment. "We kick ass."

As though someone had opened up a flamethrower inches from my face, Wyn's magic erupted from beside me, breaking through the barrier like a needle to a balloon. The translucent prison fell away as fire exploded inches from Sain's feet, the flames licking around his ankles in what was obviously meant as warning.

Sain's eyes widened at the sudden change, his demeanor shifting. For a moment, I swore I saw the sniveling father I had known for the last few months—a rat cornered by a cat.

"But you can beg if you'd like," Wyn said as she came up beside me, her hand still raised before her, the powerful heat of her magic emanating around her like a space heater.

"Not that it would do any good. For you, Sain, I would show you what my magic can really do."

Sain straightened, the weakness in his face leaving, though his eyes continued to dart around in fear.

"You should be dead, Wynifred! I saw you die," he snarled between his teeth, his voice harsh and loud before he vanished into a Stutter, leaving us staring at an empty street, at the hoard of corpses that were surrounding Ilyan and Ryland.

"He ran away? Really? How anticlimactic," Wyn grumbled, but I was already running.

"Ilyan!" I screamed the moment Sain was gone, racing to Ilyan and Ryland, ready to join the battle and take down the undead corpses.

Before we could make it more than a few steps, the bodies around them collapsed to the ground with a domino of thuds, the lights that had engulfed the street extinguished right along with them and left us standing in the dark.

My power flared, an orb of golden light floating above my hand, everyone around me following to do the same. Blue, orange, and grey they blazed, leaving us standing in an arena of strangely mutated light, the bodies still littered around us.

"Where is Sain?" Ilyan rumbled as he ran to my side, my magic connecting with his as his did with mine, both of us feverishly searching for injuries. "Where did he go?"

"Stuttered," Wyn announced, her voice far too light considering the situation we were in. "Didn't seem too happy to see me. Although, I can't figure out why you three took off without me."

"You are still on probation," Ilyan's voice was positively

acidic now, his hands dropping from me as he took a step toward the woman in question.

Her eyebrows were already attempting to disappear into her hairline. "What am I, twelve? And besides, since when has that stopped me?"

"It should have stopped you this time," Ilyan snapped, as the two faced off. Ryland looked at me as though we should just take off and let them fight it out. Maybe we should.

"What? And let you lot go off and get killed without me? No thank you." She fumed, her arms crossing over her chest in such a way that for a moment I didn't see her as anything other than a punk seventeen year old kid. "I have done worse and gotten away with less—"

"I still decide your punishments!"

"You are not my father!"

Their yelling swelled in volume as Ryland and I stepped away, tiptoeing through the thankfully still motionless bodies as we tried to move as far away from them as possible.

"I've never seen anything like that before." Ryland's voice was tense, the stress clearly still gripping him tightly, not that I blamed him.

"You mean Wyn and Ilyan fighting?"

"No," he said with a laugh, the sound still strangled by tension. "The whole zombie apocalypse thing Sain cooked up. I mean, how is that even possible?"

I shook my head, "I don't know, but I clearly have more to learn about my magic."

"As long as you leave dead people out of it..." He didn't seem to be able to get out much more than that, not that I blamed him. His eyes had gone right to where mine had— to the bodies that still remained in the pile.

360

"*Keep the magic alive, and you can use it. You can mold it into whatever you want...*" Step by step, I moved, the whispers of their dying magic flying up to me as I noticed what I was positive Sain had not wanted us to see. "These aren't Skříteks."

"I'm sorry?" Ryland asked, obviously not following.

"These are Chosen. They weren't Edmund's best men; they were just men with weaker magic that he could use..." My words froze in my throat as I stepped up to the pile, the gaunt eyes of dozens staring at me, their mouths agape in death, the sounds of cries echoing from somewhere deep inside of them.

"Do you hear that?" My voice was strangled in fear, praying I was hallucinating. The eyes of the lifeless people before me stared, mouths open that for a moment I was sure the sound was coming from them.

"Hear what?"

The sobs increased, the word 'help' now intermingled in the panic, the single word a sobbing plea that cut through me. This was not some corpse come to kill us, not with the way it cried, not with the way it sobbed for help.

"That." Looking to Ryland in alarm, he was just staring at the pile in horror.

'*Ilyan,*' I said, and the sound of fighting behind us stopped. '*Please come tell me I am not losing my mind.*'

He was with us in a second, his heart beating loudly within me.

"Be careful," Ilyan finally said, his voice shaking as he took a step toward the mound, his motions and words making everyone's fears clear. After what Sain had done, we had no way of knowing what was underneath there.

Without another word, we all moved, our motions slow as we sifted through something that I tried in vain to

361

convince myself was nothing more than a pile of rocks. It didn't work. My stomach threatened to turn itself out as we moved the bodies away, the heavy, limp masses sagging under our weight, our hands slipping on blood-covered skin. Everything smelled like blood and sweat, a vile combination that amplified as we moved the bodies, the sounds of the sobs increasing as we did so.

Wyn and I grabbed a hold of a young man, moving him aside as the blonde head of a little girl came into view, her cries beating loudly around the street as the frightened child emerged. Her motions were frantic as she wiggled out, her body covered in blood, her own blood seeping from cuts littered over her body.

With a scream of fear and relief, she broke free, wrapping herself around the first living thing she could find.

Ilyan looked to me in confusion as the tiny child clung to him.

"Please," the little girl sobbed, her voice strangled as she tried to talk through her tears. "Don't make me go back. Please. He'll hurt me. All they do is hurt me," she cried into Ilyan as she clung to him, her hands leaving bloodied prints all over his shirt.

'*Do you think she is safe?*' he asked, his voice tenser than I thought it would be given the situation.

'*She's a child.*' It was the logical answer, but one I knew didn't really qualify in this situation.

Not with Edmund.

He had used children before. He had hurt them, abused them.

Destroyed them.

I knew that this was no different, but with the way she cried, with the way she sobbed and panicked, I knew as well as he did that we didn't have another choice.

Everyone knew it.

Wyn moved toward the little girl slowly, looking from Ilyan to me before kneeling before the little girl, her motions slow as she reached for the child. The girl jerked away in obvious fear of a slap.

"You're okay," Wyn soothed, her voice soft and kind. My heart opened as I saw a side of my best friend I hadn't seen before. "We aren't going to hurt you; I promise. We're the good guys."

The little girl said nothing; she looked at Wyn, her lips quivering as the tears threatened to break free again.

"My name is Wyn, and this is Ilyan and Joclyn and Ryland. What's your name?" Wyn kept her voice calm, mellow, her motions slow.

I looked from her to Ilyan who didn't seem at all confused by this change. Ryland, however, looked at Wyn like she had grown a third head.

"Míra," the girl finally answered, her voice little more than a broken sob.

"Hello, Míra. We are going to take you to our home now. We are going to help you. Will you let us do that?"

She nodded.

CHAPTER 31

SAIN

I appeared in Ovailia's room without so much as a preliminary check. Thank goodness it was empty except for its owner. The girl in question sat in her chair, propped up on pillows as though someone was afraid she was made of glass.

I knew she was stronger than that.

"Sain!" At my appearance, she jerked, anger rumbling through the shock that was clear on her face. I guess I was lucky she didn't attack me, anyone else and she would have. "What happened? What are you doing here? Did you finish the task? Did Míra succeed?"

"She's alive," I hissed, knowing full well Ovailia had no idea who I was talking about. "They both are."

"Míra succeeded? So we are safe?" Even through her confusion, her magic pressed against me, as mine did hers, the two powers mixing delightfully. I had been right from the start, she would make a wonderful addition.

"Why didn't you kill her?" I rounded on her, it took everything in me not to kill her right then.

"Kill Míra? What are you talking about Sain?" Her magic

withdrew as her jaw tightened, fear in her eyes. It was the same as I had seen when she had faced her father. It was beautiful to see her look that way at me, to adhere to me to such a degree.

"Kill Wyn. I fed her to you on a platter. I *watched* you kill her in sight. I saw her die. Your boot moved through her skull. But her skull isn't so much as bruised."

"She's alive?"

Her shock angered me more.

"Yes, she's alive! I needed her dead. They should both be dead by now." With a growl that ripped through the room, I rushed her, her eyes widened as she straightened her jaw, the tension in her body making her look like she would fly off the couch and kill Wyn now if I gave the word.

It was tempting, but that wouldn't help, not anymore. One move, one foolish move, and everything had changed. It was too late to repair the damage. Now I needed to find a new hand to play.

I knew what that move needed to be.

"Can you walk?" I growled at the blonde beauty before me, and her eyes narrowed in obvious irritation.

"Of course I can walk. Edmund may think my magic is weak and broken, but he underestimates me all the time." Her voice was snide, powerful, all fear of the temper I had unfurled on her gone.

"Wonderful," I cooed, moving right back to her. This time, she didn't shy away, her magic moved right to mine as she sensed the change. "Because I am going to need your help."

"Anything." Her voice was light, her eyes dark.

Before I knew what I was doing, I leaned down to her, pressing my lips against hers as our magic flared in a powerful jolt. I felt her lips, felt her touch against my neck, the small pressure sending a feral growl rumbling from the back of my throat as I pulled away, eyes wide.

She looked at me with a hunger I hadn't seen before, her eyes bright, her loyalty clear.

I didn't think I had ever enjoyed a kiss as much as I had in that moment. I guessed I would keep her around a bit longer than I had originally assumed.

"Good," I replied, making her smile deepen. "Because we need to see your father."

"My father?" The hunger in her eyes vanished, hatred taking its place as she pushed herself to standing, her motions still a little stiff.

I almost chastised her for lying to me. I would have if I didn't need her, but I couldn't wait. Besides, she would probably crawl across the floor if needed.

"Yes," I whispered, taking her hand as my magic flooded into her, moving right to her spine, soothing the still tender tissue in hopes of making it stronger, at least for the next few minutes. "I'm going to need you to take out his guard. Can you do that?"

She looked at me in query, but I offered her nothing else. I needed her loyalty without question right now, something that would be put to the test shortly.

She hesitated, her eyes boring into mine until her smile returned, her hand leaving mine as she moved to the tall wardrobe at the foot of her bed. She rifled through boxes before she reemerged, a small vile clutched tightly in her hands.

"I will make sure they are as useful to my father as Thom is to Ilyan now," she shook the contents, the thick fluid moving brightly through the tiny space.

"Wonderful."

"What do you want me to do?"

"You are a smart girl, Ovi. This, I know you can figure out. Protect our lives, and everything else will fall into place."

Saying nothing more; I moved toward the door, breathing deeply as I prepared for what I was about to do. My heart thundered in a mixture of excitement and nerves I had never felt before that moment. It was an oddly intoxicating sensation.

"Take me to him," I whispered as I shifted into a cower, my body folding in on itself as I began to shake, pushing my magic back down inside my heart, knowing that, if Edmund felt even a whisper of what was coming, of what I really was, none of this would work.

Ovailia said nothing else as she flung the door open, her hand winding around the collar of my shirt as she dragged me from the room, the guard that was stationed outside straightened to attention, shock moving through his face at our sudden appearance.

Keeping my body hunched and broken, I turned my hand a fraction of an inch, letting a powerful attack move through the air and right into him. The stealthy spell sped up his spine, dislocating nerve endings, severing tendons. The man crumpled back into the chair as the magic struck his brain, the simple attack rendering him useless as it burned, his body already immobilized from the pain.

"Go," I snapped, grateful when Ovailia moved down the hall without question of what had just happened.

Ovailia pulled me around a corner, my feigned cries increased in mockery as she continued to drag my stumbling form beside her, a low grumble of irritation seeped from her lips.

"Silence," she hissed, but I simply cried louder.

One of Edmund's guards looked up from where he

stood, his lips twisting at the sight of us shuffling down the hall. His confusion at seeing us there was evident, but it didn't matter. His presence had told me what I needed to know. Edmund was inside.

"It's up to you now," I hissed to Ovailia between my sobs. "Get us in there."

Her shoulders straightened, her desperate need to impress me shining through.

"Ovailia!" the man yelled, his confusion evident as he approached us. "Sain! What are you—"

"We need to see my father." My soul shook at the power in Ovailia's voice, everything rippling over me in pride and lust as she did as I requested. "We have news."

The man looked between us, and I cried more, letting the sound flow out of me in a pathetic rumble as I pled for my life. The man stepped back in disgust before he disappeared behind the door, emerging moments later to swing the door wide in silence.

Silence was always a bad sign with Edmund.

I could feel Ovailia's hand begin to shake from where she held it against me, the soundless warning not lost on either of us. At any other time, I would run, find another way, but that was no longer an option. This was the only path left.

"Ovailia, what brings you here?" Edmund greeted us before the door had even shut, his eyes hard as he tightened a white robe around himself, his upset at being bothered without warning clear. I could already see him planning some form of punishment as Ovailia dragged me over to him, throwing me at his feet like a dog.

I howled in feigned agony at the movement, rolling myself into a tight ball as I sobbed.

"Sain was trying to hide in my room, he's back."

Edmund took a step toward me, kicking me over to face him with his bare foot as I continued to moan, my eyes wide as I came face-to-face with the powerhouse of a man I had created.

"Hiding ... Sain?" Edmund's voice was hard, and I cowered more, whimpering pathetically as he squatted beside me. "I didn't expect you back so soon ... and alone. What happened?" His temper increased with each word, the warning digging into me as I sobbed and trembled beneath him.

"Ilyan," I gasped, tears and snot dripping off my nose. "Ilyan killed them all. I barely escaped."

"Míra!" His voice was a shout, his anger boiling over.

After all, I had given him this plan. I had told him of its success. It was one little lie.

"She made it. I saw her. Ilyan took the bait." I didn't even know if that was true, but that didn't even matter anymore. That girl was on her own in there.

Edmund's toes tapped over the floor in front of my face as he bounced on his heels, obviously weighing his options. I could pray that it would go in my direction.

"Good. I would say that would secure both your lives ... but you lost me fifty men, Sain. Fifty men you insisted would be safe." His voice was a heavy weight against my back, his magic strong as his anger increased, as he made his choice. "You leave me no other option."

Unfortunately for him, it was the wrong one.

"No, Edmund." I spoke the words clearly, all trace of my shake, all trace of the role I had played for centuries gone as I uncoiled before him, my body unfurling to its full height, to its full power in one elegant move. Eyes hard, I stood to face Edmund, looking him in the eyes the way he hadn't done in centuries. "You left *me* no choice."

His eyes widened at what he was seeing, his jaw slack as he stepped back, obviously ready to attack, to call his guard on me, to beat me down in defiance.

I gave him a chance for neither.

Without warning, my magic flared, a stream of red smacking into him as I threw him into the wall, his body colliding with the old stone masonry with a smack.

His scream echoed around us as his guard moved to attention, only to have my magic move into them, freezing them in place as I brought Edmund back to me, his body little more than a rag doll as he hovered before me, frozen, my hands moving slow as I reached into my pocket and produced the sliver of Soul's Blade that I had pulled from Ovailia's body.

"I had hoped to connect all the pieces before I did this, but you left me no choice." With one wide swing the shard of red cut through the air, glinting in the light before it disappeared into Edmund, slicing through flesh and bone to embed itself into his heart.

With a sound like he had been punched, Edmund gasped, his blood spraying over me as he coughed, mouth and eyes wide in horror. My magic seeped from the guards in one quick movement, every inch of my power concentrated on the man before me, on the blade that was connecting with his magic. Freezing his magic, his body, his soul right where it was, I left him staring at me as his life slowly seeped away.

"Father!" Ovailia shouted in disbelief as my magic surged to its full potential, shielding us from the attacks of the guards who came to life within moments of my magic leaving them.

"Take care of them, Ovailia," I spat, not daring to look away from the man I held before me.

"But, Sain—"

"Now is the time to decide where your loyalty stands, Ovailia. You can be this man's slave and let him continue to destroy you, or you can be my bride and let me show you what power, love, and royalty really are!" I roared, specks of saliva flying over Edmund's face with my temper. "Decide who you stand with!"

There was a pause so silent I wasn't sure anyone was left in the room. For a moment, it was just Edmund and I, his eyes wide as life left him, as he tried in vain to understand what had happened.

"I choose you, Sain." Her answer came moments before sparks of green flew around us, Ovailia's magic erupting as, one after another, Edmund's guards fell. The men he had trained so well were felled by nothing more than a little poison.

"Wonderful," I soothed as the second to last one fell.

The last man stared at us in fear, his eyes darting around as he obviously tried to decide if he should run.

"Incapacitate the last one. Make him watch. I need a witness."

Without question, Ovailia stepped away from me, the barrier I had surrounded us with fell to the ground as her magic wrapped around the man, pinning him to the wall with a thud.

"Hello, Damek," she said, the venom in her voice taking my breath away.

"She's beautiful," I sighed as I turned back to Edmund, the fear on his face making it obvious he could feel his magic seeping away, moving into the blade along with his soul, trapping him in there for eternity. "I have to thank you for making me such a beautiful woman. She was flawed before, but now..." I smiled, looking away from him

as I licked my lips, my heart thundering through me with
need.

Beautiful.

"Sain…" Edmund whispered through the pain, his soul
and magic no more than a ghost of what they were.
"Why…?"

"Why?" I echoed, my voice heightened in false mockery.
"Why am I killing you?"

His mouth opened and closed like a fish gasping for air,
a faint sound of liquid starting to gurgle from his throat.

He didn't have long left.

"Because I am tired of being patient," I hissed, moving
closer to him, wanting to make certain he heard every
word. "I have spent hundreds of years molding you into
what you needed to be, but you didn't do what I desired.
You messed up my plan, which means I have to fix it. And if
I have to fix it, then I have no use for you."

His eyes widened as the truth of what was said hit him.
His horror increased as he tried again to talk, but the sound
of drowning came louder now, blood drizzling from the
corners of his mouth as he tried to breathe.

"When I have no use for someone anymore, I kill them.
I'd normally have you do it, but I guess I am on my own
now. I'm sorry, Edmund, but you've played your part. It's
time we throw you away." With a jerk, I pulled the blade
from his chest, his now lifeless body crumbling to the
ground in a tangle of twitches and moans as his blood dried
against the knife; his soul and his magic trapped inside.
"Pathetic."

"You," I turned to the man Ovailia still held against the
wall. Everything about him shook as I started to move
closer. "I have a job for you. Do it well, and I won't kill you.

Fail and your life will end in a much more painful way than poor Edmund finally found."

I smiled, Ovailia laughed, and the man cowered as Ovailia released him from her magic, letting him fall to the ground.

"Stand," I commanded, and he scuttled to his feet, his eyes darting away from mine in fear. "I want you to go and tell everyone what you saw here. Tell everyone of what Sain, the first of the Drak, really is. Can you do that?"

"Y-ye-yes..." he stammered as he continued to shake, the smell of urine filling the air around us.

Ovailia laughed harder.

"Good. Then, when you are done, come back to me, and I'll have another, little job for you. You have a new master now. Do you understand?"

The man nodded before he ran from us, his feet tripping over one another in his desperate need to find a way out.

"Do you think he will do it?" Ovailia asked as she stepped up to me, her body so close I could feel her warmth against my skin.

"Yes, I do. Now is when things really start to get interesting." I pulled Ovailia to me, her eyes wide as I plastered her body against mine, my arms strong as I held her in place. "Now is when everything gets real."

CHAPTER 32

JAROMIR

"Watch it!"

The voice shouted in anger, but I kept running, weaving my way through the legs of people who lingered in the courtyard, making my way around the tents in a frantic need to find out if what everyone was saying was true.

That they had found a girl... about my age.

It wasn't often anyone under the age of seventeen showed up here or even survived what the Vilÿs had done to them. I guessed this one had. It was something I had to see for myself. Being the single one in a forest of adults was boring, even with magic.

Maybe that wouldn't be the case for long.

Ducking behind a big, green tent, I moved to the little alley behind the makeshift emergency room Ilyan had put together, knowing I could get in through the window near the end. I had done it before.

Running past boarded up windows and that creepy, old door, I let my magic carefully wiggle open the pane of glass, wind moving around me as it moved me up and through.

Perfectly silent.

The first time I had done that, I had made so much noise one of the healers had scolded me for twenty minutes.

I had mastered silence quickly.

I didn't even let myself touch the ground as I opened the door, the old, wooden thing creaking loudly as it opened to a hall lined with beds, the badly burned people covered by blankets and sheets. And there, at the end...

A girl.

A few people hovered around her, their hands looking like birds wings as they talked or healed or did whatever they were doing. I knew that, if they saw me, I would get kicked out, and my better logic told me to run and hide, wait until they were gone. But I couldn't, not with something this exciting.

I kept moving forward, my eyes trained on her, eager to see her for myself, freezing as one of the healers moved to the side, giving me a clear view of the girl they had rescued a few hours before.

"Míra?" My voice rang out loudly as I saw her, her head turning at the sound of her name. Her jaw dropped as mine did at seeing her here, the adults around us looking between us in confusion.

"Jaromir?" Her voice was the exact squeak I remembered, high and deep ... even though something in it had changed.

Something in her had changed. But I didn't care.

Why would I?

She was here.

She was alive.

My sister.

My twin sister.

. . .

TO BE CONTINUED
Continue the story now with CROWN OF CINDERS.
The Imdalind Series is complete, so you can get your
binge on.

GLOSSARY

Skřítek - /skřiːtɛk/ - Meaning Elf in Czech; these people are similar to the common Fae and hold a type of magic that pulls from the energy of the earth. They tend to be tall and fair and have a rich culture of fighting and protection. Bonded and mated pairs wear their hair long and in braids. These creatures have been hunted to near extinction and their dwindling numbers still protect the source of all magic: Imdalind.

Trpaslík - /trpasliːk/ - Meaning Dwarf in Czech; these people hold a type of magic that pulls from the dark fire energy that pulls from the center of the earth. They strive best in manipulating rock and elements. They tend to be shorter in stature, but do not hold many physical differences from the mortals of the world.

Víly - /viːlɪ/ - Meaning Fairy or Sprite in Czech; these small winged creatures have jewel bright skin and stand no taller than a grown man's forearm. Their magic dwells in the souls of the world and can affect emotions or feelings. Their bite also awakens magic in mortals. These creatures have been hunted into extinction by King Edmund.

Drak - /drahːk/ - Meaning Dragon in Czech, these people hold the magic of sight. They survive off 'Black Water' that is poured from the source of magic in Imdalind. They also use that water to see in the future and the past of those who seek answers. These creatures have been hunted into extinction by King Edmund.

Silnỳ - /silːnee/ - Meaning powerful in Czech, this is the name that was given to the person that was shown in sight by the Drak to be the one to end the war over magic.

Drevo - /dreyːvo/ - A type of magical poultice that is a Trpaslík magic that when eaten can connect and embolden magic to assist in healing.

377

Vymăzat - /vee:mah:zaht/ - A type of magic burn that connects two people and allows the person who has used the magic to control the other. Once the burn is set, only death can break the control bond.

Zêlství - /zɛl:stř̥i:/ - The Czech word that is used in the magical world for when a pair is bonded or mated. For the Skřítek there is a ceremony that involves braiding and the connection or sharing of magic to complete the bond. For the Trpaslíks it is the sharing of earth and blood. The Drak's complete the ceremony through sharing of sight and water.

Tȏuha - /to:hah/ - A plane of existence that connects two people who have completed a Zêlství. This place can only be accessed through the magic of the bonded or mated pair.

Zmizêt - /zmi:zɛt/ - A shield that is used by all magical people to not only protect themselves or others from magical attacks, but for many Skříteks and others with strong magic, can bring invisibility.

Svazovat - /svah:so:vaht/ - This is a type of magic that allows a person to be present or keep awareness on an object by leaving a piece of their magic within it. For a more complex presence in the object the person may leave a piece of magic and self within the object. Sometimes referred to as a souls bind, the name is deceiving as a piece of a soul is not necessary to complete the magic. Rather, it simply needs to be something precious and meaningful that will connect the two.

Další v příkazu - /dalʃi: v př̥i:kah:zoo/ - Meaning Second in Command this is the title for those who the second or the hand to the king of the Skříteks and of Imdalind. This is also the name of the crimson ribbon that denotes the title and authority of the wearer. As the další v příkazu is traditionally a married male this has been woven into the mating braid of the possessor.

Délka vedení královského - /del:kha: v:ed:ed:ee krah:low:v:skee:ha/ - Meaning The Length of the Royal Line, this is the crown that signifies the place of the king and the Queen of the Skříteks and of Imdalind. This is also the name of the golden ribbon that denotes the title and authority of the wearer. As the délka vedení královského is tradition- ally a mated pair this has been woven into the mating braid of the possessor.

Štít - /st:i:ht/ - The 'good magic' counterpart to a Vymàzat. A Vymàzat controls, a Stit simply connects magic and supports and protects... or it's supposed to.

Zánik - /zah:n:eek/ - A fatal curse that uses ones own magic to consume and destroy the one who is cursed.

Zlomený - /zlo:me:knee/ - The name for sights that do not come to pass.

Omezující stone - /zah:n:eek/ - A stone that is found in high mountains, when consumed it can restrict the magic in **Skříteks** and **Trpaslíks**

ALSO BY REBECCA ETHINGTON

THE WORLD OF IMDALIND

THE IMDALIND SERIES (COMPLETE)

KISS OF FIRE, IMDALIND #1

EYES OF EMBER, IMDALIND #2

SCORCHED TREACHERY, IMDALIND #3

SOUL OF FLAME, IMDALIND #4

BURNT DEVOTION, IMDALIND #5

BRAND OF BETRAYAL, IMDALIND #6

DAWN OF ASH, IMDALIND #7

CROWN OF CINDERS, IMDALIND #8

SPARK OF VENGEANCE, IMDALIND #9

FLARE OF VILLAINY, IMDALIND #10

THE LAST FAE KING

CRIMSON STAINED CATALYST

GOLD BRANDED REQUISITE

ASH BURNED SYPHER

THE DARK WORLDS

THE THROUGH GLASS SERIES (COMPLETE)

BOOK ONE: THE DARK

About the Author

Rebecca Ethington is an internationally bestselling author with over a million books sold. Her breakout debut, The Imdalind Series, has been featured on bestseller lists since its debut in 2012.

Born and raised under the lights of a stage, Rebecca has written stories by the ghost light, told them in whispers in dark corridors, and never stopped creating within the pages of a notebook.

Find me online
www.rebeccaethington.com
contact@rebeccaethington.com

THE COMPLETE IMDALIND SERIES